TECHWITCH BOOK SIX

WICKED DEEDS

M.J. SCOTT

My mother was a wicked witch. She sold my magic to a demon. I thought that that was the worst that my past had to offer. Turns out, I might be wrong about that…

I survived a journey into the Fae realm that could have ended in disaster. But it was hardly a victory. The dangerous witch we were pursuing went free and a piece of my past came back to haunt me. And even though I'm back in San Francisco, there's no peace to be found.

Strange creatures are stalking the city. A disgruntled Fae lord and his minions won't leave me alone. And my worst enemy might have a connection to me that I don't want to face.

To add to my troubles, the half-Fae girl we rescued from the realm turns up on my doorstep, seeking a fresh start. Understandable but her presence might kick off a dangerous game of power that could end it all. And when the darkness that shaped my past threatens everything I've built, I'll need to embrace dangerous allies and my own magic to survive.

For my family, real, lost, and found.

Chapter One

I'VE ALWAYS DREAMED of monsters. Nightmares chase me through the dark. Well, at least since I turned thirteen and my mother secretly bound my magic to a demon. Dark things have stalked my dreams, the terror waking me from sleep to twisted sheets and my heart thumping so damned loud in my ears it's deafening.

I rarely remember much of the detail when I wake—a small mercy I'm happy to take. But some nights, the fear still lingers. It drives me from my bed to work or read or watch mindless vidstreams until the sun rises and I feel safe again. I'm used to it now. Both the nightmares and the lack of sleep. And to tell the truth, since I met Damon Riley—tech god, billionaire and the man who I know would guard me in my dreams if he could manage it—the nightmares have come less often.

Correction. *Were* coming less often. Because for the last month or so, they've been back. Only this time it's not a demon haunting me.

It's a photograph.

One that, to anyone but me, contains nothing alarming at all. Two people on a beach, smiling at the camera, wearing skimpy swimwear, tans, and the satisfied air of people having regular good sex.

The woman is beautiful. Long red hair, dazzling green eyes, a face that could launch a thousand ships if invading by ocean to steal a woman away to marry her was still a thing. The man beside her is no slouch either. His pale blue eyes are almost shocking against his deep tan and his dark hair is pushed back from his face as though it's still damp. His grin could charm a brick wall.

So, no, the photo itself isn't alarming.

But the woman is my mother, and her companion is Jack Miller, a dangerous witch who corrupted VR technology to a virtual prison, kidnapped Damon, and burned down my house with the assistance of imps. A man who consorts with demonkind can be nothing but evil.

Maybe it shouldn't be a surprise to learn they'd crossed paths at some point. My mother—Sara—always had time for men with money and an inclination to spend it on her. Until she became a mother.

Once she'd had me, she laid low, dragging us through a series of middle of nowhere small towns across half the country. But she'd often told me how she'd lived the high life before I'd arrived to cramp her style, how she could have any man she wanted. When she was drunk and bitter and ranting at me over something I didn't remember doing. I'd tried to let those moods wash over me, focusing on her body language, not what she was saying, trying to judge when I could safely retreat to bed and leave her alone with her resentment.

As for Jack, well, I don't know him. We've only crossed paths in person a few times, but he's charming. The kind of man not inclined to say no to bedding a beautiful woman who lets him think she's charmed. Sara was a master at that, though I doubted she'd ever been truly charmed by anyone. She was far too focused on working a situation to her own advantage.

I didn't know how they met. I wanted to believe they didn't. But Damon's security team had analyzed the image and hadn't found any signs of it being a fake.

So I had to assume it was real. Resulting in broken sleep and a brain spinning in too many directions, struggling with memories of not only the recent pain Jack had caused but also of my mother and a childhood I've done my best to forget.

Though my mother had always been unforgettable. Even when she was trying to blend in in small town after small town, I watched people turn to her, drawn like moths to a flame. Willing to let her spin her web of dazzling-sounding fortunes and useless potions, handing over their money and thanking her for the privilege.

She never told me who my father was. From her I inherited my magic, though it took me accidentally breaking that bond with a demon to discover my magic and my mother's lies. So I came late to my power. But I'd understood tech instinctively from the first moment I'd learned to use it. Which I didn't get from Sara—who would no more have learned to code than fly to the moon—or her parents, who were reluctantly competent users of gadgets at best.

Jack, though. Jack was a tech genius. He'd made his money inventing a refinement in holographics that helped revolutionize the industry. He'd taken the money when he and his partners received an offer they couldn't refuse and sold up. He'd grown it making smart investments in new technologies. To the rest of the world, he was a smart, savvy Samaritan, helping small tech businesses succeed. But I knew the dark side he hid so well.

Which is why the photo was haunting me. The metadata for the image was limited. We knew the location—a small private island in the Bahamas, which these days was mostly underwater—and the date it was taken.

Ten months before I was born.

The date made my stomach twist every time I thought

about it. Sara had never been one to hold on to men for long —usually because she got what she wanted and got out—but being with Jack in the Bahamas suggested some degree of seriousness.

It was possible she'd dumped him not long after, gone home and found someone new in time to get knocked up.

The island, being private and now no longer inhabitable, had no records of who had come and gone thirty-odd years ago. Damon's sources confirmed Jack and Sara's passports had been processed in Los Angeles, leaving the country on a private jet a week before the photo had been taken and returning two weeks after.

That was the sum total of information we had.

Nothing to calm my suspicions. My mother had been estranged from my grandparents well before I'd been born and they'd always told me they had no idea who my father was. My birth certificate had Sara's name only.

I had no way of knowing for sure if my hunch was right, unless I could get a DNA sample from Jack.

But there'd be no DNA if we couldn't find Jack. He'd been eluding Damon's efforts to hunt him down for almost a year now.

Did I even want to know? Jack was a criminal. Of both the human and magical varieties. I'd always clung to the hope my dad had been some poor normal dude Sara had duped along the way. She fell firmly into the category of wicked witch. I didn't want to believe I had criminals on both sides of my gene pool.

Ugh. I swiped the image closed. The datapad landed with a thump as I tossed it onto the far end of the sofa I was occupying in Damon's living room. He'd gone to bed an hour or so ago. Any sane woman would have joined him by now.

Instead, I'd told myself I'd finish some work on an analysis I'd done for a client first. I'd lasted about five minutes before I pulled up the picture again. Staring at it for most of an hour hadn't yielded any blinding insight.

Nope. All it had done was make me edgy, anxious. The kind of jittery that told me sleep was going to elude me, unless I did something to burn it off.

The sane solution was, once again, joining Damon and jumping him. My favorite form of exercise.

But Damon had been yawning when he'd arrived home. Being CEO of a global empire was hard work, even when he wasn't dealing with extracurricular issues like Jack and all the other complications the magical world kept dumping in our laps. He'd been pushing himself too hard since we'd arrived home from the UK. At first he blamed jet lag for the shadows under his eyes, but I knew better.

He was angry—and felt guilty—that Jack had once again evaded him. Angry I'd risked myself traveling through the Fae realms to try to catch Jack. Angry he couldn't protect me from things like Usuriel, the Lord of the Nichtkin, deciding to kiss me when I'd made a bargain to share memories with him to free a tanai-fol girl who wanted to return to the human world from his clutches.

I couldn't fix any of it, other than being there when he wanted to talk about it. I could, at least, let him get some sleep.

Cassandra Tallant, the head of the Cestis—the witches' ruling council—in the United States had told me to give him some time to process it all. Simply being in the Fae realm was enough to throw most humans for a loop. As she was one of the strongest witches in the country and had three decades or so of life experience on me, I was taking her advice.

So if I wanted to work off my own frustration tonight, I was going to have to do it the old-fashioned way and make use of Damon's high-tech home gym.

I'd already had a training session with Callum Dune—the *s'ealg oiche* warrior who was training me to fight demons the

Fae way—earlier in the day. I was starting to enjoy fighting with him, now I'd grown more comfortable with using a sword. Though now Callum was working on getting me to use magic at the same time as fighting, so it was harder than ever. But his sessions usually left me physically worn out. Tired enough to sleep through the night.

I could try that approach here. Use the treadmill to settle my nerves. That and one of Cassandra's always-effective herbal teas might get me to sleep. The tea was the last resort. Cassandra was an herbalist whose talent was undeniable, but she favored efficacy over taste for her concoctions. At least she did for me. Most of the things she made me drink ranged in flavor from grassy to outright compost. I put honey or sugar in them when I could, but it didn't help much.

But her teas were better than taking sleeping meds. I'd had too many nights where I'd admitted defeat, taken a pill to sleep, and wound up trapped in an unending nightmare, unable to startle myself awake. I slept, yes, but never felt any more rested.

I had to hope the treadmill would work.

I padded down the corridor toward the gym. I'd already changed into leggings and a tee before dinner, which made things simpler, and I kept sneakers in the gym. The room took up a good chunk of the rear of the house, the windows looking down into the back garden—the square footage of the grounds was too large to be thought of simply as a yard, unlike the tiny patch of land at the back of my house in Berkeley. Solar lights twinkled discreetly among the trees and flower beds and along the walls, but the light was set to low levels at this time of night, when the garden should be empty. The property had more than enough wards and mundane security measures to keep most threats out.

Damon had made his fortune young and was well-versed in keeping himself and everyone he cared about safe.

The various pieces of sleek black and silver gym equipment gleamed at me as Madge—the not-quite AI who ran Damon's systems, including the house comp—brightened the lights in response to my presence. Every weight machine you could ever want, plus a huge open area for sparring or free weights or yoga or whatever else people more excited by exercise than I was, chose to do to amuse themselves.

Then there were the cardio options. Treadmill. Elliptical. Rowing machine. All positioned in front of the windows so you could admire the gardens as you sweated. Of course, if I asked, Madge would darken the windows and project a vidstream onto them instead. Or send music to my headphones.

I slipped the headphones on. At this hour of the night, there wouldn't be much to see outside and I wasn't in the mood for a movie or the news. I stared out at the garden, not paying much attention, while I tried to decide if I wanted to choose treadmill or elliptical.

Before I'd picked my form of torture, something caught my eye. A flicker of movement between garden beds. I frowned and stepped closer to the windows. Well, French doors. They opened out onto a small deck with stairs down to the garden.

For a moment I saw nothing but waving grasses, but then another flash caught my eyes. A patch of darkness that didn't fit.

If it had been my house, I'd have assumed a stray cat but, between the height of Damon's fences and all the security, I'd never seen any animals other than birds in this garden.

Well, I'd seen an imp once. That didn't count.

The patch of darkness moved. Flowed almost too fast toward the house. I stepped back, ready to get Madge to alert the guards, when it took a running leap, landing on the deck, and suddenly I had no trouble identifying it.

Bigger than a cat, though mostly cat shaped. A foxier face with two large golden eyes. Long black and gray fur shifting slightly as it stared at me. And the dead giveaway that it wasn't a cat: two long tails, shifting slowly to trace sinuous patterns in the air.

A *nixling*. A creature from the Fae realm. I'd met one once before, traveling through Lady Cerridwen's territory with Callum and his twin sister, Gráinne. That nixling had been friendly, though Callum had told me they were excellent hunters.

Right now, I wasn't so worried about whether the nixling was friendly, as I was about what the hell it was doing here. The door to the realm was located in Berkeley, not San Francisco.

And it was, as far as I knew, still closed. Only Fae with explicit permission from the Elders were able to leave. Unlike witches, normal humans didn't know about the Fae. So random Fae creatures shouldn't be wandering the streets of the city.

The nixling yawned, flashing long sharp teeth, and sat back on its haunches, tails curling around its feet like a cat. It stared at me, head cocked slightly.

If it had been a cat, I would have read it as curious, but this was a Fae creature. Curious, maybe. Something to be wary of? Absolutely.

"Madge," I said softly, not moving in case I spooked the creature. "Call Callum."

Callum was Fae. He probably wouldn't be asleep. He should answer my call, if he wasn't entertaining himself in ways that were none of my business.

And he did. "Maggie? Is something wrong?"

"Yes," I said. "I think one of your cats got out."

Chapter Two

It wasn't Callum who arrived at Damon's house thirty minutes later.

The nixling hadn't moved from the deck, watching me curiously. Callum had instructed me not to let it in and not to try to stop it if it left. I'd told the security detail someone was coming over. They didn't mention the nixling, which made me wonder if it was using an illusion to hide from the cameras.

Which left me with not much choice but to sit and wait for him to turn up and deal with it.

But it was Gráinne, not Callum, waving at me through the security camera. She'd swapped the black leathers she usually wore in the realm for black jeans and a black leather hoodie. She wasn't carrying a sword, but I was sure she had plenty of weapons hidden under her clothes. But it was unmistakably her. Black hair braided back from her face, black metal rings in her ears. She was shorter than her twin brother—shorter than me for that matter—but she was as startlingly beautiful as Callum was handsome and her green-gold eyes were the same unusual shade as his.

"Callum sent you?" I asked through the speaker. Since our trek through the realm a month or so ago and my altercation with Usuriel, Lord of the Nichtkin, Cerridwen had started sending Gráinne to assist her brother in his training duties outside the realm. Sometimes they traded off who was in the realm versus out here. And sometimes they were both in San Francisco or Berkeley at the same time. Like tonight.

She nodded. "He was busy."

That sounded like him. "Come on in."

The gates swung inward and Gráinne strolled through, looking perfectly at ease. She hadn't been to Damon's house before—we'd been meeting at the training gym Damon owned in Berkeley—but she seemed almost as at home in the human world as her brother. Their family worked for Cerridwen—or served, I didn't know the exact term for the relationship. Their mission was to deal with demons and any other Fae creatures causing problems within the realm or outside of it. But the door to the realm in Berkeley had been closed after the Big One and only recently restored. So the city must have changed since Grainne had last spent much time here. Then again, the decade or so since the earthquake that had levelled parts of San Francisco was a blink of an eye for a Fae.

And Fae were masters at not showing their hand. Playing it cool was their superpower.

I met Gráinne at the door.

"Where is the nixling?" she asked.

Straight to the point. "Out back. There's a deck attached to the house and it's sitting there." Unless it had decided to bolt when I'd left the gym.

"It hasn't tried to get in?"

"Not so far. It's watching."

"They are nosy." Gráinne glanced right and left, brows drawing down as her eyes narrowed. "And this house is well-warded."

"It is. But it still got in somehow."

"Well, they are sneaky as well as nosy. They're slippery when it comes to wards. After all, it got through the door."

"Or someone let it out," I muttered. "If it escaped itself, what's it doing here? We're a long way from Berkeley. I doubt it rode the BART."

"True. But this house also stands out to anyone following the magic in the city, because of the wards."

"It does?" I blurted, startled. Then felt dumb. Of course it did. To anyone with magic, the warding would be obvious. I didn't know how much power Cassandra and Lizzie had sunk into the wards, but between them and me and Callum, there was plenty of magic invested in protecting the property.

"I could feel it well before I saw it," Gráinne said. "But I am Fae. Perhaps to witches, it is not such a distraction. Your magic is strange, after all."

I bit back the retort that it was Fae magic that was weird, not human. Gráinne was here to help, not get insulted. Fae were prickly beings, quick to take offense at the slightest thing. I had fought beside Gráinne and trained with her, but I'd still only known her a short time. I didn't know what might upset her.

"So it came to the city somehow and got curious?" On the scale of unlikely coincidences, that one seemed way up there.

Gráinne gave me one of those graceful Fae shrugs her brother was so good at. "Perhaps, rather than talking about it, you take me to the creature and we can find out?"

Best suggestion yet. I wanted the nixling out. Preferably without Damon waking up. He didn't need yet another piece of Fae weirdness dropped in his lap.

Righteous—as the gamers called his company, Riley Arts —were getting ready to release their newest game at their second annual tournament. Last year's had been a smash. At least as far as launching *Serenity Falls* was concerned. The game was now one of their biggest sellers. Less good was the part where Jack Miller had wormed himself into the tournament, hoping to carry out some plan we still hadn't uncovered. We knew part of it was using a method of locking people into a VR environment, overriding the layers and layers of safeguards that had been built in to prevent that very thing. He'd fled after a fight with me and some of the Cestis, which had resulted in my house burning down.

Damon was obsessed with hunting Jack down. Not only for the damage he'd done to us personally, but because he viewed Jack's corruption of the technology he loved so much as a personal offense. Trying to catch Jack was how we'd ended up in the Fae realm and met a nixling in the first place.

"Inside or outside?" I asked Gráinne.

She grinned. "Outside. A nixling does not pose much threat. They bite, yes, but so do I."

Easy for her to say. She could turn into a big-ass wolf dog, like her brother. The s'ealg oiche were shapeshifters as well as warriors.

I, on the other hand, could not grow teeth and claws. I could set the nixling on fire, but burning non-demonic creatures was not something I wanted to do. I'd feel better with a weapon. But my practice swords were back in the gym and my gun was locked in the gun safe in our bedroom.

"If you wish for a weapon, I have plenty," Gráinne added, reaching beneath her jacket. She pulled out a long dagger and passed it to me. "Not that you should need one."

I tested the dagger's weight, turning it in my hand. It was gorgeous, the hilt black metal inlaid with silver in a pattern of stars. The black blade glinted under the porch light. I didn't need to test it to know it would be wickedly sharp. It was probably Gráinne's own work.

"It's lovely." Admiration was safe enough. Better than thanking her. 'Thank you' could be taken to imply an obligation. I gestured to my right with the dagger. "It's this way."

Gráinne paced silently at my side as we walked around the house. Small lights hidden in the beds along the path brightened some as we passed, enough that there was no risk of stumbling over a stray branch or stone. Damon's gardeners kept the grounds immaculate but even they weren't on call twenty-four-seven to deal with the aftermath of weather or say, stray Fae creatures with no respect for boundaries. I always felt clumsy around the Fae, humans not being built to move with their ease. The last thing I wanted was to trip and scare the nixling away or, you know, stab myself by falling on a dagger.

My training with Cerridwen and Callum had improved my fighting skills immeasurably, not to mention my fitness. I could do things I'd never imagined even attempting, let alone pulling off, but I'd never be able to move as easily through the world as the Fae did.

Gráinne was wearing leather, but it didn't make a sound. Damon had given me a leather jacket early in our relationship. It was expensive. Handmade, nano-coated, reinforced, and soft as butter, but it still made some noise when I moved. Gráinne might as well have been wearing air.

The nixling was still perched in the same place when we rounded the corner of the house. It turned its head, golden eyes blinking once as we approached the deck.

When we were about ten feet away, Gráinne put a hand out to stop me, studying the nixling, her brows drawing down again. "That's not one of Cerridwen's."

The nixling yawned at this pronouncement, baring its teeth. I resisted the urge to show it the dagger. Show it I had pointy sharp things, too.

"Is that good or bad?" I whispered.

"There are nixling in several of the territories," Gráinne said. "But the largest populations are in our Lady's and, well, Lord Usuriel's."

Fuck. Just what we didn't need. The Lord of the Nichtkin was kind of terrifying and he didn't like me. I'd been clinging to the idea he wasn't going to be a problem as long as I avoided his territory for, say, ten or twenty years. I'd combed through the Archives to try to learn more about him but I hadn't found much.

Witches either didn't cross paths with him often or didn't survive to tell the tale if they did.

I'd asked Aubrey Carter—one of the UK Cestis—if they had anything about him or his Nichtkin and she'd found a little more from their Archives, but nothing truly helpful. Usuriel ruled one of the darker parts of Fae. He played politics, but all the Elders did. He shared Cerridwen's determination to protect the realm from demonkind but, unlike her, seemed to view me as a threat to that goal, rather than a tool to use fighting them.

So. Scary. Powerful. Not a fan of me. All reasons he might send a creature to spy on me. Though, if stealth was his aim, the nixling was failing.

"Is it one of his?" I managed over a mouth gone dry with the thought of Usuriel deciding to interfere here in the human world. "Can you talk to it?"

"I can." She turned a stern look at the cat and issued a rapid-fire stream of Fae. The only words I could make out were s'ealg oiche. The nixling's ears flicked forward and it seemed a little less certain. Callum and Gráinne and their kind weren't quite the same as the Cestis, but they had a lot of authority in the Fae. Hopefully the nixling was smart enough to recognize that and cooperate.

Gráinne waited a moment, then sighed. "It won't tell me."

"Aren't you like Fae police?"

"Not as you think of them. The nixling hasn't hurt anyone. I can take it back to the realm, but I can't force it to talk to me."

"Hasn't it broken the rules, coming through the door?"

"Yes. Passage through the door still requires authorization, and I don't think anyone is granting that to stray nixlings."

The nixling's ears flattened briefly, as though protesting being called a stray.

"Cerridwen controls the door, you work for her, doesn't it have to do what you say?"

"Like I said, I can make it return with me," Gráinne said, fixing a stern look on the creature. "It would be foolish to think it can evade me. But that doesn't mean it will answer questions. It's a lesser Fae. It might not have had a choice. And be bound not to tell. The Lady may be able to make it answer once I return it to the realm."

The nixling flicked its ear again and made a rumbling noise somewhere between a purr and a growl.

"Anything?" I asked.

"It—she—says no one sent her."

"Can the lesser Fae lie?" The Fae themselves could not, but I didn't know if the same applied to the creatures who lived in the realm with them.

Gráinne nodded. "Sadly, yes."

Not helpful. This whole conversation was useless if the nixling could lie. "How did she get through the door if no one sent her?"

The nixling's tails coiled for a moment before settling back at its feet.

Gráinne was frowning. "She says she followed someone through. And no, she didn't say who."

"Could she do that?"

"They are skilled at hiding," Gráinne admitted. "They are excellent hunters; their magic makes them hard to notice. And some of them can get around wards. So it's possible. But 'follow someone through' doesn't necessarily mean she was sneaking out. It could mean someone led her out deliberately."

"And I'm guessing she's not going to tell us which one she means."

"No."

"So, what happens now?"

"I will take her back with me and we will take it from there."

"I'd like to know why she came here."

"So would I."

I jumped half out of my skin. Damon. *Crap*. So much for dealing with this before he woke up. The man was too damned stealthy. I blew out a breath, trying to ignore the pulse pounding in my ears, and turned to face him, pasting on a 'everything's fine' smile. "Hey," I said, somewhat lamely.

One brow lifted. He wore dark gray sweatpants and a white T-shirt, his short dark hair somewhat rumpled from sleep. But there was no trace of sleepiness in his narrow-eyed glare.

Damn it.

"What's going on?" He directed the question at Gráinne.

"Maggie called me," Gráinne said, nodding at the nixling. "You have a visitor she wanted me to deal with."

"So I see." His gaze slanted back to me, the expression in his brilliant blue eyes annoyed. "You didn't think to wake me up?"

"You needed to sleep."

"You need to not take on Fae creatures by yourself," he retorted.

"I didn't," I protested. "I called Callum. He sent Gráinne. And nothing bad has happened."

"Other than that." He nodded at the nixling. "It shouldn't be here, should it?"

"No. And I will be removing it shortly," Gráinne said cheerfully. Her lack of concern didn't seem to improve Damon's mood.

His gaze returned to me. "Good. Which brings me to the question of why it's here."

"We don't know," I admitted. "The nixling isn't talking. Gráinne will take it back to the realm and Cerridwen will see what she can find out." I tried to match Gráinne's cheerful, nothing to worry about tone.

He lifted one dark eyebrow at me again and then turned to Gráinne. "Do you need a car to take you back to the Rose Garden?"

"Yes, that would be useful." Gráinne pounced, grabbing the nixling before it could try to get away. It didn't struggle, but instead just lay in her arms like an overgrown housecat, only the twitch of its tails suggesting it might be annoyed. Though even annoyed, apparently it knew better than to take on one of the s'ealg oiche.

Damon glanced up at the nearest security cam. "Madge? We need a car out front."

It wouldn't take long. Sure enough, by the time Gráinne had carried the nixling around to the front of the house, the gates were swinging open to admit Boyd driving Damon's usual sleekly expensive but unremarkable town car. Damon opened the door as soon as the car came to a stop and Gráinne climbed inside with one last instruction to me to check the wards, just in case.

Boyd drove back out through the gates and they closed again, leaving Damon and me alone outside the house.

"There," I said brightly. "All taken care of. Let's go back in."

Damon was staring at the gates as though expecting them to open again and more trouble to saunter through.

I nudged him with my shoulder. "Inside. Sleep."

He shook his head. "Mitch will be here soon."

Well, crap. I thought I'd avoided Damon's security getting involved.

"Can't he wait until morning?"

Damon shook his head. "That thing got in here without setting off any warnings, despite every way this house is protected. He's going to want to do a full sweep."

He would. And no doubt he'd be asking me some questions. Mitch Angelico, Damon's head of security, was a man who left no stone unturned. Ever. He was annoyingly efficient at his job and annoyingly thorough. I could probably kiss any thought of getting to bed in the next few hours goodbye.

"In that case, inside and coffee." I suppressed a sigh. "I'll send Cassandra a message, let her know what happened, too."

Which would no doubt result in a lecture from Cassandra as well, even though none of this was my fault. I hadn't let the damned nixling in. I hadn't even been near the realm recently, so it couldn't have followed me out. Or, if it had, it had taken its damned time following me home.

Damon nodded and held out his hand. I took it gratefully, recognizing the gesture for what it was. Him letting me know he wasn't mad with me. Falling for me had brought a lot of complications to his life. Just as falling for him had complicated mine. Dating a billionaire had shoved me into a world I knew nothing about, at the same time I was learning I had magic. It had been an adjustment for both of us, one that had torn us apart at one point.

But we'd made our way back to each other and mostly by agreeing to take the good with the bad. If we wanted each other, then that came with security teams and restrictions and paparazzi, as well as magic and Fae and other weirdness.

Still, it was hard sometimes, in my weaker moments—like when I was sleep-deprived and stressed—not to worry Damon might one day decide it was all too much.

Chapter Three

While Damon made coffee, I did a lap of the house, running my hands along the walls and inspecting the wards for weak spots. Nothing. The wards were intact. After all, the nixling hadn't managed to get inside the house. Not that it had tried.

Gráinne had said something about some nixlings being able to get around wards. Did other lesser Fae share that talent?

Damn. I hoped not. Even without the photo of Jack and my mom, some of the creatures we'd encountered in Usuriel's territory were enough to give me nightmares.

Nope. If I thought about that, I'd never sleep again. And if it was a common ability, surely Cerridwen or Callum would have mentioned it by now.

So I was going to be all Pollyanna and assume the house was secure.

One less thing to worry about, unless Mitch's team came to a different conclusion. Knowing Mitch, there'd be at least one extra guard taking a shift in the garden for the rest of the night.

Normally Damon's team monitored the house from a

neighboring property he also owned. They did patrols, but there were no permanent gate guards as such. Damon always said he didn't want to feel like he was living in a prison, but having more of his team on hand was one of the conditions Mitch had set after Jack had taken Damon. Along with more bodyguards for Damon. I had one when I went anywhere by myself as well. Which was still weird, but one of those things I'd had to accept was part of life with my favorite billionaire.

I didn't try checking the wards along the boundary fences. I wasn't keen on going into the garden alone. Better to wait for Mitch and Maia Lin, my bodyguard, who no doubt would accompany him. She was the strongest witch in the security team.

I slurped coffee—willing the caffeine to push some clarity back into my brain—pondering my next move. It should be to call Cassandra and let her know what had happened.

I didn't want to disturb her but, as head of the Cestis, she needed to know there'd been a rogue Fae creature in the city.

The last time that had happened, it had been a *bruadhsiu*—a nightwalker—and people had died. The nixling was not the same level of threat but, still, another breach of the door—if that was what it turned out to be—was Cestis business. So, as much as it was tempting to ask Madge to route me through to her message service rather than calling her directly, I put on my big-girl pants and went to make the call.

I carried my coffee out to my office, but nearly spilled it when the call notification on my datapad chimed before I could even pick it up.

Cassandra's name flashed on the screen. Great, she'd heard the news. Which saved me a call, but I wondered if it had been Mitch or Gráinne who'd spilled the beans. Possibly both.

"Cassandra, hi," I said. "You heard?"

"Yes," she said dryly. The image of her on my screen shifted as she covered her yawn with a hand and settled back into her chair, her large golden brown eyes alert. Her silvery hair was pulled back in a bun that was messier than usual, but that was the only sign she'd just been woken. She had on a crisp cotton shirt in a vivid shade of red. No taking vidcalls in her pajamas for Cassandra. At least my gym clothes weren't sweaty.

"Why don't you tell me what happened?" Cassandra asked.

"I'm going to assume you already know there was a nixling. But there's not much to tell. Other than it being here, nothing happened."

"Define 'nothing'."

"No one's hurt or bleeding, and nothing's on fire."

When had that become my standard of something being an emergency or not? I drank more coffee, trying to drive away the sudden chill in my stomach. When had I reached the point where random magical creatures didn't faze me unless they were actively trying to hurt someone or wreak havoc in some obvious way?

Cassandra grunted. "Hmm. But it did get inside the grounds?"

"Yes," I said. "I've checked the wards on the house and they seem fine. But I haven't had time to look around outside yet. I wanted to wait for Mitch and Maia. Safety in numbers and all. Gráinne said something about some of them getting through wards easily. So there might be nothing to find."

"Let's hope not. And where is the creature now?"

I did the math after checking the time. By my estimation, Gráinne should be back at the Berkeley Rose Garden where the door to the Fae realm was hidden. At this time of night, traffic should be light, and it'd been thirty minutes or so since she'd left.

"I would imagine nearly back to the door, if they're not inside already," I said. "I called Callum. Callum called Gráinne. Gráinne came and grabbed the critter." Fae pest control. Of a kind. Not that the nixlings were pests, as far as I knew. Callum and Gráinne had been friendly with the one we'd encountered in Cerridwen's territory. They weren't like afrits, which were the cockroaches of the demon world. If cockroaches were amenable to following orders, had magic and were able to, you know, kill people.

"It didn't put up a fight?"

"No."

"Does she know why it was there?"

I shrugged. "She talked to it—it seems they have that same telepathy thing Gráinne and Callum can do, but I couldn't hear it. It wasn't being cooperative. She said she didn't think it was from Cerridwen's territory."

"That's not concerning at all," Cassandra said, shaking her head

"Don't panic. Gráinne said they're found in a few territories, and, you know, if they're like cats, maybe it got curious and let itself out the door."

"Did Gráinne think that was likely?"

"No," I admitted, "and neither do I. I mean, if it was curious about a source of power it was feeling, then your house is much closer to the Rose Garden than Damon's."

"Exactly. Did she happen to mention if nixlings live in you-know-who's territory?"

Cassandra, I had noticed, didn't like saying Lord Usuriel's name out loud any more than I did.

"She did," I said, "and they do, but that doesn't mean this one does." I was trying to be optimistic. It was hard. There were probably other Fae Elders who didn't like the idea of a witch who'd fought with a demon and survived, but Usuriel was the only one I'd tangled with in person.

"I guess we'll see," Cassandra said. "But for now, let Maia and the others inspect the wards. If they don't find anything wrong, I'll send Lizzie or Zee in the morning, just to be safe. If they give the all clear, we'll have to assume the creature got through them without damaging them. If there is an issue, call me back."

"I will," I agreed, somewhat relieved she wasn't going to charge straight over here. Yay. I wouldn't have to deal with a grumpy witch on top of a grumpy Head of Security and a grumpy Damon. That made me happy. "I'll talk to you tomorrow." I was still trying for that optimism thing. It didn't always come naturally to me.

"Let's hope so," Cassandra said. She hung up before I could, and I carried my coffee back to the kitchen, where Damon was drinking his and watching the feed of the front gate on a holoscreen.

I was refilling my coffee when the gate swung open, a Riley Arts security Jeep drove through, and Mitch, Maia and two other members of the security team climbed out of it.

"The cavalry's here," I said, jerking my head at the image on the house-comp screen.

"Well, I think Gráinne was the cavalry." Damon said, "But let's see what Mitch has to say."

"He'll probably want me to check the wards again with Maia or whoever he brings."

Damon shrugged. He'd pulled an old Righteous sweatshirt over his T-shirt, but it wasn't doing much to hide the fact that he'd been woken up in the middle of the night and wasn't happy about it. "I would imagine so. I can't be much help in that department. I'll stay inside." He gestured at the datapad on the counter. "I've got Madge analyzing the non-magical security data. She says she didn't note any glitches, but I asked her to run it all again. So I can keep doing that while you do your—" He wriggled his fingers in a 'you know, magical stuff' gesture.

I rolled my eyes. "I don't actually wriggle my fingers."

He grinned. "I know. But I don't know the correct gestures for checking a ward."

All the more reason for him to stay inside. Him not

arguing about it was a relief. It might even improve Mitch's guaranteed-to-be-cranky mood. Usually he had to try to argue for Damon to be sensible when there were unexpected magical adventures, but it seemed today Damon wouldn't need encouraging.

I finished my coffee and was contemplating whether I wanted to eat something to soak up some of the caffeine and give me some hope of sleeping once Mitch was satisfied all was well.

"Mitch and the team are here, Damon." Madge's calm tone interrupted my contemplation of the contents of the refrigerator.

I closed the door and waited as the team made their way inside.

Mitch practically marched into the kitchen. The severe black of the Riley Arts security uniform emphasized his ex-military posture. He ran a hand over his short more-gray-than-red sandy hair and regarded me with somewhat exasperated blue eyes before he muttered a gruff "Hello, Maggie."

Maia Lin stood behind him, seeming more amused than annoyed. Dark haired and dark eyed, she was much more cheerful than her boss. Though no less effective at her job. Jake Kennedy stood beside her, all tall, brown-haired muscle. His gray eyes also looked entertained as Mitch rapid-fired a plan in which Maia and I would focus on the wards while he and Jake rewatched the feeds of the 'incident' and then I'd answer questions.

I found myself back out in the garden, moving somewhat warily around the walls, but despite Maia and me doing our best, we didn't find any holes in the wards.

Whatever the nixling had done to get in, it hadn't damaged anything.

When we went back inside Mitch made me tell him what had happened in minute detail. I'd been expecting the questions and answered them as quickly as I could.

Damon confirmed his part, and I decided to see if I could make a strategic retreat while the team reviewed the security recordings. Maia had already started testing the house wards, repeating the checks I'd already done.

They didn't need me. They all knew what they were looking for in the recordings and I didn't feel like answering the same questions all over again. Mitch was a stickler for detail and could find ten different ways to ask a question when he was in a mood. And while he was fond of me, and had accepted I was likely a permanent fixture in Damon's life, the magical problems that trailed in my wake did tend to put Mitch in a mood.

I retreated to my office, staring at the screen on my desk comp. I could try to work, but doubted I'd manage anything actually productive. But I didn't want to end up staring at the damn photograph again. Instead I pulled up a vidstream, scanning through idly for some entertainment that might take my mind off everything.

The list of offerings didn't really appeal. I was saved when the little light above Aubrey's name in my chat list blinked on, meaning that she'd just logged on.

The system clock showed nearly two a.m. So, nine a.m. or near enough in London.

Sometimes time zones were convenient rather than annoying.

I sent her a 'hey, you free' message. Aubrey and I weren't friends, but we had been talking regularly since Damon and I had returned from the UK. I wanted to know how Gwen Jones, the tanai we'd helped return from the realm, was adapting back to life in the human world. Poor kid had no family and I knew how it felt to feel unwanted. Also, I was trying to at least get one of the UK Cestis to like me. Damon wanted to digitize their Archive, the same way he was ours. Establishing friendly relations might help.

To my surprise, Aubrey replied almost immediately.

Good morning, Maggie.

I could hear her clipped British accent in my head as the words flashed up.

You're up late. Is something wrong?

No, nothing.

I didn't need the Cestis on two continents worrying about nixlings gone astray.

Something I can help you with then?

Just working late. Damon had a thing. I saw you come online so I thought I'd check in on Gwen. How's she doing?

Gwen was something of a mystery. Her father was human, but he hadn't raised her. Once the Cestis had her back in London and started digging into her background, identifying him was proving challenging.

She didn't know her Fae mother. She'd never acknowledged her and Gwen had no idea who she was. She hadn't learned she was tanai until she'd finished school.

She'd been raised by a woman she thought was her aunt until she was ten, when she was packed off to boarding school and only saw her 'aunt' during vacations. She'd grown up thinking her father and mother had died in an accident.

When she turned eighteen, her aunt had turned up at the school, handed her an envelope full of information, including bank accounts set up for her, and informed Gwen that she wasn't really her aunt, that she'd been paid to care for her until she was an adult, and that Gwen was now on her own.

Understandably, Gwen had gone a bit off the rails after learning the truth. She'd started her university degree, but met some tanai on campus who recognized her as one of them—

another bombshell—and it seemed she'd followed one of them into the realm, perhaps drawn by the thought of finding her mother.

Which she never had. Gwen's Fae parent hadn't chosen to acknowledge her and no one knew who she was. I didn't know if that was part of the reason why Gwen had wanted to come home, but from what I could gather, it hadn't made Gwen's time in the realm any easier.

So there was no one to help her get used to being out of the realm again. The Cestis were looking for her dad, but it turned out the name on her birth certificate was fake. At least, the Cestis hadn't been able to identify anyone with that name who'd been alive at the time Gwen was born.

My datapad pinged again with a vidcall request. Aubrey wanted to talk face to face.

Unlike me, she was wide awake and perfectly groomed. She had on a white silk shirt with pearls at her ears. Her blonde hair was pulled back into a perfectly sleek updo and her makeup was immaculate.

I ran a hand over my own hair, hoping there wasn't a stray leaf or anything stuck in it after getting too close and personal with some of the bushes along the boundaries to get to the wards.

Aubrey's mouth curved briefly in a smile, amusement flashing in her icy blue-gray eyes, but she didn't comment.

"Hi," I said again. "Sorry to interrupt your morning."

She dismissed this idea with an elegant wave of her hand. "I was just getting started. It's no trouble."

As the youngest member of the UK Cestis, I knew she had a schedule as tight as Damon's most days, so I took this with an enormous grain of salt. I didn't want to take up too much of her time.

"So. Gwen. Any news?" I asked.

Aubrey shrugged. "I'm not sure. She's quiet. We got her access to her bank accounts back, so that's helpful. She doesn't have to worry about money. Whoever her parents were, they at least left her financially secure."

Which didn't make up for the part where they'd rejected and/or abandoned her, but money was better than no money if you were left on your own with no family.

"She's still talking to the healers," Aubrey continued. "Therapy. She says it's helping."

Something Gwen had resisted at first, but the Cestis had made it a condition of them continuing to help her. I imagined Aubrey would love to be a fly on the wall for those conversations but no self-respecting healer would reveal anything about their patients without consent. Same as a human psychologist. With the usual exceptions for being worried about crimes or self-harm, but I didn't think Gwen was a criminal mastermind. While she'd had something of a rough time in the realm, she—from what Aubrey had told me —hadn't shown any signs of wanting to do something stupid.

"And we've been looking at some university options, but she hasn't made any decisions yet," Aubrey continued.

"What was she studying?" I asked.

Aubrey actually smiled. "Believe it or not, she was doing a technology and media degree. Intending to major in VR game design."

"That's interesting." I kept my face neutral. Was Aubrey hoping that Damon might be able to help? He could probably place a call and get anyone admitted to any VR degree in the world.

Righteous sponsored what was now considered the world standard program right here in California at UC. It was where my sometimes-intern, all-the-time-computer-genius friend, Yoshi Liebfield, was studying.

I just didn't know if Damon wanted anything to do with anyone so recently connected with the Fae and Lord Usuriel. And after the nixling, it wasn't the night to ask.

I also didn't like asking him to pull strings and avoided it where humanly possible. There were enough people in his life who only saw him as someone who could do things for them. My goal was to never be one of them.

To be the person he could just be Damon with.

Aubrey was waiting for me to continue.

"Do you think that's what she still wants to do?" I asked, keeping my tone neutral. I didn't want to offer any encouragement.

Aubrey shrugged again. "I'm not sure. She's still adjusting. She'd have to make up her mind fast to start in September. It might be easier for her to take a job somewhere for a year while she gets her feet back under her."

It was a sensible idea. After all, Gwen's first attempt at university had ended with her vanishing into the realm. Though, that might be unfair. Maybe after getting free of the realm she was going to be focused on making sure her life went where she wanted it to this time. "Has she been hanging out with any tanai?"

"No. I offered to introduce her to some of the smaller families here in London, but she refused. Perhaps it's just as well. Better for her to avoid the Fae for a time, while she settles in. The tanai here are much more connected with their Fae than yours in San Francisco."

True. Though that was starting to change, according to Pinky. Now that the door to the realm in Berkeley had opened again, some of the tanai who had left when the Fae did were starting to make noises about coming back. Which was making those who'd stayed behind nervous. But San Francisco was a big city. Room enough for both kinds of tanai. I hoped.

"I can understand her staying away from them. She's probably had enough Fae for now."

Behind me, I could still hear Mitch's team moving around the house. I'd drawn the blinds when I'd retreated to my office, not wanting to see them prowling around the gardens, probably checking the wards all over again.

I knew it was sensible, but it was also irritating. Sure, they had more experience than me, but I knew the wards around Damon's house as well as anyone. I hadn't found any holes, Maia hadn't found any holes, and I doubted anyone else Mitch cared to task with checking would.

He could just accept that, for now, the emergency was over and send everyone home so we could all go to bed. But doing things the easy way was not in Mitch's DNA. Not when it came to keeping Damon safe.

Which I couldn't be annoyed with him about.

I stifled a yawn, focused back on Aubrey. "Do we know if she has magic?" I asked.

"She has an aura. She looks like a tanai to me, but if she has any power, she is being tight-lipped about how she might use it."

"Well, I guess it's up to her." It was her decision whether or not to embrace her power. Fae magic didn't work the same way as a witch's. Witches who weren't taught to use their power could have unpredictable results, but there were tanai who ignored their magic quite happily. And Gwen's couldn't have caused her any problems when she was younger because she hadn't learned she was tanai until she got to university.

But if Gwen had no interest in magic, that was one less thing to worry about. Her Fae heritage might make it tricky if she decided to go back to studying VR. She'd need a chip eventually and not all tanai could tolerate them. My friend, Pinky Andretti, also a tanai, had one, but she was lucky. Iron didn't bother her at all.

"Yes," Aubrey agreed. "And if she doesn't want anything to do with Fae, it's probably just as well if she's happy to leave any magic she may have learned there behind." She tucked a strand of hair that had dared to break free from her bun back behind her ear and straightened. Shifting back into Cestis mode. Hopefully preparing to get on with her day rather than drop some Cestis bombshell on me.

"Well, keep me posted if there's anything you think I need to know." I stopped myself from offering any more help. The Cestis had managed the magical affairs of the United Kingdom for centuries without any assistance. Gwen wasn't the first tanai they'd helped return from the realm. She wouldn't be the last. If Aubrey wanted our help, she'd ask.

Aubrey smiled. "I will. Say hello to Damon for me."

"Sure." I paused. "Any decision yet on your Archives?" Damon would ask, if I told him I'd been talking to Aubrey.

Aubrey shook her head. "No. We had a few things come up in the last few weeks along with helping with Gwen, so we haven't had time to talk about it as a group, but it's on the agenda for our next official meeting, which is at the end of next week. We'll discuss it then."

"Do you think they'll go for it?"

Aubrey pursed her lips, considering. "Ralph, I think, can see the benefits of the idea, though he has his reservations. The others, well, they're harder to read. They play their cards close to their chests. The biggest sticking point will be Leo. He's a bit of a stickler for tradition. And I'm sure Isolde will have legal questions about how the information will remain protected."

"Cassandra had her doubts, too. I'm sure she'd be happy to speak to them if you think it would help."

"Yes, I'm keeping that in mind." She hesitated. "But…"

"Let me guess, a vote of confidence from someone over here is not necessarily going to be helpful?"

"Relations between Cestis can get complicated."

I nodded. I understood. Aubrey had been frosty enough herself when I'd first met her when she'd come to learn about how the Cestis here were embracing tech in the name of efficiency. "I hope you can get them to see the benefits. It would make it easier for the Cestis to help each other. Leaving aside how much they actually want to cooperate."

It would be much easier if I could log in to the UK Cestis

Archives and access their massive collection, which was far older and more extensive than the ones Cassandra maintained beneath her house. For one thing I wouldn't be waiting on Ralph to dig up more information on Lord Usuriel, I could have found it for myself.

Aubrey nodded, glancing down off-screen. "I'm doing my best. Now, I'm sorry, Maggie, but I have a meeting shortly and you should probably go to bed."

"Yes. I should." Footsteps still clomped up and down the corridor beyond my office. Sleep wouldn't be happening as long as Mitch and the team were still doing their thing. But that wasn't Aubrey's problem. "Talk to you soon," I said.

Aubrey nodded and ended the call.

Leaving me to contemplate nixlings and Fae and Usuriel. And that damned photo.

Chapter Four

THE SECURITY TEAM finished up around three a.m., when I was just getting to the point of being so tired I wondered if I'd imagined the whole thing. Mitch left Maia to bunk down in the guest room we kept for the security team and Jake on patrol in the garden.

I didn't argue. It was his job to make the calls when it came to our safety—at least where it didn't interfere with me helping the Cestis—so whether I liked it or not, he was in charge.

Damon and I crawled into bed, too tired to do anything but fall asleep, curled around each other as comfort against any more things going bump in the dark.

Damon's alarm went off far too early. I barely managed to open an eye and mutter something as close to 'see you later' as I could manage on three hours sleep before pulling the pillow over my head and falling back to sleep until my own alarm went off around eight. I cut it off with a wave of my hand and forced myself out of bed, heading for the shower before I could give in to the temptation to ignore the alarm and sleep the day away.

I used every 'wake me up' option Damon's complicated

shower offered, alternating pummeling jets of water with cold bursts that made me yelp and regret my life choices.

Five hours sleep wasn't much better than three.

I was staring at myself in the mirror, trying to ignore my dark circles, my long brown hair falling damp on my bare shoulders, when Madge announced Lizzie was at the gate.

"Let her in. Tell her I'll be five minutes."

I hastily threw on some clothes, dried my hair as best I could, and then followed the smell of coffee to the kitchen where Lizzie was perched on one of the stools at the counter, watching Maia make coffee. Maia was in her usual black, everything immaculately ironed, and her dark hair braided away from her face. Lizzie, in contrast, wore a daffodil-yellow sundress with bright-blue combat boots. She'd left her hair loose for once. It was nearly true silver, almost sparkling in the sun pouring through the windows.

I assumed it was some kind of nano effect, but required caffeine before I could form the words to ask.

Real coffee was one of the perks of dating Damon I would never take for granted. Maia tried to pass me the mug she'd just poured, but she had had as little sleep as me so I made her take it and waited for the machine to produce the strongest espresso it was programmed for. Damon usually made the coffee himself, overriding the programming. I knew how, but this morning I was happy to let the tech take care of it and save my brainpower.

We all drank coffee silently for a few minutes, Lizzie unusually quiet despite the sunny outfit. There were faint dark smudges under her eyes. Had she had an interrupted night as well?

When she yawned and stretched and I spotted the familiar sheen of a spray bandage on her left arm, I answered my own question.

I pointed at the bandage. "What happened there?"

Lizzie grimaced. "It's fine."

"That's not what I asked."

"Zee and I were doing another sweep through Dockside. Someone reported a 'giant bug' climbing a wall to the police."

"And the police responded?" Most of Dockside was a no-go zone for cops. The city had essentially abandoned the area. Too much damage and no one willing to step in and spend the money to restabilize the docks and build the infrastructure to keep back the water. It had been tried on other parts of the city's shorelines with varying degrees of success. Some areas had recovered, some were still teetering on the edge of might make it back, and Dockside had been declared a failure. So, no cops. Not unless a VIP got into trouble down there, and even then it would have to be someone *very* VIP.

"The police recorded the call in their system. The Cestis has been monitoring for key words and phrases, as usual. And 'giant bug' was one of them, so we got pinged."

The Cestis operated independently of the other arms of the law when it came to magic users, but it also piggybacked off existing infrastructure where it could. I didn't know the full extent of its resources, or how many witches Cassandra and the others commanded, but I knew they couldn't hope to cover the whole country without using other agencies. They just had to do it discreetly.

"So, an afrit?" Maia asked.

Lizzie shook her hair, the effect somewhat mesmerizing as the silver sparkled. "Not that we could find. Of course, down there, it could have been someone having a really bad trip."

"So officially it's a figment of a Dockside-induced hallucination?" I said.

She nodded but her mouth had flattened into a dissatisfied line.

"And unofficially?"

"I'm not sure. We'll keep looking. But it's been, what, more than a month since you killed yours? It could have been a loner." She ran her hand down her arm, stopping where the spray bandage started, massaging the skin above it gently, as though it was annoying her. Or the lack of success finding the afrit was.

Afrit, though not common, did sometimes turn up in the city. Anywhere there'd been imps or lesserkind who used them for various low-level tasks and mischief. They could climb walls, burrow underground, and infiltrate places imps couldn't. The Cestis rooted them out and killed them where they could, but it was nearly impossible to find them all.

Without any other demonkind directing them, they seemed to live like large bugs, eating—I assumed—rats and pigeons and garbage and avoiding contact with humans unless something magical caught their attention.

"Right. A loner," I echoed Lizzie as Maia rose to refill her mug.

Lizzie's brown eyes were skeptical. My gut agreed with her. And wasn't happy about it.

"So we just keep monitoring the reports?"

"Yes," Lizzie said. She and Zee and Cassandra had spent more than a few nights working their way around Dockside since Callum and I had killed an afrit down there. Callum and Gráinne and I had, too, under the guise of training. None of us had found any trace of other afrit, but they could hide in places impossible for humans to follow and if there weren't groups of them and they were mostly dormant, they didn't leave a strong enough magical signature to trace easily.

Though I was much better at sensing even faint traces of demon magic these days.

"Do you want Maia to look at your arm?" I asked Lizzie. She was rubbing the spot above the bandage again.

"No, I'm icy. Scratched it on some chain link. Zee cleaned it out for me." She moved her left hand around in exaggerated bends and swoops, demonstrating it was fully functional. "See."

Except for the part where it was hurt, probably. But my

skills at healing were limited at best, so I had to take her word for it. Zee wouldn't take any chances when it came to Lizzie, though, so if he'd cleaned and dressed the wound, it would have been thorough.

"Fine, fine. I'll stop nagging. I'm sorry Cassandra dragged you out here," I said with an apologetic grimace.

"Not a problem. It is, after all, my job."

One of her jobs. Like Aubrey, she was the youngest on the US Cestis; at twenty-three she was eight years younger than Aubrey, who was my age.

But Lizzie wasn't content with merely helping police the magical world. She also worked part-time at Spark, a charity for kids with troubled backgrounds. She didn't need to, but if push came to shove, I would bet good money she'd choose helping those kids over the Cestis and magic. They were a cause too close to her heart.

Her father was an exceedingly wealthy man. But also a massively controlling and abusive asshole. He had, thankfully, dropped dead a few years ago.

Lizzie ran away from home at fourteen, somehow ending up in San Francisco, though she'd grown up on the East Coast. She'd lived on the streets, or in squats. Luckily she'd fallen in with a group of guys around her age—including Zee —who had been more interested in gaming than drugs, and the four of them had managed to eke out an existence in game clubs and doing odd jobs for a couple of years until Lizzie had crossed paths with Cassandra, who'd helped them all get back on track.

Cassandra pulled strings so Lizzie got her trust fund early, and her mother added to it after her father died. But, as far as I knew, Lizzie had no other contact with any of her family on either side. She and her mother loved each other, in their way, but the fact her mom had stayed with her dad had fractured their relationship in a way that, so far, Lizzie didn't seem interested in fixing.

So she knew what the kids she tried to help were going through and gave up time she didn't really have, to see if she could change their lives the way Cassandra had changed hers.

I was surrounded by a bunch of overly-dedicated-to-their-jobs enthusiasts. Or workaholics to put it bluntly. Not that I was any better. Note to self: make some friends who liked doing things like taking lazy island vacations and brunching and could teach the rest of us how to relax. I didn't like my chances of meeting anyone like that at Riley or through the Cestis. And I didn't want to think about island vacations because right now, the main thing islands brought to mind was the damned photograph of my mom and Jack.

Time to work. I needed something to focus on if I wanted to avoid finding the nearest comfortable flat surface and napping.

"Where's Jake?" I asked Maia. After a night patrolling the garden, he deserved coffee, too.

"He reported in thirty minutes ago and Mitch told him he could go home. There weren't any more incidents."

I already knew that. Jake would have raised the alarm if he'd spotted another nixling.

"Maia said you both checked the wards and couldn't see anything," Lizzie said, putting down her empty mug with a wistful glance at the coffee machine. Her 'more coffee will be bad for me later, but I'd *really* like it now' face. I knew how she felt.

Lizzie had more willpower than me when it came to caffeine, so I restrained myself so I wouldn't tempt her into another cup. She deserved to sleep well when she finally got to go to bed. "No. Everything looks normal. I'm not sure if that's a good or a bad thing."

"Well, it means nothing else got through them. We need to ask Callum if he has any ideas about how to keep nixlings out, or whether it's a waste of time trying," I said.

"Agreed," Lizzie said. "I'll go over the wards, so Cassandra is happy, and then you and I can go to Berkeley and see what Callum has to say." Her hair shimmered as she considered me. "Unless of course you had something else to do this morning?"

Technically I had client work, but it was just data analysis I could run in the background and read the reports later. I had a couple of jobs to finish up before I started my stint working on Damon's new game. That would keep me busy for a month. I also had to go through my current list of project offers and make sure I had work lined up for when I was done at Righteous. Damon would have happily employed me full-time, but I'd worked too hard at my business to give it up just yet. And sure, ferreting out problems for some of my other clients wasn't always as fun or cutting edge as working for him, but it was still interesting, and people still wanted my help.

I was hoping Yoshi might have some time to help me out over the summer, before his classes started up again. He always made the workload lighter, but I also wanted him to enjoy his summer vacation time. Like the rest of us, he had workaholic tendencies, between looking after his sister and trying to cram in vacation internships at various tech companies. So I'd have to see what he wanted to do.

"Nothing urgent." I nodded my head toward the fridge. "Do you want me to help you with the checks, or do I have time for breakfast?"

"Eat. Maia can take me round. She knows the wards as well as we do."

Well, she knew the witchy parts of them and the ins and outs of the security system. Callum was the one who'd added some additional Fae touches. I knew enough about those to know how to spot a problem, but I didn't yet know enough Fae magic to alter them myself. Neither did Lizzie, but she might see something I'd missed.

Lizzie was thorough. It was more than an hour before she and Maia came back into the house.

I'd started working but focusing was proving difficult. I kept thinking about the nixling and what it could have wanted.

Not a useful train of thought. I had no way of knowing. I shut down my desk comp when I heard Lizzie's footsteps coming down the hallway. Maia wore combat boots, too, but hers were military grade and she managed to be stealthy in them. Lizzie stomped cheerfully when she didn't need to be quiet.

She poked her head through the door. "I didn't find anything. Let's talk to Callum."

Callum was still using my house in Berkeley as a base. Which gave me an excuse to put off making the decision as to whether I was going to keep it or not.

On the one hand, it used to be home. My grandparents' house, the house where I'd first found a real home when I'd come there after my mother had died. On the other hand, it had been destroyed once in the Big One and then again by Jack. I'd rebuilt it twice now and with each passing week it felt a little bit farther away from my memories and a little bit harder to justify why I was keeping it when I was basically living at Damon's.

Still, I didn't have to make my decision while it offered a handy base for Callum and Gráinne when they were training me or doing whatever arcane Fae things Cerridwen set them to do in the city.

She'd seemed happy enough to add Gráinne to the roster, claiming it was easier to have two of them working outside the realm to train me and Pinky and help the Cestis see if they could hunt down stray afrit. I pretended to believe her, but the other reason—the one no one was talking about and that I didn't really want to think about too hard—was that I'd potentially made an enemy of Lord Usuriel. Fae weren't supposed to interfere with humans, but Usuriel hadn't struck me as a rule follower.

And Cerridwen hadn't invited me back into the realm yet.

Which I assumed meant she was still trying to calm things down and didn't want to risk my safety. The thought of Lord Usuriel on the warpath made me more than happy to have an extra s'ealg oiche on my team.

The Lord of the Nichtkin scared me.

We found Callum sitting out back, sipping tea out of one of Lizzie's sparkly pink 'Unicorns are real' mugs. The matching teapot was sitting on my cheap wooden outdoor table. Somehow, despite the wonky table and the silly mug, Callum, dressed in a white linen shirt and dark jeans, managed to exude elegance.

He nodded a greeting as we came down the steps. "That was fast."

"Not much traffic." Lizzie dragged the chair next to Callum's away from the table, sat and turned her face up to the sun, eyes squeezed shut.

Clearly she needed a moment.

My neighbor's dog, Ted, realizing Lizzie and I were home, started barking eagerly from behind the fence. I went over, climbed up the rail to say hello. He wagged his tail as I rubbed his ears but started barking again when I stopped. He was still wary of Callum, which Callum didn't seem to take personally.

Ted pointed his nose in Callum's direction and barked again.

"I know, I know. He can do things you don't approve of. But he's fine." I rubbed his ears again, appreciating the simplicity of a happy dog that wasn't a Fae creature.

But I couldn't use Ted as an excuse for too long. I heard Lizzie yawn behind me. The faster we got this over with, the faster she could get some sleep. I lowered myself down from the fence and joined Lizzie and Callum, wishing we'd stopped in the kitchen to make coffee. The steam drifting from Callum's teapot smelled like mint and something I didn't quite recognize. I doubted it contained caffeine.

"There were no gaps in the wards?" Callum asked Lizzie.

She shook her head. "No. Any idea how it got in?"

"They are curious creatures," Callum said. "And some are resistant to certain forms of magic."

"So they can really just walk through the wards? Even your wards?" I asked.

The s'ealg oiche fought demons. Their skills at warding were second to none, according to the information I'd found in the Cestis's Archives. And Callum himself.

"They can get around many things," Callum said. "We are not entirely sure how. It's a secret they do not care to share."

"So you're telling me anyone could slip a creature into my backyard at any time?" I asked.

Callum shrugged. "The bigger question is how it got out of the realm. They can get through wards, but the door is another matter."

"Did it say anything when Gráinne brought it back?"

"Not that I've heard. Which means it wouldn't talk to Cerridwen and probably comes from a territory that isn't necessarily friendly."

Like Usuriel's. "She wouldn't hurt it, would she?"

He shook his head. "No. It didn't harm anyone, and it isn't one of ours. She marked it with a charm that should stop it getting through the door again and sent it out of her territory. It can make its own way home. Maybe it slipped through behind someone who didn't notice. Creatures will get out from time to time."

The back of my neck prickled. The last time a creature had slipped out of the door, it had been a bruadhsiu, a night-walker. A nightmare creature feeding on people's dreams and draining their life force.

We'd killed it in the end, but not before it had done some

killing of its own. Damon's driver, Boyd, had nearly been one of its victims. And we'd never figured out how it had made it through the door.

The nixlings were nothing like nightwalkers, but I'd still prefer it if the Fae could make sure nothing got through their door without permission.

"But it's more likely someone let it out, right? Do you think someone was trying to send a message?" I asked. "You know, 'hey, look, we know where you live'."

Callum grimaced. "Perhaps."

Was he being diplomatic? It seemed the most likely scenario to me. The Fae were supposed to stay unseen in San Francisco. It was part of the contract they had with the Cestis. They couldn't harm humans, and they were not allowed to show their true forms if they did get permission to leave the realm. And one day soon, the restrictions on the door would lift. After all, it had been over a year since it had been reestablished, and it seemed to be stable.

But there was dissension among the Fae at the best of times and reopening the door to San Francisco wasn't a decision all of them supported. It had been necessary to stabilize the realm. but some thought it was too soon to reconnect to the part of the world with the most known demon activity in recent times. It was not much more than a decade since a demon had caused the Big One and less than that since a demon had come for me. The Fae hated demons more than the Cestis did. A demon gaining access to the innate magic of the realm could destroy both the realm and the human world.

"You think Lord Usuriel?"

"He does seem the most likely candidate." Callum put down his cup with a sigh. "Lord Padran isn't fond of you, but he doesn't command nixlings. His realm is mostly water, and nixlings do not love getting wet."

I pictured the nixling's fluffy coat. They could probably

swim—cats could—but I doubted it would be fun to dry off afterward.

"Will Cerridwen talk to Usuriel?"

Callum poured more tea. "That may depend. Things are still…delicate."

Confirming what I already knew.

Between rescuing Gwen and crossing Lord Usuriel, I hadn't made myself any more popular with the members of the Elder Council, who already didn't like me.

I assumed I wouldn't be going back into the realm for some time yet, and Callum and Gráinne would train us here. I was happy with that plan. I knew Pinky was, too. She was even less fond of the realm than I was, seeing as technically Cerridwen could command her fealty at any point and put her to work.

But I would have thought a month might start to ease the tension. After all, I hadn't broken any rules. If anything, Usuriel had. But maybe denting his pride was worse than breaking rules. I'd just have to wait it out until he cooled down. I didn't exactly miss going into the realm, but I missed Cerridwen's lessons. I didn't want to forget the Fae magic I'd fought hard to understand.

But my sense of time wasn't the same as a Fae's.

"Alright," I said. "So is there anything we can do to stop this happening again, or do we have to be on alert for extra weirdness?"

Callum's mouth quirked. "Gráinne and I can extend the wards, give you more warning if anything of concern approaches the house. Most of the creatures you need to worry about can't get through wards the way the nixlings can. It would take a great deal of force, the kind that can't be achieved with stealth and that would be an undeniable breach of the contract. If you come across any of them, well, you know how to defend yourself against demonkind. Most of the things effective against them will work against beings of the realm."

Mostly the way I killed demonkind was with fire. Callum had made me a far better fighter—though I had a long way to go to get anywhere near as skilled as he or Gráinne were— and Cerridwen had begun teaching me Fae magic to add to my arsenal, but so far I hadn't mastered anything advanced enough to kill a demon.

"What about bullets?"

His mouth pursed. The Fae, as a rule, didn't approve of guns. Fair enough when guns were made from iron and steel and so were many of the bullets they fired. Damon had swapped all our ammunition over to steel casing and cores after our first encounters with the Fae. A pure iron bullet would wreck a gun after a few shots, so it was the best we could do. For now.

"A bullet could kill some. Weaken others. Others, you would merely anger unless you have iron ammunition," Callum said. "In some ways it's a pity we cannot put on some show of strength to let them know you are not defenseless."

"Such as?"

He shrugged. "Well, if they sent something more dangerous than a nixling, killing it would have sent a strong message that you are not easy prey."

"I'm not about to start killing things that haven't even made a move against me," I said.

"An admirable position," Callum replied. "But while the nixling didn't seek to harm you, locating your house and breaching your wards is a move in itself. Particularly if we are to assume it did not decide to seek you out on its own."

Apparently he'd come round to my way of thinking.

"So I'm in a game of chicken with an unknown Fae?"

Callum squinted at me. "I fail to see what poultry has to do with it."

Lizzie snorted. "'Chicken' is what we call a dumb game

where two people run or drive at each other. The one who gives in first and dodges, loses. It's epically stupid."

"Ah. I am familiar with such contests. The Fae know such games of dominance. Though I fail to see why it would be called chicken. Are human fowl particularly cowardly?"

"They're smart enough to run away, if you charge them," I said. "That's not cowardly, that's just good sense when you're not a predator."

"Dumb name for a dumb game," Lizzie agreed.

"So it seems," Callum said. "But perhaps the lesson to be had is that in games of dominance, it might be wiser to be the predator than the prey."

Chapter Five

"Wanna come play predator?" Lizzie asked.

"Are you talking about gaming or Cestis business?" I hadn't expected to hear from her again today. On the datapad screen, the circles under her eyes were deep, despite her makeup. After we'd left Berkeley, she'd gone to Spark. I'd come home to Damon's place where I'd worked for a few hours, crashed for two hours and then gone back to work, eating dinner at my desk because Damon was still at the office. Now it was nearly nine p.m. and I'd been contemplating an early night when Lizzie called.

Lizzie swept a hand at herself. "Do I look like I'm dressed for gaming?"

She wore black. A long-sleeve tee. When we went to gaming clubs with Zee, Lizzie usually dressed in an even brighter version of her neo-anime-meets-chaos-witch style. Not black. I sighed. "No. So what's wrong?"

"A friend called me. She's worried about a house in her neighborhood."

"And this requires me? Not say, Zee or Trick or Cassandra or Ian?"

"Zee has a tournament. Trick is out of town. Cassandra

and I discussed it, and she said it would be educational for you. Callum's coming, too. So, are you joining us?"

That made me feel slightly better. Callum could deal with just about anything we might encounter. And Cassandra wouldn't send me with Lizzie if it was something she thought I couldn't handle yet. "This is one of those 'it's really more rhetorical' questions, isn't it?"

"Yep," Lizzie said with a tired grin.

Guilt twinged. I doubt she'd managed to work a two-hour nap into her day

"Sure," I said. "Where are we going?"

"Sea Cliff. We'll swing by and pick you up," Lizzie said. "Callum's on his way. Have coffee ready."

———

From the outside, the house, though small, was nothing out of the ordinary. Nondescript even. White, boxy, two stories, with a grayish roof and front door.

The grass was mown and the low maintenance bushes planted in the garden beds trimmed, but there were no plants on the small porch or any other signs of life.

This section of Sea Cliff was hanging on so far, but we passed one other empty house in the street, and there'd been more than a few vacant blocks on our way.

The ocean-view mansions that had lined the cliffs before the Big One were a thing of the past. The cliffs were crumbling and unstable. The houses that survived the earthquake had been declared unsafe. So it had gone from being an enclave for the rich and famous to one for regular people, full of rebuilt properties that attempted to mimic something of the area's original style but in sensible, smaller, quake-proofed homes.

The fact that some of those were empty in a city that had lost a chunk of its residential space told me people weren't so keen to make a bet on a suburb so close to the ocean.

It wasn't a part of the city I'd ever spent much time in. I'd done the obligatory school trips to the old Legion of Honor Museum and the bus drivers had always driven us past all the ritzy real estate as part of the experience, but they'd moved the museum further in toward the center of the city when they'd rebuilt it as the New Legion of Honor, so I hadn't been back. But even though it wasn't as upscale as it had once been, it also was nothing like Dockside. It was still a livable neighborhood where people worked, raised families, and played. Quiet at this time of night, but only because most people would be sleeping or getting ready to. It wasn't the 'no one's here because it's abandoned' or 'no one's out because it's not safe' vibe of Dockside. Just an average-looking suburban street.

Hardly the kind of place you'd expect magical oddities to spring up. And it didn't seem like a place you'd find afrit running around. Certainly I couldn't sense any trace of magic.

But what did I know?

Lizzie was studying the house, hands on hips, her expression tightly focused.

"You said your friend told you this place was empty, right?" I said.

Lizzie nodded. "Yeah, she's lived about a street back from here for nearly a year, but she walks her dog in this street. She said this house has never had anyone living in it all that time. No cars or people. No lights at night."

Someone was cutting the grass, but all that proved was someone was paying for lawn maintenance. "Someone's taking care of the lawn. I guess that means it's not just abandoned?"

"Probably."

"And what bothered your friend?"

"She said she saw lights a few nights ago, but no signs of

anyone having moved in. She told the police, but they came around and couldn't see anyone."

"Did they go inside?"

"No. I checked their report. No cause to enter. And then yesterday she felt something weird as she was passing."

"Weird?"

Lizzie wriggled her fingers. "You know, *magically* weird."

Callum looked unimpressed with the description. Maybe for a Fae, it would take a lot for magic to be weird.

"Okay. So bad vibes," I said. "Got it."

"Yep. When she was walking her dog this morning, she got the same feeling. So she called me."

"What does she do?"

"Well, she's an attorney. But she's also a witch."

So, potentially someone who wasn't deep in the magical world. But obviously someone Lizzie considered credible. And in the end, Lizzie, as a member of the Cestis, had to make the call about what got investigated and what didn't.

I glanced down the street. The houses all had their blinds drawn, most of them with no lights shining around the edges. The only things moving in the street were us and the wind through the trees planted next to the sidewalk in front of every other house.

This wasn't Dockside. It was the sort of place where, if someone spotted three strangers dressed in various forms of tactical black, complete, in my and Callum's cases with weapons strapped to our backs and thighs, in front of an abandoned house at this time of night, they'd probably call the cops.

And because Sea Cliff was still a neighborhood, not an abandoned hellhole like Dockside, the cops would respond.

Lizzie would no doubt handle them. Pull out her Cestis badge or whatever it was she actually used to prove her credentials, but better if she didn't have to. "We should get moving," I said. "Or your friend won't be the only one noticing something weird." I took a step toward the front gate.

"Wards," said Lizzie.

I froze. Damn. Rookie mistake. I knew better. But I hadn't had a full night's sleep in several days and it was starting to show. I stepped back as Lizzie raised her hands, shifting my sight to study the property.

I couldn't see much. A few faint shimmers at random intervals along the fence but nothing resembling a fully functional ward. Whoever was paying for the yard work wasn't paying for the wards to be maintained.

Lizzie seemed to come to the same conclusion.

She dropped her hands and stepped back, looking at Callum.

"What do you think?" she said. "All I get is remnants."

"That is what I also see," Callum said. "There were wards once, but they have long since been broken."

Lizzie nodded. "I checked the records. The house still has an active connection to the solar grid, so someone's paying the power bill. Couldn't find any record of a current vidlink."

No vidlink equaled no communications. And hopefully no monitored security. But it didn't rule out your basic 'make enough noise until the neighbors call the cops' type alarm. "Do you know who owns the place?"

"No. We can dig into that later. But if there's power, there could be an alarm system." She studied the house. Probably looking for cameras.

"We can check out the battery array. The control box should tell us what's connected. If there's an alarm, well, you two are the ones who sneak around at night for a living. What do you usually do?"

"It is not my area of expertise. Wards, yes. Alarms, no. I do not usually have a need to break into human houses," Callum said.

Lizzie smiled smugly. "Sometimes I do."

Did she mean recently or when she'd been living in abandoned buildings as a teenager? Probably not the right time to ask.

"Then you can figure out what to do if there's an alarm," I said. "I vote we go around the back, scope out the battery array, take it from there."

I peered at the house, wishing there was more light. There were no obvious cameras, but cameras could be tiny. Or tucked away in places we didn't have a line of sight to. Two standard exterior lights were positioned on the front of the porch, either side of the stairs. I found a loose stone on the street and threw it toward the front door. The clatter it made landing on the porch was way too loud, but no lights came on. "No motion sensors. That's helpful."

Lizzie waited, watching, but must have agreed with me because she headed for the gate, motioning for us to follow.

Like most of its neighbors, the blinds in the large windows were drawn. Lizzie skirted the direct approach to the porch, instead heading left, where access to the backyard was blocked by a wooden fence with a locked gate. I boosted Lizzie over and Callum helped me. He, of course, almost vaulted over it. Mere mortal gates were no obstacle when you're a Fae warrior.

Lizzie rolled her eyes at me as he landed. I hid a smile. Callum was showy and cocky, but his confidence was warranted, backed by his magic and his centuries of experience. I didn't want him leaving in a huff. We kept moving. No lights came on, no alarms blared, and I began to relax a tiny bit. It was probably messed up that I was more worried about the police arriving than an afrit, but I was confident that Lizzie and Callum could take care of an afrit. Whereas I didn't need the headache of the newslinks getting wind of Damon Riley's girlfriend being caught breaking and entering.

The paparazzi were bad enough, even when I wasn't doing anything illegal.

The backyard wasn't much bigger than the front and not much different. The grass was trimmed and the beds planted with the same generic green blob bushes. Zero sign of anyone living in the house.

No shoes at the back door. No kid's toys or play equipment. No garden tools. No table or chairs on the tiny patio area.

The place felt empty in a vaguely disturbing way.

So much for starting to feel relaxed. Something about the house made my instincts nervous. I looked again for wards, but still nothing. The faintest of gleams on one side of the back door, perhaps. I squinted at it and then decided to leave it to the experts and turned my attention to the battery array.

The control panel was in the usual place. A basic model. Though there were some old screw holes in the wall above it like someone had had a more sophisticated system set up and removed it when they moved out.

I'd grown spoiled living with Damon. I had to remember normal people didn't know that things that went bump in the night were real, didn't have to deal with potential kidnappers and crazy fans, and didn't need twenty-four-hour live monitored security and state-of-the-art vidlinks and house comps.

Most people would put in a security system they could afford and call it a day. This one didn't even have a palm scan to open the metal control box. It was locked with a padlock.

"This looks easy enough," I said, waving Lizzie forward.

She took my place, peering at the box, while pulling on a pair of latex gloves. No fingerprints. Right.

"Oh, yeah. I know this kind. Icy." She produced a set of lockpicks from a pocket inside her jacket and made short work of the padlock. She and Zee had taught me to pick locks when I'd found them practicing one day a few months ago. I could handle basic locks now, but I wasn't anywhere near as smooth as Lizzie.

She swapped the picks for a penknife one-handed as she

flipped open the control panel door, in an impressively well-practiced move. She selected a blade and did something I couldn't see to the interior of the box. Something else I should ask her to teach me.

"Done. Alarm connection taken care of." She straightened, closed the panel and replaced the padlock.

"What happens if there's stuff inside? Valuables or whatever. People might steal it if there's no alarm?" I asked.

"I'll ward the control panel and send someone round to fix the connection. No one will even know we were here. Speaking of which." She paused and dug into yet another pocket. "Gloves." She passed us each a pair. "No point leaving fingerprints if we can avoid it."

"Do the gloves not interfere with your magic?" Callum asked, pulling a face as he slid his on.

"Not so far," Lizzie said. "Though, Maggie, I wouldn't recommend throwing flame with them on. They might melt. That would be unpleasant."

Couldn't argue with that. I pulled on the gloves. "What exactly are we looking for?"

"At a guess, traces of magic," Lizzie said.

"Your friend didn't mention giant bugs?"

"No. Lights. Weird vibe. Something setting off her spidey sense, but not giant bugs."

"Is she the kind of witch who would know what an afrit is if she saw it?"

Lizzie shook her head. "I don't think so. But a hella big bug would have caught her attention. And if she does know, well, she would have mentioned it."

"But if there is an afrit?" Fire was the easiest weapon against demonkind. Though starting one inside a building was a bad idea. Fighting Jack's imps had left me with a shell of burned-out walls instead of a house.

"Let me and Callum take care of it," Lizzie said.

"And if there's a silent alarm?"

"Stop worrying so hard. I'll deal with an alarm if I have to. But I don't think there is one."

I hoped not. But she was probably right. The system was cheap and we hadn't tripped anything so far. It seemed unlikely anyone was monitoring the house. But someone could still show up. It's not like someone had helpfully invented teleports so a security team could instantly be on-site. After we'd returned from the realm I'd asked Damon if he thought humans might ever invent something close to the Ways the Fae used to cover distances fast, but he'd said he had no idea. Sigh. With all the traveling between San Francisco and Berkeley I did, a teleport would be handy.

But for now I was stuck with commuting, and trusting Lizzie to deal with rent-a-cops if they arrived.

I joined Lizzie at the back door while Callum watched us. There was a palm scan by the door but whatever Lizzie had done had disabled it, too, because it didn't light up when she waved her hand near the plate. Satisfied, she demonstrated her lockpicking skills yet again and cautiously pushed the door inwards, leaning forward to peer into the darkened hallway. No lights sprang on. So we could rule out a rat or something setting off a sensor light to explain what Lizzie's friend had seen.

I extended my magic, searching for traces of demonkind, but got nothing. I twisted back to Callum. "You should go next."

"You won't learn if you always go last."

Maybe not, but in this situation, I was willing to hang back. Whatever we found in the house, I'd be more use backing Lizzie and him up than trying to lead the charge.

Lizzie moved deeper into the house and Callum glided after her, moving in the silent way he always did in our training sessions. A s'ealg oiche on the hunt. Focused and deadly.

I should attempt to channel that energy. I was a hunter, too.

I followed Callum, closing the back door once I was inside. The hallway was dark without the moonlight, and I blinked, trying to get my eyes to adjust. I could barely make out Callum's hand stretched toward what I assumed was a light switch.

"No. I don't want to draw attention," Lizzie said. She summoned a globe of dim light in her left hand. "This will do."

"Ah," Callum said, "Yes, that is sensible." He followed Lizzie's example and also summoned a small light, setting it to hover by his shoulder. I couldn't do the hovering part yet, but I could summon a light to my hand, like Lizzie.

My sight adjusted to the small amount of light, showing me a central hall painted some light color that was hard to make out by the witchlight. There were two doors on each side, painted a deeper shade of whatever the color was, then the hall ended at a more open area at the front of the house.

The air was musty, like the house had been closed up for a long time. Someone might have been taking care of the garden, but no one was coming in to clean judging by the layer of dust gathered on everything and the cobwebs stretched over some of the doors.

I shivered at the sight of them. Since the bruadhsiu, spiders creeped me out. And the webs reminded me of the sticky sensation of Cerridwen's lure. The one that had drawn an afrit in. I reached for my magic. I didn't get the same sensation here, but that didn't mean anything. There are many different types of afrit.

I took a few more breaths of the stale air, but all I got was dust and the fading heat of the day. None of the acid-rot smell of demonkind.

I blew out a breath, some of the tension in my shoulders easing.

Lizzie pointed down the corridor, gesturing at the doors. "Which one?"

One of them might hide a staircase, though that was more likely to be near the front. More likely the doors led to the kitchen and laundry room. Maybe a powder room and home office. The bedrooms were usually upstairs.

"Can you hear anything?" I asked Callum. His hearing was way more sensitive than ours would be. It might be smarter to check upstairs first, make sure the place was truly empty. But if it was, it didn't make much difference what order we checked the rooms.

"No," he admitted.

"So we take one room at a time?" I asked. "Stay together."

He nodded. "That seems wise."

Lizzie opened the nearest door, the first room to the left, revealing a laundry room. Washer, dryer, laundry sink with a floor-to-ceiling cabinet next to them lined one wall. A counter with cabinets above and below filled the other. They might have been white, but mostly looked grimy gray under the dust.

The appliances were covered in dust, too.

Lizzie opened the tall cabinet. Her brows drew down as she stared at the contents.

"What's wrong?" I asked.

She waved a hand at the cabinet. "Whoever lived here left a bunch of stuff."

I peered past her shoulder. She was right. The cabinet was full. Iron and ironing board, a robot vacuum on a docking station and shelves full of the random junk that accumulates in cabinets. Garbage bags, detergent, cleaning supplies.

"Well, some people are messy when they leave," I said. "Or it could be a furnished rental?"

"Who leaves a rental empty long enough for all this dust to accumulate in this city?" Pivoting she started opening the cabinets on the other wall. They also held cleaning supplies. "I think they left in a hurry."

"If they did, it wasn't recently," I said. "Let's keep looking."

Lizzie grimaced but nodded. With three of us, it didn't take long to go through the cabinets. No sign of afrit or magical artifacts of any kind.

We moved on to the next room. An office but, unlike the laundry, it didn't look well-used. There was a large desk in the far corner with the kind of starter kit office chair you buy from big box office supply stores tucked up against it. Most of the wall opposite the desk was taken up with built-in storage cabinets that, unlike the laundry, were empty. And lacking any of the scuff marks or left behind bits and pieces to suggest they'd ever been in use. I mean, if whoever lived here had vacated in a rush, surely there'd be crap in this room, too?

The only evidence humans had ever been inside this room, other than the furniture, was a charging cable plugged into a socket in the wall.

My turn to frown. "If they used this as a home office, there should be more stuff in here. And if they didn't, why isn't it a junk room?"

"Some people are tidier than you," Lizzie said with a grin.

"I'm tidy enough. Most people still end up with junk in a spare room, even if it's temporary." I shot a glance at Callum. I didn't know if he had a house in the realm, though the fact that Lady Morgain had called him Lord Duinne at some point suggested he did. If he did, I couldn't picture it as anything less than immaculate. No junk rooms for Fae. "Unless, of course, they can magically expand their houses."

"Going to guess that doesn't apply here," Lizzie said. "But there's nothing we need to worry about."

We moved on. The second door on the left was a powder room. Not many places for afrit to hide there, unless they were swimming up and down the sewer lines. I shuddered at the thought and pushed it away. That was one nightmare image I didn't need.

Backing out of the room, I stopped for a moment and studied the floorboards.

Lizzie almost crashed into me. "What are you looking at?"

"The floor is too clean," I said. "Everything else is dusty but there's a clear path along the corridor. Someone's swept or vacuumed or something."

"Could be a cleaning service?"

"A cleaning service that only does a strip of floor? Nope."

"Someone covering their tracks," Callum said. "If the floor was deep in dust, there would be footprints."

Exactly. But there were none. And it had to have been recent because the dust hadn't yet started to spread out over the surface again.

Lizzie crouched down, one hand spread, fingers touching the floor lightly. She closed her eyes, forehead wrinkling in concentration. She climbed back to her feet. "Well, if someone was here, they didn't clean the floor with magic."

"Your friend said she saw lights. Someone moving around in here is the simplest explanation," I pointed out. At least it possibly ruled out demonkind. I doubted imps cared much about housekeeping and afrit couldn't use a broom. But a human trying not to leave traces behind might clean up after themselves.

I extended my magic again, feeling for anything strange. But no. Nothing. More points to the no-demonkind theory.

I walked up to the end of the corridor, sticking to the clear parts of the floor. As I'd suspected, there was a staircase leading up to the first floor on the left and to the right a living area. Two beige sofas were angled toward the far wall where a monitor hung. No pictures, no knickknacks.

The place was beginning to creep me out again. There was no trace of anything indicating demonkind, but Lizzie's friend was right. There was a weird vibe. I would be happy to get out of there and never come back. Callum tipped each of the sofas up onto one end in turn, moving the heavy furniture as easily as I might pick up a cushion, but nothing scuttled out from under them.

"Kitchen, then upstairs?" I asked.

Lizzie nodded. Her expression was focused as she scanned the room a final time. "Kitchen."

The kitchen didn't make the creepiness any less. When we opened the door, there was a sour smell that had me reaching for my gun. Until Lizzie said, "Well, whoever lived here, they didn't take out the garbage when they left."

The kitchen was a mess. There were fast-food bags on the table, and unwashed—now covered in mold—plates and glasses in the sink. Lizzie flicked on the fan over the stove but it only made the smell worse. Callum, covering his mouth with one hand, grimaced, then waved his hand in a complicated gesture. The room instantly smelled fresher.

Lizzie arched an eyebrow. "What was that?"

"A scent ward," Callum said. "The smell is still there but we won't notice it."

"Right," Lizzie said. "Handy. Can you teach it to me?"

Callum nodded with a half-shrug I interpreted as 'I can try'. Fae magic and witch magic were different. I had a better chance of learning Fae magic, because I hadn't been steeped in witch magic since I was thirteen like most witches. So, depending on how Callum's ward worked, it might not be something Lizzie could replicate.

Without the smell, it was easier to focus on the room, not the garbage. Whoever built the place was team storage. Lots of cabinets. A bonus if you wanted to live there. Less so if you were hunting creatures that could fit in small spaces. I decided to start with the pantry. When I pulled the double doors open, a light inside came on automatically, nearly blinding me.

I threw up a hand, eyes watering. "Crap." I blinked back the tears, and froze as my vision cleared, revealing what was on the shelves. Bags of chips and other junk and a bunch of canned sodas and bottled water filled the middle shelf, convenient for grabbing stuff, but otherwise the shelves were full of things that could be used for doing magic.

"Maggie?" Lizzie asked, straightening from where she'd been examining the cabinet under the sink.

"I think you should come see this," I said, trying to sound calm. No need for immediate panic. I couldn't feel any magic. I hadn't tripped a ward. There were magical supplies, yes. But they were dusty like everything else. Whoever had been using them hadn't been doing so lately.

Lizzie joined me, scanning the shelves quickly. "Huh."

"That's a lot of candles and salt," I said. And herbs and other powders and liquids in clear glass jars.

"Sure is," Lizzie said. Her fingers tapped out a slow rhythm against her thigh as she studied the collection.

Callum peered over my shoulder. "Human magic."

Fae magic didn't require any assistance. They grabbed the energy they wanted and made it do as it was told. Of course, it helped that the realm was swimming in magical energy.

"No one's used any of it in a while," I said, swallowing, still scanning the shelves. Candles and salt. Which suggested protective spells or…a summoning. And so far everything I'd learned about witchcraft told me nothing good ever came from a summoning.

"Right," Lizzie said. "Let's speed this up. I want to clear the upstairs, then we'll call Cassandra." She waved her hand at the pantry. "I can't see anything obviously illegal, but we'll need to work out what's inside all those jars. But upstairs first."

My pulse rang in my ears as we climbed the stairs. My hand kept straying to my gun. I had to force it back. With Lizzie in front of me, pulling a gun was a dumb idea.

"*Breathe.*" Callum said gently. "*Focus on that. Clear your mind.*"

Great, he could tell how nervous I was. I obeyed orders and slowed my breathing, trying to clear my head. A pantry full of magical supplies was strange, but not an immediate threat.

The stairs led to a small open area. There was another monitor on the wall and a leather recliner positioned in front of it. Stacked on a small table against the wall was a viddeck and two headsets.

I stopped at the sight of them. I knew the model of the deck. It was a few years old now, but had been expensive when it first came on the market, one of the earliest home models with a chip connection. My former best friend, Nat, had had it on her wish list.

"Are you sure there's no vidlink?" I asked Lizzie.

"I'm sure. Why?" She looked puzzled.

"This is a couple of thousand dollars' worth of gear." I put my hands behind my back, not wanting to touch it. "It's one thing to leave appliances behind, but this deck is a lot of money for someone to give up. If we had a link, we could find the ID on the system."

"Later," Lizzie said. "Let's finish the rooms first."

The first door we tried led to a bedroom. At first glance, it was the same as the other rooms—dusty and unused. The closet was empty except for a pair of black sneakers and a black raincoat shoved on the shelf above the hanging space.

The queen-size bed was made up with a dark gray jersey comforter. It gave me a 'male who wants something cheap and easy' vibe. I made my way around to the nightstand on the side closest to the windows and pulled open the top drawer. A bottle of ibuprofen lay on its side next to a box of Kleenex.

I pulled the box forward gingerly, hoping whoever had stashed it there had allergies rather than having another reason for wanting Kleenex at close hand in their bedroom. Behind the box was a familiar looking badge, lying face down.

A rectangle with angled corners. Matte black with white around the edge. I froze, trying to tell myself I was wrong, but I knew I was right.

If I turned it over, it would have a name. Or an initial and a surname. Next to a Riley Arts logo. On campus, most of the Riley Arts security team wore their uniform, but those who were on an assignment that required them to wear civilian clothes—like, say, escorting Damon to a function during the day—wore name badges. A visible symbol so if something happened and the security team member gave orders, they were followed, no arguments.

In a company as huge as Righteous, no one knew everyone's faces. And yes, the staff wore ident tags, but in an emergency the badge was quicker.

I reached for the badge, but I already half expected what I'd see when I turned it over.

And I was right.

I straightened, turning to hold the badge out toward Lizzie with trembling fingers.

"Maggie?" she said. "What is that?"

"It's a Riley Arts security team badge," I said. "And it belonged to Ajax Fields."

<h1 style="text-align:center">Chapter Six</h1>

For a long second, Lizzie just stared at me. I saw the moment when her brain made the connection. She went very still.

Ajax *fucking* Fields.

Someone both Damon and I had once trusted. He'd been close to Nat before she died. He'd been on Damon's security team, for fuck's sake. And then he'd betrayed us both by somehow getting involved with a lesserkind.

He'd hidden his new allegiance well until he kidnapped Damon and me, to try to force me to agree to being bonded to a demon again.

His gamble hadn't paid off. He'd died for his stupidity and the Cestis hadn't figured out how he'd ever found a lesserkind. They'd reinforced Riley Art's security processes after the issues with my demon. So either he'd managed to slip under the radar or the lesserkind had found him after he'd already moved from the testing team to security.

I thought I'd heard the last of him. But sadly, not.

"This is what we're going to do," Lizzie said in a tightly controlled voice. "Maggie, put the badge down. I want you and Callum to go back downstairs. In fact, go back to the car.

Callum, call Cerridwen. Maggie, call Cassandra, tell her what you found, tell her the address. When you get outside, take those gloves off, leave them on the back porch. There's salt in the back of the car and purified water. Wash your hands, both of you. Callum, check her for any demon taint. Check yourself, too."

Demon taint? Fuck.

I put the badge down as gingerly as though it were a live grenade, swallowing against the urge to puke. If Lizzie could be calm, I could be calm. Panicking never helped anything.

Easier said than done, but I tried to shove the fear away. "What are you going to do?"

"Start looking for traps."

Hell, no. "If it's not safe for me and Callum, it's not safe for you. You should come with us. Wait for the others."

"Maggie, I know you're freaked out right now, but this is my job, remember. I'll be careful." Her expression was all business, no hint of fear in her brown eyes.

I knew she was right, but I hated the thought of leaving her on her own in this house. "I could help."

"No, I need you out of this house. You were one of Ajax's targets. If something is triggered, we don't want you within reach if something comes through."

"You think there's something like a summoning set up to trigger?" I swallowed. Part of me wanted to bolt for the door and not stop until I was far, far away. But I couldn't leave Lizzie.

"I don't know, but I'm not willing to take the risk if there is. If one of the other rooms has any kind of ritual work set up, I don't want you anywhere near it."

There was only one room we hadn't checked. Most likely a bathroom. Surely no one summoned demons from their bathtub?

"There is a door missing," Callum said suddenly.

"What do you mean missing?" I asked.

He jerked his head toward the bedroom door. "The rooms on this floor, they do not take up the right amount of space. Unless the bathroom is a peculiar shape, there's a space on the other side of the wall."

Lizzie twisted to face him. "Are you sure?"

He shrugged. "Not certain. But something feels… strange."

"Warded?" she asked.

"Perhaps. I can't feel one."

"Line a room with the right things before you ward it and it's possible we wouldn't," Lizzie said, sounding grim.

Callum's expression matched her voice. "I will look deeper."

Lizzie shook her head. "I want you both outside. Make those calls. Callum, you stay with Maggie. If something happens, you're the next line of defense."

He shook his head, looking stubborn. "We should do it the other way around. I am much harder to kill than you."

"No. This is my job and you're Fae, not human. The Cestis has to take point on this."

Callum shot a glance at me. "Take point?"

"Be in charge," I translated.

Callum shrugged. "I do not know that Cerridwen would necessarily agree, if there is a demon here."

"If there was a demon here, we'd be dead already. What I'm worried about is relics of spells. Or deliberate traps. Things we could trigger without meaning to. Especially if you're right about there being a hidden room. The external wards have faded, but that doesn't mean all the magic has. Not if they concentrated whatever they were doing in one room. And not if someone was in here, messing around with something recently. This is human magic, and while you might be able to help contain it, we're the ones who know how to undo it. You're strong, yes, but brute force isn't necessarily the answer." Lizzie put her hands on her hips. "So, no more arguing. Both of you *go*."

The tone of voice was so much like Cassandra that I was moving before I realized it. Callum gave Lizzie one last unhappy look and then strode out of the room. I followed, staying close, straining my magic to feel for any wards. We moved fast and silent until we were outside again, blinking in the moonlight.

"Gloves," Callum said gruffly.

Right. Lizzie had said to leave them. I stripped mine off, balled them up, and left them with Callum's outside the back door.

"Come on." Callum took my arm and walked me back around the house yard, moving faster now we were outside.

"Do you think she's right?" I asked him, half jogging to keep up with his longer stride.

"About her knowing better than me?" he said. "That remains to be seen."

"No," I said, "About me being in danger if something triggers?"

"Yes."

The answer felt like a slap, making me dizzy. Well, I'd asked. I tried to focus on breathing until we crossed the property line and were back at the car. I glanced back. So far there was no sign of any activity from inside the house.

"I'll call Cassandra," I said.

"We will use the salt water first. In fact, stand still."

I did as instructed.

Callum muttered a few Fae words under his breath, holding his hands either side of my face for some time. He huffed out a breath, lowering his hands. "Let me see your hands."

I lifted them obediently and he slowly passed his over mine. "Can you see anything?" I asked, nausea rising again. I hoped not. And I really hoped the Cestis wouldn't want to use demonstone on me again. Twice in one lifetime was two times too many.

"No," Callum said, relief clear in the word.

"Can you check yourself?"

"No need. I would know if something was wrong," he said. "Cerridwen will confirm when she arrives. Let's go. We must rinse our hands with salt water."

We could ring the whole damned car with salt as far as I was concerned. But I didn't think it would make much difference. "The car's not going to help us if a demon comes through."

"No, but if we sit in the car, we are less likely to be noticed. The last thing we need now is nosy humans interfering."

"They'll notice if a whole bunch of cars turn up at this hour," I objected.

"Yes, but it will be Cassandra's task to explain. I'm sure she is more than capable of dealing with them."

"Aren't you?" I asked, trying to lighten the mood.

"Yes, but you do not approve of my methods," he said.

Right. When we'd fought the afrit we'd been interrupted by a squatter in the building we were searching. Callum had put him into some sort of magical Fae sleep. And casually dropped the fact that the guy would never wake up if Callum didn't choose to wake him.

The thought of being trapped asleep until you eventually died of old age gave me the heebie-jeebies. So, yeah, better not to leave crowd control to him.

I glanced back at the house again as I hit the remote to unlock the car. I hated the idea of Lizzie being alone in the house, but I also knew she could handle herself. The fact that she was younger than me didn't mean she was less powerful. In fact, quite the opposite.

Callum and I rinsed our hands with salt and water. Then climbed into the car and did as Lizzie had ordered.

I called Cassandra while Callum called Cerridwen. Cassandra backed Lizzie up when I explained the situation, telling us to stay put and wait.

"Should I call Mitch?" I asked.

"No." The response was sharp. "Damon's crew can't go anywhere near the house until we know it's safe. What's the address?"

I gave it to her.

"Alright. Don't move until I get there."

Callum and I spent the next quarter of an hour sitting in the car, which was kind of awkward. I stared up at the second story, but with the blinds closed I couldn't even see the glow from Lizzie's witchlight. I gritted my teeth, telling myself no news was good news.

Just when I was deciding whether to disobey orders and go after Lizzie, she came around the side of the house. Relief stole my breath. I was remembering to breathe in when Lizzie reached us. "Anything?" I asked, lowering the window as Callum climbed out of his seat, the bag of salt in one hand and a bottle of water in the other.

"I'm not sure," she said. "Callum was right. There's a wall where there shouldn't be one, but I can't find a way in."

"It might be mechanical rather than magical. Damon or Mitch could probably help with that," I said.

"Not until it's safe," Lizzie said. "What did Cassandra say?" She took the salt and water Callum offered and rinsed her hands carefully.

"She's on the way. Stay put until then."

"Right," Lizzie said. She shook her damp hands as though working off some nerves. "Callum, can you check me before I get in?"

"Of course," he said. "Hold out your hands." She did and he repeated what he'd done with me. "Nothing."

Lizzie's expression was as relieved as Callum's tone. She climbed into the back seat, with a sigh.

Callum passed her backpack over. "Here. You should eat and drink. This is going to be a long night."

He was right. Cassandra arrived with Radha and Ian, the other two members of the Cestis, hot on her heels. A few minutes later, Zee pulled up, too. Either his tournament was done, or he'd bailed. He made a beeline for Lizzie when she got out of the car to go talk to the others, gathering her in for a hug before inspecting her with serious dark eyes, reassuring himself she was all right.

They all conferred for a few minutes before Cassandra came over to the car and knocked on the window.

I wound it down.

"Maggie, you might as well go home," she said. "I've let Mitch know the address and that you found something related to Ajax. He's going to dig into who owns the house, see if that tells us anything, but there's nothing more you can do here."

I hesitated, not liking feeling useless. Part of me wanted to stay and help, and part of me wanted to run far away, but the choice was out of my hands, and arguing would only slow the rest of them down. "Mitch should check the gaming gear inside. They might get an ID off the system."

Cassandra nodded. "I'll see that he does."

She didn't say anything else. Clearly, I was dismissed. "Right. I'll get out of your hair."

"I take it Mitch called?" I asked as I walked into the kitchen. Damon was seated at the table, working away at something on his datapad. He still wore jeans and a somewhat wrinkled white shirt. Clearly he'd had no intention of going to bed before I got home.

"Yes." He stood and met me halfway across the room, hands catching my shoulders. He looked me over with the same intensity that Zee had looked at Lizzie.

I smiled up at him as the familiar buzz of knowing I was the center of this man's world stole through my veins like a slow shot of tequila. "I'm fine." I put a hand on his cheek, and he leaned into the touch. "I'm fine," I repeated, stepping back. He'd want a debrief and if I was going to talk, then I wanted snacks.

It was too late for coffee, but I wanted something hot and comforting to drink. I had some of Cassandra's teas, including a soothing one that tasted less bad than a lot of her concoctions. Accompanied by a cookie or three, it might be just what I needed. Damon waited for me to fill a mug. I could feel the weight of his gaze as I moved around the kitchen, as though he was still making sure I was really okay. "Tea?" I asked, holding up the teapot.

"No. Are you going to tell me what happened?"

I explained what we'd found. He listened, shoulders set in a hard tense line, laser focused as I talked.

"Where's this house again?" he asked, when I finished.

"Sea Cliff." I carried my tea and cookies back to the table and Damon followed, taking the chair next to mine. "One of the rebuilt parts. Nothing special."

He shook his head, mouth twisting. "Ajax didn't live in Sea Cliff. He was close to Riley. We never found anything at his apartment relating to demonkind or magic."

"Which makes sense now we know about this place." I sipped tea, closing my eyes for a moment as the heat and sugar soothed me.

"Nothing to indicate he owned a second property, either."

"I'm sure Mitch will find out if he did. We'll know more soon enough." I swallowed tea, trying to focus on the warmth. If Ajax didn't own the house, who did? Had he had accomplices we knew nothing about? He couldn't have been renting. Surely, his family would have terminated a rental agreement when they dealt with his estate. And the house wouldn't still be empty. I shivered involuntarily. Who owned the damned house?

Damon seemed as though he was thinking along the same lines, something hard and distant in the depths of those blue, blue eyes. "I guess we will."

"Yeah." I covered his hand with mine. "We should probably try to sleep. They'll let us know if they find anything."

"Yep," he agreed. "Something you should probably see first."

"Now what?" I asked. I wasn't sure how many more surprises I could take in one day.

"Nothing as eventful as yours, but the security team sent me a clip earlier. Madge, can you pull up a holoscreen and play the video from Rufus?"

"Of course, Damon," Madge said.

A holoscreen appeared above the counter, showing me a security clip of the garden. Dammit. What now? As I watched, I couldn't see anything but a section of the path and the plants around it, moving slowly with the breeze. "What am I looking at?"

"Just wait," Damon pointed at a section of the screen. "There."

I leaned closer. Yep. Barely visible among the bushes were two twining furry tails.

Well, crap. "*Another* nixling?"

"Yes. But as far as we can tell, it's gone."

"You went out there?" I squeaked. Damon had no magic to defend himself.

"No. Jake and Rufus did a sweep. But no sign of your fairy kitty."

"Not *my* fairy kitty." I leaned in to examine the image. "Who knows if it's even the same one."

"Not me. But I thought you'd want to know."

I sighed, finished my tea and pushed the plate of uneaten cookie away. There wasn't enough sugar in the world to soothe me at this point. "And now I do. We can tell the others in the morning. Not worth interrupting them for this."

A nixling, while disturbing, was not as important as working out what the hell Ajax had been doing in that house.

***

"Would you mind coming back to the house before you return to the city?" Callum asked. "I have something to discuss with you."

I stopped chugging water and wiped my mouth. We'd been sparring for twenty minutes, and I was sweating like a pig. But the workout had helped, making me forget about Ajax and demonkind and nixlings for an hour.

Two days had passed since we'd found the name badge at the house.

Turned out Callum's instincts had been right. There had been a hidden room and the Cestis had managed to break into it.

The walls were lined with steel and iron and layers of other protections, which explained why we hadn't noticed it when we'd entered the house. Ian and Trick and Cassandra were still working on cleansing the space completely. But there'd been no traps. No demons suddenly sucked into the world from their dimension.

Not that Cassandra had allowed me near the place yet. Mitch had been equally adamant Damon stay away. The house was owned by a private company. One owned by a succession of equally private and mysterious corporations, culminating in one incorporated in the Cayman Islands. Damon had his lawyers and accountants working on who was behind it all, but if Ajax had been working with others, we were no closer to finding out who.

Which left me and Damon with a lot of frustration without many outlets. Turns out there are only so many times you can have 'I'm annoyed, take my mind off it' sex before it starts to feel weird.

Which was why I'd been relieved when Callum had called me earlier and said he was free for a training session. I'd been reading the pre-release story bible for *Infinite Rise*, Damon's next launch, trying to get a feel for the game, but the details wouldn't stick. I'd jumped gratefully at the chance to take my frustration out in a more direct way.

It had worked while we sparred. Having a Fae warrior swing a freaking big sword in my direction always focused my attention.

But now the tension came back with a rush. "Is something wrong?"

He shook his head. He, of course, was annoyingly sweat-free, his dark gray workout gear as pristine as it had been when we'd started the session.

Damned Fae. But I'd made him at least start breathing harder. One day I'd make him sweat. Until then I tried to think of him as more an early model avatar—when they didn't show details like sweat or hard breathing——rather than admit he was barely exerting himself against me.

Better for my ego.

In contrast, I was a mess. The air-conditioning in our training gym was perfect, but while it kept out the midsummer heat, it couldn't counteract the fact that fighting Callum took nearly everything I had. I put down the water bottle and reached for a towel, mopping sweat off my face and neck. Ugh. Maybe it wasn't the exertion that heated every cell of my body so much as the burn of having my ass handed to me three times in an hour.

If we'd been fighting for real, I'd have been dead, dead and, oh yeah, more dead.

"I have to be back in the city in a couple of hours. Damon and I have a charity thing tonight. Is this thing a long discussion or something quick? I might have to rain check if it's long. Unless it's urgent." I stared at him for a moment, looking for any clues in his face as to what this was about. But the Fae do inscrutable better than anyone.

"Not urgent. And it should not take long."

I glanced around the empty gym. Pinky had a deadline for her latest movie score, so had passed on today's session. Maia was out in one of the other rooms. She didn't watch me every minute I was with Callum now. Fine with me. Being beaten every time was less embarrassing without an audience. "And we can't talk about it here?"

"No," he said. "It will make more sense at the house."

Okay. Now I was curious. But I knew him well enough to know that Fae surprises weren't always the fun kind. But non-fun surprises seemed to be par for the course for my week, so why the hell not? "All right. Let's go." Good or bad, I might as well find out.

"Quick detour by my place," I said to Maia after I'd done a lightning quick change back into my street clothes. I regretted skipping a shower, but I didn't have time.

"Will that leave you enough time? You have your glam squad coming at five." She pulled up something on her data-pad. Probably my schedule. No doubt Cat, Damon's assistant, had been reminding her tonight wasn't one of those nights we could be late.

"We'll make it." Or they would wait. Damon paid the makeup artist and hair stylist I used when we went to god-tier rich people events like this evening's. The ones that cost eye-watering sums for a ticket and involved people who would never give me the time of day if I wasn't with Damon. I kind of loathed them, but I never wanted to let Damon down by not looking like I belonged there like all the other partners who spent large chunks of their time every week to ensure they always appeared immaculate. I, on the other hand, spent mine , wading through obstreperous code or reading ancient documents or trying not to get stabbed by a Fae shapeshifter.

So now I had a *glam squad*, as Maia and Lizzie delighted in calling them.

It was their job to try and turn Cinderella into the belle of the ball when I needed to be. Or as close as I could get. They knew what I liked and were both excellent and fast at what they did.

Though tonight it didn't matter what I liked. It mattered that I fit in. Everyone would be dressed to outshine, outdo and, bluntly, assert their dominance. I didn't want to win whatever contest most of them—men and women—seemed to be playing. I wasn't interested in billionaire power games. I had enough to worry about between witches and Fae. But Damon's world had rules and I wasn't going to break one unless I absolutely had to.

Back at my house, Callum offered tea and I declined. Which didn't stop him making himself a pot.

Maia tapped her wrist, looking stern. "Don't forget, we're on a schedule here."

Callum remained unperturbed. Kind of his default. Whether he did it to be irritating or whether it was the result of centuries playing Fae politics, I was never sure. But it annoyed Maia and if she showed it, he'd only slow down more.

I caught her eye and tilted my head toward the door. "It's fine. Go wait in the car, I won't be long." I intended to be done with whatever this was and headed home as soon as possible. The house was cool, but I was regretting the not-showering decision. I felt grimy and sticky underneath my clothes.

A shower was definitely a nonnegotiable step once I got home. My gown for the ball had cost several small fortunes. So I needed Callum to say what he had to say so I could bail.

"So, what's this about?" I asked, not willing to wait for Callum to finish fussing with his tea before we talked. Tea could be a whole ritual with the Fae, but today I didn't have the time.

Callum spooned pale green leaves into a small sedate black teapot I didn't recognize. Chinese, or maybe Japanese? I didn't know enough about tea to know. Perhaps Callum had had enough of unicorns and acquired a pot more to his taste. After the third scoop of leaves, he put the spoon down and closed the tin of tea slowly.

I took that to mean he would take as long as he wanted. I chewed my lip to stop myself telling him to hurry the hell up.

"I had an idea about the nixlings," he said while he poured boiling water into the teapot.

"Which is?"

"Have you ever heard the expression 'set a thief to catch a thief'?"

My shoulders tensed. "Yes," I said warily.

"Then this should be simple."

In my experience, rarely could anything involving the Fae be called simple. "Define 'simple'."

He flashed me a grin. I was used to how handsome he was now, but that didn't make it any less distracting when he exerted himself to be charming. Though I'd learned to be wary when he did.

"Let me demonstrate." He pursed his lips and whistled three short notes.

The door to the laundry room, which I hadn't noticed was ajar, pushed all the way open and a nixling walked through and jumped up on the counter to perch next to Callum's teapot.

No cats on the counter. I could hear my Gran's voice, and the memory cut through my surprise. He'd brought the nixling back out from the realm? "Is that..." I started to ask but stopped.

This wasn't either of the nixlings we'd seen. It was lighter. Still shades of gray, but no black as they had. Instead its fur was banded with light and dark gray stripes. The tips of its tail, ears, and a patch of fur on its chest were more silvery, and its eyes were a luminous gold with a near metallic sheen.

It stared back at me while I studied it. Then, apparently tired of waiting, it made a purring chirrup of a noise, twin tails curving curiously.

"Maggie," Callum said, "this is—" He spoke a rapid string of Fae words that merged together in a musical lilt that took me a minute to untangle.

"Right," I said, struggling to translate with my basic vocabulary. "That means she who hunts softly?"

"She who hunts in silence like the breeze in the east."

Of course it did. "That's an impressive name." And quite a mouthful I stopped myself from adding.

Callum smiled. "You can call her Lianith if that's easier."

It was. And I wasn't going to ask what Lianith translated to. If the nixling liked it, it was fine by me.

"And what am I supposed to do with tha—with her," I amended when the nixling hit me with a slit-eyed look I could only describe as judgmental.

"She can patrol your garden for you. That should keep other nixlings out. If one should come, she can deal with it, or perhaps convince it to talk to her."

"And why would it do that?"

"She assures me that they will. It's a nixling thing. They have hierarchies, even if the other one doesn't belong to Cerridwen."

Of course they did. They were Fae creatures. The nixling certainly looked regal. "And she's high up the chain?" I asked.

"Yes."

I pictured Damon's face if I came home bearing a magical cat queen. Or boss. Or whatever. He liked Ted well enough, but I didn't really know if he was an animal person.

Even if he was, liking normal human world pets and wanting a Fae beastie living in his house were two very different things.

"It does not have to be forever," Callum said, seeing my hesitation. "But for now it is an added layer of protection more likely to help than anything else I can think of."

Dammit. If he couldn't think of a better option, there probably wasn't one. "I see." Other than Damon, I couldn't think of another objection. Not if Lianith could keep the other nixlings away. I met her gaze. "And you're happy to do this?"

She nodded, a movement that was disconcerting coming from something my brain still insisted was a cat despite the two tails.

Two tails. Right. That was a problem.

How was this going to work? Damon's grounds were extensive, but he still had neighbors and nixlings could climb. Unless we kept Lianith inside—which defeated the purpose of having her—there was a chance someone might see her. Some of Mitch's team knew about the Fae but Damon's gardeners didn't. His housekeeper, Amy, knew I was a witch but she didn't know about my past or that things like demons were real.

"She doesn't look much like a cat," I pointed out. "That's going to be confusing for people if they see her."

"It won't be a problem," Callum said. "We can cast an illusion on a collar."

I blinked. "She's happy to wear a collar?" Her neck was bare now. A collar seemed a very human thing. And not in keeping with her being high up the nixling pecking order.

"I do not know if happy is the precise word, but she has consented so it can carry the illusion. She understands it is necessary."

"Okay, well, it's worth a shot. But if Damon disagrees we are going to have to come up with another plan."

"Your Damon is a sensible man," Callum said. "He will not argue when it comes to your safety."

He was right. That was the one argument that almost always worked with Damon. Though I wouldn't blame him if he decided a live-in nixling was not something he was on board with.

I turned my attention back to Lianith. She stretched her front legs, bowing like a dog, and yawned, baring very long, very white, pointed teeth, before sitting back, casually raising her front paw and unsheathing equally long claws before starting to clean them with her tongue.

Apparently I was boring her with my questions. And I was running out of time. "Okay," I said. "I guess we'll try it. What does she eat?"

No doubt there were mice and other small critters in Damon's garden, but the nixling was large. Too big to live on mice. And I didn't want her hunting birds or deciding to go farther afield in search of prey.

"Raw meat," Callum said. "Beef or lamb, chicken. Fish. Not pet food," he added, wrinkling his nose. "I have smelled what they feed Ted. It would be unacceptable."

Ted seemed happy enough to scarf down what I knew was expensive gourmet pet food. But he was a Labrador and I don't think he'd ever met a food he didn't like. But raw meat was easy enough. I'd add it to the shopping list on the house comp and Amy would work her housekeeper magic to make it appear in the fridge.

I looked at Lianith. "Let's go for a ride."

Chapter Seven

"Not so fast," Callum said, standing up abruptly. "Collar first."

"Oh, right." I'd forgotten.

He pulled a delicate-looking leather collar out of his pocket. It was a rich charcoal gray like Lianith's fur, with a pattern of embossed leaves and fish, and an elaborately engraved silver buckle.

"Gráinne's work?"

Callum nodded. "Yes. The Lady and I did the charms, though."

I held out my hand.

His eyebrows lifted. "You want to put it on her?"

"Well, I'm going to be the one who has to take it off or put it on once we're at the house. Better to find out now if she's going to let me."

"You should keep it on, if you can. It's designed to be difficult to remove."

"Is that safe?" Cats weren't allowed outside these days, but Lianith would need access to the garden and I knew collars were dangerous. I had visions of her stuck in a tree, the leather hooked on a branch.

"It will come undone if she needs it to." He passed me the collar.

"Good." I hesitated. Should I ask her permission before putting the collar on? If so, how? "Okay, this takes care of what she looks like," I said, letting my sight slide into the magic as I examined the collar, trying to see if I could understand the illusion. Parts were familiar but there was a complexity to the way the magic twined around and through both the leather and the silver, that I didn't know how to unravel. I couldn't quite figure out how it had been built. "Which brings us to another issue."

"Which is?" Callum asked.

"How is she going to talk to me? Can she do what you do?" I gestured vaguely near my temple to indicate the mind-to-mind speech he and I used.

"Mostly," Callum said. "Not as strongly and she does not have a great facility with English. She will most likely respond in Fae. Cerridwen put something in her charms on the collar to facilitate the process, but if Lianith speaks to you in English, it will be basic. Even her Fae may be…unusual. They don't think about things the same way we do."

I wasn't sure there was a 'we' in there. Fae thought differently from humans about a lot of things. So if Callum thought that nixlings thought strangely, well, that was going to make things complicated. "That's not super helpful. I'm still learning Fae."

He smirked, amusement flaring in his green-gold eyes. "Cerridwen thought this would be excellent practice. You should be able to communicate well enough. She'll get the point across, I promise. And if she needs to tell you something complicated and you don't understand, you can always call me or Gráinne."

I looked dubiously at Lianith. "So how does this work? Talking to her, I mean." Callum and I just talked to each other. I didn't have to put any special effort into it. Which had been a shock the first time he'd done it. But so far the nixling hadn't said anything to me.

"If you think something at her, she should hear it, or if you ask her a question out loud, she'll answer you in your mind."

"*It may be fainter than me,*" he added mentally.

"Lianith, say something to Maggie."

I stayed quiet, trying to listen. At first, I got nothing but then, faintly, I heard "*Hael,*" in my head.

That was one Fae word I knew. It was their equivalent of hello.

"*Hael,*" I thought back. "Hello," I added out loud so Callum would know I'd heard something. The nixling blinked at me and I got a sense she was pleased. Her voice was not like Callum's. He came through clear as day. This was more subtle. Like a voice carried on a breeze or twisted through the rustle of leaves. I was going to have to pay attention.

Though Lianith could probably shout if she wanted to.

"Any Fae words you think I should know to make this easier?" I asked Callum. "Like what she wants to eat?" Most of the Fae I knew revolved around being polite to Fae or magic and fighting demons. We'd skipped over things like cooking terms.

He ran quickly through the various words for beef, lamb, chicken, and salmon. Then added inside and outside.

"Okay," I said, "I can remember those. Send me a voice note with any others I might need." My datapad, still in my leather backpack, chimed suddenly. Reminding me I was supposed to be home, getting ready for tonight. "I need to hit the road. Is there a carrier?"

Lianith's ears flattened slightly, her eyes sparking brighter gold.

"She knows how to behave in a car." Callum said, "She will sit on your lap."

I was fairly sure that was illegal. Pets were supposed to be restrained in vehicles. But I wasn't going to try and shove a Fae creature her size into a cardboard box or crate against her will. Even if the thought of her digging those claws into my leg if she spooked wasn't appealing.

I nodded at Callum, then focused on Lianith. "Time to go. Let's put this collar on and then I can carry you or you can follow me? To the car."

Callum must have translated for me, because the nixling stretched out her nose toward me and sniffed my hand and pressed her head into my palm, like a cat or dog asking for scritches.

I scratched her ear tentatively, and, when she didn't object, slipped the collar on, fastening the buckle. The shift in her appearance was instantaneous. Suddenly there was a large long-haired gray cat, with similar silvery tips to her ears and her single—albeit very fluffy—tail sitting on the table. I blinked twice, startled by how well it worked. Though I shouldn't have been if Cerridwen's magic was involved. Cerridwen could change the appearance of the realm around her with a thought. Charming a relatively small animal was hardly a challenge. I reached to pick Lianith up and almost staggered when she weighed more than my brain expected. Illusions can't change the mass of an object. So I had to remember I was lifting a nixling, not a cat. I hoisted her more securely in my arms and carried her out to the car.

———

Lianith sat on my lap, ears pricked and occasionally flicking back and forth, gaze fastened on the scenery passing by as we headed back to the city. She didn't offer any comments. Probably just as well. My Fae wasn't up to translating nixling feelings about the San Francisco skyline.

Maia stayed silent until we were back across the bridge, when her curiosity got the better of her. "So is this a case of nixling versus nixling?" I'd explained what Lianith really was when I'd carried the seemingly-a-cat out to the car and Maia had hit me with a 'why the hell do you have a cat?' face.

I shrugged. "That's what Callum said. Lianith here should be able to scare off any others that try to make it past our wards."

"Right. Well, it's a reasonable plan," Maia agreed. "But I don't think Mitch is going to like it."

I was sure he wouldn't. But I'd rather have Mitch cranky at me than Cerridwen, and she must have given her blessing to Callum's plan. He wouldn't take a nixling from the realm without her permission.

At least I hoped not.

The real wild card was Damon. He mostly rolled with the magical punches these days and I figured he'd be happy to trade one Fae creature who was on our side for a random assortment of others that weren't. If he wasn't, I had ways to make it up to *him* that I couldn't use on Mitch.

Still, I was somewhat nervous when I arrived home. Madge informed me Damon was in his office. I walked down the hallway, Lianith padding behind me, head swiveling from side to side taking in her surroundings. Damon's office door was closed.

I bent down to Lianith and slipped her collar off. I wanted Damon to see her in her true form for this introduction. She made a soft inquiring chirrup noise at me as I tucked the collar into one of the pockets of my workout jacket.

"I hope you understand this, but I need you to wait here, okay?" I said softly, wracking my brains for the Fae word for wait. When it finally popped into my head, I repeated it silently to Lianith.

She sat back on her haunches, tails curled around her feet. Message received.

I hoped. I knocked on Damon's door, slipping inside when he told me to come in in a distracted tone.

He had all the screens in the room up and they were displaying a bunch of different data analysis sets that made me glad, once again, that I wasn't him. Code was fun. Running a global empire was not my jam.

"Hey," Damon said, pushing his chair back from the desk, looking vaguely guilty. "You're home. Have I lost track of time again?" He tugged at his white T-shirt. "Do I need to get ready?"

"Not yet." I swept a hand down my active wear. "But ask Madge to ping you an hour out if you're in data absorption mode."

He grinned, which I was happy to see. His smiles had been few and far between the last few days. "Don't worry. She won't let me be late. Cat will have set reminders. Cinderella must get to the ball on time tonight."

"Personally, I'd be happy to miss it all together," I said. "If you're too busy…."

"Nice try. But no. Though I promise I'll make it up to you."

Now, that I could get on board with. "I'll start thinking of how."

"Oh, I have plenty of ideas." His grin returned.

I matched it. "Then we'll need plenty of time to get through both lists. Maybe you could get Madge to clear your schedule tomorrow," I said, wishing we could get started on those lists right now. I could tempt him into coming and scrubbing my back in the shower. But no, he had to work and I sadly had no time for shower sex. Tomorrow was Saturday. Damon usually worked at least a few hours every day but we usually had us time on the weekends. "*Do* you have anything on your schedule tomorrow?"

"Nothing major." He stretched his arms out, cracking his knuckles. "But I should finish this." His gaze flicked back to the nearest screen. "Did you need me for something?"

I knew the signs of a geek wanting to get back to the job at hand. "One quick thing and I'll get out of your hair."

His expression turned instantly wary. I hated that when it came to news from me, these days his mind seemed to go straight to worst-case scenario.

"You're not hurt? You were training, weren't you?"

I shook my head and then did a quick twirl. "All in one piece. Nothing bruised but my ego. As usual. But Callum came up with an idea for a solution to our nixling problem." Hopefully I sounded like I was happy about it.

Damon raised an eyebrow. "Am I going to like this solution?"

"I don't know? How do you feel about, er, a guest?"

"A guest? Who?"

"Easier if I just introduce you." I went and opened the door. Lianith was still sitting outside.

"Come on in," I said.

Lianith strolled into the room, twin tails curving question marks over her back.

Damon shoved back from the desk, coming to his feet. "That's a *nixling*." He raised his eyebrows, huffing out a surprised breath.

"Yes." I filled him in on Callum's basic theory that Lianith would be able to scare off other nixlings.

"So she's like, what, a nixling warrior or something?"

"I'm not sure. We didn't really get into the details. Callum seemed confident, though."

Lianith took a few steps forward and sprang onto Damon's desk from about ten feet away, landing lightly enough not to disturb anything. To his credit, Damon didn't so much as flinch.

"Impressive," he said drily, looking down at her as she settled herself on a pile of paper. "Right. So she's up to the job. But what are we doing about the whole…not really looking like a cat or a dog situation?" He gestured at the tails now curving over her front paws. "She's going to upset the neighbors."

I pulled the collar out of my jacket pocket and held it up. "This." I came over to the desk and fastened the collar into place.

Lianith morphed back into a cat.

This time Damon did flinch slightly before he caught himself. He narrowed his eyes at me. "You could have warned me. But I see that works. She looks like a what…Maine Coon, is that what those big cats are called?"

"I think so. Callum picked the biggest cat he could find to model the illusion on." These days, of course, people had all sorts of designer pets. Gene coding and DNA manipulation were tightly controlled, but cosmetic changes to fur color and pattern and size were allowed, if expensive. "It's only an illusion, so you don't want something too small. It would be strange if she appeared normal cat sized but could reach things a normal cat couldn't for example."

"Okay," he said. "And you said 'guest'. So not a permanent addition to the household?"

Seriously, he was taking this way better than I thought he would.

"No," I said slowly. "She's volunteering to help us out for a while." Lianith was cute but I didn't think she would want to live outside the realm permanently, even if Cerridwen would allow it.

"What's her name?" Damon asked.

"Oh," I said. "Sorry, it's Lianith. Lianith, this is Damon. He's my…er, mate?"

That got me a response. Not really a word, more a sensation of amusement.

I must have looked startled because Damon said, "What?"

"She just laughed. I think."

His eyes widened. "You talk to her like you do Callum, when he's wolfed out?"

"Yeah. Though she only speaks Fae. She understands some English but it's not quite the same." She seemed smart, so hopefully, as Callum had said, we'd learn from each other.

Damon was holding his hand out to Lianith who sniffed it politely. "We need to get her settled somewhere for the night. I'll take care of it. You need to shower before your squad gets here."

"You were working," I objected.

"It can wait. And it won't take long to see which guest room she likes," Damon stroked Lianith's ear and smiled when she butted her head into his hand like she had with me. Letting them bond might make this all go more smoothly. "Callum said she eats raw meat."

"I'm sure we'll find something." He stopped patting Lianith, came around the desk and kissed me fast. I leaned into it, heat rushing though me as it always did, but all too soon he ended it.

"Go on, go get pretty."

"I'm already pretty," I said, pretending to be offended.

"I know," he said, "but go get even more pretty so everyone will be jealous of me tonight at the gala."

I laughed. "No. Everyone will be jealous of *me*."

Chapter Eight

"Just out of curiosity, how hard is it to get you out of that dress?" Damon asked, grinning at me from the far side of the back seat of our limo.

I glanced down at the mounds of embroidered midnight-blue silk satin spilling out over the seat. There was a reason Damon was sitting over near the door. My dress took up enough room for three people. Beautiful, but unwieldy. Like the ornate deep-blue sapphires spilling from my ears in loops and whorls. I'd used an illusion on the bracelet Cerridwen had given me, to make it look like sapphires, too. I could remove the illusion now, but the rest would have to wait. The gala had wrapped up before midnight and we were headed home.

Where I would get rid of the dress and drag the man into bed. So, I could be patient. As much as I wanted to let Damon take my clothes off, the dress had cost a mint. One of the ones he insisted on paying for because the theme for the evening required an actual damned ball gown not a mere evening gown. So I wasn't going to let him ruin it. My girlfriend-of-billionaire dresses got resold or donated to charity auctions when I wasn't going to be able to wear them again. This one fell firmly into that category.

"Too hard to contemplate in the back of a limo," I said, holding out a hand to ward him off. Not really necessary with the wall of skirt acting as a barrier.

Pity. We didn't often use a limo, but tonight had been the kind of event where you had to arrive in style and the gown wouldn't fit into a regular car. The best thing about the limo was it had a lovely soundproof partition between the driver's section and the back. And I could reinforce it with an aural ward if Damon and I wanted to indulge in other activities on the way home.

But tonight we were going to have to wait. Which was a waste of the massive back seat.

I pouted. Ball gowns were ridiculous, and this one was worse than most. The bodice was fastened with tiny buttons and the skirt had about a thousand layers of tulle supporting it. It did, however, have pockets hidden in the side seams. I insisted on them whenever it was possible. There had been a couple of slinky evening gowns where I'd had to go without, but the designer had managed it this time. But even with pockets, it was a hundred percent impractical. The satin was treated with nano tech to stop it wrinkling, but nothing could alter how much space it took up.

"It's unfair that they wrap you up in these beautiful things and then make you hard to unwrap," Damon said.

I shrugged. "Well, you know, you can complain to the people who put on your galas about their dress codes." Tonight had been a Marie Antoinette theme. A bit on the nose for billionaires, but at least they hadn't gone full fancy dress.

As much as I didn't enjoy wearing ball gowns, I did love Damon in a tux. Something about the black and white against his dark hair and brilliant blue eyes just did it for me. Even more than usual.

"Hmm, if I can't take it off. What about an alternative approach so to speak?" Damon asked, loosening his seat belt and sliding a little closer, pushing more of the fabric into my lap.

At least it wouldn't wrinkle. But I still didn't think he was going to get far. As much as I wanted him to, as I watched his eyes go hot and intent. "I'm warning you, there are about fifty layers of tulle beneath this." I flicked my fingers at one of the roses embroidered on the skirt.

His brows flew up. "Isn't that…scratchy?"

"Welcome to women's clothes," I said, teasing him. "They're often dumb, or hadn't you noticed? But there are layers of other things between me and the tulle." I wasn't an idiot. I could put up with a dress that was tight or heavy or awkward, but I wasn't going to put up with one that was actually painful.

"So you're just too hot, not itchy?"

"Fortunately I know how to do a cooling charm now. So as least I didn't sweat my way through six courses."

The ballroom of the Phenix Hotel had been decorated with extravagant garlands of white roses intertwined with tiny golden bees and lilies. In between the flowers were tall white candles in golden candlesticks. On the tables, on stands around the room, and lighting the elaborate chandeliers.

Glorious to look at, but the candles only added to the heat in an already crowded room. And, as always, I wondered why they didn't just ask everyone for a donation and give that plus the money they would have used putting on the event to the charities they were trying to support. Lizzie had explained to me that people wanted a reward for their money. She agreed it was dumb, though.

But when you played at certain levels, you had to do certain things for show. Damon donated a lot of money he never talked about, even outside his own foundation. But there was something about being seen to be charitable that seemed to matter.

"Let's just make out," I said, "Save the rest for when we get home."

His grin widened. "I am on board with that plan."

I thought about Lianith waiting at home for us.

Damon had put her in one of the guest bedrooms with two pounds of top-shelf steak, retrieved from the refrigerator, and several water bowls. Callum claimed she knew how to use a toilet for her…needs. I hoped so. Offering a litter box to a creature who could talk to me seemed wrong somehow

I'd ordered a couple of fancy water fountains and food bowls and a few large plush pet beds while I was being curled and primped and polished but they wouldn't arrive until the morning. Hopefully nixlings were like cats and she had napped a lot.

I wriggled—as much as my skirts would allow—closer to Damon while Boyd pulled up to a traffic light.

But before Damon could lean in and distract me, something caught my eye out of the window. Something dark, skittering up the side of a building.

I went cold and hit the intercom button without thinking. "Boyd, pull over please."

"What?" Damon said, twisting around.

I pointed out past his shoulder. "I saw something on that building. Something climbing up the wall."

"A person?"

"No, smaller."

He watched a moment before turning back to me. "I can't see anything. Probably just a trick of the light."

"No," I said, "I definitely saw something." I didn't want to be right about it, but the skittering motion reminded me of an afrit. Too small to be an imp and I had no idea if imps could even climb a wall. Afrit could though. "I need to check it out."

"Are you sure?"

"Lizzie and Zee got called out about a 'giant bug' earlier

this week," I said. "They didn't find an afrit but that doesn't mean there wasn't one. I can't take that chance."

His mouth went flat as he gestured at my gown. "You're not dressed for chasing afrit around in the middle of the night."

"It was headed for the roof, I just need to get up there. I'll take Maia." I hit the button to lower the partition between us and the front seat where Maia was sitting with Boyd. "Maia, I need you to come with me."

"You're just going to waltz in there? It's nearly one a.m." Damon objected.

I eyed the building. It had to be an office block or apartments. Eight floors. No one had rebuilt any skyscrapers in San Francisco after the Big One.

"I'll figure something out." My training sessions with Callum, chasing illusionary creatures around the city, had taught me there was a way to get into most buildings. Or there was always Lizzie's lockpicking lessons to fall back on.

"Luckily you won't have to," Damon said, reaching inside his jacket for the tiny datapad he carried to events.

"Why not?"

"I own it." He swiped something on the screen and said, "Mitch? I need you to contact whoever's on security at the office building we bought last year in Alamo Square. Maggie and Maia need access immediately. Tell them to give Maggie anything she asks for, but otherwise stay the fuck out of their way." He listened for a moment. "Yeah, one of those things. I'll let you know if we need any help."

"There's the usual in the trunk?" I asked him when he ended the call. He nodded. We kept go bags of gear and weapons for both of us close at hand these days. I didn't love that we needed them, but it was useful to have them for moments like these. I didn't have time to change clothes, but I could grab a gun.

"All right," I said, reaching for the door handle. "Call

Cassandra. If she doesn't answer, call Callum. Tell them I think I saw an afrit."

Maia had already retrieved my gun from the trunk by the time I'd wrestled the dress out of the car. I took it from her and shoved it into my pocket. I had a license to carry a gun—but no point causing a scene if I didn't need to.

At least my shoes had low heels. I'd figured no one would see them under the gown anyway and it was heavy enough to make it tricky to walk in without adding stilettos to the mix.

I grabbed the skirt with both hands, lifting it so I could move more easily and followed Maia as we headed for the building.

I should have let Damon mess it up after all. If we had to fight an afrit, I wasn't sure it would survive in fit condition to be donated anyway.

But there wasn't much I could do about that. If we waited for Cassandra or Callum, the afrit could be long gone. And I wouldn't have spotted it in the first place, if I'd given in to back-of-the-limo sex with Damon.

The weight of the gun in my pocket was reassuring, but my heart was speeding up. Afrit usually traveled in groups. And those groups were usually being directed by an imp, if not lesserkind.

The Cestis hadn't found any signs of imps or lesserkind when they investigated the afrit I'd killed with Callum, and last night's call had been a false alarm according to Lizzie. But maybe not. Maybe the caller had seen something and the Cestis hadn't arrived in time.

Not that the presence of an afrit downtown was proof there'd been one in Dockside.

"How do you want to do this?" Maia asked as we neared the entrance.

"I think the roof. It was climbing and there's no reason to think it got inside the building." Afrit might be the cockroaches of the demon world, but they couldn't creep in through the kinds of tiny cracks and crevices actual bugs could. It would need an open door or window or an uncovered vent into a heating or cooling system. If Damon had bought this building I knew it would be all up to code. Which for office buildings required windows that didn't open and a top-class security system.

"Okay, straight up then," Maia said. She had one hand on the gun at her hip, ready to draw. I slid a hand into my pocket and closed my hand around the pistol's grip.

The entrance into the building was floor-to-ceiling glass. A guard in a dark-green uniform waited inside the door. Mitch worked fast. The guard—a black man with his hair buzzed short—nodded as we approached and hit a button on the datapad he carried. The doors slid open smoothly and closed as soon as we were through.

He raised his eyebrows at my dress before he wrestled his expression back under control. "How can I help?"

"No one else gets in unless you get the okay from Riley Security," I said.

"Sure thing, ma'am," he said. "There's a service entrance at the back, but we don't have any deliveries scheduled tonight. So everything's locked up tight."

"Please keep it that way. We need to get to the roof," I said.

He pointed at the elevator across the lobby. "You can take the elevator to the top floor and the fire door's down the corridor, to the right."

He handed me a security pass, old-fashioned, but faster than setting up a palm screen.

"This will let you up. Don't lose it. The door will lock behind you."

"Okay, thank you."

I handed the pass to Maia, who slid it into one of the many pockets in her jacket. She was wearing the formal version of her uniform, a sleek black blazer and pants with a crisp white shirt that blended in better at black-tie events than their standard uniform. It looked like a normal suit, but it was made of some kind of tactical nano fabric and had a lot of concealed pockets and pouches to let the bodyguards carry all their gear.

"If you see anything odd, call Riley," I said to the guard. "They'll deal with it."

"What kind of odd, ma'am? There's a bunch of clubs a few blocks down from here. This time of night, the foot traffic leans rowdy."

"Anything other than your usual," I said. I had no idea where he stood on witches. Plenty of humans lived most of their lives ignoring us, and some actively disliked us. Regardless of his stance on magic, there was no way I wanted him to find out about demonkind tonight. That would be a whole other level of trouble. "Do you have cameras on the roof?"

"Only one, by the exit."

"Can you show me the feed?" I nodded at the datapad.

"Sure." He pulled it up. I studied it briefly. No sign of an afrit. But the field of vision showed a wide stretch of the roof. Which was a problem. I didn't want him watching us if we did have to deal with an afrit. And if we didn't, I didn't want any chance of the papps hacking the security to get footage of me running around like a crazy person in the middle of the night. "Okay. You need to cut that feed."

His mouth flattened. "Ma'am—"

"You won't get in trouble," I said. "This building is owned by Riley Arts, right?"

He nodded slowly. "Since last year. Gaming company. They run the building management through a subsidiary. But they don't have any offices here."

"No." I pointed out the window. "See the limo? The guy in there is Damon Riley. And I have his permission to do what I need to do in here. So cut the feed, please. If there's any trouble down here, call the Riley head office security team. Don't try to intervene."

He bristled slightly, but nodded, "Yes, ma'am."

At least I wasn't going to end up on a newsfeed or explaining to Cassandra that she needed to deal with a human freaking out about demons. Maia and I headed toward the two elevators on the opposite side of the lobby. It was all gray and white with touches of gold in the lighting, the planters, and the frame around the currently dark information screen above the reception desk.

The guard must have called the lifts down because the doors opened instantly when we hit the button.

I waited until they closed again, hoping the security guard wasn't nosy enough to try to listen in to our conversation after I'd already told him to cut the feed. But I kept my voice low just in case. "Alright, if it's an afrit, we should try and trap it and wait for Cassandra or Callum to get here. It may be helpful if they can see it alive."

Maia pursed her lips, considering. "It would be safer to fry it."

"Yes. And we'll do that if we have to, but there's only so much Cassandra can tell from a dead one. If we can keep it alive, she can study it and then fry it when she's ready."

"Alright," Maia said, "but that's only going to work if there's something up there we can trap it with." She looked me up and down like the guard had. "You're not going to be able to move fast in that damned dress." She reached around behind her back and pulled out a Taser. "I have this. It has a decent range so you can stay out of reach."

Solid plan. But I didn't know whether a Taser would stun an afrit or kill it. Or just feed it a bunch of energy it could use to fight us.

"Let's stick to guns and fire. If we can't trap it, we shoot it. Or fry it. The first priority is that it doesn't get away."

"Fire is safer than the guns. It will draw less attention. Though, worst-case scenario, I have a silencer."

So did I. But bullets could ricochet and do weird things. I preferred to stick to fire. I doubted there'd be much junk up on the roof. Damon set strict safety standards for all the properties he owned, so I doubted frying an imp would do much damage.

It was only seven floors, but the elevator ride seemed to take forever. By the time we came to a halt, I was tapping my foot impatiently, trying to ignore my speeding pulse. We stepped out and the elevator started to descend again.

The door to the fire stairs was right where the guard had told us. Maia pushed in front of me and opened the door, scanning the stairwell before stepping through the door and doing a more thorough inspection.

"Clear," she said. She blocked me as I moved to join her. "I go first."

"Have you ever fought an afrit before?" I asked

She'd been practicing with the training program Damon had developed for me, but I didn't know what she'd done in real life.

"No," she said. She lifted her palm and summoned a flame. "But I have the general idea."

"That'll do it. So you go first, but you have to let me do what I need to do." That was the rule with bodyguards. Let them protect you. But when it came to magic, I was stronger than Maia. I'd managed to fry an imp without knowing what I was doing. But she was better trained. Not just in witchcraft, but in half a dozen forms of martial arts and self-defense.

Not to mention all of Damon's security people had stringent training in firearms and other weapons, as well as close combat.

If the afrit was up here and we could get to it, hopefully we should be able to contain it.

And hopefully there was only one—my brain added less

helpfully. If there was a whole squad of them, we would need a different plan.

Maia had just reached the landing after the first flight of stairs when I heard the door open behind me.

I readied myself to tell whoever it was to fuck off when Damon stepped through. Which didn't change my impulse. I held my arms out, blocking his way and scowled. "No. You can't be here."

He stood in the doorway, leaned against the partially opened door to hold it in place and folded his arms, matching my scowl. "Clearly I can."

"Funny. You're funny. You know what I mean."

"Yep, and you know I'm not going to sit in a car downstairs while you do this."

Heartwarming but exasperating. Was that a thing? If it was, he was it. "You don't come on training sessions with me," I said.

"No. But that's different. And you can stand here and argue with me and whatever it was you saw might be gone by the time you get up there or you can accept I have your back."

Fuck. "Okay, but if it's anything bigger than an afrit you have to promise me you'll get out of harm's way." We stared at each other for a long moment.

Eventually he nodded. "Okay."

I didn't totally believe him but he was right, we were wasting time. And he was a better shot than me. "Let's go," I said to Maia.

Chapter Nine

WE CREPT up the fire stairs. I followed Maia's lead, moving cautiously as I wrangled the dress. I didn't see how anything could get into the stairwell, but better safe than sorry. Particularly when hampered by yards and yards of fabric.

Damon stayed behind me and I tried to focus on the job at hand rather than how angry I was he'd followed us. Ahead of me Maia reached the top landing where an exit sign glowed above a door marked ROOF in large red letters.

Helpful.

"Slowly," I said when Maia went to swipe the security pass. "We don't want to let it in the building if it's waiting by the door." The back of my neck prickled with nerves. Demonkind. Never good. Afrit were the smallest and easiest to kill but I didn't want to deal with anything to do with demons.

Maia shot me a look back over her shoulder that suggested she wasn't an idiot and she knew how to do her job.

Fair call. My nerves, not to mention Damon tagging along, were making me speak before I thought. Dumb. I had to keep my wits about me. I sucked in a deep breath and blew it out. "Go on."

She eased the door open. There was no immediate scurrying, skittering rush of clawed feet. Just the sounds of the city below suddenly audible again. A faint hum of traffic. A police siren somewhere off in the distance, and the thump of synchro-pop music off to our left. One of those clubs the guard had mentioned. Maia gestured for me to hold the door and then slipped through.

There was a long pause while my heartbeat thudded too loud in my ears, drowning out the city noise. Then Maia said, "Clear. Come on." She held the door for me.

As I maneuvered sideways, I wished I'd asked Maia for a knife to cut the damned skirt off, but too late now. I stepped onto the flat concrete, every nerve tensed. Damon followed and pushed the door shut. The click of the lock hit me like a shock.

Time to get to work.

Damon came to stand beside me.

"Remember what I said." The words felt tight in my mouth. "Too much trouble, you get clear."

"Don't worry about me, go look for your devil bug." He smiled. It was a fraction too tight for him to be as calm as he sounded, but he still exuded confidence.

I scowled at him and turned to survey the roof.

It was mostly empty. There was a water tower, the small structure surrounding the door, and a bunch of stuff I figured was to do with the HVAC system or whatever it was office buildings required to function.

The whole space was plain gray concrete broken only by the yellow safety line painted a few feet inside the edges. Those were protected by a glass barricade about four feet tall, anchored in about a foot and a half of concrete. Tall enough that no one was at any risk of falling off without making considerable effort to do so. Not that it would prove much of a deterrent to an afrit.

Despite the barrier, the breeze was strong enough to ruffle the skirt of my dress and bring out goosebumps along my arms. After the heat of the Phoenix and the warmth of the limo, it was cold.

It was never truly dark downtown but other than the small exit sign over the door, there wasn't any lighting to illuminate the inner part of the roof. There were lights along the edge, outside the glass, but they all angled down toward the building's exterior. The back glow from them provided enough light at the edge to make the shadows around the various structures appear even darker. Perfect for an afrit to blend into.

I reached out with my magic, trying to see if I could feel it, extending my reach slowly, so as not to immediately tip it off if it could feel me. It was the mental equivalent of walking in the dark, holding my hands out in front of me, hoping I wasn't going to stumble into a spiderweb or worse. There was a trace of something. But not strong enough for me to tell if it was still here. My kingdom for more light.

As though she heard me, Maia reached inside her jacket again and pulled out two tiny flashlights, handing me one. I snapped it into place on my gun. I didn't routinely carry a light for it, because I could make my own, but Maia was always prepared.

I scanned the roof again with the flashlight, looking for movement.

Nothing.

The only thing moving besides us was a piece of paper stuck under a pile of industrial buckets stacked near the edge of the roof opposite us. They stood next to a couple of metal containers I guessed held some type of cleaning product, a pile of tarps, several neatly coiled ropes and a plastic crate stuffed with something I couldn't quite make out. Window cleaning gear.

I pointed at the gear and mouthed, "There?"

Maia shook her head once and made a circling motion, pointing to her left.

Right. Best to check behind us first. We started to ease

around the doorway structure. It was only about ten square feet but it was high enough to stop us seeing anything on its roof.

My skin crawled picturing an afrit sitting there, waiting to leap. But there was nothing I could do about the possibility, so I followed Maia, putting everything Callum had ever taught me about moving silently into practice.

Not so simple wearing fifty layers of tulle.

Damon moved behind me. I avoided looking at him. I couldn't let my focus stray. Had to trust him to protect himself. And me.

I could yell at him later. And let Mitch yell, too.

Maybe even Cassandra.

Imagining it calmed me down a little as we cleared the section of roof behind the door and kept moving slowly forward, Maia sweeping ahead of me. There was nothing near the water tower or any of the other permanent structures.

So either the creature had continued over and down the building and disappeared into the night or it was hiding in the window cleaning gear.

I tipped my head toward the nearest bucket.

Maia grimaced but nodded and crept closer until she was within arm's length. "Cover me," she mouthed before she reached out and upended the bucket in one swift move.

Empty.

I almost sighed in relief. Maia tucked the handle of the bucket over her arm and studied the pile of gear. The containers of detergent or whatever they were only had small screw on lids, too small for an afrit to crawl into, even if it had wanted to coat itself in chemicals.

Which left the remaining buckets and the crate. Now we were closer, I could see it was stuffed with rags and old towels. The piece of paper that had caught my attention initially still flapped slowly in the breeze.

It made the faintest rustling noise but was clearly just paper. Afrits didn't use illusions.

Maia watched it too, then turned her attention back to the buckets. Before she could make her next move, I heard something new.

Something not papery. More like fabric moving against a hard surface. Along with the faintest suggestion of a hiss.

Maia heard it, too, her eyes narrowing and her body language sharpening as she shifted her focus to the towel-filled crate.

Damon stepped up beside me, his gun at the ready. Three for three. I wasn't imagining things.

I sent my magic out again and got a far stronger sense of wrong, wrong, wrong. Maia looked at me and I nodded. Her mouth went flat as she put a finger to her lips, telling us to stay silent.

I tightened my grip on my gun. Maia pointed to it and lifted the bucket she held, miming tipping the crate over, then slamming the bucket down.

As methods of catching an afrit went, it wasn't the smartest but I didn't have a better one. Not if we wanted to catch it alive.

Maia mimed again, nodding toward the crate and scowling at me. I really didn't want to pick up a crate containing an afrit, but too bad for me.

Going against every instinct I possessed, I motioned for Damon to move back a couple of feet. I inched closer to the crate, gun ready, trying not to think about what would happen if the afrit was in there and it charged me rather than Maia. The idea of it getting under my skirt made me want to puke.

So I had to act before I could psych myself out. I bent forward, grabbed the back of the crate with my free hand and tipped it over, sending the contents spilling out. I scuttled backward instinctively, a move that nearly resulted in me tripping over the stupid gown.

Nothing happened for a long moment then came a hiss that sounded like a furious cat crossed with a big-ass snake. The hairs on my arms stood on end. A large black bug-like creature with weird scaly skin burrowed out of the pile of towels and charged straight at Maia. As it moved, long thin black spines shot up out of its back, turning the afrit into a nightmare hedgehog-cockroach combination that made my brain stutter for a moment, stuck on wrong-bad-*run*.

Thank God for Maia's training, because she reacted like lightning to slam the bucket down over it before I could panic.

The hissing increased, more screechy and angrier. The bucket wobbled despite the fact Maia was leaning her whole weight against it.

Which she wouldn't be able to do for long.

I grabbed one of the tubs of cleaning chemicals and placed it on top of the bucket. The wobbling stopped and all three of us breathed identical sighs of relief.

"Now what?" Damon asked from behind me.

The angry screeching hisses continued, punctuated with tapping sounds like it was using its legs or feet to figure out its next move.

Maia was talking into her headset, alerting someone—I hoped Cassandra—we'd caught the afrit. I kept my gun aimed at the bucket.

The hissing subsided suddenly and I waited for another round of creepy tapping. Instead there was a soft *splat* and a tiny hole started to melt through the plastic about halfway up, a clear thick liquid spilling over the edges and starting to slowly slide toward the concrete.

"Fuck. It spits acid," I said.

"So I see," Damon said slowly. "Now what?" He moved up beside me.

I shot him an annoyed look. "We could start with you leaving."

He grinned tightly. "Not going to happen, baby. One afrit we can handle."

The hole stopped growing but another splat came from within and more liquid goo trickled out of the first hole as another one started to form beside it. Afrit might be the dumbest of the demonkind, but this one could obviously think itself out of a trap. Some of its acid goo reached the concrete. There was a tiny sizzling noise and the concrete went white before starting to pit.

So, really *strong* acid.

Perfect.

"We don't have anything else to contain it," Maia said. Her gun stayed trained on the bucket.

"No. So. Plan B?"

"What's Plan B?" Damon asked.

"Kill it with fire," I said.

Maia grinned approvingly. "Plan B it is. You want to do the honors, or should I?" She started to put her gun away.

"Wait," I said.

"What?" The gun came back out as though she thought I'd seen something.

"If we're going to do this, we need water. To put the fire out."

"Right," she said. The gun lowered again and she scanned the roof.

"If there's been window cleaners up here, there must be a faucet or something they use to fill the buckets. They can't drag buckets up from inside surely? Maybe on the cooling tower?" I suggested.

She nodded, went back to the pile to grab another bucket, and jogged off toward the cooling tower. "Score," she called. "There's a hose connector up here and a valve."

Something creaked, followed by the sound of running water.

I willed her to be fast. Under the influence of whatever it

was the afrit was spitting, the hole in the bucket had widened to about the size of two quarters. As I watched, one long leg extended out. It was covered in short black spines ending in three claws that glistened in the moonlight in a way that told me they were very sharp. And wet.

Claws covered in acid were nothing I wanted to get up close and personal with.

I took a half step back, bracing myself to shoot.

Maia arrived back with her now full bucket and came to stand next to me. "Do you want to be fire or water?" She put the bucket down between us.

"Fire," I said. I'd never actually managed to call lightning a second time, but otherwise, fire was my thing.

"We want like a concentrated stream," she said. "Let it burn for a minute or so, then I'll dump the water on it."

"Okay," I said. If a minute wasn't long enough to kill it, we had a bigger problem and we were going to have to shoot the afrit, no matter what reaction gunfire might bring.

The bucket over the afrit was plastic. It would melt.

I raised my hand. Then paused. The cleaning fluids. Also in plastic containers but the contents were chemicals. And some chemicals were flammable. Or explosive.

I jerked my chin at Maia. "Move that cleaning stuff. We don't know what it's made of and I don't want to make some-thing go 'boom' accidentally." The afrit made another splat and the hole got bigger. The leg wiggled, claws scraping the concrete. The bucket rattled.

"Good idea," Maia said, "but someone will have to hold that bucket down once I move those."

"I will," Damon said. He moved before I could stop him, damn the man.

The afrit's leg withdrew from the gap, like it was following his movement. My skin crawled. I could smell it now. Acid and rot, a scent my brain and body associated with terror and death and danger. I had to fight to keep my breathing steady. I knew I could kill it, but it still terrified me. It was demonkind. The enemy. Demons, given a chance, would devour our world and everyone in it.

Damon gripped the so-far-intact side of the bucket. His face was taut. Determined. But also possibly trying not to breathe too deeply.

"Alright," I nodded at Maia, wanting to get on with it. "Take the cleaning stuff."

She moved fast, lifting the containers and carrying them to the far side of the roof. Damon's knuckles whitened as he tightened his grip on the bucket. As though it had sensed the changing weight, the afrit thumped against the side of the bucket, making it shake. It screeched again, the sound like nails down a demonic chalkboard.

I resisted the urge to order Damon to swap places with me. He was behind the side with the hole. That was hopefully safer as long as the damn afrit didn't decide to spit upward.

"Can you burn it from where you are?" Maia asked as she returned and picked up the water bucket.

"We're about to find out." I stretched out my hand, pulling on my magic, and summoned a flame, thinking about shaping it into a spike like a miniature lightning bolt.

The flame rose in my hand, brilliant orange. Hot enough to burn through anything I aimed it at, though hopefully not through the concrete roof before we could put it out.

"Alright," I said to Damon. "On the count of three, let go of the damned bucket and get the hell out of there. Once you're out of the way, I'm burning it."

He nodded, mouth grim.

I turned to Maia. "Ready?"

The water bucket was at her feet but she had her gun out, ready in case the afrit got free. "Ready when you are."

"One, two….THREE." I yelled at Damon.

True to his word he let go and bolted sideways, back toward the doorway.

I waited until he was fifteen feet away before I sent the flame arcing down.

The plastic went up with a *whoomp*. The afrit started screaming, the sound of it physically painful. Bad enough that it made me want to stop my fire so I could clamp my hands over my ears. Somehow my brain knew it didn't come from the throat of any creature from the human world. But I held my ground and the flame. After about thirty seconds, the noise stopped. I waited another thirty seconds before I stopped feeding the fire.

Maia held up a hand. "Wait."

We stood in silence, watching the flames dance. The stench of burning plastic made my eyes stream but there was no movement from within the fire. Maia held her forearm over her mouth, coughing. The smell was as bad as the shrieking had been—the combination of burning plastic and afrit was stomach churning—and the breeze was blowing in her direction.

After a minute or so she said, "Okay, enough."

I pulled my gun back out of my pocket just in case, and she dumped the water over the molten mess of burning plastic.

Fortunately, it went out, hissing steam, which made the stench worse.

Ewwww. I coughed, wishing I could cover my mouth and nose, but I needed both hands for my gun.

Maia put her bucket down, gaze still fastened on the steaming pile of ash and melted plastic.

Nothing moved.

Thank God.

"You want me to check it out?" Maia asked, nodding at the mess.

I shook my head. "Let's wait."

At least the death cries hadn't summoned any friends. Afrit

often moved in packs but this one seemed to be alone. Like the one Callum and I killed in Dockside had been. Weird.

Damon came back to my side. He wrinkled his nose at the smell but smiled at me. "Well, that was exciting. But good job. You, too, Maia."

"Thanks, boss," she said.

"You could go back downstairs now," I suggested.

"Nope." He slipped off his tux jacket and held it out to me. "Put this on, you're shivering."

Excellent idea. I pocketed my gun and slid the jacket on. It was warm and smelled like him. Way better than fresh fried afrit.

Warmer, I stared at the remains. Two afrit in a month. Not to mention the other potential sightings and finding Ajax's secret lair. What the hell was going on?

Maia refilled her bucket and poured a second load of water over the remains. The concrete around the pile of melted plastic was scorched, but less steam indicated it was cooling down. Promising. No doubt Riley Arts were going to have to get the fire department or something to check the damage—after the Cestis had removed any sign of what had actually been burning. Maybe the fire department would believe that the cleaning chemicals had started all this?

Not my problem. The Cestis were the ones who dealt with covering up demon activity with the non-magical first responders and legal system.

"All right," I said, starting to believe the afrit was dead. "Now we call Cassandra."

Maia tapped her earpiece. "No need. She's already here."

Chapter Ten

I KICKED my shoes off as soon as we walked through the front door. Cassandra, after seeing what I was wearing, had sent us home after a few questions. Maia had stayed with her to help with the cleanup.

I was getting sick of being sent home while the big kids finished the job, but my feet were damned happy to be out of the shoes. Low heeled or not, they weren't designed for afrit hunting. I headed on autopilot toward our bathroom, where I could ditch the dress, shower to get the smoke scent out of my hair, and finally get to bed. I was struggling with the clasp of my necklace when Damon appeared behind me, the mirror showing him frowning down at his datapad.

More than a 'we just chased an afrit' frown.

"What's wrong?" I asked, freezing with my hands behind my neck, wondering if this night was about to get worse.

He held up the screen to me and tapped it.

I squinted, then sighed when I recognized the security feed from the garden. Dim blobs of plants moving in the night air. "What am I looking at?"

"Wait."

And I saw it. A flicker of two tails going behind a bush. Another nixling. Not Lianith. She'd had her collar on while the glam squad worked on me and I'd left it on when we headed out.

I groaned, dropping my hands. "Another one."

"Yep," Damon said.

"Is it still here?"

"No, watch."

I kept watching. After another thirty seconds or so, Lianith came tearing into view, her faux-Maine coon tail fluffed in outrage. The nixling bolted and Lianith chased it out of frame.

"I should talk to Lianith," I said. I put my hands on the edge of the sink, resisting the urge to bang my head against the marble counter. My kingdom for one uninterrupted night. Or Damon's maybe. My kingdom was tiny.

I straightened with a sigh. "I take it Mitch already knows?"

"Yes. Do you want to call Callum?"

"If it's already gone, I'm not sure there's much point." I hesitated, considering. Callum and Gráinne were hunters. It was possible they could track the nixling and find out where it had run to. I took the datapad and replayed the footage. It was high quality, but even the best night footage was still mostly shades of gray in low light. The nixling was dark like the others but I couldn't see enough detail as it fled to know if it was one that had visited us before.

"I'll send Callum a message. He can decide what he wants to do. I need to get out of this dress and shower. Then I'll talk to Lianith"

"Alternatively, wait to send the message, and I'll help you out of the dress. And in the shower." He pulled me close for a second, pressing his lips to my temple.

Which I was pretty sure smelled like fried afrit, but it didn't seem to bother him.

"I don't like when you go running off to kill random demon creatures," he muttered.

"I don't love it either," I admitted, resting my head against his chest. Then I pulled back, frowning up at him. "You shouldn't have followed me. That was…not optimal." There. More diplomatic than 'kind of dumb'.

"It was fine."

"It could have been very not fine if there'd been more of them."

He dismissed this with a wave of his hand. "There weren't, so stop worrying. Turn around and I'll see if I can pry you out of this thing. Is there a zip somewhere?"

"Nope, just buttons."

He sighed. Buttons took time. "Go get Lianith. Talk to her while I unbutton. I want to shower in peace."

Good idea. I started to pick up the skirt of my dress to turn around, then stopped. Maybe Lianith could hear me without me leaving the bathroom.

"*Hael,*" I sent in the direction of the guest room.

The response was almost immediate. "*Returned.*"

"*Yes.*" I switched to English. "*You chased off another nixling?*"

"*Yes.*"

"*Did it talk?*"

"*No. It ran.*" She added something I thought might be coward in Fae, her tone distinctly unimpressed.

"*Any idea where it's from?*"

"*Not time. Couldn't tell much. Not Lady.*"

"Okay, thank you." She hadn't learned anything but she'd done her job.

Damon was watching me with an odd expression.

"What?"

"Were you talking to her?"

"Yes."

"Weird," he muttered. "What did she say?"

"It ran when she chased it. She didn't get anything out of

it. But hey, it might spread the word that she's here now and we won't get any more visitors."

He didn't look convinced.

"Let me message Callum."

He grunted a 'yes', then gestured for me to turn around so he could start on the buttons.

Typing the message to Callum didn't take long, and an answer pinged back. He would come by in the morning. It was already closing in on two a.m., so fine by me. I put the datapad on the counter and worked on unpinning my hair while Damon worked on the buttons. I finished before he did, but not by much. The last button came free and the weight of the gown pulled it down to the floor.

I let out a groan of pleasure. "I tell you what. All those women back in the day must have been fit hauling all this around every day." My fingers were already working the fastenings on the petticoats, and I stepped out of those as well to find Damon watching me with a glint in his eye that made my fingers suddenly unsteady. I stopped what I was doing. "Something you wanted to say?"

"Maybe I have a thing for petticoats," he said.

He moved around me, trailed a finger across my collarbones and back. I shivered happily. "Well, you'll have to be happy with just me. I'm not going to be voluntarily climbing into another gown anytime soon." Without the petticoats, I was left wearing only stockings, a garter belt and panties. The dress's boning had ruled out the need for a bra. I bent to release the first clip on my stockings.

"Let me." Damon dropped to his knees, his hands moving mine out of the way. He pressed his lips to the small, reddened mark on my skin where the clip had pressed into it. Heat bloomed in the wake of his kiss and when he moved his mouth a little higher I was very tempted to let him keep going. But both of us smelled like barbecued afrit, which was ruining the moment.

"Stick to the task at hand," I said. "I want my shower."

"More than this?" He kissed my thigh again.

"Yes. I love you, but the eau de afrit is killing the vibe."

He laughed. "Can't argue with that."

He stopped with the kisses, which made me regret my life choices. But I held firm while he flicked each fastener open in turn before rolling the stockings down my legs and shoving them into the pocket of his tux jacket.

Damon in a tux. My favorite thing. Other than naked Damon. "Why don't you go turn on the shower. Get rid of your own clothes."

Tuxedos were faster to remove than ball gowns. I'd barely peeled off what remained of my underwear when naked Damon gestured at the shower.

"Ready when you are," he said with an inviting grin.

I scanned him from head to toe. One of my favorite parts of him was definitely ready. But it would have to be patient until we were both clean.

The warmth of the water pounding down on me was so good, I wanted to cry. I stood there, letting it soak me, unable to move.

"You're tired," Damon said, pressing a kiss to my shoulder.

"Frying afrit is hard work." It hadn't been that much magic, but it had been a long day.

"Let me wash your hair."

I wasn't going to say no. He had magic fingers when it came to head massages. And other things. But right now I was interested in the head massage. And the clean-hair part. "Thank you, that sounds divine."

For a moment, he pulled me back against him, wrapping an arm around my shoulders. His erection pressed against me but he didn't try to do anything about it. He didn't even try to kiss me. We breathed together, both of us needing the reassurance that everything was fine. That, once again, we'd survived.

We stood for several minutes before Damon reached for the shampoo and set to work. I tipped my head back, letting his touch ease the tension out of my body, then handed him the conditioner for the second round.

Once my hair was clean, I reached for the shower gel and let the spice-scented suds get rid of the last lingering smells of afrit before washing my makeup off as well.

Then I turned back to Damon, who was still too quiet as he stood watching me, water cascading down every gorgeous muscle and plane of his body. I knew what he was thinking.

"I'm okay," I said, "*We're* okay."

His blue eyes watched me, the expression in them turning soft. Almost wondering. "Always," he said, and lifted me out of the shower.

He wrapped me in soft warm towels and carried me into the bedroom. And then he pulled me close again, one hand stroking my cheek, before he kissed me so softly that at first it felt like I was imagining it. We kissed for a long time, making out like teenagers. I wanted nothing more than the taste of his lips on mine, his breath, his hands in my damp hair. We were trying to find each other, lost in each other, telling each other the things we sometimes couldn't bring ourselves to say out loud. That we were both still there and what we had was more important than any heat-of-the-moment arguments about who should be doing what in dangerous situations.

Our lives were never going to be simple. But this—the love and the need and the undeniable something that drew us back together every time—this could be simple.

As simple as breaking our kiss and pushing his head down. As letting my legs fall open as he kissed his way down my body. As giving in to the swooping rush as his tongue touched my clit and he did his best to set me alight and the world closed in to the sensation of his mouth on me, of the sounds he drew from me with his tongue and fingers, driving me higher and higher, the weight of him keeping me anchored as I twisted and arched and begged him for more and more and more.

I never knew what I said. Incoherent and needy. Wanting this burning, consuming pleasure only he could give me. He pushed me up and up and then over the edge, but tonight he was hungry, too. I had no time to catch my breath, to come back to myself. He pushed my legs wider and then drove himself home, the feel of him so hard and strong inside me, while I was still half-coming, nearly pushing me immediately over the edge again.

"Wait for me," he growled. "This time. Wait for me."

My head was spinning, my heart pounding as the need clawed through me, but his words were their own brand of magic. I wanted only to do as he said, to give him the same fierce satisfaction he gave me. I wrapped my legs around his hips as he thrust and growled heated praise against my neck and my lips and whichever parts of me he was kissing, until his words broke into pieces that stopped making much sense until he rumbled 'now' as his blue eyes burned into mine and I arched and broke beneath him as he cried out my name.

I woke when something landed with a thump on my bed. I almost screamed before I realized it was Lianith, not an afrit or worse.

"Madge, lights," I croaked, mouth gone dry from fright. The lights blinked on. The nixling was perched on the space between me and the edge of the bed, golden eyes wide, one paw raised as though she had been about to tap my face if I hadn't woken up. Damon was nowhere in sight. I'd crashed early, before he'd come home. Two days had passed since we'd killed the afrit and he'd been burning the midnight oil. He might still be at the office. I gave myself a few seconds to calm down.

"What is it?" I asked, stomach sinking. Lianith had so far proven to be an excellent house guest. She spent her nights since chasing off the first nixling patrolling the grounds and most of the days sleeping inside. According to Callum, nixlings leaned nocturnal anyway.

I kept practicing talking to her, but the process was slow and the conversation so far had to be simple. But she said she was happy. When she wasn't sleeping or stalking through the garden, she usually came and sat somewhere near Damon or me, watching us curiously.

Humans were odd but interesting, was the only opinion she shared. I'd had to ask Callum what the words she used were and he'd laughed for at least a minute before seconding her sentiment.

Her head swiveled back toward the door and my stomach clenched. "Something you want to show me?"

Her response was to jump back down off the bed, looking over her shoulder as though to say, 'come along'. I'd learned to see through the illusion—so I could see the tips of her tails twitching in different directions—but it worked wonders for anyone without magic. Certainly, Amy and the gardeners hadn't reacted to her appearance, taking our story that we were cat sitting for a friend of mine at face value.

I shoved my feet into the closest pair of sneakers, thankful I'd gone to bed in pajamas. "All right, show me."

I followed Lianith through the house to the gym. I had a fair idea of what I was about to see. Lianith hadn't interrupted us sleeping since she'd arrived.

Sure enough, there was a nixling sitting on the deck staring back at us through the window.

Well, crap. After a lack of nocturnal visitors, I'd started to hope that whoever had sent the first two had decided to give up.

"Is this the same one as before?"

Lianith jumped up to balance on the handrail of the treadmill, her tails twitching. Fae I was learning. The intricacies of nixling tail gestures might take me longer. "*Same?*" I sent.

A smidge of Fae floated into my head, faint and hard to make out, but I thought it was a 'no'.

I concentrated, waiting to see if she was going to add anything else. But nope, apparently Lianith understood 'no' was a complete sentence. Right. So. Not the same nixling. Which made it number three? Or was it four?

Regardless of the number, it was starting to piss me off.

Lianith made an impatient sound and I dragged my thoughts back to the present. The nixling on the deck hadn't moved. Its tails twitched, long fur ruffling with the movement.

"Some of us want to sleep," I said to it. "You should leave." I made a shooing motion. It stared back at me, unmoved.

Irritation sparked through me. I was sleep-deprived and cranky. "Right," I said to Lianith. "Let's do this."

Her answering chirp sounded pleased. She sat back on her hind legs, reaching a paw toward the door in the windows.

"We'll go out the front. Otherwise it might just run."

She dropped back to all fours, grumbling, but she followed me when I headed to Damon's office to grab my gun. I didn't want to shoot a nixling, but I would if this went badly.

But I hoped it wouldn't. Much like with the afrit, I didn't want the security team to come running, which they would if I fired my weapon. Mitch had reluctantly agreed to let Lianith and I deal with another nixling, should one appear, so they wouldn't intervene unless I asked. Madge had ears on the entire property. She'd hear if I yelled for help.

Lianith walked ahead of me on the path, picking her way silently, tails up. So far, reading her body language like a cat's had worked well enough, so I figured she wasn't particularly worried about confronting the other nixling. Maybe I shouldn't be either.

Still, I kept a tight grip on my gun as we came around the back of the house. The nixling had descended from the deck, sitting at the base of the stairs waiting for us.

Lianith walked until she was about three feet away from it and then made one of her chirping noises at it, this one sounding like a demand, with an edge of something closer to a snarl. The other nixling—which, like the first two, was darker than her—didn't reply, and I waited to see what would happen next.

"*Stranger,*" Lianith's voice came a little louder in my head this time. "*Should go.*"

"*Do you know where it's from?*"

"*Nichtkin.*"

Ugh. Not what I wanted to hear. "*Can you ask it who sent it?*"

She made another, more aggressive noise, tails twitching.

The nixling spat something back and Lianith hissed, taking a half step forward, fur bristling.

This was not going as smoothly as I'd hoped. Callum had said Lianith could handle other nixlings, but I didn't want her to actually fight and get injured.

So I decided to join the discussion. I took a full step closer, so I was slightly in front of Lianith. I kept my eyes on the strange nixling. Its eyes flicked back and forth between us, as though it couldn't decide who was the bigger threat.

I straightened my shoulders. Make yourself look big. Wasn't that what cats did? "This is my territory and Lianith's. You are not welcome here. I cede no loyalty to the Nichtkin. I am allied with Lady Cerridwen. If someone has sent you here, tell them they can speak to her or me directly. But I will not have my territory invaded. There will be consequences for the next one of you who shows up." I emphasized that last word by drawing a flame to my hand, letting it dance there.

The nixling flinched back at the sight of the flame.

"Yes, I have magic of my own. I can defend this territory, and I will defend it." I let the flame flare for a few seconds before pulling it back. Lianith bared her teeth.

The nixling didn't move, though its tails were twice the size they had been. I didn't want to set it on fire, particularly not after spending a few days with Lianith and learning how cute nixlings were, but I wasn't going to be pushed around in my own house. I took a step closer, let the flame brighten slightly, and the nixling backed up to the next step.

Lianith let out a noise that was far more a growl than previously. That seemed to be the deciding factor.

The nixling turned, bolted up the steps and across the deck, diving off the other side.

Lianith gave chase but returned within a minute or so. "*Gone,*" her voice said in my head loudly enough that I had no trouble hearing a certain degree of smug satisfaction in the statement.

I allowed myself a fist pump. "*Thank you.*" Hopefully the nixling would return to the realm and report back to whoever had sent it. If it was from Usuriel's territory, well, I'd deal with what happened next. If he was trying to see if he could push me around…well, yes, he was scary, but that didn't mean I wasn't going to push back.

Chapter Eleven

"COME TO MAMA." I sniffed the aroma of strong coffee happily as I poured a fresh mug. After Lianith and I had dealt with the nixling intruder last night, I'd informed Cassandra and Callum and decided whoever was on night duty could update Mitch. Then I'd gone back to bed and surprised myself by crashing out instantly, waking only enough to register when Damon finally made it home. When my alarm went off, he was gone again.

I'd decided checking in with him could wait until I'd showered, refueled and caffeinated. I'd achieved the shower, and coffee and breakfast were imminent. But before I could settle at the table with my caffeine fix and one of Amy's breakfast muffins, Madge chimed an alert.

"Yes?" I said before taking a bite of the muffin and chewing happily. Amy swore the muffins were healthy, and I'm sure they were, but she was a goddess of the kitchen who knew how to make a healthy muffin taste like the regular loaded-with-fat-and-sugar kind.

"There is someone at the gate, Maggie. She says she knows you."

"She?" I ask curiously. "Can you put the feed on the screen, please?"

Madge already knew all the people likely to visit me. This was probably some random Damon groupie, trying to weasel their way in using my name.

That was the problem with dating a famous guy. People knew my name. And, worse, tried to use it to their advantage. A problem compounded by the fact that it's impossible to be as famous as Damon is and keep your address secret. And made worse by Damon insisting on living in a normal neighborhood. If by 'normal' you meant 'full of rich people'. But it wasn't gated, and he hadn't bought a property out in the country somewhere we could have miles and miles of land between the front gate and a house and taken to commuting via chopper or something. Though come to think of it, it was entirely possible he did own a farm or a ranch or an estate or whatever the hell you called it. Or several.

He had houses and apartments in multiple cities and I hadn't even been to all of those yet. But I knew it was unlikely he'd ever abandon San Francisco as his base. Not when he'd fought so hard to help rebuild the city.

A holoscreen blinked into life at eye height, showing the security feed from the front gate. To my surprise, I recognized the face looking up at the gate camera.

Gwen Jones.

What the hell? I dropped the muffin back onto the plate, wondering if I was mistaken. It wasn't even a week since I'd talked to Aubrey and she'd said nothing about Gwen planning to come to the States.

I zoomed in on the image. Yep, it was her. She'd chopped her long pale-blonde hair to shoulder length since I'd seen her last, but it was definitely Gwen.

What the hell was she doing here?

"Connect me to the intercom, please," I said to Madge.

"Of course, Maggie. Connecting now."

The picture zoomed in on Gwen's face. She was chewing her lip, looking worried. "Gwen, hi" I said, keeping my tone neutral. She jumped a little anyway, blinking up at the camera, her eyes widening.

"Sorry. Didn't mean to startle you. This is Maggie," I continued. "Do you want to come in?"

Her expression turned nonchalant, but I could see she was trying to be casual. "Maggie, hi. Yes, please."

Her accent wasn't as posh as Aubrey's, but it was still what I thought of as well-off English. She sounded tired, though, her voice raspier than I remembered. Which was not surprising if she'd just spent eleven or so hours on a plane. I zoomed the picture out. Even though she sounded tired, she was still startlingly pretty, her Fae blood clear in the elegant curves of her face and the gleam of her skin, even through the vidfeed. A massive, well-stuffed green backpack rested on her back and one hand gripped the handle of a large suitcase.

More luggage than someone planning a short visit might need.

Perfect. She'd run away from home. Or whatever the adult equivalent was.

I rubbed my forehead, glad she couldn't see me. "Great, come on through. I'll meet you at the front door." I cut the connection, my jaw clenching. Another complication.

"Madge, can you bring up the file I had started on Gwen Jones?" I'd made notes of everything Aubrey had told me about her since we'd brought her out of the realm. It wasn't a lot, but I didn't know what might be helpful. I skimmed it quickly, refreshing my memory.

Gwen's expression flashed relief when I opened the door, before she went back to cool. I showed her through to the kitchen, biting back the hundred or so questions whirling in my head. No point scaring her off. She dumped the backpack by the counter, sighing out a breath, and parked her suitcase next to it. Then rolled her shoulders, as though happy to have ditched the weight, as she looked around, taking in the kitchen. Which was sunny, light-filled and welcoming, but also screamed expensive if you had an eye for interior design.

"Nice place," she said.

Nice was an understatement but that might be English politeness or simple exhaustion. "Thanks," I replied warily. "So, what brings you to town? Aubrey didn't mention that you were leaving England."

Her pale blue eyes narrowed. "Aubrey didn't know." She paused for a second. "Do you talk to her often?"

"Often enough to know she'll be worried about you."

Gwen rolled her shoulders again, the gesture part shrug, part nervous twitch. "The Cestis...well, I'm an adult. I can do what I want."

Her tone sounded more defiant teen than adult. But I didn't react. She'd not long turned eighteen when she'd gone into the realm. She wasn't a normal twenty-two-year-old. Plus she'd had a bad time with Usuriel and maybe even in Morgain's realm. Gwen had claimed she was happy enough being a servant, but it didn't ring completely true. Not when she'd made a deal with Usuriel because she'd wanted out.

"Sure. No one's going to argue about that," I said. "But I'll have to let them know you're here."

That earned me another shrug that reminded me of Yoshi when he was in one of his rare moods. I could introduce him to Gwen. He could show her how to be a semi-normal young adult. Though his background wasn't any happier than hers.

Gwen kept stretching. Her clothes were creased, her hair messy and her eyes tired. I always felt like death warmed up after a long flight, so I could give her the benefit of the doubt and chalk the weird attitude up to exhaustion.

"You look as though you had a long flight." Gwen's unknown father had left her money, but I didn't know if she was comfortably off or wealthy enough not to have to think twice about traveling suborbital versus commercial airlines. Commercial, London to San Francisco was an eleven-hour flight, which was a slog. "Would you like coffee, breakfast, shower? Do you have somewhere to stay?"

She nodded. "I booked a hotel, but coffee and breakfast would be brilliant."

"Okay," I said. "Let's do that."

I teased out of her what she might like for breakfast and hunted through options while the coffee machine did its thing. Gwen was mostly silent. I hoped it was jet lag, rather than attitude.

As I slid a plate of bacon and eggs in front of her, along with a coffee, Lianith wandered into the kitchen, presumably drawn by the smell of food. Callum had said she would prefer raw meat, but we'd discovered she loved bacon. She'd even learned the English word for it.

At the sight of her, Gwen froze, fork halfway to her mouth. "That's a nixling."

Right. She was tanai. She could see through the illusion. "Yes," I said, trying to sound soothing. "It's all right. She's friendly."

She put her fork down, looking more alarmed than surprised. "Why do you have a nixling?"

"That's a long story," I replied. "Eat your breakfast."

She stared down at the bacon and eggs and, to my horror, her lip quivered, as though she was about to cry.

Had she had a bad experience with nixlings? "What's wrong?" I asked, making a little shooing motion at Lianith. The nixling twitched her tail, turned, and stalked back out of the room. A vague *"humph"* hit my mind.

"I came to San Francisco because I wanted to get away from the Fae. And I knew you lived here, so I'd know someone at least, and that there are tanai here who didn't leave when the Fae left, who got free..." Her breath hitched.

"Oh," I said. "Well, yes, that's true. Some tanai didn't

follow their Fae relatives when the door closed. But you know the door here is open again."

She swiped at her eyes with the back of her hand.

Great. I really didn't want her to start crying.

"But it's not free traffic in and out of the realm here yet. Not the way it is in London." I didn't tell her that was because there'd already been trouble with the door. Unlikely to be reassuring. "But the nixling won't bother you if I ask her not to." At least, I hoped not. Lianith had definite opinions about what human things were orders she would follow versus suggestions she could ignore.

Gwen said nothing.

"Drink some coffee," I said, "or eat. You'll feel better. I know someone—a tanai—who's from one of the lines that stayed. Her family doesn't have much to do with the Fae. I can ask if she'll talk to you." I cocked my head. "She can tell you about how their families work. But you don't know who your mother was, do you? So is it her you're trying to avoid, or something else?"

"Just Fae," she said. "In London, there, there are too many of them. I don't want to have...I don't want to go back there." She pushed her plate away

Was she worried about being taken or being tempted?

I rubbed my temples for a moment, starting to feel frazzled myself. "Eat," I said again, pushing the plate back. "You'll feel better with a full stomach, and then I can get someone to take you to your hotel. Or," I added, wondering if she might just run again if left to freak out on her own, "you could stay here for a few nights."

"Damon wouldn't mind?" Gwen sniffed and wiped her eyes again.

"No." I pulled a box of Kleenex out and passed it to her.

"Alright. Thank you. "She blew her nose and picked up her silverware, taking a bite of bacon. She made an appreciative noise then attacked the food like she was starving.

"Good. You finish that. There's plenty more if you want." I said. "I'm going to let Aubrey know you're here."

Gwen looked up. "Why?"

"Because the Cestis have been helping you, and they're going to freak out if one of them tries to contact you, and you've vanished. Aubrey mentioned you're still seeing Padma? So you must have a schedule."

Gwen hunched. "They can't make me go back."

"Of course not. You can go where you want. You haven't broken any laws—" that I knew about "—so the Cestis don't have authority over you. But they were helping you, so I'm going to let them know where you are." Along with Cassandra.

Gwen looked mutinous.

"And," I added, "Aubrey helped get you out of Fae. Without her, I wouldn't have known how to get Lord—" I stopped as Gwen flinched.

Right. Don't talk about Usuriel.

"About how to get *you* out of the realm. So we will do her this common courtesy and let her know you're safe. They can't make you go back if you don't want to. You got this far, so I'm assuming you have your passport and a tourist visa. That won't last forever, but we can deal with that when it comes to it, if you decide you want to stay." I tapped my finger on my now-cold mug of coffee. "You were studying game design, weren't you?"

She nodded, then flinched again. "I don't want you to think I came here to try to get Damon to help me with that. I knew you were here and I knew you were kind to me back in England and—" She waved a hand in a vague 'over there' gesture, which I took to mean in the realm.

She was in a bad way if she couldn't even say the words.

"Damon might not mind if you stay here a few days," I said. "And he will know what programs are best, if you were interested in going back to school. There are international scholarships and things."

"I have money," Gwen said. "I'm not a beggar."

"Well, that's great to know," I said, "but school's expensive here. San Francisco's an expensive city in general."

"So is London," Gwen pointed out.

I couldn't argue with that. "Eat," I said again sternly. "Lianith might come back. She won't hurt you. She likes bacon. Give her some and she'll leave you alone. Do you know how to talk to nixling?"

Gwen nodded.

"Well, tell her to leave you alone if you want."

I went back into my office to call Aubrey.

Thankfully, she picked up. This was not news I wanted to break in a voicemail.

"Maggie," Aubrey said. "Is something wrong?" She was sitting in a car. Driving in fact. Flashes of other cars moved in and out of the background.

"Does something have to be wrong for me to call you?"

"No," she said, "but it's the nature of the beast with my job. I tend to assume the worst when someone from your part of the world calls me out of the blue."

"Ah," I said, "sorry."

"What can I do for you?"

"I wanted to let you know Gwen just turned up at Damon's house."

"What?" Aubrey's mouth dropped open, her normally serene expression vanishing. "She's in San Francisco? Since when?"

"Well, I don't know when she landed, but she arrived here about thirty minutes ago. So if any of you were expecting to see her soon, there's been a change of plans."

"Did you ask why?" Aubrey asked, sounding half exasperated.

"I think she's looking for ways to make sure she doesn't

have to deal with the Fae. Too many in London. But that's all I know so far."

Aubrey sighed. "Yes. Padma mentioned she'd been talking about that in her last few sessions. Damn. We should have seen this coming."

I raised an eyebrow. "Should Padma be telling you what she and Gwen talk about?"

"Yes. She doesn't tell us the details of their conversations, of course, but we're kept informed of Gwen's general progress."

"Well, she's here now," I said. "She mentioned she'd booked a hotel; I've invited her to stay with me and Damon for a few days. She's pretty freaked out about the Fae. Said she wanted to come here and meet the tanai who stayed behind. Did something happen to set her off?"

Aubrey frowned. "I have no idea."

"Well, I'll see if I can find out. And if Pinky is willing to talk to her. That might make her feel better. But…" I trailed off, unsure how to phrase what I wanted to say diplomatically. "But I wouldn't bank on her coming back to England any time soon."

"Thank you," Aubrey said. Her mouth twisted with frustration before she got her expression back under control. I sympathized. She and the others in the UK Cestis had put a lot of effort into helping Gwen reestablish her life and now she'd…well, run away.

"It will be all right," I said.

"I hope so." Aubrey shook her head. "But she's an adult, so we can't stop her doing what she wants. She'll make her own choices."

"She will. I'll keep you posted."

"Right," Aubrey said. "Call me if you need more help or if she says something more about why she left."

"I'll ask. But she might not tell me."

Aubrey sighed. "She can be little prickly. Young for her

age, even though she hasn't had it easy. Padma thinks that spending so much time in the Fae as a servant means she hasn't learned to assert herself in an adult way. But tell her we're here if she needs to talk. To Padma, or me, or any of us."

I was raised by a mother who had the ego of a perpetual teenager; I understood something of that problem. Yoshi might, too. Though he was her opposite. A teen who'd had to be an adult too soon. He was, if anything, too responsible. "Right now, she's tired. Let's give her a couple of days to get over the jet lag and I'll see what else she has to say and if I can set something up with Pinky. I'll keep you posted."

I went back to Gwen. I wasn't surprised to find Lianith perched on the chair next to hers, cleaning her whiskers. Gwen's plate was empty but she was still sipping her coffee. "I see you two have bonded over bacon."

"I only gave her a small piece." Gwen's tone was defensive.

"It's fine," I said. "Better for you two to get along."

"What did Aubrey say?"

"She was happy you're safe. Said to call her or Padma if you need anything."

"She wasn't mad?"

"Surprised, but not angry," I reassured her. I nodded at her plate. "More?"

"Toast? Do you have marmalade?"

"No. But Amy, Damon's housekeeper, makes great jam. I'll find you some of that. Then you can shower and take a nap and I'll see if Pinky's free any time this week. I know she has a work deadline soon, so you might have to be patient."

Chapter Twelve

Pinky arrived at my Berkeley house about five minutes early. I'd called her while Gwen was napping after her shower the day before and she'd said she could do lunch today if we could do it in Berkeley, where she was working with some session musicians in a local studio. Handy. She hugged me fast and then peered past me up the hallway. "Is she here?"

"She's setting up lunch in the kitchen." Setting up being the operative word, because I'd raided Damon's freezer for some of Amy's stashed meals and added a bunch of salads from the nearest grocery store. I'd had dinner with Pinky and Ivy at their house a few times and they were both excellent cooks. I was adequate, at best, and even if Gwen could cook, why add the stress of cooking for a stranger on top of everything else?

"One thing about you, your life is rarely boring," Pinky said. She looked me up and down. "You need sleep."

"Right back at you." She had the edgy air of someone on a deadline, her pink hair messily braided around her crown and her fingernails chewed. Her charcoal linen tank and baggy pants looked like chic meets nouveau punk, the tank revealing the vibrant tattoos covering her arms.

"Mine is work. What's your excuse? Continuing to live in interesting times?"

"I'd take some boring times," I said. "There's been a lot going on."

"I heard about your nixling problem from Callum," Pinky said. "What does Grandma have to say about it?"

"So far nothing she's cared to share with me. I haven't been back to the realm." And Cassandra had sent me home from Ajax's house long before Cerridwen arrived. Had Pinky heard about that, too? I didn't want to talk about demons in front of Gwen. I had no idea how much she knew about them. Presumably something because she'd been living in the realm when the Fae had been debating whether or not to reconnect the door in Berkeley. Lady Morgain was one of the Elders who'd been strongly in favor.

And Gwen knew I'd killed a demon, because Usuriel had talked about it in front of her. But this wasn't the time to remind her about my past. Until she was settled back into human life it was going to be easier for everyone if she was somewhere close to some Cestis member. If not London, then San Francisco was the next best thing. So we didn't need her freaking out and deciding to move again.

"Nothing?" Pinky's eyebrows shot up.

I shook my head. "Let's not talk about that now."

"But Gwen is fine with you having a nixling in your house? You said she was staying with you, right?"

She was. I'd convinced her it would be better than a hotel, plus she'd have some company. Damon agreed with me. "Yes, and she doesn't seem to mind Lianith. But Gwen doesn't know all the details about why Lianith is there, and I don't want her thinking about Usuriel. So don't mention him. We're trying to get her settled. She wants to know about avoiding the Fae."

"Kind of ironic when you're…you know…you." Pinky smiled wryly.

"Well, she knows I have some involvement with them. She

met me in the realm. But I don't want to rub her face in it. I'm trying to give her a few days to take a breath. She needs to make some decisions. I've asked Yoshi if he can show her around his campus sometime. Aubrey and the others were trying to encourage her to go back to school."

Pinky pursed her lips, considering. "You really don't know why she's here? She just turned up out of the blue?"

"Yep," I said. "I talked to Aubrey last week and there was no hint of Gwen wanting to leave. And then, bam, she took a plane ride. She says she wants to learn from the tanai here how to stay away from the Fae."

"It doesn't involve special skills," Pinky said, shaking her head. "You can just avoid them."

That was an oversimplification, I was sure. "I'm not sure that's so easy in London. Particularly not now she's spent time in the realm. Some of the Fae there must know her. Maybe she thinks she can be anonymous here."

"But she doesn't know who her mother is?"

"No. And I think she's keen not to find out. She doesn't want to be dragged back in there under some obscure parental claim."

Pinky shrugged. "Well, I can set her mind at rest about that, at least. The Fae can't force anyone into the realm. Of course, if she goes in willingly, then that would change things. Like what power her mom might have over her." She sighed. "But, hey, let's not have this conversation here. Let's have it with Gwen in the room."

"Sure," I said and headed for the kitchen where Gwen was nervously realigning the silverware. She'd bought gorgeous pink and peachy dahlias at the grocery store and had arranged them in a low bowl in the center of the table. My china was plain white and so was my only tablecloth, so they added a splash of color. The pink almost matched Pinky's hair. The whole thing was simple, but prettier than I could have made it. Or would have thought to. My Gran always made things feel cozy and comfortable but, beyond making sure I had all the life skills required to be a functioning adult, she'd abandoned trying to turn me into a domestic goddess when it became clear that computers were always going to be way more interesting to me than making sure my baseboards weren't dusty, and my china matched my tablecloth.

Maybe Gwen learned the knack at boarding school. Or maybe serving in the realm had made her more sensitive to such things. The Fae had firm views on hierarchy and proprieties.

"Gwen? This is Pinky Andretti. Pinky, this is Gwen Jones."

"Hi," Gwen said awkwardly. She leaned over and moved the bowl of flowers half an inch to the left. She had on a deep-blue sundress, her blonde hair clipped back in a half-up, half-down style. She looked almost delicate, despite the fact she was short and had more curves than your average Fae. The sun glinting off her hair revealed the almost pearl-like edge to the blonde. If Pinky hadn't already known Gwen was tanai, it would have taken her approximately a second to figure it out.

"How's it going?" Pinky asked with a smile.

Gwen managed a smile, but it was wobbly. "Very well, thank you." Her accent sounded more clipped. Nervous.

Pinky let the silence stretch before she relented. "Maggie said you had some questions. About the tanai here?"

Gwen nodded, still looking uncomfortable.

"Why don't we eat?" I suggested "Gwen can ask her questions afterwards."

"Sure," Pinky said easily. "What's for lunch?"

"Amy's vegetable lasagna and a few other things. Plus brownies for dessert."

Pinky's face lit up. "Oh, yay, Amy cooked."

I laughed. "I'd take that as an insult, but I agree with you."

I served the meal, thankful for Amy's skills. For the first few minutes, we all ate, mostly in silence. Amy's cooking deserved close attention. When I managed to slow down from scarfing pasta, I asked Pinky about her current project. She'd been working on a movie score on and off over the last year.

"It's going well enough," she said. "They're behind in their primary filming, which makes it more complicated. I've got a lot of the score written, but fine-tuning it for the edit is always the hard part. But I'm sure it'll all come together. It always does."

If she was like Damon it came together by her pulling crazy long hours for several weeks at the end of the project. But, like Damon, she loved her job, so she probably loved that part of it, too.

"And Ivy?"

"She's in the middle of an important case, so it's hard to get much time together right now. Ivy's my wife," she added to Gwen.

"Cool. What does she do?" Gwen asked.

"She's a lawyer. Corporate stuff. I don't understand most of it, but she's loves it."

"Must be useful to have a lawyer in the family," Gwen offered.

"If you need a lawyer," I said, "I'm sure we can find you one."

Gwen paused, a forkful of lasagna halfway to her mouth. "Why would I need a lawyer?"

"If you decide you want to stay, you'll have to deal with visas and immigration. Which is lawyer territory." I didn't know a lot about green cards, other than they were hard to get.

Pinky blinked. "You want to stay in America?"

"I'm not sure," Gwen said. "But the schools here are great. The colleges, I mean."

"They are." Pinky nodded, her tone encouraging. But she slid me a dubious glance.

"I haven't quite decided what I want to do. I'd only

finished my first semester when I, you know, went into the realm." Gwen put her fork down, reached for her water glass.

"How long ago was that?" Pinky asked.

"A little over four years," Gwen said.

"So you were eighteen when you went in?" Pinky shot me another look.

I wasn't entirely sure what she was trying not to say. It would have been useful if she could talk to me mentally like Callum.

Without that, I decided to try to keep the conversation flowing, rather than trying to figure out what Pinky was worried about. "Yep, but, you know, plenty of people take a while to figure out what they want to do," I said cheerfully. "So Gwen's got plenty of time now she's back."

"And you're sure you don't want to go back? To the realm?" Pinky asked.

Gwen visibly shuddered. "Absolutely not. I was trying to get out for a while, even before Aubrey and Maggie came. But I hadn't finished out my service with Morgain."

Which was why she'd made a deal with Usuriel, which had been flat-out dumb in retrospect. It could have ended horribly for her if she'd wound up trapped in his court rather than with Lady Morgain.

"You left without your Lady's permission?" Pinky asked, looking surprised.

"Technically, under the contract, no one without a familial claim can keep her in there," I pointed out. I'd spent a long time familiarizing myself in more detail about the terms of the contract between the Fae and the Cestis since we'd all returned from the realm. I doubted this would be my last entanglement with some of the Fae Elders, and it was handy to know the letter of the law, even though understanding the legalese made my head hurt.

I'd probably driven Cassandra half-mad asking her questions. In the end, she passed me over to Ian, who, being the second oldest of the Cestis, had the most experience with the Fae after her. He'd been delighted to explain the terms to me in minute detail.

"Yoshi's going to show Gwen around his campus," I said. "Show her all the options in the program he's doing." Yoshi was a genius, but if Gwen had been accepted into a game-design program back in the UK she must be smart, too.

"Maggie said you wanted to do game design?" Pinky asked when Gwen smiled at the mention of touring UC.

"Probably," Gwen said. "Something creative, anyway. I like the storytelling and the art."

"Plenty of opportunities to use those," Pinky said. "It's a very competitive field, but if you're good, that doesn't matter." She shrugged with the confidence of someone who was top of the class when it came to her job. She had an Oscar amongst her many awards. "Yoshi will be able to tell you about all the options," Pinky said. "He researched a lot of schools before he picked UC. If you decide to stay, having an offer from a school would probably help with a visa. But, if you want to avoid Fae completely, well, San Francisco isn't the best city for that. Not since the door reopened."

"I want to be somewhere with tanai. People who know what it's like. But not where the tanai are super chummy with the Fae," Gwen said. "Since the door opened, you haven't changed your life have you?" She started eating again.

"My mom hasn't changed hers," Pinky said judiciously. "She stays away. I'm a little bit more involved since I met Maggie, but I wouldn't say I was chummy."

I shook my head ever so slightly when she turned to me. Better not to go into the whole 'Cerridwen asked her for a favor and she couldn't say no' thing. "But I'd say I'm one of the exceptions among those of us who stayed behind. And it will be easier for you if no family has claimed you. Lady Morgain hasn't been in contact since you left, has she?"

Gwen dropped her fork. "Why would she?"

"Well, if you swore to her to serve her for a period of time, yes, there's the contract, but they don't like broken bargains."

Gwen's expression turned alarmed. "Maggie? Is that true?"

I shook my head. "I'm not sure." I tried to summon a soothing expression. "I'm sure Aubrey would have thought of this and dealt with it somehow. The UK Cestis have a lot closer contact with the Fae than we do."

"You can ask her," Pinky said.

"She would have told me," Gwen objected. "What does it matter if I'm never going back? Someone can't come out and take me, can they?"

"No," Pinky said firmly. "Not legally, but never is a long time, and if you ever do have to go back, it's better not to have one of the Elders thinking they have a claim on you."

Gwen hunched.

"We'll talk to Aubrey," I said reassuringly, hoping I was right and it would have been taken care of. Aubrey was not the kind of person who left any i's undotted and t's uncrossed if she could help it. Though I wondered why she hadn't told Gwen, if she had sorted things out with Morgaine. But maybe she hadn't wanted to trigger Gwen's anxiety about dealing with the Fae.

"Can we call her soon?" Gwen asked.

"Of course," I said. "But let's eat lunch. No one's coming to grab you from the house. It's fine." Gwen had been a little nervous when I'd told her we were meeting Pinky in Berkeley, not liking the idea of being close to the door. But I'd reassured her it was still strictly controlled.

I pointed my fork at Pinky. "Why don't you tell Gwen a bit about how the tanai here live?"

"It's not terribly exciting," Pinky said. "Those of us who stayed behind, well, most of us have pretty normal lives. We do what we do and we don't deal with the Fae. It was difficult at first. The Fae weren't happy, but the contract says they can't force anyone living outside the realm to enter it. And everything was chaotic after the earthquake. They wanted to close the door. That took precedence over trying to convince every last tanai to come with them. Mostly."

"What do you mean mostly?"

"In some ways, it depends on the family. Lady Cerridwen, who is my, well, call her my grandmother, to keep it simple. She gave her tanai the choice. So did some of the others."

"You mean some didn't? They *forced* their tanai to go with them?" Gwen said.

"Forced is a big word," Pinky said. "Let's just say they incentivized people to move. The Fae have plenty of money to throw at people if they choose."

I was sure there was more to it than what Pinky was saying. Had there been Fae who'd flouted the contract and compelled their tanai to leave with them?

"But some tanai cut ties completely and left San Francisco to move to places with no Fae populations. A few have moved back since, but as I said, we mainly live normal lives. My mom already kept away from the Fae even when the door was here. I grew up with her in Oakland. I knew I was tanai, but it didn't mean much. And even less after the door closed. Mom didn't even tell me we were related to Cerridwen until I asked her when I was fifteen. She doesn't use her magic.

"Do you use yours?" Gwen asked.

Pinky tucked a stray strand of pink hair back behind her ear. "Do you?" she countered.

"In the realm, a little. I can use the everyday charms the servants use, but didn't really need to do more," Gwen said. "I haven't tried since I got back. When I was in school, I had no reason to try. I didn't know I was tanai. And it's not like I accidentally levitated a bed or anything. If that's even possible."

"That would depend entirely on who your mom is and how strong your magic is. It will be more difficult out here," Pinky said. "It depends on what you're trying to do, but the realm, well, it *is* magic. So it will take more effort to do anything out here, unless you're quite strong. If you never had any weird stuff happen growing up, maybe you're not." She paused, as though inviting Gwen to tell us more. Gwen shrugged.

Was Pinky right? Did Gwen not using her magic before she'd gone into the realm, mean she wasn't strong? Or, like me, had she never considered the possibility of having magic and therefore never tried anything? Yes, my magic had been bound, but it had still taken me being in fear for my life for it to surface once the bond had been broken. If Gwen had never been in the kind of mess where she might instinctively use magic to save herself, it might never have been an issue. I'm sure girls in boarding schools generated drama, but not life-or-death situations.

"I don't have a lot of power," Pinky continued. "I can do some basic magic and in the realm I can do more, but it was never something I was particularly worried about. My mom taught me enough to let me do things like light a candle or warm myself up if I ever wanted to, but we didn't use magic at home. And I was never that curious. So I left it alone."

She sat back in her chair. "That's what it boils down to: being willing to leave the magical world alone and live normally. There's no reason to go into the realm if that's what you want." She tipped her head at me. "Most tanai even steer clear of witches. Not all of them know about the Fae, and we have to obey the part of the contract about not revealing ourselves to normal humans. So it's easier to not hang out with witches. Some of them can spot the magic and they get curious and then it can be a whole thing to avoid explaining."

I hadn't thought about that, but it made sense. Fae magic appeared somewhat different to my sight than human did, but if a witch didn't know someone was tanai, I could see how they might think a tanai's aura, or their energy field, however they saw it, was slightly strange. I could also see how it might lead to some awkward questions.

"My advice," Pinky said, "is to go back to school, get your degree, find a job, build a life. I mean, you don't have to stay in San Francisco after you graduate."

"It's kind of one of the best cities if I want to be in game design, though," Gwen said.

"There is that," Pinky said. She was looking at me, not Gwen. "Maggie will tell you there's not many witches who work at Riley Arts. If they do, they're not there because of their magic, at least other than the security people like Maia." She smiled suddenly. "You don't have a desire to be a bodyguard, do you?"

Gwen, who was a good half a foot shorter than me, laughed. "No. I don't think that's my calling. They probably have a height requirement."

"Yeah," Pinky said. "All of Damon's security people I've met are tall."

"Like Maia?" Gwen nodded. "She's an amazon. And she's cool, but that's got to be a weird job, right?"

"I agree," I said. "But I think Pinky's right. Focus on what you want to do with your life, go back to school and take it from there. Unless you have a burning desire to keep using magic, you should be able to stay free of trouble easily enough."

"Is that what you do?" Gwen asked.

Pinky coughed and I glared at her. Staying out of trouble was not precisely my strong point.

"I'm not tanai," I said finally. "So, me and magic, that's a different proposition. Witches have to learn to use their magic, or it's dangerous."

"But you do stuff for the Cestis?"

"The Cestis have been teaching me. I came to my magic late," I said. "So, they want to make sure I know what I'm doing."

"But you fought a demon," Gwen said. "That's what Lord…" She paused, wincing. "What, *he* said back in the realm."

Damn, she remembered. "I did. And that's a long story. But, again, most people, including most witches, go their entire lives without getting so much as a sniff of demonkind or Fae. So, things will work out. You can play tourist for a few days. Take the tour with Yoshi. I'm sure Damon can organize someone from his recruitment team to speak to you. I know they have programs on a lot of campuses to help people who are interested in the industry."

Gwen's expression eased. "That would be helpful, I'd appreciate it." She glanced at Pinky's wrist. "You have an interface chip. Like Maggie."

Pinky's tattoos flowed around the chip, making it obvious. She held out her arm, so Gwen could get a better look. "Yeah. I sometimes compose for games. These days, that makes a chip necessary."

"It doesn't interfere with your magic? The tanai I knew in London…they thought chips wouldn't be an option."

"They can be, for some people," Pinky said. "But it varies. I don't know many tanai with one, but there are a few. But Maggie knows a great healer and one of the best chip surgeons in the country. I know they've been working on ways to make the chips work for witches—some of them have issues, too—I think there are some tests now?" She aimed the question at me

"There are. I'm sure Meredith—that's my healer friend— would know how you can get tested. Might be better to find out sooner rather than later if it's going to be an issue for you. Not having a chip would affect some of your choices." The cost of chips was dropping. Once they reached a certain price point, they were going to take over from headsets as the dominant way to access games and all the other forms of VR. I'd seen the Riley Arts data modeling about it.

There would always be people who didn't want a chip, but the best VR companies like Riley weren't going to be hiring game designers who couldn't work with full VR. "I can ask her. It might be expensive. Health care isn't cheap over here."

Gwen lifted her chin. "I have money. That's the one thing my father—whoever the hell he is—did do for me."

It would be rude to ask her how much, but I had to admit I was curious. Maybe it showed on my face because she said, "I'm not Damon rich but I'd probably be fine never working in my life. But that sounds dull to me."

"Yes, way too boring," I agreed. "So we'll add getting you tested for compatibility with a chip to the list, when you're ready."

Chapter Thirteen

I TRIED a few gentle questions on the ride home to see whether Gwen wanted to talk about anything that had come up at lunch, but she shut me down, yawning and staring out the window, so I wasn't sure whether she was jet-lagged or avoiding the conversation.

Once we were home, she crashed until dinner when she emerged to eat, still looking half asleep. We watched a vidlink of an old movie she liked for an hour or so, before she fell asleep on the couch. I shook her awake gently and shooed her back to bed.

The next morning she slept late. I'd been up and working for most of the morning before I smelled coffee coming from the kitchen. Coffee seemed like the perfect excuse to see how she was doing.

"Good morning," she said, stifling a yawn.

"Hey." I poured coffee, not pushing for a conversation. I drank half a mug and found a cookie, eating it before I spoke again. "Got any plans today? We could do some sightseeing, if you'd like."

"I'm still kind of tired," she said, shrugging. "There'll be plenty of time for sightseeing."

"Alright," I said. "Anything you would like to do?"

"Do you have any games?" she asked eagerly.

I stifled a snort. "You're in Damon's Riley's house. Yes, we have games. You want to play something?"

"That would be awesome."

Games, I could do. Especially if it would build some trust with her. "Let's go."

"Sweet setup," Gwen said when I showed her the gaming room.

"It's one of the perks," I said, with a grin. I pulled a couple of headsets out of the cabinet where we kept spare gear and handed one to Gwen.

She took it, then hesitated. "You have a chip."

"Yeah, but it always feels uneven if one person is playing with a headset and the other has a chip."

"Does a chip give you that much of an advantage?"

"It makes the sensory sensations more realistic and a tiny bit faster. I think it helps your reaction time, though Damon says they adjust for that when the players are using mixed access modes," I said. "But you know how it is sometimes. Half a second in making a decision can be the difference between success and, you know, dying in some embarrassing way."

"Thanks, that's nice of you."

"Pick a chair. The system is set up to go to a foyer, the usual kind of thing. We can choose from there." I said. "Hang on, I need to set you up first. Madge, can I have a holoscreen?"

"Of course," Madge said.

A screen appeared in front of me, and I swiped my hand down to summon a keyboard as well while Gwen settled into one of the game chairs. "I'm going to set you up an account." I typed in the commands. Damon had set up an account for Gwen on the house comp so she could check email and calls and have access to our general link feeds, but I knew he'd locked everything else down.

I didn't know if he'd done the same with the game collection. We had Riley betas and even pre-beta concept games loaded on our servers. I locked those off Gwen's menu, making sure she would only have access to released games.

There were more than enough to choose from. Damon collected games as well as making them. His game library was vast. Name a game and he probably had it. He certainly had hundreds I'd never even heard of. He got some kind of weird geek kick out of converting old games to run on new tech.

So it didn't matter if Gwen hadn't gamed for four years. She could probably find anything she liked from her teenage years and far earlier.

"There," I said when the system confirmed the account. "Come over here and let Madge scan you again so you can use facial recognition to log in."

"Brilliant," she said. "No passwords to remember."

I laughed. "Most things tend to use biometrics now."

"If you're fancy," she said. "If you're playing with an old deck at boarding school, then passwords are definitely still a thing. Even at university. Some people in halls had ancient systems."

"Halls?"

"Halls of residence. A dorm I think you'd call it?"

"Right," I said. Of course she would have lived on campus, though she presumably could afford not to, but maybe it was a rule over there like it was here for most first years to live on campus

Yoshi had an exemption because of his sister.

"Alright," I said. "Log in and see you in the foyer."

I settled myself back and put the headset over my temples. The bonus of this being Damon's system was as soon as I had the set connected, Madge logged me in without me having to activate anything.

I blinked my eyes and I was standing in the white square foyer. Gwen was there, looking around curiously, wearing a default avatar with a black skin suit and her own face.

"Do you have an avatar?" I asked. "If you don't, you can build a basic one via the menus." She could build something much better than basic, but I didn't want to stand around waiting.

"I'll decide once I know what we're going to play."

"Sure." I waved a hand and brought up the game menu, scrolling through slowly. "See anything you like?"

Gwen made a little 'go on' gesture. After a few more scrolls she gestured for me to stop. "What's 'training ground'?"

Crap. I'd forgotten Damon's monster simulator was sitting on our main menu. I hadn't blocked it.

"That's something Damon built for me so I can practice… well…witch stuff."

Gwen leaned a little closer to the menu. "Fighting? You know the s'ealg oiche, right. The ones who were with you in the realm?" she said. "I assume they're training you to hunt or something?"

She was clever, I had to remember that. She had made some bad decisions in the realm, but that didn't mean she was stupid. And she probably knew more about Fae creatures than I did.

"Or something," I said, not wanting to tell her more.

"Can I see it?"

I hesitated. For someone who didn't want anything to do with magic, it was an odd thing for her to be curious about. "Not just yet. I need to talk to a few people and get permission. A lot of the information in here belongs to the Cestis."

She didn't argue, even though her face fell. "Okay."

"What was your favorite game before you went into the realm?" I asked, wanting to get us heading in the right direction again. If this was going to work as a bonding session, then Gwen had to enjoy the experience.

She named a space exploration game.

"You might like *Serenity Falls*," I suggested. "That's Righteous's newest sci-fi game. Actually we're going to Decker's tomorrow night. Damon's playing an exhibition bout of Serenity."

"He games publicly?" Gwen's eyebrows shot up.

"Not often. This was a contest that Decker's ran back in April. Proceeds go to charity. The winner gets to play Damon. He does a couple of these a year. You can come along, if you'd like."

"Is he good?"

"He's hard to beat," I said. "I mean, he's not a pro-gamer, but he could have been." If he hadn't decided making billions inventing games was more fun. "Plus he knows the games inside out."

"I guess that helps."

"It doesn't hurt," I agreed and started the game.

By the time we got to Decker's on Sunday night, Gwen had started to relax. She'd spent most of Saturday with Yoshi, touring UC and had arrived back at the house practically bubbling over with excitement. She'd talked Damon's ear off at dinner asking him for his views on various options for studying. He'd answered patiently, but after about an hour had retreated to his office to finish up some work, leaving Gwen to research schools and courses on her own.

She'd spent most of the day continuing her research. I'd reminded her about the event and it seemed a game club trumped wading through course catalogs because she'd been ready thirty minutes early.

Decker's was crowded, which I'd expected. Damon's public sessions were always sold out. The crowd was a wall of noise and only grew louder as we were escorted down from the private rooms on the upper floor to the main gaming stage. But they stayed mostly respectful as we moved through the room surrounded both by our own security and the club's.

Damon climbed the stairs to join the MC onstage, and Jake and Maia shepherded Gwen and me over to a small area to the left of the stage to stand with some VIPs and the competition winner's family and friends.

Damon walked out on stage and the whole place went crazy.

Gwen's hands flew to her ears, her mouth dropping open, eyes wide as she watched the reactions. Knowing Damon was famous and seeing the reality when he was surrounded by fans, was a bit of a mind-fuck. I'd seen it enough times now to get used to the adulation, but it was *loud*. Loud enough that the instinctive part of your brain interpreted the sound as danger as much as appreciation.

I had no idea how rock stars got up on stages in front of tens of thousands of people screaming at them. Maybe all they felt was the enthusiasm and love. Knew how to ride the emotion to fuel their music.

Damon, I knew, would have preferred to stay out of the spotlight, but he did whatever he needed to do for Riley Arts and he did it well, charming the crowd with the full wattage version of his charm-the-universe smile and waiting the noise out. After a minute or so, the roaring and applause died down enough to let him make his speech, congratulating Lia Wang, the woman who'd won the right to play him, before taking his place in one of the two game chairs and logging in.

The crowd roared again as the *Serenity Falls* title sequence started to roll on the massive screen set at the back of the stage, filling the back wall above the level of the game chairs and then split into two, showing Damon and Lia's individual views of the game. Damon's avatar appeared in the familiar room at the hostel, looking down on the market, ready to start his adventure. Lia, in a different room, was doing the same.

Neither of them wasted any time. But as Damon left the hostel and entered the market, looking to buy some extra equipment, I faded back a little. I didn't need to be in the front row. I'd played *Serenity Falls* quite a bit. It was the game that had led to me meeting Cerridwen, but I enjoyed it enough that I'd pushed through those associations to play quite a bit with Damon. And it was one we'd tried with Callum, though he seemed to prefer historical games. Gwen had loved the game and we'd played several sessions since our first one. Gwen was a bit rusty, though improving fast enough I could tell she would be great if she practiced enough.

Damon's bout with Lia was scheduled for an hour. The Righteous programmers had developed a separate shorter route through a few key sections of the game. The full version of *Serenity Falls* could take months to play through. An hour was only a taste, though I was sure it would be a close contest.

But I'd spent a lot of time in game clubs watching other people play and supporting Nat back in the day. It had never been my favorite activity and it still wasn't. Not even when it was Damon. Surely no one would mind if I went to the bar? Nobody would pay any attention to me with Damon playing on stage.

I cast a glance over my shoulder toward the nearest bar. I knew my way around Decker's and security had cleared the club before we arrived. I felt like being normal for once. The bar was about twenty feet away. Maia would still be able to see me.

I sidled over to her. "I'm going to go get a drink."

She frowned. "Someone can bring you one."

I shook my head. "It's fine. It's just over there." I pointed to the bar. "You can see me from here. And everyone's watching the stage. No one will bother me." Decker's had a couple of floors, but the two top ones were for VIPs or pro team gaming. The second floor was filled with rows of gaming booths on each side of several long hallways. Those were open to anybody who paid the fee.

The first floor, once you got past the entry where people paid their fee, checked gear, and were scanned in to confirm their rank if they were pros, was one big square with the main gaming stage at the far end. There were a few larger gaming booths along each side, strategically interspersed with bars. The rest of the floor was set up with seating to watch the main stage or the screens streaming games from the other floors if people chose to stream. Though tonight, those were all showing the main stage. Now that Damon and Lia's game had started, the seats were all full, with more people standing behind the seats. From what I could see, there weren't many people at the bars.

Maia scanned the crowd and then the bar, lips pursed. I gave her my best version of puppy dog eyes. If she said I had to stay put, I'd stay put. But my pathetic look must have worked.

"Don't go anywhere else," she said, sternly. She tapped my wrist. "And use your panic button if you need to."

"I won't need to. But I won't leave the bar," I promised. "Watch Damon. This should be fun." He and Lia were now walking out of the town toward the first bridge.

That was one of the first tests in *Serenity Falls*. Also the part of the game that had led to me finding out Fae were real. I had no particular desire to see the circle of rocks where Cerridwen had hidden a summoning rune again, so I turned on my heel and wriggled my way through the crowd to the bar.

As I expected, nobody paid me much attention. A few people nodded as I walked past, but no one tried to block my way or start a conversation. The bar itself only had a couple of people waiting to be served.

I slid into a space between a tall blond guy and a shorter one with spiky red hair who looked barely old enough to be able to play at Decker's—which was an eighteen-plus club—let alone buy a drink. The bartender, a pretty black woman, was checking his ID with a scanner, a skeptical expression on her face. Her eyes were a coppery shade too metallic to be natural. Her long thin braids echoed the metals, dyed shades of bronze, copper, and gold. Her makeup was the same colors. In her black uniform she looked like a futuristic goddess.

She took my order of straight whiskey with a nod, asked my preference as to brand, and smiled approvingly at my choice before pouring it into a heavy glass and putting it down in front of me with a bowl of the little spicy things Decker's always served with booze to make you drink more.

I pulled out my datapad to pay and she shook her head. "Mr. Decker said you drink free tonight, Ms. Lachlan."

I hid the wince at the fact she knew who I was. "Thanks." A few years ago, Nat and I would have been more than happy to score free drinks at Decker's but now, when I didn't need it, it felt weird.

But Damon was making Decker's plenty of money with his appearance tonight and by running the tournaments, so I guessed it worked out.

I took a sip, letting the whiskey's smoky burn distract me from the restlessness I knew was leftover adrenaline from the last few days. Between Gwen and nixlings and afrit, the week had been crazy. And it wasn't over yet.

"How is the whiskey?" the blond man asked.

"Not bad," I said absently, not really looking at him. I had no particular desire to make small talk with a random stranger.

I took another sip, starting to turn away, looking down to try to let him know I wasn't interested, preparing to go back to the others if he wanted to pester me.

The stranger held up a hand. "Not so fast, Maggie Lachlan."

My head snapped up. I knew that voice. Knew in the pit

of my stomach, rapidly turning to ice, all the pleasant warmth of the alcohol vanishing.

He was wearing dark smoked glasses, which was not a completely unusual fashion choice in a game club. But as I watched, the glass cleared, leaving me with a clear view of completely black eyes. No whites, just bottomless pools of darkness.

The face was unfamiliar, but I knew those eyes. All too well.

Usuriel. Lord of the Darker Hours. Who should be safely in the Fae realm, not anywhere near me.

"What are you doing here?" I hissed, bracing myself to run. The bartender was serving another woman, not looking at me. I tried to keep my face calm, not wanting to drag anybody else into this.

Usuriel's hand was still raised. A subtle whisper of magic brushed by me. Fae magic. The sound of the club receded.

Fuck. He'd cast an illusion around us. Probably to anyone watching it would look as though we were having a friendly chat. Question was, was it only an illusion or a physical ward? In other words, could I walk away?

Don't panic.

Easier said than done. I took another swallow of whiskey, hoping it might burn out the shock at seeing him here. It seemed to work, the thump of my pulse in my ears died down to normal levels. I squared my shoulders. I had broken Usuriel's magic before. I could do it again, particularly out here in the human world, where his magic would be slightly weaker. But only slightly. He was an Elder, like Cerridwen. One of the greater Fae powers.

"You told my watcher you wanted to speak to me in person," he said, coolly. "I thought it was only polite to comply with your request.

"So you *did* send the nixlings. What the hell are you doing spying on me?"

He shrugged and tiny pinpoints of rainbow light shimmered over his black shirt. I would have sworn it was silk but watching the glimmers of light, I wasn't so sure. It was beautifully tailored, setting off his pale skin and the hair that was shorter and several shades darker than it was in the realm.

The face was different, too. Human, not unearthly Fae lord. Which was a relief. It made it slightly easier to control the fear still prickling down my spine. I could probably see through the illusion if I tried hard enough, but I didn't want to waste my power in case he tried something. My hand slid into my jacket pocket, seeking the familiar smooth disc of my panic button. I could activate the one programmed into my chip with a flick of my wrist, but I didn't want the movement to draw his attention. And I didn't want to pit Maia or Jake against Usuriel, let alone any of Decker's staff, none of whom were witches.

Safer to see what he wanted and try to get him out of the club as fast as possible. "I asked a question."

"Not so much spying as observing," he said.

I frowned, lifting my chin. "Sounds like the same thing to me."

Another liquid shrug.

Irritation crawled up my spine, tightening my shoulders and jaw. Were they all taught to do that? Callum, Gráinne and Cerridwen were all masters of the ambiguous gesture, which could mean any number of things. Perhaps in a society where people couldn't lie and acknowledgment could be taken as a debt, you had to develop other ways to deal with nuance and fill spaces where it would be dangerous to say something definitive.

"Very well, why are you watching me?" I asked, trying to temper my tone to something more polite. Not pissing off the scary Fae lord seemed like the smart thing to do. Particularly when I didn't want to test my magic against him. Especially when I could hardly set him on fire like an afrit. Crowded club aside, I was sure there would be nothing but a world of hurt waiting for me if I physically attacked an Elder.

I could defend myself under the contract, but crossing Usuriel in the realm had so far led to me being persona non grata for over a month. If I actually injured him—let alone killed him—I doubted I'd ever be allowed back.

"I have learned more about the person you were pursuing through the realm."

Chapter Fourteen

Jack? He'd found out about Jack? Fuck and double fuck. How? And *what* had he learned? I clenched my teeth shut. I really wanted to know. I couldn't ask. Usuriel would want something in exchange for the information. And I had no intention of ending up in his debt. I forced back all the questions and let the silence stretch.

"He is someone to be concerned about," Usuriel said.

"He is a criminal," I agreed carefully. "But that doesn't explain why you are…watching…my backyard. I can guarantee he's not hiding there and it's unlikely he'd try."

"I would not be so certain. This man seems to feel some connection to you. Did he not try and take the man you share your life with?"

"He did," I said, "but he was trying to steal from Damon's company. He didn't want me." I didn't know if that was strictly true. Yes, Jack kidnapped Damon, but we didn't know what his ultimate goal had been. He may have wanted Damon to help him with some aspect of whatever plans he had, or he may—as Usuriel suggested—have wanted me. But without knowing how much Usuriel knew about what had happened, I wasn't going to mention anything other than the first option.

"Even if that is true..." Usuriel's tone suggested he didn't think it was. "You now live with Damon. It is his territory I have been watching. And, regardless, you frequently attract trouble. Witches. Demons. A man who seeks the Greater Dark. One does not need to be Lady Morgain to know that your fate is a complicated one. And that we should all be watchful because of that."

"I do not 'attract' demons," I snapped, trying to keep my voice low. The bartender was ignoring us. Hadn't even glanced in our direction since Usuriel had started talking. The illusion was working on her, too. Hopefully it would keep her safe.

"You can speak normally. We cannot be overhead." Usuriel waved a hand in her direction and she still didn't react. Her expression was faintly glazed but she moved down the bar to serve another customer, so whatever the spell was, it wasn't preventing her from doing anything other than seeing us.

I took a sip of whiskey, trying to think. "Did you do something to her?"

"No," Lord Usuriel said, "Merely a ward so no one can hear and a little encouragement not to look at us. Or be curious if anyone does."

"You can't cast Fae magic on humans, it's against the contract." I was on solid ground there. The Fae got to keep their doors and their realm, the Cestis kept the fact of their existence secret and, in return, the Fae weren't supposed to use their magic on humans. No luring people into the realm with glamours or compulsions or other magical trickery. No keeping humans who wanted to leave the realm there against their will. Of course that one was harder for the Cestis to police. And, of course, most of the Fae who ventured outside the realm were capable of being very charming. Add in their beauty and you got temptation personified. So humans still followed them into the realm for other more human reasons. Like lust, curiosity, or the always classic sheer stupidity.

"I am aware."

"I'm human," I pointed out.

"I did not cast it on you," he said with a smile that was somewhat chilling. "I cast it around myself. You just happen to be within the boundaries of the spell."

Ah, that was the kind of Fae dancing around the edges of a rule I had been warned to watch for. "And is anything stopping me from removing myself from within those boundaries?"

"No. But you were the one who invited me to talk."

"Only so I could tell you to stop spying on me. You're wasting your time."

"Unlike you, Maggie Lachlan, I have an ocean of time at my disposal. I could watch you for the rest of your human life and it would be a mere blink of an eye to me."

And that wasn't creepy at all. I stared at him, trying not to shudder. Hopefully he meant fifty or sixty human years were no time at all to an ancient Fae lord, rather than that he intended to see to it that my life was short.

"It would still be wasted because you would get to the end of my lifetime and have nothing to show for it." I put my unfinished drink down. "Ward or no ward, you probably only have a few minutes before my bodyguard comes looking for me. And this ward may not break the rules of the contract but anything else you actively do to anyone in this place would. I assume you would prefer not to start a war with the Cestis right now, so I'm telling you again. There's no need to watch me. I am no danger to the realm and your people."

"Why would you object to extra protection freely offered?"

I actually laughed before I managed to choke it off. "Last time we met, you tried to stop me from removing a human—"

"A tanai," he interjected.

"A human," I continued, unmoved. "You did your best to

stop me removing her from your court, you sent your subjects after other humans with the apparent intent to hurt them, and you tried to invade my mind." And he'd kissed me. Not through any desire, but because, as far as I could tell, he thought it would upset me enough to make it easier for him to break my shields and yank whatever memory he'd been seeking out of my head. "Why would I believe that you want to protect me? Any of us could have been killed." Or all of us.

"I was annoyed at the time," he said, as though that was a perfectly reasonable excuse for attempted murder.

"And you usually try to kill those who annoy you?" I asked, a chill traveling down my spine. My fingers flexed at my hip. I was used to being armed when I was dealing with Fae. But Decker's had stringent security. Damon's security team carried guns but Decker's security only used stunners as far as I knew. No guests were allowed any weapons. No exceptions. No even for Damon Riley's girlfriend

Damn it.

"Sometimes," he said, in the same 'no big deal' tone. He paused, frowning at me, perhaps reading something of my fear in my face.

I tried to wrestle it back under control.

"One does not become Lord of a Fae realm by being eternally nice. And you cannot fight the Greater Dark with kindness. You should know this. You have known Lady Cerridwen long enough. She is no less ruthless than me."

True, but she'd never tried to kill me. In fact, she'd actively tried to help me. So, there was a difference. If Usuriel had decided the only way to fight the Greater Dark—demons—was by becoming a monster himself, then it was all the more reason not to trust him. "Still," I said. "You have to admit, it's quite a leap to go from viewing me as a threat to wanting to protect me."

"Let us say that I believe in keeping my options open."

"Then let us say that I believe in not having your creatures in my backyard."

"Your backyard, or Damon's?"

"It's our backyard," I said, realizing it was true. I no longer thought of my house as home, but Damon's. Huh. "And if you don't leave us alone, I will have to bring this up with Cerridwen and the Cestis. I doubt either of them will be thrilled about you overstepping your bounds."

He tilted his head, studying me in a way that made me think of an eagle or a shark. Something predatory and entirely emotionless about the fate of their intended prey. "Not many people are so forthright with me, Maggie Lachlan."

"Yeah, well, I'm sorry, but you're not my lord. I'm not tanai. I'm a witch. Cassandra gets to boss me around, not you."

"And the Lady Cerridwen?"

"We have a mutually beneficial arrangement." Did he know Cerridwen had kind of stalked me to begin with? Or at least magically compelled me to meet with her by booby-trapping one of Damon's games? If he didn't, I wasn't going to be the one to give him ideas.

"You and I could have a mutually beneficial arrangement."

"I would have to trust you to agree to that," I said. "If you are concerned about the things that the Lady usually handles, then I suggest you make an arrangement with her."

"And you would work with me if I did?" he asked.

Fuck. I wanted to say no. But I wasn't sure the choice would be mine. "If the Cestis and the Lady were satisfied it was safe, I might consider it. If it was within the terms of the contract. Which this conversation, my lord, is not. My understanding is that access through your door is still restricted."

One side of his mouth curved upward. "So cautious."

"Only idiots aren't cautious when it comes to…certain things."

Usuriel looked past me, to the stage. I risked following his gaze, twisting to see. Damon was currently running down a steep rocky hill, guns drawn, shooting at something. "And is your Damon Riley cautious?"

"He defends what is his. And you don't get to be as successful as he is without knowing how to manage your risks. He knows his way around a contract. And so do I. Now, do you want me to call the Cestis and see what they think of your being here?"

Usuriel returned his gaze to me, toasting me with his glass, seemingly not worried at all about me telling on him.

Which worried me. I pulled out my datapad. "Shall I make the call?"

He grinned suddenly but shook his head. "Well, this has been enlightening but I think it is time for me to go."

Enlightening? Only if your definition of enlightened was full of confusion. But if he wanted to leave, I wasn't going to stop him.

"I wish you a swift return to the realm, my lord."

He smirked. "I'm sure you do."

I tracked Usuriel's progress through the crowd, trying to keep sight of him through the heaving bodies. His head turned toward the stage at one point before he moved on.

God. I hoped he hadn't spotted Gwen. If he was upset with me for taking her, I doubt he was happy with her for leaving.

The farther away he got the hazier he appeared. Magic swirled around him. Another fucking illusion obscuring my vision. So I couldn't tell if he'd actually left. Bloody Fae. But the magic seemed to be receding, and he was almost at the exit, then, at least as far as I could tell, he was gone.

I watched a few seconds more, relief weakening my knees. When I was sure I could walk steadily, I made my way back to the stage. If Usuriel hadn't left I wanted Maia and the rest of Damon's team guarding my back. And Gwen's.

Gwen's attention was firmly focused on the screen above the stage. Damon and Lia were breaking into a rustic-looking building. I recognized the scene. An airfield where they had to try and steal something to fly to the nearest spaceport. Gwen's face was tense with excitement as she followed the action. She didn't notice me at all.

Maia, however, did, moving to her usual position beside me. She seemed relaxed. "Good, you're back."

I pulled her off to the side, out of Gwen's earshot. "Were you watching me?"

"Not the whole time. Who was that guy you were talking to?"

She'd seen Usuriel. I wasn't sure if his illusion allowed that much. But then again, it would have been strange if it made it look like I was talking to myself. And would draw attention if I vanished altogether. "What did he look like to you?"

"I don't know, kind of an average guy. I didn't think he was bothering you."

Damn Usuriel was good. Maia was a witch, a strong one. If she hadn't noticed any hint of magic, then Usuriel was very slick. Or very sneaky. But maybe she hadn't been watching for it. As far as she knew, I was just making small talk. No reason for her to suspect magic.

Some of that must have showed on my face.

"Wait. Who was it? Was someone using an illusion?" Maia demanded, suddenly fully focused.

I didn't want to say his name in case he was still in the club. "Let's just say someone from another place who really shouldn't be *here*. Someone I met on my trip to that other place and who doesn't have much reason to be fond of me."

Her eyes narrowed. "You mean Lor—?"

I made a cut-it gesture with my hand across my throat.

She clenched her teeth shut before his name left her mouth, and pulled me two steps farther away from the stage.

"What do you mean *he* was here? He's not supposed to be out of the other place, is he?" Her voice was almost a hiss.

"I don't know," I whispered back though semi-clenched teeth, trying not to let any emotion show on my face. No doubt there were people in the crowd watching me. Hopefully not Usuriel. "I don't know how closely you have to stick to the rules when you're as powerful as he is."

Maia's face went professionally calm and controlled. Which told me she wasn't calm at all. "I have to tell Mitch."

"Yeah, and I have to tell Cassandra." I turned away, looking for Gwen. She was still so focused on the action, I doubted she'd even noticed I was gone, but I wanted to make sure. "Gwen didn't see him, did she?"

Maia made a 'maybe' gesture with one hand. "She's been watching the game. She might have got a glimpse of who you're drinking with, but, if she did, she didn't show any signs she recognized him."

Well, that was a relief. I didn't need her to be freaked out. I was freaked out enough for both of us. Gwen might be okay with my magic but I doubted she'd be anything resembling calm if she knew Usuriel was nearby.

"Is he still here?" Maia demanded.

I shook my head. "I invoked the contract on him, told him to go. Hopefully he did. But someone like him, well, I don't think he feels any obligation to stick to the rules." He'd done his best to trick us in the realm. I wasn't going to trust him to do any differently out here.

"This is not good. Combined with your furry visitors, I don't like it."

"Me neither." It was one thing to deal with a nixling or two. Another to deal with the one who'd sent them. But it was also my fault. I issued the ultimatum. "But they're kind of the same thing. He sent the nixlings."

"He did? Why?"

"He said he's concerned about Jack. And no, I don't know why that equals keeping tabs on me. I told him to leave, but there's nothing I can do if he didn't. Not unless he decides to show himself." I glanced back at the stage, where Damon was running across the airfield, pursued by his competition. "How long do they have left?"

The timer in the top corner of the screen said thirty minutes but that was in-game time. I didn't know if they were taking breaks.

"Do you want me to pull him?" Maia asked.

"No. I think you-know-who has gone. Stopping the game would be more trouble than it's worth." There would be a shitstorm in the gaming world if Damon pulled out of a competition bout like this for anything less than a true emergency. And as much as Usuriel was a boatload of trouble if he chose to be, currently there was nothing to indicate he was an immediate threat. I didn't need Damon to get bad publicity because of me.

"All right." Her voice was reluctant. "But I want you standing by the stage where we can all see you. We'll be escorting you out the back of the building as soon as he's done with all his obligations. No flashy exits to please the papps, okay? Everyone got enough shots of you coming in."

That was part of the deal with Decker's. A mini red carpet with Damon and I and various celebrities, gamers and staff from Riley Arts on the way in. Damon and I had posed. Gwen had stayed in the background with Maia.

What else had Damon signed up for? I pulled up the schedule Cat had sent me for the event. "There's supposed to be a meet and greet after this, but that's it unless Damon's having drinks with Alexei after." Alexei Decker owned the club. He owned several of the most popular game clubs in the city.

"If he did, try to get him to back out. Tell him you have a headache."

I was hoping for hot sex tonight, so a fake headache was not my preferred plan A. But nor was telling him that Usuriel had been here. I wanted one night with no drama. Was that too much to ask for? "I'll tell him Gwen's tired. He'll think she still has jet lag. But there'll be more pictures after they're done playing. He won't be able to skip those." I resisted the urge to scowl. It was going to be a long night, even if Damon did only the bare minimum.

Maia scowled for both of us. "Just try to wrap things up fast."

"No arguments here."

I went to stand with Gwen. She was still fully engrossed in the game; the fascinated expression on her face was familiar. Nat used to wear it when she watched gamers. Benji and Eli and the other Righteous programmers still did. So did Zee. All the people who'd made games a huge part of their lives. Gwen would fit right in.

I nudged her gently, and she blinked, half-startled, and turned to me.

"Having fun?" I asked softly, trying to sound perfectly calm.

"Yes. They make it look so easy." Her mouth twisted a little as though she was judging her own performance against theirs and not liking the result. She'd done well when we'd played. She had a knack for puzzle solving and held her own in combat. *Serenity Falls* was more gunfights and spaceship encounters than hand to hand, but she'd flattened an NCP who'd tried to hit on her in a bar with a couple of well-placed punches.

I didn't know if she could fight in real life but her avatar could handle herself. "They've had a lot of practice. Lia is a pro. And Damon's, well, Damon. But hey, you have plenty of time to practice. I'm sure Damon would play against you if you asked him. He can show you plenty of tricks."

Her face lit up. "That would be brilliant. I'll ask him, thanks."

"Not a problem." I nudged her attention back toward the screen.

Damon was climbing into a rickety gyrocopter, one of the better forms of transport in the first stages of the game. He wasn't in danger, but it still made my heart catch slightly to watch him soaring to the air in a temperamental bucket of bolts inclined to not infrequent sudden explosions in the game. I'd died that way once, and the sensation of falling toward the earth before the game cut in and removed the sensory feedback because I was dead, had been distinctly unpleasant enough to make me vow never to parachute in real life.

Fortunately Damon stayed unexploded and escaped to the next sector, the last one of the bout, involving breaking into a black-market spaceport to make off with a small planetary transit ship to get to the next stage. There were many ways to die. But Damon knew the game backward and so did Lia, based on what was unfolding on the screen.

When the game ended, Damon was fractionally ahead on points. When he logged out and disconnected from the chair, he was grinning. Lia shook his hand, and Damon bent to say something in her ear. She'd probably scored herself and her team a wild-card entry into the next tournament, judging by the ecstatic smile that spread across her face as she blinked at him as though not believing what she'd just heard.

Maia sidled up to me as Damon and Lia posed for photos. "The meet and greet is upstairs in the VIP area. We've done several sweeps. The guy you spoke to seems to be gone. We go straight up there and then straight down to the car, once Damon's done, got it?"

I nodded, and Maia settled into place behind me.

"Is something wrong?" Gwen asked.

"No, they're always on high alert in crowds like this. It's hard to predict what Damon's fans will do." I touched Gwen's wrist, trying to reassure her. Decker's was not one of the clubs that allowed illegal drugs, but there were plenty of legal stims that could make someone cross the line from fervent fan to dangerous in the blink of an eye. "It's nothing you have to worry about. The team are pros and they've got this covered."

She looked back at Maia, Jake, and Rufus standing behind us. "Three of them doesn't seem enough."

"There's more than three of them. There are others upstairs, there are guys outside, plus all the Decker's staff. You don't have to worry, okay? Relax and enjoy the night. It'll be a bit of a crush upstairs, but we can just hang back and grab a drink or whatever. Damon's the one who has to press the flesh."

"Is it always like this? So…crazy?"

"He doesn't do a lot of smaller events like this these days. This is only because of the lead-up to the tournament. It's great publicity. He does the rounds at a few of the big conventions, but that's more keynotes than meet and greets these days. That only means when he does do one, it's crazier than ever," I admitted. "But mostly it's not like this. We go to business things, fundraisers and galas and many long dinners with boring speeches. At those they're more worried about playing power games with him than getting his autograph."

She pulled a face. "Rather you than me."

"Well," I said, "it does have its perks. After all, I get Damon. But, yeah, it can be a lot. But then again my life isn't always a bed of roses for him."

"I guess not."

Damon was descending the stairs off the side of the stage. He came over to us and bent down to kiss me quickly. I could tell he was riding the high of the game. He didn't often get to play for the fun of it, and even though he was probably under some pressure tonight to win, I knew he loved when he got to play with his own creations and show them off to a bunch of people who appreciated the amount of hard work and genius that went into them.

"Congratulations," I said when he set me free.

"You can congratulate me later," he laughed.

"Oh, I will," I said, slipping my hand in his. "Now I think the gang's eager to get you upstairs so you can meet all your adoring fans."

His smile slipped for a second. Short enough that no one else would notice. He was never rude to his fans, but I knew at times dealing with crushes of people like this was over-whelming for him, too.

"It's not that many," he said. "I think Alexei said fifty. Just a quick hello and a picture, and the team will move them on fast. We'll be home before you know it."

I squeezed his arm. "We're fine. After all, there's free booze, and I'm sure upstairs there'll be some of those excel-lent snacky things they do."

"Alexei knows how to throw a party."

He turned to Maia. "Right. Let's do this."

She tapped her earpiece and muttered something under her breath, and two more of his security team appeared through the crowd. With one of them either side of us, two in front and two behind, we moved through the crowd easily enough. Once we reached the stairs, there was no one in our path.

Upstairs, the noise level fell considerably. Can't have the VIPs annoyed by the masses.

One end of the room was set up for the meet and greet, with a backdrop of artwork from *Serenity Falls* and a couple of blinding photographic lights, along with a vidstream team and a photographer. The queue of excited Righteous fans were corralled behind a red velvet rope line.

Three of the guys accompanied Damon in that direction while Maia pulled Gwen and me over to a booth toward the back of the VIP space, mostly out of sight. "You and Gwen can wait here. Someone will come to take your orders if you want anything." She scanned the crowd, screwed up her nose. "Fifty people, a couple of minutes each should be two hours at the most."

Two hours was hardly short, but I hoped that she was right. It was going to be midnight before we got out of here at that rate. We retreated to the booth, which was covered in soft black leather. A trio of tiny brass lanterns sat in the center of the table, casting soft light. Larger versions of them hung above us. I settled back with a sigh and tapped the nearest lantern to summon the holomenu. One of the servers arrived at the table almost immediately. Gwen ordered chili fries and a salted yuzu margarita. I stuck to club soda and some sliders. Dinner felt like a long time ago and if we were going to be stuck here for two more hours, I wanted fuel.

The food arrived and we dug in. Gwen was full of questions about *Serenity Falls*, and I answered them as best I could. She'd almost finished the plate of chili fries when there was a crash of glass and a loud bang and something fell from the ceiling. Gwen cried out as it hit her, and then bounced, crashing to the floor, glass spraying everywhere.

Chapter Fifteen

I DUCKED INSTINCTIVELY at the sound of shattering glass but nothing hit me. I twisted back to Gwen. "Are you hurt?"

She gaped at me, eyes wide with shock. "What was that?" she said, her voice high and thin. She gasped, bending forward in pain.

I slid around the booth to get closer to her. "What's wrong?"

She straightened, still gasping in pain, and I saw the gaping slice in her forearm.

I didn't have much more time to think anything but 'long' and 'bad' before blood started to well out of the wound and my attention shifted from Gwen's state of mind to 'shit, stop the bleeding'.

I grabbed a napkin, realized it was heavy paper not fabric, and swept everything off the table so I could use the tablecloth instead. I wrapped it around Gwen's forearm and applied pressure.

"Gwen, can you lift your arm a little?" *Slow the blood flow. I have to slow the blood flow.* The first aid lessons Mitch had insisted I have had apparently stuck in my brain. "Gwen. Lift your arm, it will help stop the bleeding," I repeated, tapping her elbow gently when she didn't immediately obey.

She blinked at me, her blue eyes huge, her face white. She was biting her lip hard enough I was surprised it wasn't bleeding, too.

Shock. Which might be useful for a minute or two. Because once it wore off, her arm was going to hurt like a motherfucker.

But she lifted her arm. I needed something to support it, so she could keep it there but I didn't want to release the pressure. The tablecloth was already turning red. "Stay calm. Deep breaths. Close your eyes and focus on just breathing, okay. Help is on its way."

As though to prove my point, Maia reached us at a run, barking orders over her shoulder.

Rufus was close on her heels.

"Maggie, what the hell happened?" he asked.

"I don't know, the light, I think." I tipped my head back to inspect the lights. Sure enough, there was a gap in the row. "One of them fell. Or exploded. I'm not sure."

"Are you okay?" he asked.

"Yeah, I'm fine."

"There's glass in your hair," Maia said, her dark eyes sweeping over me. "Are you sure you're not cut?"

Nothing hurt. And I couldn't feel anything damp in my hair like I might be bleeding. "I'm fine. Let's focus on Gwen."

"An ambulance is on its way," Maia said. "Five minutes out."

She dropped a backpack at my feet. The emergency kit one of them usually carried. All our cars carried a first aid kit capable of treating most things from bullet wounds down. They even had antidotes to common poisons and pathogens. Which was why Mitch had insisted on me learning to use most of them.

"Keep pressure on it until I tell you to stop," Maia said to me. "Rufus, take off your jacket, put it under Gwen's arm." She kept talking to the three of us while she pulled supplies from the kit.

I focused on doing as I was told, trying to ignore the still spreading blood stain on Gwen's makeshift bandage. My own breathing had gone shallow and I tried to slow it down. Fainting wasn't going to help anyone.

"Maggie, I'm going to need you to let go. Gwen, this might hurt," Maia said.

I removed my hands. They were stained with blood, too red under the lights, and my vision went spotty for a few seconds. Maia moved with speed and precision, no wasted movement, undoing the tablecloth and re-bandaging the wound with actual bandages, all the while talking to Gwen softly.

I closed my eyes for a minute, trying to fight off the shakiness from the adrenaline rush.

"Maggie," Damon said, softly.

I opened my eyes. He was standing at the end of the booth closest to me. "I'm okay," I said. I clenched my hands shut, not wanting to see the blood.

Damon noticed, his eyes darkening with concern. "Are you sure? I'll cancel the rest of the meet and greet and come with you to the hospital."

Hospital. Right. Gwen would need stitches, if not surgery. She was even paler, her eyes still closed, but she was responding when Maia asked her questions.

Where was the damned ambulance? I sucked in a breath. *Get it together, Maggie.* I was fine. Gwen was not. But she would be. And if Damon stayed, we wouldn't wake up to headlines about explosions at Decker's disrupting the night. It was just a freak accident. Nothing newsworthy.

"No," I said firmly. "You stay here and finish up, if the team thinks it's safe. It was an accident. I'll be fine at the hospital."

No doubt his team would be scrambling to search the place for threats, but there'd been no follow up to the light. No other explosions or attacks. And it had exploded over Gwen, not him. Barely anyone knew she was in the city. If Usuriel had spotted her and decided to take her, she'd be gone. I couldn't have stopped him on my own. There was absolutely no reason to think anyone else would target her. It was a bad bulb and bad timing.

Damon stood his ground, the muscles in his jaw tightening as he stared down at me.

"Seriously," I said, "I'm fine and you can't do anything I can't at the hospital. I'll make them take us to St. Isidore's. Meredith will help us." Or if she wasn't on duty, there'd be another healer in the hospital. The healers who worked in hospitals knew tanai existed. We'd be fine.

He nodded, but waved off the Decker employee who was standing at a not-so-discreet distance, obviously ready to usher him back to the meet and greet. Half the people still in the queue were gawking at our table, trying to see what was happening.

"Get everyone back in line," Damon said, his tone as close to a snap as he allowed himself to get in public. "I'll be over in a few minutes. I need to make sure everything's okay here first."

"Of course, Mr. Riley," the employee said and backed off.

The paramedics arrived next. They didn't fuss with Maia's work, just took Gwen's vitals, got us to repeat what had happened, asked Maia what the injury was, and then bundled Gwen onto a stretcher to be carried out.

The shorter of the two, a black woman with close cropped curls, who was in charge, asked, "Who's coming with us?"

"Me," I said, pushing out of the booth. "We need to go to St. Isidore's."

"St. Isidore's? Is this a healer situation?"

That was the delicate way of asking if Gwen was a witch.

"Yes." I wasn't going to explain she was tanai. It was enough that they knew I wanted a healer to examine Gwen first. Meredith would know if Gwen's parentage would cause any issues.

But the paramedic didn't ask for any clarification. "Fine. Let's go."

I turned to Maia. "Call ahead. Let Meredith or whoever the healer on duty is know we're coming."

The ride to the hospital didn't take too long, though the medical smells made my pulse pound. Hospitals brought back too many bad memories

Gwen's new bandage was stained by the time we reached the hospital. The paramedics had dosed her with a hypo of painkillers and hooked her up to an IV they assured me was just saline.

When the ambulance's doors swung open, Meredith was waiting for us. She looked like it had been a long day already, the green scrubs under her white coat wrinkled, but she smiled at me, pushing the long brown braid of her hair back over her left shoulder.

"Maggie, hi," she said. "Hang on." She turned her attention to the paramedics, letting them update her. When they were done, she stared at Gwen for a long moment before stepping back and nodding at the paramedics. "Okay, let's take her through to the ER. I've got an exam room ready." She watched intently as the paramedics unloaded Gwen and trundled her off in the stretcher.

Meredith turned to me. "Are you hurt?"

"No."

"There's glass in your hair."

"So people keep telling me."

"I'll get a nurse to clean it up for you." She glanced down at my hands. "You can clean those, too. What happened?"

"A light globe exploded. Or the fitting fell. Or both. Glass and metal falling from the ceiling, anyway. Gwen was in the way."

Meredith was too professional to wince but she made sympathetic noises as she led me toward the ER.

"It looked bad. Lots of blood," I said, clenching my hands again. The blood was mostly dry now and the tight sensation was nearly worse than the fresh blood had been.

"We'll take care of it," Meredith said. She lowered her voice. "She's tanai?"

I nodded. "Yep, her mom is…from there."

We'd reached a door labeled 'Exam Room 5'. Meredith waved to the nearest nurse, a slightly frazzled looking redheaded guy who had a datapad in one hand and a box of bandages in the other.

"Pete, this is Maggie. She had a close encounter with an exploding industrial light bulb. Her friend got the worst of it but can you find someone to get the glass out of her hair. Examine her scalp, too. And the rest of her clothes. There could be glass shards anywhere. And she needs to wash her hands. Once she's done, she can come back here. No need for a patient record, I'll take care of that."

Pete nodded. "Sure thing, Dr. Dempsey." He nodded his head at me. "C'mon, we'll use one of the cubicles. It won't take long."

He started walking and before I knew it I was seated in a curtained-off cubicle while he angled a bright light at my hair and picked glass out with tweezers. After he made me put on a gown so he could check for cuts and shake out my clothes. For once my game club casual had paid off. My jeans and leather jacket had protected me from the glass. Pete declared me glass-free and pointed me at the sink so I could finally scrub the blood off my hands.

When I was done, Pete escorted me to the exam room, where Meredith was rebandaging Gwen's arm.

"Okay, so it's not too bad," she said, with a quick smile as I came in. "It's a long cut, about six inches but actually not too deep. But the bleeding is still…active, so we're going to take her up to an OR, let a surgeon look at the vascular structures, then stitch her up. Anyone who needs to know she's going into surgery?"

"No. She's from the UK. No relatives here that I know of."

"Well, she's awake enough to consent, so that's not an issue. It shouldn't take too long. I think she's possibly nicked a small artery and I've given that a boost to help it heal. The surgeon will clean it up if they need to. If the artery's fine, it's a straightforward job to close the wound. They'll use a nerve block not a general. She'll probably be able to go home in a few hours. You can wait in the VIP waiting room, if you want. Or you can go and we'll keep you updated."

"She's staying with me and Damon. I'll wait." I wasn't leaving Gwen alone in a hospital where she knew no one.

"I thought you'd say that. So let's get you settled in."

She walked me out of the ER and up a floor to a waiting room, scanning me in with a palm scan. She pointed at a screen on the wall. "If anyone else is going to join you, you can page me there and I'll make sure reception gives them access."

"Is Gwen really going to be okay?" The memory of the long bloody gash on her forearm was fresh. Too much blood.

"Yes. She was lucky. Didn't sever anything muscular, as far as I can tell. Her hand and fingers are all moving fine, so if there's any nerve involvement, it's minimal. Once the surgeon is done, I'll give her another boost but I'm not expecting there to be any complications. She'll be sore for a few days, but that's what the good drugs are for."

"Are there any issues because she's tanai?"

"I don't think so. Gwen said she's never had an allergic reaction to anything. So, fingers crossed, it's all smooth sailing. Sitting here and waiting is the hard part. Info about access to the public link is all on the screen there so you can hook up if you need to."

I didn't. The signal on my datapad was fine without the hospital's link, but I couldn't focus. I updated Damon and left a message for Aubrey. Then sat and tried to be patient. Meredith's estimate was right on the money. It only took a few hours before a nurse came to take me to Gwen's recovery room. I tried to be quiet as I entered the room. Gwen seemed small on the big hospital bed, her eyes closed, her chest rising and falling. Asleep, probably. Meredith stood next to the bed, focused on Gwen, one hand hovering over her chest. Checking her energy field.

I did the same. Gwen's was a pearly blue, with a hint of the smokiness I associated with Callum and Cerridwen. Her Fae heritage, presumably. But it seemed pale. Too translucent. And she was too still, though the rise and fall of her chest was regular.

"I thought you said it would be a nerve block?" I asked softly.

"It was. But she's been through a lot. She's sleeping. Which is the best thing. There's no nerve or muscle damage and she's all patched up."

Gwen's arm was now stained with iodine, but the gaping cut had turned into a neatly stitched wound covered by a surgical shield. She was still hooked up to a drip and a few other things; monitors were beeping softly in the background.

"The drip is hydration and some antibiotics," Meredith said. "We'll send her home with painkillers, but the nerve block will last about twelve hours. Hopefully more like a day. We'll keep her a bit longer for observation, then you can go." She nodded at a chair on the far side of the room. "You can wait in here. There'll be nurses in and out and I'll update you in an hour or so."

Right. She had other patients to see.

"Thank you," I said and started to move around the bed

toward the visitor's chair when all the monitors started beeping wildly.

I froze as Meredith headed toward the bank of screens.

"What's going on?"

"I'm not sure," she said as Gwen started gasping for air. "Looks like an allergic reaction. Could be the sedatives or the antibiotic."

She hit a button on the wall and laid one hand on Gwen, sending a jolt of magic into her.

A few seconds later, a nurse came running through the door carrying a thick plastic syringe with a bright orange cap on one end.

"What's that?" I asked, trying not to panic.

"EpiPen," Meredith said as the nurse handed it to her. "It will take down the reaction if that's what it is."

She put the EpiPen against Gwen's thigh under the surgical gown and hit it home. Gwen squeaked in pain and them slumped back against the bed.

After a few seconds, the machines started to calm down.

"Maggie, go wait outside," Meredith ordered.

I stood out in the hallway, trying not to panic, and wishing the recovery room wasn't so well soundproofed. I got brief bursts of noise when various hospital personnel ran in or out of the room but no one stopped to update me. I leaned against the wall, beating off incipient panic as the sounds of machines beeping and rushing feet triggered too many memories of too many hospital visits. Gwen would be okay. She was young. Strong. Stronger than most humans, with her half-Fae blood.

I won in the end, maintaining some semblance of calm. When they let me back in, Gwen was lying with her eyes closed, several blankets piled over her.

Meredith stood by a bank of monitors, looking at the readings and typing numbers into her datapad.

"Is she okay?" I asked, the words almost snapped.

Gwen opened her eyes. "I'm fine."

She didn't look fine and she sounded wiped out. Still a few shades too pale underneath the flushed cheeks. Blood loss, surgery, and an adrenaline shot will do that to you.

"She will be fine," Meredith confirmed, turning away from the monitors. "The allergic reaction is under control. We think it was the antibiotic. Gwen, I'm going to ask you a few quick questions now you're back with us. I take it you've never had xenocylicate before?"

Gwen shook her head. "I never get sick much. And I've never had a bad injury. Or surgery." She gestured at the bandage wrapping her arm.

"I've made a note on your medical records, but it's not a medication many people react to," Meredith said. "Do you know if your human parent had any allergies? It could come from the Fae side, but it's not a known contraindication. I'll need to send a request up through the Cestis to follow up on that."

"Is that a thing?" I asked.

"Yes. Tanai react differently to some medications," Meredith said. "But this one should have been safe. It's synthetic, it doesn't contain any plant-based material, no iron. Gwen, any family history?"

Gwen closed her eyes again. "I don't know my father. I don't even know who he was."

Meredith shot me a confused look. "Long story," I mouthed.

Her mouth turned down as though she was all too familiar with that kind of long story. She focused back on Gwen. "Unusual allergies can be inherited. Have you ever had your DNA run?"

Gwen opened her eyes, sitting up a little straighter. "The Cestis in the UK, they did it when I…er…"

"Came out of the realm?" Meredith prompted.

"Yes, that. But they were looking for a parental match, so they could make an information request to try and find my father. Nothing came up. They didn't say anything to me about medical stuff."

"Nothing came up in the UK database," Meredith corrected. "The privacy laws are extremely tight. There's no automatic sharing beyond the immediate jurisdiction. Those have to be requested additionally and usually there needs to be a good reason before most countries allow searches by non-citizens. If the Cestis thought you were English, they could only run it there. But with a medical reason, we can do it here."

"How does that work?" I asked. "Running her DNA if she's tanai?" DNA analysis for medical problems had become a lot more accessible. But as the technology had improved, various companies had failed as their methods became outdated. Then had come a bunch of very expensive lawsuits about who got the data and in the end, in most countries, the databases were now run by the government.

"We have ways," Meredith said. "The databases the Cestis control pick out only certain genetic information to match against the general population databases. Nothing that stands out as…different. It works."

That made sense. "And you can search for relatives here because it's a medical issue?"

These days the legacy DNA sites that people used to trace their genealogy were highly regulated when it came to living people. In cases where a child had been conceived via dona-tion or had proof that a parent who raised them was not their biological parent, they were able to get medical history, along with the relevant genetic data for medical issues, if the databases had a match, but they received nothing else about the individual they matched with, unless both parties consented.

"Yes, because it's an unusual allergy and Gwen doesn't know her parents, we can request a broader medical history search as well as a parental match," Meredith said. "If there's a parental match, then your father would, of course, be informed that there's a match and that his medical history was accessed, but you don't have to agree to release any information to him. Of course, neither does he, beyond the medical history."

Gwen nodded. "Yes, that's what they told me in London."

"If your DNA is already on record, this is all fairly simple," Meredith said, "I make a request from the Cestis's UK database, they send the profile, and we do the medical history search via the US Annex site—that's the Cestis-controlled database. Though, if you don't want to know, we can just check your profile and see if it identifies any of the known allergy markers."

"No, I'd like to know. If he's out there. I mean, I'm not sure I want to know who he is, but I'd like to know the medical stuff."

"It does make things safer." Meredith pulled up a form on her datapad. "Read this and authorize with a palm scan."

Gwen read the form, chewing her lip. But she scanned her palm at the end, handing the datapad back.

"Great. We'll have the medical scan back in a few hours. We'll see with the history. But, like I said, don't get your hopes up about any contact."

Gwen nodded. "I'm not expecting anything from my father at this point. He washed his hands of me when I was born. But that's okay. I don't need him." The defiance in her voice was undercut by the slight quaver. She looked very young. And I knew what it felt like to be young and abandoned or betrayed by everyone who should have protected you.

"No," I said, gently. "You've done fine. You know, my mom was, well, difficult and I still turned out okay. You'll find a whole different kind of family as you find out what you want to do and where you want to be. It will all work out."

"And it will work out even better if you know what medications to avoid in the future," Meredith added cheerfully. "So I'll get this started and we can check your profile for allergy markers and anything else. Whether or not there's a match in the database is just a bonus."

Gwen managed a half-smile. "I'd like to know where I'm from at least. I always thought I was English, but it looks like I'm not."

"You were born there. You're English. And your father might not have ever had his DNA profiled," Meredith said. "That's one reason for no match."

Or he had dumped Gwen in England because he didn't want anyone to be able to find him. He'd left her financially well off, so he probably had enough money to not have to skimp on medical care. But not everyone thought DNA testing was a good idea.

"Either way, we won't know until we get this all underway," Meredith said. She swiped up on the datapad and did her own palm scan. "There, that's the request sent. I want to keep you here for observation another hour or so, and we should know the basics by then. If everything's under control, we'll send you home."

She fixed me with a stern look. "You did say Gwen's staying with you? I don't want her alone in case she has another reaction."

"We'll watch her," I said reassuringly. "Don't worry."

"Okay," Meredith said, "Well, you two hang out here. I'll get some coffee and food sent for you, Maggie. And Gwen, you can eat something in a little bit once we're sure your stomach isn't going to react to the antihistamines."

"I'm not hungry," she said.

"No, but between the surgery and the adrenaline and the antihistamines and your injury, your body has burned through a lot of fuel in the last few hours. You'll feel better if you eat. Even if it's just jello or something to start with. How's your pain level?"

"My arm doesn't hurt at all."

Meredith smiled. "That's what I like to hear. The nerve block is holding. I'll send you home with some pain meds. You can start taking them tomorrow morning before the block wears off. But hopefully you'll only need them for a few days. The cut should heal easily enough. I'll leave you two alone, but you can ask the nurses to page me if you need me."

By the time Meredith reappeared a couple of hours later to see how Gwen was, she was looking almost back to normal, sitting up in bed and talking about Damon's game tactics. That she understood a lot of what he'd done and how it affected the flow of the gameplay boded well for her potential as a game designer. She could *think* in game, the same way Damon and the other game designers I knew did. I could follow the storylines and figure out tactics, but when they started brainstorming worlds and all the interconnected threads, my brain noped out after a certain point.

Plus, the bonus side effect of her being so caught up in the match was that, as far as I could tell, she hadn't noticed Usuriel.

I wasn't bringing him up. She'd had enough shocks for one night.

"Okay," Meredith said when she came back into the room. "Gwen, I need to let you know there were two matches in the DNA database. So we have the medical histories, but there's nothing on them you need to worry about. So we're just going to write this off as a strange reaction and take it from there. It's on your medical history now, and I'll send you the information about the medication. It has a few brand names so it's good to know so you can tell your doctors in the future."

"Okay, that's good," Gwen said. She chewed her lip for a moment. "Was one of them my dad?"

Meredith nodded. "Yes."

"Oh." She didn't say anything else and there was a long silence. I stayed quiet, giving her time to process. It was one thing to know your dad might be out there. Another to know that he was out there and had ditched you. At least, I imagined it was. Another layer of hurt.

Gwen eventually heaved a sigh. "Right. So he is out there somewhere. Well, I have what I need from him, I guess." Her mouth twisted and then her eyes widened. "Wait, you said two matches?"

"Yep, two. The search looks for parents, siblings, other close relatives like aunts, uncles, first cousins." Meredith replied.

"*Siblings*? I could have a half brother or sister out there?"

"It's a possibility. It could be a cousin," Meredith said gently. "But remember, they'll be notified that a match has been made, but it's up to them as to whether they want to release any more information. If someone has their profile locked down, the medical history is all you'll get. Outside of parents, there's no automatic access to how the person is related to you."

Gwen's mouth turned down. "That seems unfair. Aren't there medical things where it might be more likely you have the same thing if it's your sibling versus say a cousin?"

"Once you have the history, that becomes a bit of a moot point," Meredith said gently. "It's to protect people's privacy. And, sometimes, their safety. People can choose not to have any other contact.

"Do people really not want to find out?" Gwen asked. "If they have a brother or sister out there?" She sounded bewildered. As an only child she'd probably grown up dreaming, like me, about a big happy family.

Meredith hesitated. "Families are complicated. And if you didn't grow up with your biological siblings then there's usually a reason. Affairs, or messy divorces, egg or sperm donation in the parent's past they never told their kids or even their spouse about. Abuse, sometimes. Not everyone wants to know. Or deal with it if they do. And speaking of dealing with it, you should sleep on this. Take a few days to think about it. Wait and see what happens. If someone initiates a contact, you can take it from there. If they don't and you decide you want to know, then you could send a contact request. Or there are other legal processes if there're valid reasons you would need to know their identities."

Like a false name on a birth certificate? Would a court give Gwen the name of her dad if she wanted?

Gwen nodded, looking more than a little overwhelmed.

"That all sounds sensible to me. Can we get out of here now?" I was starting to feel like Gwen looked. Exhausted and not entirely sure I was awake. The clock in the room told me it was nearly five a.m. Mondays were never my favorite day of the week, but a Monday on a couple of hours sleep was going to be a real bitch.

Meredith moved closer to the monitors, pressing various buttons and comparing the readings against Gwen's chart.

"I think so. I'll just check her aura," Meredith said. She studied Gwen for a time and then asked, "May I touch you?"

Gwen nodded and Meredith rested two fingers on her forehead. Curious, I let my sight shift into the magic, to see the aura for myself. It was stronger now, not as misty as earlier. And I couldn't see anything unusual. Meredith would be doing a deeper scan, using whatever magic it was that healers did to see all the things that I didn't even know to look for.

Whatever she saw, it seemed to satisfy her because she moved back, smiling. "Perfect. Let me get you set up with some pain meds and you'll be out of here."

Chapter Sixteen

As PREDICTED, hauling myself out of bed a few hours after getting home was no fun at all. But I had one last client report to complete and today was the deadline.

I padded down the hallway and eased Gwen's door open. The room was dark, and she was a lump under the covers, dead to the world. Good. She needed the rest. I needed caffeine. All the caffeine.

After coffee, breakfast and a shower, I felt human enough to tackle the report and managed to finish it in an hour. I moved straight on to the Archives metadata I was working on for Damon, rather than giving in to the urge to take a nap.

I finished the first batch of entries, processed the changes, and got ready for batch two. We'd been refining the taxonomy as we increased the number of volumes scanned and updating entries was complicated. Ralph had shared some information about how the UK Cestis cataloged their collection and it was even more complicated than Cassandra's method, so Cassandra wanted some additional data added.

It wasn't the most exciting task in the world, but if I logged in to do any testing prep for Damon, I'd have to talk to the rest of the team and, knowing Righteous, word would have spread about the accident last night. I didn't want to answer a thousand questions.

I tagged entries for forty minutes before my caffeine-fueled determination to be productive flagged. When my inbox notification chimed, I gave in to the lure of distraction. The first one was from the National Genetics Registry.

What the heck? Was Meredith sending me Gwen's results?

Sure, my DNA was in the database. When my grandparents had taken me home after Sara died, they'd asked me if I wanted to try to find my father. At the time, thirteen-year-old Maggie had wanted nothing more. I tried one more time when I was eighteen. Still nothing. After that I'd locked my profile down and forgotten about it. I'd never had any requests for medical information.

Frowning, I opened the email.

"Dear Margaret Diana Lachlan," it read. "This is a mandatory notification that your medical history has been utilized." Followed by a lot of boring legalese about the relevant laws and a plain English explanation of what had been released, which boiled down to gender, genetic traits for any diseases, and any other known conditions where the genetics hadn't fully been nailed down yet but were suspected to have hereditary factors. As far as I knew, I didn't have anything to report.

"Should you wish to know more about this match, please access your file via the Annex site. Authentication by palm or retina scan is required to access the match." Annex site? Oh, right. The database for witches. I should ask Cassandra about that. As far as I knew, my grandparents had used the regular site. After all, they thought I had no magic. Had the Cestis moved my record?

I sat back in the chair, stomach churning. Who the hell had I matched with? I knew all my immediate relatives on my mother's side. There weren't many of them. My grandparents had both come from small families—one sibling each—and neither my great-aunt nor great-uncle had had children. They'd died before my grandparents. And, of course, my mother was an only child.

Obviously there were more distant cousins I'd never heard about. Maybe one of them doing a search?

I read the email again and something moved uneasily in my stomach, my intuition pinging. Weird timing. Gwen does a search and I get a match? Surely it was a coincidence? It had to be.

I couldn't have matched with Gwen. She was English. I had some Irish and Scottish blood, but my family had been in the US for more than a century.

Vaguely queasy, I opened a connection to the Annex database, logged in, provided the palm scan and checked my notifications.

Which didn't tell me much more than the email. My medical history had been provided following a duly authorized request. As my account was locked down in relation to other information, no other information had been provided. I could request the nature of the relationship via the relevant form. As this was the Annex database this process could take up to five business days due to privacy and blah blah blah. It also gave me the process to initiate a search for relatives.

I shut down the site, wondering why I was so uneasy. It had to be a coincidence, right?

But my nerves didn't settle so, acting on instinct, I vidcalled Meredith, expecting to leave a message. But instead I got her, looking neat and tidy as always in a misty green T-shirt that matched her eyes under her white coat. She leaned closer to the screen, looking worried.

"Maggie, hi. Is something wrong with Gwen?"

"No, sorry. Didn't mean to alarm you. Can I run something by you, if you have time."

"I have about ten minutes, then I have another patient. Is that okay?"

I had no idea if it was enough time, but I wasn't going to waste the chance. "I got a notification from the genetics database this morning."

"Oh?" Her brows drew down.

"Yeah, it says my medical history was accessed. That's never happened before."

"Never?" Her frown deepened.

"Small family on my mom's side and all the ones I know about are dead."

"And you don't know who your father is?"

"No."

"You never searched for him?"

"My grandparents put in a request when I was thirteen. There were no matches. I put one in again when I was eighteen. Still no matches. I haven't tried since. My profile is locked down."

"And, most likely Cassandra had you flagged as a witch once she found you, so you'd be in the Annex. That's an added complication. More hoops to jump through to put in contact requests. That's the easiest thing to do, if you want to know."

"Yeah. But something's bugging me about it. Gwen put her request in last night and suddenly out of the blue I get a notification."

Meredith's eyebrows shot up, surprise replacing concern. "You think it could be Gwen?"

I knew it sounded ridiculous but I couldn't shake the feeling. "You have to admit, it's a weird coincidence. She got two matches, and now this is the first time I've ever matched with anyone."

"Have you told Gwen yet?"

"No, she's still sleeping. I figured she needs the rest."

"Good call. In that case, you could both put in requests. Or I could compare the history she got with yours if you both give permission."

"I don't have much of a medical history," I said. "I mean I had that weird reaction to the chip. But that was because of the demon. Otherwise, I've been healthy. Will there be enough to compare?" I'd been in hospital only once as a kid. When I turned thirteen. At the time it had been chalked up to a severe bout of fever due to an unknown virus, but I knew now it was either from being bound to a demon or a reaction to whatever Sara did to me to make me forget the ritual. Any other childhood bugs, Sara had handled herself with her healing skills.

"Yes, in cases, where there's not much to report, there's still a genetic marker comparison to establish the relationship. I'll be able to tell if the one she got matches yours."

"Right." So I had to wake Gwen up and tell her we might be half sisters? That was…crazy. I had no idea how she was going to feel about it. I had no idea how *I* felt about it.

"Maggie," Meredith said gently. "Gwen aside, if it's her, you've found your father as well. Gwen got a parental match, too."

Crap. I'd been focused on the half-sister part. But half sister in this scenario meant same father. My father. After all these years. I had no idea how to feel about the possibility. "There's no chance it's a match with her mom?"

"No, it was a paternal match. Besides which, I'm willing to bet quite a lot of money that no Fae has ever allowed their DNA to be sampled. Even most of the tanai tend to steer clear of it. Cassandra could probably tell you what percentage of the Annex records are tanai."

"Cassandra?"

Meredith looked at me as though I was being dim. "She's the head of the Cestis. So she's the boss of everything that falls under their jurisdiction."

Right. "I know that." Logically, yes. But I'd never considered how broad that role was. I had only seen the tip of the iceberg when it came to the Cestis.

"But regardless of Fae DNA, Gwen's first match was her

father. So if you matched with her and you're half sisters, then he's your dad, too."

I swore half under my breath. I'd made my peace with not knowing who my father was more than a decade ago. I still didn't want to know, and seeing the photo of Sara and Jack hadn't changed my mind. But a sister…even if a half sister. That was different. I swore again. Then made an apologetic face. "Sorry."

Meredith grinned. "It's not an uncommon reaction. But if you're right about Gwen, even if you have no interest in finding out who this man is, I recommend you get the medical history. It's useful to know."

Maybe. But Gwen had that information. Maybe she would share. And Meredith had said last night there was nothing to be concerned about, anyway.

I nodded. "Let me think about it a bit. When Gwen wakes up, I'll talk to her. That's going to be a fun conversation."

Meredith's expression turned sympathetic. "You could leave it a few days."

Yeah, and how would I explain putting it off to Gwen when I finally decided to tell her? Hey, Gwen, I've known for a few days we might be related but I didn't want to mention it? I didn't need magic to know that was a bad idea.

But if she *was* my sister and we shared a dad, well, suddenly I couldn't get that picture of my mother and Jack on the island out of my brain again.

"I think this is more a 'better to rip off the Band-Aid' situation," I said. At least as far as Gwen was concerned. Jack… well, I'd have to think about that part.

"Well," Meredith said, "let me know if you two want me to compare the records. You can download a copy of your history and the match from the database. Send it through to me, if you want. I'll send you a secure upload link. Then if you decide to go ahead, just let me know. Deal with the sister part first, then worry about the other one."

Crap. What if Gwen freaked out about the possibility of me being her sister? Me with all my magical drama. She might hate the idea. Want nothing to do with me. But she'd said last night that she'd be interested in a sibling.

"Whatever you decide, the protocols are there to follow" Meredith continued.

I nodded, but my brain was whirling. If there was any possibility Jack was my father, I absolutely didn't want him finding out I was his daughter. I was assuming he didn't know, of course, because it was the only thing that made sense to me. He could have played things very differently at the *Serenity Falls* tournament if he wanted to waltz into my life as my long-lost father.

Instead he'd revealed his true colors. And I didn't want anything to do with them.

So it might be in my best interest—and Gwen's—to see if those protocols were truly as ironclad as Meredith thought.

After all, I knew a bunch of genius computer geeks. And I knew damned well some of them skirted the wrong side of the law at times. If I asked Damon to hack a database to find out if the guy who'd matched with Gwen was Jack, then he'd try his best to do it. And his best was damned good. Surely we could find a way for me to follow this thread without Jack finding out.

Meredith was still talking and I tried to pay attention, but nothing she said was sticking. Which she didn't miss.

"Look, you both need some time to sit with this. Talk to Gwen. Call me when you two have a decision. I need to get to my patient."

We said goodbye and I slumped back in my chair, feeling as though someone had turned the world upside down and shaken it around. Lianith wandered into the room and jumped up onto the desk, angling her ears for scratches. I obliged, still lost in a whirlwind of chaotic thoughts.

The person I really wanted to talk to was Damon, but he'd

already left and I knew he had a morning of international calls.

I left him a message, made sure I had all my privacy settings set on the highest levels in the Annex database, downloaded my medical history, and double-checked my notifications. Still only one. I downloaded it, too. So whoever Gwen's mystery man was, he hadn't yet been connected to me. And if he did, I wanted to make sure he didn't get anything more than I was legally obliged to give him.

When I logged off the database, my hands were trembling.

I had to work off some adrenaline. I could call Callum to come over and let me try to beat him up, but it would take him some time to get here and I didn't want to wait."

So I did the next best thing and logged myself into Damon's training program.

Escaping into the virtual world and beating up some imps or something was just what the doctor had ordered.

We'd added a few of the creatures we'd encountered in the Fae realm, but I stuck to imps. No worrying about whether they were bad or not. And the handy part about VR was that it seemed to work the same way as real-life exercise when it came to stress reduction.

I didn't really pay attention to the time as I squared off against a series of imps. So I almost lost my virtual footing, only narrowly avoiding falling on my ass, when Madge interrupted me with an in-game message.

"Maggie, Gwen would like to speak to you."

Oh God, she was awake. No more hiding away in VR. I had to tell her the news.

Crap. My avatar was sweaty, my limbs felt heavy from exertion. I no longer felt shaky, but this was a conversation I wasn't so sure I was ready to have.

But I couldn't see another option. Not if we were sisters.

A *half-Fae* sister. Would my life ever stop getting weirder and weirder?

My grandmother, I knew, would have been delighted, even if the half-sister bit came from my unknown father. She'd always wanted more children, but it hadn't worked out. She made a point of semi-adopting any friends I brought home.

I disengaged from the game and opened my eyes. Gwen was sitting in the chair next to mine and I nearly jumped out of my skin.

"Holy crap," I wheezed. "Can we ease back on the jump scares?"

Gwen yawned. "Sorry, I didn't think." She wore pink-and-white-striped pajama pants and a tank top covered in some pink-and-white anime character I didn't recognize. Her hair was half falling out of a short ponytail. But even in 'just rolled out of bed' mode, she was beautiful. She was staring at the monitor above the chairs, so I took the opportunity to study her. Short, blonde, and nothing like me. But, quite possibly, my sister.

Genetics were weird.

Her incision under the surgical shield looked normal. Nothing red or crusty or bleeding. She had a bit of color back in her face and she seemed alert enough. So, no medical reason to put off telling her the news.

"Is that your training game?" Gwen asked, pointing at the monitor.

Well double crap. How much had she seen? I hadn't yet talked to Cassandra about letting Gwen see the program. "Yes. But how about you forget you saw it?"

"What was that thing you were fighting? A lesser Fae?"

"No, an imp."

"An imp?" she said. "A *demon*?" Her eyes went wide. Under the bright light of the monitor, they were almost silvery blue.

I hit the button on the arm of the game chair to turn the monitor off. "Not a demon. Demon*kind* but not a demon."

She shuddered. "Whatever it was, it was creepy."

True. Imps were disturbing. At least she couldn't smell the

damn thing. The smell of demonkind was unmistakable. And unmistakably vile. And Damon had done far too good a job of replicating that in the simulation. "I'm sure you saw some creepy things in the realm."

"Well, yes," she said, "but nothing quite like that. Lady Morgain's territory is mostly peaceful and she doesn't let Nichtkin come there. That thing would fit right in with the Nichtkin."

Usuriel had Fae that resembled imps in his court? Great. Or was Gwen projecting and his subjects were just creatures— or people, I guessed—whose forms weren't human. Frightening didn't necessarily equal evil. And Gwen had never faced an imp in real life. I'd fought Nichtkin. None of them had that same terrifying feeling as demonkind.

"Lord Usuriel is firmly in the anti-demon camp," I said. "I doubt there are any imps in his court. There are no demonkind in the realm." If there were, well, there wouldn't be a realm and humans would all be demon fodder. But if Gwen didn't know that already, I wasn't going to tell her. "Hopefully you'll never have to meet an imp or anything out here." And maybe if she was creeped out by one measly fake imp, she might not be ask to see any more of the training program.

"No," she said. She pulled her gaze away from the monitor, yawning again.

"Coffee?" I said brightly. "I need more coffee. How about you? You should eat."

"Sounds good."

Right. Plan A. Feed her up and get her blood sugar stabilized before I hit her with 'so, hey, we might be related'.

We headed to the kitchen and I grabbed a canister of Amy's homemade granola along with yogurt and fruit from the fridge. "Cereal might be easier to eat. Unless you're queasy from the meds? I can do toast? You only need one hand for cereal, so you can rest your arm. How's it feel?"

"Still numb. I don't think the nerve block has worn off yet. And I'm hungry. My stomach is fine. I'll try the granola."

"Meredith said to start on the painkillers by midday at the latest," I reminded her, nodding at the packet of pain patches still sitting on the counter with the other bits and pieces the hospital had sent her home with. "Start those before the block wears off. It's nearly eleven now, so you'll need to put one on after you've eaten."

She pulled a face. "Yeah, okay."

I poured granola into a bowl for her and pushed the yogurt and a spoon across the table so she could help herself, before filling another bowl for me. Fighting virtual imps was hard work. I deserved second breakfast.

Lianith came bounding into the room, joining us on the table with an inquiring merping trill.

"No bacon this morning. I don't think you'd like cereal." I said to her.

I didn't need her mental *"bah"* to understand her disappointment.

"She might like yogurt," Gwen said.

"I'm not sure dairy is good for her."

Lianith blinked at me slowly, her golden eyes gleaming. I sighed and got up to spoon yogurt into a bowl, putting it down on the floor near her fancy water bowl. "Don't blame me if you get a stomachache."

Gwen crunched through her bowl of granola at high speed. I went more slowly with mine, hungry but nervous about what was to come. Lianith wandered back to join us, and perched on the chair next to Gwen's, cleaning her whiskers with a paw as delicately as any normal cat. She seemed fond of Gwen.

I tried to work up the nerve to tell Gwen the news, trying to figure out what to say as she ate. Finally I decided to just get it over with. "I need to ask you about something."

She tensed, pushing her bowl away. "What?"

"You're not in any trouble," I said. "It's...look, there's no easy way to say this. I got a notification this morning from the database."

"The database?" Her brows drew down and she tilted her head, making loose hair fall across her face. She pushed it back without taking her eyes off me.

"The National Genetics Registry."

"Oh," she said. "You have your DNA in it, too?"

"Yeah. I don't know who my dad is either, so my grandparents did it a long time ago."

"You never found him?"

"No, there weren't any matches back then, and I stopped looking. I made up my mind a long time ago that I didn't need to know."

"Yeah, me too." She grimaced and picked up her spoon, twirling it between her fingers. "I don't know how I feel about knowing he's out there somewhere."

I knew how I felt about it. If it was Jack, I wanted nothing to do with him. Less than nothing. But I'd deal with Jack after the first hurdle of this little chat.

"Well, it doesn't really change anything, like Meredith said," I said, trying to sound casual. "You don't have to contact him." In fact, I was going to do my best to make sure she didn't.

"Yeah, that's true," Gwen said, still twirling her spoon. It danced through her fingers with the ease of long practice. Or innate Fae grace. "So you got a notification?"

"Yeah. And it's weird timing because I never had one before. I don't come from a big family on my mom's side. And I guess my dad's relatives aren't team DNA testing." I waited a moment to see if she might make the connection I had.

She didn't. Just twirled the spoon and watched me, waiting for me to keep talking.

"I was wondering if it might be you," I said in a rush.

Gwen's mouth dropped open. The spoon dropped to the table with a sharp clang. "*Me?* Why?"

I understood the surprise. "For one thing, I'm not fond of coincidences. The timing is suspicious, don't you think? I mean, sure, lots of people must be searching every day, but, you know, you put yours in last night, and suddenly I have a notification that my medical history was accessed."

She looked as shocked as I had felt earlier. "You think you're my sister?" She shoved a hand into her hair, pulling out her hair tie, as she shook her head. "We don't look anything alike." She tugged at her perfect blonde hair, then nodded at mine.

"I'm aware," I said drily. "But genetics aren't straight-forward."

She blinked slowly. "Still. Sisters? Us?"

I held my hands out, palms up. "I don't know. But it's possible. And I know it's weird. But I wanted to tell you straight away."

"How do we find out if you're right?"

"Well, we can clear up the half-sister part," I said. "We can both send a contact request."

It sounded simple enough. But the knowing wasn't the complicated part of all this.

"What if it's not me?" Gwen objected. "Do you want to contact some stranger?"

Probably not. Not without some time to think. But Gwen wasn't a random stranger. "Meredith said if we both give her permission she can compare the history you received to mine. That's the other way."

"You talked to Meredith about this?"

"You were asleep," I said, suddenly defensive. "And I wanted to know if she thought I was being an idiot to think it might be you."

"I take it she didn't?" Gwen suddenly sounded very English.

"No. Which is why we're having this conversation. And like I said, I know this is weird. But I think it's better to know."

She started to nod, then froze. "If we're half sisters, my father is yours, too."

"Yeah."

"You didn't get a notification about him?"

"No. But I didn't initiate a search, so that tracks."

"You really don't know anything about your dad?"

I shook my head but couldn't stop myself from flinching slightly.

Gwen's eyes narrowed. Short, blonde and gorgeous didn't equal stupid. She'd seen my reaction. My cheeks went hot.

"What? Do you know who he might be?" Gwen demanded.

"Nothing concrete," I said, voice a little too high.

"But you have an idea?"

I sighed. Rip off the Band-Aid time. "Yes. Do you remember why Damon and I were in the realm?" She'd been out of it when we'd reached Ljubljana. I had no idea what she remembered.

"You were chasing some guy. Jack something? He did something…er, bad?"

So Aubrey hadn't provided her with any more details. Good. It was Damon's business. Nothing to do with Gwen.

Except if he's our father.

Still, I didn't know how much was okay to tell her. So safer to stick to the basics for now. "Yeah, him. Ralph found a photo of him with my mom before I was born. Ten months before I was born."

She blinked and I could see her doing the math. "So you think he might be your dad? Our dad?"

Her face fell, the color draining from it. "*Oh.* He's not a good guy."

I sympathized with the horror in her voice. I mean, she couldn't have thought her father was a saint. He'd abandoned her. But there's a difference between deadbeat and straight-out criminal.

"No," I said. "So I think it would be better, for now, at least, if you don't put in a contact request to your paternal match."

"No." She swallowed hard. "No chance we're related on the maternal side?"

"No. My mom was a witch, not Fae. I'm sure of that. And Meredith said there are no Fae in the database. We have to share a father."

"Right," she said. "So, what do we do?"

"What do you do about what?" Damon asked from the doorway.

Chapter Seventeen

Damn it, I hadn't heard him come in, and Madge hadn't let me know he was home.

I stood, trying not to look guilty. "Hey. What are you doing here? I thought you had meetings all morning?"

"I decided to work from home. Wanted to make sure you're both okay after last night."

I smiled automatically, happy to see him. He wore dark jeans and a white shirt, far more pulled together than either of us.

He smiled at Gwen. "I'm so sorry about last night. How are you?"

She mumbled something like "good," but she looked pretty shell-shocked, so I wasn't sure it was that convincing.

"Alexei will cover your medical costs from last night. He wants to apologize in person when you're up to it," Damon said.

Gwen nodded, still looking distracted.

He shot me a glance, obviously wondering if she was okay.

I felt my smile turn lopsided. "So there's been a development. I told you that Gwen had some matches on the DNA database."

"I remember," Damon said, his smile turning tight. Our conversation after Gwen and I had finally arrived home had been short, but Damon hadn't let me get to sleep until I'd filled him in on all the pertinent details.

"Well, this morning, I got a notification from the national DNA database that my medical history had been accessed. That's the first time that's ever happened."

He made the link almost instantly. "Wait, you two are related?"

His head turned from me to Gwen. I wondered what he saw. She was short and blonde and beautiful. I was tall and mousy-haired and…well, he thought I was beautiful, but I wasn't half-Fae gorgeous. I had my mom's green eyes. Gwen's were blue.

Pale blue, like Jack's, I realized. His were the same ice-blue shade. Another nail in the coffin of coincidence. "Possibly half sisters." Cousins was possible, but my gut said no.

"So you'd have the same dad? I mean, her mom is Fae, right?" Damon asked.

"Yep," I agreed.

"And she got a match with her dad, too?" He was watching me intently. Probably trying to figure out if I thought this development was good or bad.

"Yep."

"Do you know who he is?"

"You don't get that information from the database," I said. "Only the medical history. You can send a contact request, but Gwen hasn't—"

"You didn't get a match with him, too?"

"I didn't do a parental search recently. And my info is locked down. So, no. Whoever it is should only get a notification about his medical history being released, same as me."

"Well, she should do that," Damon said. "That would be amazing, if you knew who…" He trailed off and I knew he'd remembered the photo when he muttered something distinctly impolite under his breath. "That photo of your mom. You think it could be Jack." He stared at Gwen intently. "She doesn't look like him."

"He has eyes like hers. Such a pale blue isn't common."

"Jack has blue eyes?" Gwen interjected.

"Yes, like yours," I said.

"The color could be a Fae thing?" Damon suggested.

"It's possible," I said in a tone that was more 'probably not'. If Gwen's eyes were purple or some absolutely non-human color, I could chalk that up to her being tanai, but pale blue was still human.

Damon pressed his hand to the back of his neck, digging his fingers into the muscles as he locked eyes with me. "You could do the search for your dad."

"I told you I've done it before and never had a hit. So, if it is Jack and his DNA is in the database now, it's been a recent addition, or, at least, sometime since I turned eighteen."

"He worked in medical holographs, you'd think he'd be into medical tech," Damon muttered.

"You tech boys are always the ones paranoid about data safety," I pointed out. If Jack was Gwen's father, he knew he'd left a kid behind in England. He'd made arrangements for her. Left her money. But if he didn't want her to find him, that was the perfect incentive not to add his DNA to a database. So why had he changed his mind? And when? Did he know Gwen's was here in San Francisco? That she'd come out of the realm? Or that she'd gone in there in the first place? Had he kept tabs on her from a distance all this time?

Too many questions. I regretted my second breakfast, as my stomach flipped and churned.

"Right," Damon said. "Dammit. He'll have the notification that his history was accessed, too, won't he?"

"He already knew about Gwen. So it wouldn't be a surprise," I said. "He walked away from her. Maybe he won't care."

"Do you think he knew about Sara getting pregnant?"

"I doubt it. She made it very clear my dad had no idea I existed. I threatened to run away once and she told me there was no one else who knew I'd even been born. I thought my grandparents were dead until the police located them after her accident. Jack had money. If Sara had wanted something from him, she would have figured out how to get it."

Which suddenly made me wonder why she hadn't extracted every penny she could from Jack. My mother never met a dollar she didn't like. So, why hadn't she worked Jack like all her other marks? Had she...?

A thought struck me like a bolt out of a clear sky. She'd wanted to use me for the demon all along.

Bile rose in my throat. Was it possible? Could she have planned that far ahead? Had a kid because she thought she could make a bargain with the demon for whatever it was she wanted? It was the only thing that made sense to me for her not wanting to stick with Jack, at least long enough to saddle him with me and leave with a nice payoff.

Holy *shit*. Was that why she'd gone underground in middle America? Determined he'd never find out about me until she knew whether I had power and could be traded to a demon? I bent over, bracing a hand on the back of a chair, trying to remember how to breathe. Had my mom really been that callous? Or crazy? Jack was no picnic, either. What the hell did that say about me if those two had provided my genetic material? Was I one short straw away from cracking and trying for world domination?

"Maggie?" Damon said, crouching down beside me. He put a hand on my back, rubbing it gently. "What's wrong?"

"I'm sorry. I just figured out my mom was worse than I thought." I stifled a half hysterical laugh and straightened. Gwen stared at me, looking thoroughly confused and paler than ever. "Can we find out if it is Jack?" I asked Damon. "Another way, I mean. A...less direct way?"

He frowned. "I'm not sure. Those databases will be locked down tight."

I raised an eyebrow. "Are you telling me you couldn't do it?"

"Don't look at me like that," he said. "I'm not supposed to break—"

"Not 'supposed to' being the relevant part of that sentence," I said, making air quotes. "We need to know. Jack will have been notified his medical history was accessed, too. I mean, he knows about Gwen, but what if he decides he can use her in some way? She's half-Fae…" Half-Fae and half-witch. Untrained. Vulnerable.

"Fuck," Damon pulled a face.

"Exactly," I said.

"Someone want to tell me what's going on…what did Jack do?" Gwen asked.

"We can't tell you. Not without the Cestis okaying it," I said. "We can ask Cassandra when we tell her about this."

"Why would Cassandra need to know?"

"Because Jack's a witch. Which makes you…well, I'm not sure. More than tanai. I don't know how common that is, but we have to tell Cassandra."

Gwen half rose from her chair, as though she was going to flee. I put a hand out, catching her arm instinctively. "Hey, none of this is your fault. No one's going to be mad at you."

Mad, no. Concerned about her magic, yes. I didn't need to be Cestis to realize that.

"It will be okay." I put gentle pressure on her arm and she thumped back down into her chair.

"She doesn't necessarily have witch magic, does she?" Damon asked. "Not all witch's kids do."

Gwen perked up. "Yeah, maybe I don't."

"She has some magic. She's tanai. I don't know about the other part." Other than Jack was strong. You couldn't summon imps if you weren't.

"You can't tell from her—" he waved his hand at Gwen, an encompassing swirl of his hand around the general outline of her body. "You know, energy field."

"It looks a little smoky, like Callum and Cerridwen. Other than that, well, she hasn't used magic around me. And, if she did, I'm not sure I could tell whether it's Fae or witch magic she was using. Cassandra probably could."

Damon shook his head. "So we ask Cassandra."

Gwen slumped back in her chair. Obviously not so keen on the idea of the Cestis here getting interested in her.

"Which brings us back to who her—our—dad is. And why we need to know. If it's just Joe Normal from the middle of nowhere, then we can all relax." How Joe Normal would meet and knock up a Fae was the hole in that argument. I mean, it had happened back in the day…Fae stealing humans away, but not since the contract.

"Gwen can refuse a request if he tries to make contact," Damon said. "Doesn't that solve the problem?"

"She can refuse the request," I said, "but we know Jack has friends who have no scruples crossing the lines of data privacy and hacking. He might choose to pursue other avenues of access, too."

Damon's expression turned dark. He could hardly argue that Jack was going to play by the rules. I could see him turning the possibilities around in his head, his brain running at its usual genius speed as he analyzed the problem. I let him think until he shook his head once and squared his shoulders. "So the first thing we want to do is get your records out of the database. He can't hack information that's not there."

He had a point. "How?"

"Your information is in the Cestis database, right?"

I nodded, not surprised he knew about the Annex database.

"So ask Cassandra. She's in charge. The Cestis database interfaces with the regular ones. But the Cestis control it. And

I'm sure it's well protected. They wouldn't want the government having access to the names of every witch in the country, would they?"

"No," I said. The relationship between witches and humans hadn't always been friendly. There were still countries where magic had been made illegal and witches were underground if they hadn't fled. So I couldn't imagine the Cestis would give the government any more access to the database than was strictly necessary. "You're right. So we need to call Cassandra. And Meredith. But Cassandra first."

Gwen looked like she wanted to object. I squeezed her arm again. "It will be okay."

She started gnawing on the thumbnail of her free hand.

Damon passed me his datapad and I called Cassandra, putting the call up on a holoscreen.

"How do I get my record out of the Annex DNA database?" I asked when she answered, skipping even a hello. "And Gwen's."

She frowned at me, her initial smile when she'd answered the call replaced by her eagle-eyed, no-nonsense expression. Her Cestis face where the normal silver-haired, curvy, non-threatening, sweet old lady meets Mrs. Claus persona she used to make people comfortable around her vanished and you were left with no doubt you were dealing with someone of vast power and authority. Someone not to be messed with, because they would probably mess you up with ease. "Good morning to you, too, Maggie. You have to put in a request."

"How long does it take?"

"A few days, a week. I'm not sure how often they review these days. We get reports, of course, but that's always been more Ian's thing. He liaises with a lot of the government departments we have to work with."

"Okay, can it be faster?"

"I can authorize a priority request." She leaned forward, her eyes glowing gold through the screen.

"Great," I said, looking down. "Let's do that. Gwen and I need to get our records out fast and you need to tell them to be on the lookout for hacking attempts."

Her gaze sharpened even more. "Back up. Tell me what's going on."

"Well, first thing you need to know there's a possibility that Gwen's my half sister and the second is, if she is, Jack Miller might be our father."

Chapter Eighteen

"PLEASE HOLD," Cassandra snapped. Her image froze and we waited. My grip on Gwen's arm slid down and I found her hand. She held on, fingers curling around mine, gripping me like I was her anchor in the world. Her hand was warm even though her face was still pale. Smaller than mine.

But very real. My *sister's* hand. I suddenly knew I didn't need the DNA to convince me. I'd do whatever was necessary to keep her out of Jack's path.

Neither of us spoke. And Damon left us to our silence.

After the longest five minutes in history, Cassandra's image began to move again. "Your records will be removed. As soon as possible. I've got the team checking the security logs, but we could be too late. Though, there are quite a few layers of encryption between the information in the database and anything that identifies you. And he'd have to go back to the UK database for Gwen's original information. We'll remove that, too. I've contacted Isolde."

Well, it was something, at least.

"If you need any help working out if there was a breach, let me know," Damon offered.

"Thank you," Cassandra said. "Let's hope that's not

necessary. But now that's taken care of, Maggie, explain to me why you two think you're related and Jack's your father? Does this have anything to do with the accident at the club last night?"

"It does," I said and gave her the rundown of the DNA testing and about my notification.

"So, so far this is a theory?" Cassandra asked, not sounding skeptical, but somewhat less tense. "You haven't asked Meredith to confirm?"

"Not yet. If it is Jack, he will have gotten a notification like me. And we figured he might try to get in touch with Gwen. After all, he knows about her even if there's been no contact. Even if he didn't want to make contact officially, there's always the possibility he'd try to find out where she was through less official channels. Try to hack the database and trace the match. Given he's, well, Jack, we don't want him tracking Gwen down. So we called you first." I didn't mention I'd been about to ask Damon if *he* could hack the database to trace the match in the other direction and find out if it was Jack. I wanted her to help me, not chew me out.

"Well, I can't fault you for that, but before this goes any further, why don't you make sure? Call Meredith."

"You can't get that info from the database?"

"Meredith already has the data she needs. St. Isidore's will have Gwen's information from last night, including the medical histories from the matches. I'm assuming, Maggie, that you downloaded yours. She can compare those. If you didn't, I can arrange for it to be sent to her. Your records will be removed from the Annex and placed somewhere more secure, not deleted entirely. Call her, and by the time I get there, you'll know for certain if you're sisters, and we can proceed accordingly."

"You're coming here?" I asked, somewhat startled. "You don't want to wait until we know for sure?"

"I was coming into the city today anyway. And it's best to

deal with this kind of thing in person. No chance of anyone listening in who shouldn't be. And even if Meredith says you're not sisters, that still leaves the question of whether or not Jack is your father. A question I'd rather have answered quickly, so we need to work out how."

Right. Damon's place was as secure as a house could be. "Good point. Okay, we'll call Meredith."

"Amy is supposed to be working this afternoon," Damon said. "Do you want me to give her the day off?"

"Yes," Cassandra said. "We want to be able to talk freely. I'll see you all soon." She ended the call.

Gwen and I stared at each other for a moment. We were still holding hands.

"Do you want to call Meredith, or should I?" I asked.

Gwen swallowed. Hard. Then lifted her chin. "Let's do it together. You said she would need permission from both of us, right?"

"Yep." I turned my attention back to the datapad. It only took a couple of minutes for Meredith to confirm we were half sisters.

"Congratulations," Meredith said after she gave us the news. "Will you be contacting your father?"

"No," I said. "In fact, we need you to make sure any files you have on me and Gwen are as secure as you can make them."

Her congratulatory smile vanished. "Can I ask why?"

"Long story. Short version is there's a possibility it's Jack Miller. If it is, well, Gwen doesn't want anything to do with him, and I don't want him to discover he's related to me."

"You don't think he knows?"

"If he did, I think he would have pulled some sort of 'Maggie, I'm your dad' crap the last time we crossed paths. And my mom went off-grid for a reason. Other than her being, you know, generally shady. That's not enough to hide the way she did. The only reason I can think of is that she didn't want anyone else with a claim on me showing up to ruin her plans."

Meredith's face turned grim. "Right. I'll make sure your files are secure. Gwen, how are you? Did you use one of the patches?"

Dammit, we'd forgotten the patch. "She slept in. I told her to put one on after she ate." And wow, that sounded totally like a bossy older sister.

"The patches are right here on the counter," Gwen said. "I'll put one on now, but so far the block is holding."

"Good. But you want to start the patch before the block stops or you'll be in a lot of pain. Better to stay on top of it. Right, I'm sure you both want time to talk. Call me if Gwen has any issues with her arm or if you need anything else."

She leaned closer. "It's a bit early for me to be prescribing a stiff drink and Gwen shouldn't have alcohol while she's using those patches. So, I'm going to say, eat some ice cream or something sugary and bad for you. Doctor's order. If you want to go wild, drink some herbal tea. Something soothing."

I managed a smile. "Cassandra's coming over, I'm sure she'll take care of that."

After Meredith ended the call, and I'd messaged Cassandra the news, Damon offered ice cream. Gwen and I both refused. Did her stomach feel as queasy as mine?

I slipped my hand free and went to grab her pain patches, bringing them back to the table with two cans of soda. They at least had sugar and my stomach didn't rebel at the thought of drinking one.

I cracked one open and pushed the other toward Gwen.

She studied the can. "Cranberry, pomegranate and yuzu?"

"You ordered a yuzu margarita last night. I thought you liked it."

She half-smiled. "I'm not even sure what it is."

"It's a citrus. I think." I swigged my soda. It was just sweet enough, the sharpness of the fruits offsetting the sugar rush and washing the sour taste of adrenaline out of my mouth. "Try it. It's good."

She looked dubious, but opened the can. Damon was watching both of us, one finger drumming on the table. No doubt he'd prefer it if he could swing into action. Be all 'master of the universe' and deal with all of this with a wave of his bank balance, but he had to wait like the rest of us mere mortals. He could work his own brand of magic once Cassandra told him how he could help.

Gwen downed her soda fast. Then burped and immediately clapped a hand over her mouth, turning scarlet.

I laughed. "Good to see my sister is classy." Gwen turned an even deeper shade and for some reason, I lost it completely, doubling over with laughter. Damon joined in and after a few seconds Gwen did, too.

"It might not be him," Gwen said when she finally stopped.

"It's possible." My gut told me otherwise, the brief tension relief from the laughter fading fast as it tightened all over again.

"We'll figure it out soon enough," Damon said.

"How do we do that without making contact with him?" Gwen asked.

Damon and I exchanged a long look. I waited to see what he proposed. I wouldn't push him to do something not strictly legal if he didn't want to.

"I'll get Mitch to talk to the lawyers," he said. "Jack is wanted in this country, so we may be able to get a court order to break the privacy on the database."

"How long will that take?"

"Through the courts? Probably a while." He sounded displeased at the prospect.

I suspected the instruction that Damon was going to give Mitch would be more along the lines of 'by any means necessary'.

"We'll have to wait and see," Damon continued. "Don't worry, my lawyers are the best."

"What if he used a fake name on the database?" Gwen asked. "Like on my birth certificate."

Crap. I'd forgotten that.

"There are other routes," Damon said. "We know his real name and we can track down other relatives. From what I understand it's difficult to submit a sample these days without having your identity thoroughly confirmed. So maybe we won't have to. We can start with when your father's sample was submitted to the database and take it from there. In fact, when Cassandra gets here, we should get her to start that process. He can remove his records just like you two can. And he might if he tries to find Gwen and her record vanishes. It could tip him off we're on to him. Though he doesn't have the advantage of having Cassandra on his side to expedite his request. Particularly if he went through the regular database. She might be able to freeze his record. Though that could tip him off, too." He paused, looking into the distance, thinking hard. "Cassandra should just copy the record. So we have his analysis even if he manages to pull it."

Gwen was starting to look overwhelmed again.

"We'll take it one step at a time," I said, trying to sound confident. "Cassandra will be here soon and we'll figure this out."

Cassandra arrived about forty minutes later. I took her back to the kitchen and introduced her to Gwen, who was sitting at the table, still looking pale and pushing the empty package from her pain patch back and forth with anxious flicks of her fingers. She'd asked to see the picture of Jack. I'd sent a copy to her email. She'd stared at it for a long time before she said, "Your mom was very beautiful."

To which my reply was, "Only on the outside."

Cassandra said hello to Damon, asked if we'd confirmed we were sisters and when I said yes, smiled approvingly and informed us she'd requested the name of the man who had matched with Gwen using her authority as Head of the Cestis.

I avoided looking at Damon. Friends in high places were good. Especially if that meant he wouldn't have to crawl around in the low ones to help me out. "Thank you," I said.

"Thank you," Gwen echoed.

"You're welcome." Cassandra nodded, eyeing Gwen. Her head tilted and her eyes narrowed slightly. I recognized the look. Someone was about to get tea. I stifled a sigh.

"Maggie, why don't you show me Amy's herb garden?" Cassandra said. "I'll make Gwen something to help with her healing. Gwen, you wait here, we won't be long. Then we can all talk."

I let her hustle me out of the house.

"What's wrong?" I asked when we were admiring the neat rows of herbs that Amy grew in the small kitchen garden the gardeners had ceded to her. She'd explained the whole system to me once when I'd asked her for some mint to practice something Cassandra had been teaching me. There were strategic shade panels and UV blockers that protected the plants from getting fried, a recycled water irrigation system— Amy's explanation of that had gone over my head—and solar lights along the paths, highlighting the neat labels for each group of plants.

Cassandra smiled approvingly as she moved along the paths between the beds. I didn't have to look to know she was building extra layers of wards. I felt them as they wrapped around us, ensuring privacy. Lianith would tell me if there were any nixlings nearby and I doubted anyone short of a Fae Elder or a demon could get through Cassandra's wards, even if they managed to get through all the other layers of protection around the garden without alerting us.

Her emerald-green shirt went well with the plants. The sunlight caught her silver hair as she tugged a leaf off a mint plant and crushed it between her fingers, before inhaling the scent. "You realize if Jack is your father, Gwen has the potential to have both witch magic and Fae magic."

"Yes, I worked that out. Is it a bad thing?" I asked.

She pursed her lips. "It's unusual, and if she's untrained, she's either potentially vulnerable or potentially dangerous…"

I didn't need her to finish the sentence. I knew it was dangerous to not control your magic. I'd burned myself the first time I'd used mine. And Gwen was half-Fae, too. Who knew what she might be capable of?

"Is there a way of testing her to see if she has both kinds of magic? Are they so different?" Cerridwen had told me I could learn the Fae way of doing magic, because I hadn't been taught to think like a witch since I was thirteen. But I could do witch things in the realm and some of the Fae things outside of it. It was just harder without the inherent magic in the realm.

"Witches can see the magic and we can change its energy, but we expend energy to do so. Fae, for lack of a better explanation, are connected to that energy. And they can make it do what they want. A witch can burn their power out. I doubt a Fae can."

I still wasn't sure I understood the difference and trying was making my head ache. "Doesn't that mean the Fae side would dominate? So she should just be a more powerful witch?"

"Perhaps. Regardless of how she does magic, the issue is more whether she can control it. Within the realm, she may not have used her power much, so we have no idea how well she's trained. Or how that would translate to her control out here. If she can't control her magic, she's vulnerable. And out here, she doesn't have someone like Lady Morgain protecting her. The Cestis can't be everywhere."

Vulnerable. She meant to demons. Though, being in the realm hadn't been entirely without risk. Gwen should have been safe in Morgain's court, but Usuriel had still somehow managed to reach her. Not that he was as bad as a demon. Maybe.

Damn. Usuriel. I should tell Cassandra about him. Ugh. I rubbed my temples and Cassandra bent down and picked another sprig of mint.

"Sniff this if you have a headache."

I doubted mint was going to fix things, but I took it anyway. The smell was calming, if nothing else. Though right now I would have preferred it in a mojito.

"If Jack is your father, I think it would be best to assume Gwen inherited his talents as well as her mother's," Cassandra said. "And if she has a leaning toward game design, she could have inherited his skills for technology as well."

Ugh. "Do you think that's why I can do what I do?" Jack had made his fortune in early holographic and VR tech. I'd read articles about him describing his talent for making connections and innovations in the early stages as 'uncanny'. Much like my own skill for solving bugs no one else could.

"There's no way of knowing, really. Don't doubt yourself. You are not your parents, and you know that."

I did, but it felt hard to remember when faced with a whole other level of who they were. Double ugh. I didn't want anything from Jack. Let alone the talent I'd built my life around. "Let's hope Gwen takes more after her mother," I muttered.

"I would prefer that she took after the woman who raised her. Who seems to have been kind and dutiful at least." Cassandra's hand drifted over the tops of more plants, the green scent of them filling the air.

"Ignoring the part where she was doing it for money and working for a criminal."

Cassandra picked another sprig. Rosemary this time. "I doubt she knew who Jack was, even if it was dubious to agree to pretend to be Gwen's aunt. Still, a mercenary-minded human is a known quantity. As is Jack, to a degree. We don't know what kind of Fae her mother is. This would be easier if we did."

"Perhaps. But the only people who know that are Jack and her mother, and her mother has so far stayed away." I paused, considering. "Do you think Cerridwen would be more interested in helping Gwen find out who her mother is if she knows about the witch thing?"

Cassandra's face hardened. "I think I would prefer not to tell any of the Fae about this yet."

"Why not?"

"Well, for one thing, we already know some of their factions are suspicious of you, because you've encountered a demon. If we tell them Gwen's a tanai with witch magic, that she's likely very powerful, they're going to primarily see her also as a tempting target for a demon."

Was that how Cassandra saw her? "Why? She can learn to protect herself."

"It takes time," Cassandra said, "and it could be complicated by her heritage."

"All that means you should tell Cerridwen," I pointed out.

"I will. But I need to pick my moment. And we don't want them trying to use this to claim she should return to the realm."

"Could they do that? I thought because she's human she has rights."

"She has rights as a witch, yes. She has rights as tanai, but there are provisions in the contract about threats to the realm, and you already know they view demons as a threat."

"But there is no demon."

"There are afrit. And someone was in Ajax's house," Cassandra said. "Just because we haven't found out who it was, or why they were there, doesn't mean there isn't any connection to whatever Ajax's plan was. And then there's Jack to consider. If he was keeping tabs on Gwen and lost track of her when she went into the realm, well, now he knows she's back."

"You think he'll come after her?"

"I don't know. He must have had his reasons for having a baby with a Fae in the first place, not to mention keeping the child. The Fae don't have children easily, and it would have taken some convincing to get Gwen's mother to agree to give up a child."

"Not so hard when that child is tanai, perhaps," I said, my mind still chewing on the fact that Cassandra was worried about demonkind. The threat of a headache was turning into a full-blown one at the thought. I'd been training to fight demonkind, but part of me had never thought I'd have to do it again. At least, not anything bigger than an afrit. I shivered despite the warmth of the sun beating down on us. Then forced my mind back to Gwen. "The Fae don't view tanai the same way as they would a full Fae." That much I knew from Pinky. The Fae, well, certain families, viewed tanai as slightly better than humans perhaps, but still in the category of possessions to be told what to do, rather than living, thinking beings with a right to control their own lives.

"Still, I'd like to know what Jack offered Gwen's mother. And I don't think we should let Cerridwen know about Gwen and Jack until we have to. Usuriel wasn't happy about letting the two of you leave the realm. If he finds out Gwen's half-witch, he might be difficult."

"Usuriel was at the club last night," I admitted in a rush.

For once I'd managed to genuinely shock Cassandra. Her jaw dropped. "And you're just telling me this *now*?"

I gestured back at the house. "There's been a lot going on. And he only wanted to talk to me."

She muttered something under her breath. It didn't sound complimentary, but I wasn't sure if it was aimed at me or Usuriel. "He shouldn't be outside the realm. I'll have to tell Cerridwen. What did he want?"

"I'm not sure. He admitted he sent the nixlings. Said he wanted to keep an eye on me. Somehow he found out Jack was the one we're hunting and that Jack has dabbled with demonkind. I don't know how much more he knows, but he said he wanted to watch for him."

"And you believed him?"

"Not completely. But you know, the enemy of my enemy is my friend and all that. If he wants to help stop Jack, that's fine with me."

"You don't think he was there because of Gwen?"

"He sent the nixlings before Gwen arrived in the US. And I don't think he saw her. So, no."

"Still, it will be safer if he doesn't find out."

"I'm not sure how we prevent that," I pointed out. "If he's moving outside the realm and watching us still, he'll see her sooner or later. Or his spies will." He had more than nixlings at his disposal. But that though made me think of something else. "Usuriel's not the only one with a spy."

Cassandra looked confused.

"Lianith," I continued. "She belongs to Cerridwen. Or serves her or whatever you want to call it. I'm not sure how much of all this she understands but she's overheard some of our conversations. She could tell Callum or Cerridwen." For all I knew, she had already.

"Has Callum been here?"

"No, but she has the same mental speech he does. I don't know if that works long distance."

Cassandra sighed. "If it does, then I expect I will be hearing from Cerridwen sooner rather than later. But I'll cross that bridge when I come to it. Just be careful. With her and with keeping Gwen safe."

"We're always careful. This is one of the most secure places in the city. Probably in the whole damned country. But I get it. I'll watch out for Usuriel. Can we not tell Gwen, though? She is not a fan. And if we're trying to reduce her stress level to avoid a magic flare, this won't help."

"She has to know eventually."

"Let's give her a few days to adjust. She's been through a lot recently. Let's see if we can find out if Jack is our father, before we hit her with the news Usuriel's stalking me."

"Very well." Cassandra didn't look entirely happy about it, but she didn't argue.

"Can we ask Callum to figure out how well Gwen has been trained in Fae magic? We don't have to tell him about Jack. He knows she's tanai. I'd like to ask him to teach her that trick of his to break out of VR." Callum had been able to get out of the re-creation of Jack's locked VR. I could usually manage to exit a VR magically when I was sufficiently scared or angry, but I couldn't do it reliably otherwise. "Maybe she'll figure out a different way to Callum. Something easier for the rest of us to try to learn."

"And safer for her if Jack decides to take an interest?" Cassandra said.

"Yeah, that too." I rubbed the now nearly pulverized mint savagely between my fingers. Fuck Jack. Teaching anyone how to escape a locked VR should never be necessary. But thanks to him, and whoever his twisted cronies were, it was. Yet another reason to hate him. "Are you sure there's no way of hexing Jack or something? If he died, that would solve a lot of problems."

"As much as he's broken enough of our laws to warrant it, sadly, no. That kind of thing is black magic or worse. We'll have to do this the old-fashioned way. Catch him, bring him in, and then deal with him."

"He burned down my house. He summoned imps. Doesn't that warrant ending him?" I asked, bitterness burning my tongue and sharpening the words.

"We want information from him first. Like who he's working with. Don't worry, he will get the fate he deserves."

But how much harm could he do before he did?

Cassandra touched my arm. "You know, none of this is your fault," she said. "You don't know him, you didn't know about Gwen and you weren't any part of Jack's plans."

"Sara knew him," I said bitterly. "She made a baby with him."

"Well, I doubt he told her he was consorting with demonkind. In fact, I doubt he even was back then. Thirty-odd years is a long time for a witch who has anything to do with demons to survive. Perhaps Sara sensed something about him. After all, she hid you."

"Because she didn't want him to take her handy little demon sacrifice away." My voice hitched, the bitter taste in my mouth matching the ache in my chest.

Cassandra touched my cheek gently. "Your mother was not a good person. She made bad choices. But you have not. You have Damon, who loves you. Your grandparents loved you, too. Lean into the love, not the regrets. And now you have a sister. Think of her, rather than Jack. We'll find him in the end. And deal with him."

"And then I'll have a father who's a known criminal."

"We can keep your connection with him quiet," Cassandra said. "We have a lot of leeway for that kind of thing. His crimes won't require a high publicity trial. He falls under our jurisdiction, not the human one."

I stole a sideways glance at her face. Which was grim. "What does that mean?"

"As far as the wider world is concerned, he'll quietly disappear and be declared dead a few years later. So you don't need to worry. He's not going to be a problem you have to deal with long term."

Hearing her say her plan was to execute my father should have made me feel bad, surely? But instead, I could only agree with her. The problem was catching him, so justice could be handed out.

She nodded back at the house. "Gwen should be thankful he left her alone and didn't come back for her. He hasn't pulled her into any of his crimes."

"Logically, yes," I said, "but that's hard to explain to her. She doesn't know the whole truth about him yet."

"And you're right, we should take it slowly with Gwen," Cassandra said. "She's had enough shocks in the last few days."

So had I. But Cassandra was right. I should focus on Gwen.

"So how do we find out about her magic? I don't like the idea of her doing something like I did and throwing fire accidentally."

"We ask her what magic she learned in the realm and then go to Callum and the Lady. They can confirm her Fae magic. We'll figure out the witch part. I don't want her wasting too much energy trying to do magic while she's healing," Cassandra said. "And I need to search the Archives. See if we have records of half-Fae, half-witch children. Which means consulting with our British friends. I don't remember any cases here, but they may have had some over the years."

"Fun times," I said.

"Yes," Cassandra said. "So, let's pick some of this mint and a few other things. Everyone here could probably use some nice soothing tea."

Chapter Nineteen

DAMON INTERCEPTED me as we came back into the house. "Cassandra, I need to borrow Maggie for a moment."

She raised her eyebrows but nodded. "Tea will be ready in about ten minutes."

I smiled weakly. Maybe she'd make it taste nice for once. Take it easy on Gwen?

Damon watched Cassandra walk into the kitchen before pulling me into his office, closing the door behind us. The room was soundproof, so I didn't worry about warding.

"So, what was all that about?" he asked, his eyes searching mine.

"Cestis business," I said, trying to dodge the question.

He was having none of it. "Maggie, I deserve to know what's going on."

I sighed. Cassandra hadn't explicitly told me not to tell Damon. "All right, but you can't mention any of this to Gwen."

"Of course not," he said. "She has enough to deal with. But before we get into this, how are you? This is," he waved back in the direction of kitchen, "a lot. A half sister and maybe a father."

"Well, there's definitely *a* father. I've always known that."

"You didn't always know it might be Jack."

"I've had my suspicions since I saw the photo. You know that."

"Sure, but suspecting is different to knowing." He pulled me close, hugging me before dropping a kiss on the top of my forehead. "Don't worry, we'll know soon enough, and we'll make sure he doesn't find out about you. He won't get anywhere near you."

"He's had thirty-plus years to have something to do with me if he did know, and he's never made the attempt. I don't think he knows."

Damon made a noncommittal noise. "Good. But I care about you, not him. Are you okay?"

"I don't know," I said. "Yes for now. Yes, it's a lot, but for now, I'm all right."

"A sister. That's kind of cool, right? More family for you." He sounded happy.

I pressed my face into his chest. "By blood. We're still strangers. Which sounds bad, I know, but it's the truth. We'll have to take some time and see how things work out."

"Do you want a sister?"

"Not sure that's something you get to choose. It seems I have one."

"Yes. But that doesn't mean you have to be close. I mean, I'm not suggesting we kick her out onto the street, but if you need space I can find her somewhere else to stay. Or Cassandra can if she wants to keep an eye on her."

"I'm not sure another rejection is what Gwen needs right now. And I'd like to get to know her. I just wish we could do it without...."

"Without Jack?"

"Yes. And without all the weird stuff." I flailed an arm in a frustrated circle.

Damon caught my wrist, pressed a kiss to my palm. "I'm

not sure there's any circumstances where finding out you have a sister you never knew about at your age wouldn't be weird to some degree."

"Yeah, but there's weird and then there's *weird*."

He put a finger under my chin, lifting it so I had to meet his gaze. "You eat weird for breakfast."

I wrinkled my nose. "I'd prefer to stick to cereal. And I'm not sure how Gwen will take my weird. She came here to get away from the Fae and magic. I'm stuck with the Fae for now."

"True. That's something the two of you need to figure out. Once she's happy no one's coming from the realm to steal her back, she'll relax about it all."

Coming from the man who once broke up with me because of my magic, I wasn't sure if that made me feel better or worse. He'd overcome his feelings about magic because he loved me. Gwen had no reason to care about me and my feelings other than a shared crappy dad.

"It would be useful if I could see the future," I said. "See how it all works out."

"I don't know. I think it's better not to know. Think of Morgain. That's what her magic is, isn't it?"

Lady Morgain could read the fates. And she constantly shifted form, moving through her own timeline, perhaps, to do it. "Not that much of the future. Just enough to win the lottery." I lifted my head to smile at him.

His answering smile was cocky. "You've already won the lottery; you have me."

I snorted. "Maybe you won the lottery when you found me."

"Oh, I did," he said, pulling me close again. I pressed my face back into his chest, wishing I could stay there forever.

"So, what can I do to help? Gwen doesn't seem to need money, but if she wants to go to school here I can clear that pathway for her. Let her see we're on her side."

"Well, I'm not entirely sure what her side is," I said. "And I don't want her to think we're just going to throw money at her and try and buy my way into a relationship with her."

"No. I don't want that, either," Damon agreed. "But I can talk to people when she's ready. She'll still have to meet the academic requirements, but a recommendation will help." He let me go, stepped back. "So, what did Cassandra want?"

I sighed. "She's concerned about Gwen's magic. If it is Jack. The half-Fae, half-witch thing."

"She agrees that's a problem?"

"It's uncommon and Cassandra is concerned it would make Gwen a target for you-know-whats. And it could also make the Fae…uneasy." I threw up my hands. "I don't know. I'd like a rewind, please. Life was a lot simpler before that damn door opened again."

"I agree," Damon said. "But this is where we are. So deep breaths and one step at a time, like usual."

"Okay. But is it too early for a whiskey?"

"Yes," he said, "but how about head-banging sex instead?"

"Not while Cassandra is in the house. Thank you, but no."

"We could make out a little," he said, stepping into my space.

"That's the best idea I've heard all day," I said and let his kisses chase the world away.

When we got back to the kitchen, Cassandra was standing by the open French doors, talking softly but fiercely to someone on her datapad. I could smell mint and other things in the air and our largest teapot sat on the counter, steam issuing gently from its spout. Whatever tea Cassandra had made was steeping away. Gwen was still at the table, looking somewhat wild-eyed and nervous, Lianith on her lap. Which meant Cassandra hadn't banished the nixling from the room.

I waved Damon over to the counter, making gestures I hoped he would correctly interpret as 'find something to eat with the tea'. When he started rummaging in cabinets, I went to sit with Gwen, wondering what Cassandra had said to her.

"Everything okay?" I asked.

Gwen's eyes darted in Cassandra's direction and her fingers stroked Lianith's fur faster. "She's very intimidating." She was nearly whispering.

"Comes with the territory. You don't get her job without knowing your shit and knowing how not to put up with any. And you've dealt with the Cestis in the UK. As long as you're not committing a crime, their bark is usually worse than their bite."

Gwen smiled tightly. "Their bark can be unpleasant, though."

"Something in particular you're worried about?" I asked.

"She said I'll need to learn magic, if Jack's our father. Said I need to control it, even if I don't use it." She looked queasy at the thought. Or perhaps ready to run again. Better to nip that idea off at the bud.

"She's right. You could hurt yourself otherwise. You don't want that, right?"

She bit her lip. "I don't know."

"Basic control shouldn't take long. You said you learned some magic in the realm."

"A few charms. Not real magic. Anyone can do a warming charm or freshen a room or clothes."

Those didn't sound so basic to me. "Well, if you can do those I'm sure it wouldn't take you long to get to the point where the Cestis are satisfied your shields are adequate and you're not going to set anything on fire." Or herself.

"It's not the same out here, is it? How do we even know if I can learn?"

"You're half-Fae, half-witch. I think you'll be okay. The Cestis will help. They want you to do this. Uncontrolled magic is unpredictable." I didn't know what Cassandra might have said about learning to shield. "And you can protect yourself, once you know what you're doing. Stop anyone taking advantage. If you know shields and wards, you won't have to worry. You don't have to use magic for anything else."

If she wanted to stay away from the Fae and away from magic that had to appeal, right?

Her expression turned mulish. "You have shields and wards and you get into trouble."

"I'm…different," I said.

"Because of the demon?" Her fingers tightened in Lianith's fur and the nixling narrowed her eyes at me.

"Not my fault," I thought at her.

"No speak demons." Lianith's tone was adamant.

"She brought it up."

But Lianith was right. Better to keep Gwen's thoughts off demons for now. "Because I've agreed to help in the magical world. But you don't have to if you don't want to. Learn how to protect yourself, and then you can go off to school and find a job and live whatever life you want to live."

She didn't look entirely convinced, but she no longer looked as though she wanted to bolt for the door.

An improvement.

Damon, as though sensing it was a good time to interrupt, came over with a plate of cookies and crackers. And, accepting the inevitable, four empty mugs for Cassandra's brew. "Snacks," he said with an encouraging smile.

Gwen's answering smile attempted to be grateful and she took a cracker, pretending to nibble at it. I still wasn't hungry, my stomach tight and uneasy. I was trying to stay calm for her sake, but the knowledge I could be Jack's daughter still swam through my brain, making my thoughts slosh together uneasily.

Cassandra ended her call and joined us. I started to ask if

her tea would be ready, but something in her expression changed my mind. "Is everything okay?"

"I have the name from the database of the man who matched with you."

So fast? Sometimes I forgot the sheer power of the Cestis. Cassandra asked and people sprinted to do her bidding.

"And?"

"It's not Jack Miller. At least, that's not the name on the account, and the ID used to open it matches the name."

I blinked. Wait, it wasn't Jack? That seemed all too easy.

"What was the name?" Gwen asked.

"Edward Wheatley," Cassandra said.

The cracker shattered in Gwen's fingers as her hand clenched, spraying crumbs in every direction.

"Gwen? Does that name mean something to you?" I asked.

She shook her head. "Not Edward. But John Wheatley Cornelius is the name on my birth certificate. The fake name, I mean."

"Yeah, that's not a coincidence," I muttered. My tiny spark of hope that it wasn't Jack sputtered and died. "Damon, does Mitch or whoever is overseeing the hunt for Jack have a list of known aliases?"

"We have a few. Not enough, unfortunately." He pulled out his datapad and started typing furiously.

"Can you find out if Wheatley pops up anywhere?"

"That would be sloppy. Jack isn't sloppy," Damon said but he kept typing.

"He could have tried to leave a clue for Gwen?" I said.

"I doubt it," Gwen muttered. "He could've just used the same name. But it's nearly twenty-three years since he used the name on my birth certificate. He probably forgot."

"I've got a search happening to see if we can get any information on this Edward," Cassandra said. "IDs can still be faked if you have enough money."

Lack of money not being a problem for Jack.

"Thank you," Damon said. There was something fierce and focused in those laser blue eyes. He'd been looking for a new lead on Jack for weeks.

And I knew who else I could ask about names Jack might use.

If I wanted to owe Usuriel a favor. I gritted my teeth in frustration. Better to try the regular way before I went looking for answers from the Lord of the Nichtkin.

"Okay. So Damon's team will dig into the aliases, Cassandra's people will verify the ID. We'll get an answer. In the meantime, I think there's been enough excitement for one morning. I, for one, need to blow off some steam. Gwen, want to come kill some virtual bad guys with me?"

"No," Gwen said firmly.

I blinked. "Sorry?" Damn it, was she mad at me for all this? Hardly my fault, but maybe I was the nearest target.

"I want to know more about Jack," Gwen said. "About why you've all been looking for him."

"He did bad things," Cassandra said bluntly.

"Yes, I know. But what bad things?"

"Most of it is falls under the category of confidential," Damon said.

Gwen's chin jutted out. The defiant expression on her face made me suck in a breath. For the first time, I saw a resemblance. My sister was as stubborn as me. It almost made me smile. Almost. I stifled the urge. Gwen probably wouldn't see the funny side.

"You don't think I have a right to know if you think he's going to try to find me?" Gwen asked.

Cassandra matched her chin tilt, folding her arms across her chest for good measure. "You said you didn't want to be involved with magic. So we can't tell you about Cestis investigations. That information is need-to-know only."

"So is the Riley Arts investigation," Damon added.

Gwen didn't back down. "Don't I fall under the category of need to know? If he's my father?"

Cassandra shook her head. "We don't know that for sure. And I'm sorry, Gwen, but we don't know you very well either."

"What, you think I'm working for him?" Now she looked mad, not stubborn. Her eyes burned almost silvery. Curious, I peeked at her energy field. Brighter. But not like she was actively using magic. Interesting.

"Well, you have turned up here at a very coincidental time," Cassandra pointed out.

"Because I wanted to get away from this kind of thing, not because my evil father sent me." Gwen's voice was sharp.

"Couldn't she sign an NDA?" I interrupted. Provoking Gwen into a rage didn't seem like a sensible plan if we wanted to avoid accidental magical outbursts. "Or whatever the Cestis equivalent is?" Or both, if necessary. "It's not unreasonable for her to want to know."

Damon and Cassandra gave me identical 'you're on her side?' expressions.

I raised my eyebrows at them, adding my own chin tilt to let them know I was, indeed, on her side. "Well?"

"Is that a good—" Cassandra started

"I understand what an NDA is," Gwen interrupted. "I'm not an idiot."

"If I bind you to Cestis confidentially," Cassandra said sternly, "you'll most likely end up in jail if you break it."

"Same if you break a Riley Arts NDA," Damon added. "I have the best lawyers in the country, and I pay them well. Plus, I can get you blackballed in the industry. Which won't matter if you're in jail."

Sheesh. Talk about bad cop, bad cop. "Back off," I mouthed at him.

He ignored me, keeping his attention on Gwen. "So, if we tell you, you don't get to tell *anyone* else. No matter what you find out. You talk to one of us, you talk to Maggie. A few others we okay. Anybody else and the consequences will be unpleasant."

Gwen threw up her hands. "Who am I going to tell? I don't have any friends here on the outside. I spent my teen years in a boarding school full of girls I didn't have much in common with. I never really had a best friend. Even the ones I was friendly with have probably forgotten who I am now. My mother is unknown. My 'aunt' dropped me the second her legal agreement was over and, as far as Aubrey knows, left the country for parts unknown. There's just me."

I tapped her foot under the table, nudging it with mine, hoping she'd take it as a 'not just you now' gesture of support. For a few seconds she ignored me, then gave a tentative tap back. Her posture eased a little.

"What about Fae?" Cassandra asked. "Do you have friends in the realm?"

"Does it matter if I'm never going back there?"

"You think that now. But things change."

"Well, in the unlikely circumstance I change my mind, I'm sure you could get Lady Cerridwen to put a binding even more effective than yours on me. The Fae have ways of making people stay silent, too. The kind you probably don't want to know about. I want to know the truth. I'm sick of lies and being kept in the dark."

Understandable.

Cassandra gave her a hard stare before turning to Damon. He nodded sharply.

"Very well. Give us a moment to talk," Cassandra said.

"We can go to my office," Damon suggested.

The two of them hurried out, leaving Gwen and I sitting in silence.

"Fight?" Lianith asked.

"Just a disagreement. Everything is okay." Hopefully.

"Tell big witch, trust." Lianith nudged Gwen with her nose

and Gwen patted her a little more calmly. *"Keep Gwen safe. No tell secrets."*

I blinked at her. Apparently nixlings picked their own sides.

"Trust," Lianith repeated firmly before closing her eyes and starting to purr, the noise loud but soothing.

Gwen didn't look particularly soothed.

"It's not personal," I said, knowing damned well it must feel personal to her. "Cassandra and Damon, they have responsibilities to uphold. The kind of responsibility you and I can't really understand. I don't think anyone can, unless they're in the same position. They have to follow the rules. And keep everyone safe."

"Aren't I part of everyone?" Gwen asked plaintively.

"One part. But in their jobs, sometimes the greater good beats the individual. Particularly for Cassandra. The Cestis keep the peace between witches and normals by doing what they do. We don't want to go back to the bad old days. So the Cestis keep secrets. Actually," I tilted my head at her. "I'm surprised Aubrey or someone didn't give you some version of this speech already."

"They did. The 'no talking about demons or Fae to any normals' part, at least. Even most witches. Not that I know how to tell who's a witch."

"You don't?"

She squinted at me. "You do?"

Right. She'd only done magic in the realm. You didn't have to look for the energies in there. You could just assume that everyone had magic and were using it to some degree most of the time. Or could do so as easily as breathing whenever they wanted to. "Witches can see other witches using magic. When we choose to look."

That didn't seem to help.

"Look at what?" Gwen asked.

"At the energy fields."

Gwen still regarded me as though I was talking gibberish. Or maybe sprouted an extra head.

"Like an aura," I added.

"Auras are real?"

Okay, so she'd been exhausted and medicated in the hospital. So maybe she hadn't understood what Meredith meant when she said she wanted to check her aura. "Well, energy is real. And witches can see it. I'm not sure the old hippy version of an aura was ever true. Maybe there were people with very weak magic who caught glimpses of the energy field, but never knew what it was before the witches went public."

"So you can see magic?" Blonde brows drew down. "Can you show me?"

"I think it would be better to wait until Cassandra gives the okay. I take it Fae don't do the same thing?"

"I don't know about out here, but in the realm it's more a sensation. If you're paying attention, you can sense the magic flowing to and from people. Unless they're cloaking what they're doing. That makes it tricky. You learn to recognize other signs. But you *see* the magic? Like a color or something?"

"Yes. But I can also feel the energy sometimes. It's different for different people. Yours is kind of a smoky blue. I think the smoky part is a Fae thing. Cerridwen and Callum have it, too." I stopped for a moment. Her energy was blue. So was mine. Mine lacked the smoky tinge but it was blue. Another confirmation we were sisters.

"Huh." She looked intrigued, despite herself. "Do you think Cassandra will show me how to see them?"

"I think she'll insist on it, if it turns out Jack is our father. It's part of controlling magic, learning to see the energy. At least for a witch. If not, well, I'm sure we could ask Callum if there's someone who can teach you the Fae equivalent. Or one of the tanai, if that's what you'd prefer." If she wasn't half-witch, Cassandra would be less concerned. We could leave it up to the tanai to explain to her what she might be able to do out here if she wanted to. Before Pinky had done her favor for Cerridwen and wound up being trained with me, she had lived quite happily not using her magic, so maybe it wasn't a problem for them.

Gwen sighed, and reached for another cracker, this time taking a proper bite. She chewed, swallowed. "This is not what I intended when I came here. I thought it would make things simpler."

"Well, you couldn't have predicted exploding light bulbs or finding out you have a half sister." I hesitated. "How do you feel about it? Be honest. You can say it's weird if that's how you feel, you won't hurt my feelings."

"Is that how you feel?"

I half shrugged. "It's weird, but not bad weird. Does that make sense? I'd like to get to know you, if that's what you want. But we don't have to be in each other's pockets, if it's not. Maybe it's like meeting a new friend…we have to see if we get along."

She nodded. "It is weird. But…you saved me, back in the realm. You've always been nice to me. I'd….I'd like to get to know you. I don't know if I'm going to be any good at being a friend or a sister. My aunt, well, she was chilly. She did all the right things, but she wasn't affectionate. During my holidays, she took me to museums and lectured me about art or whatever. We went to the theatre, or movies she deemed suitable. When we were home, I had chores or stuck to my room. She wasn't sociable. We definitely didn't hang out. Not once I was old enough to be at school. She played with me when I was little, but she didn't love me. Not really. Though I didn't know any different at the time."

"At least she did all the right things. My mom didn't always do even that," I said. "But I was lucky. After she died, her parents—my grandparents—took me in and they did love me. But I know what it's like, having a rough childhood." Mine had been rough in different ways to hers. It didn't sound as though she'd ever worried about there being enough money or having to pack up and leave in the middle of the night. So hopefully, unlike me, she didn't know what it was like to go hungry. But neglect took many forms. "And hey, we both like games, that's a start."

Gwen was probably farther down the gaming rabbit hole than I would ever be. Like Nat had been. But since I'd dated Damon I'd had an increased appreciation of VR. After I was sure I wasn't going to be stalked by a demon in a game again.

"A start," she agreed.

I studied her face, but found no trace of me. But maybe I couldn't see it. I had my mother's eyes and hers were that icy blue. But I couldn't argue with the DNA. She was my sister. I wanted to know her.

I tried to think of something to suggest, something we could do together. Sister bonding time. But Damon and Cassandra came back into the room before anything sprang to mind.

Gwen shifted in her chair. "What did you decide?"

Damon nodded. "Mitch called. They found another Wheatley in the list of aliases we have for Jack. Spelled slightly differently, but I think it's enough for now. Unless Cassandra's team finds proof that the guy in the database is real and living his life somewhere, we're going to assume it's Jack."

Well, fuck. I tried not to let the slice of jagged fear that hit my stomach at the news show on my face.

Gwen wasn't so well controlled. She looked scared. "So, what happens now?"

Damon held up his datapad. "Now, if you want to know more, you sign an NDA. And Cassandra does whatever she needs to do with you from a Cestis point of view."

"Oh, we have NDAs as well," Cassandra said.

"Sure," Gwen said, holding out her hand for the datapad.

"Wait," I said.

She frowned at me.

"You need to read it. Never sign anything without reading it. It's like asking a Fae for a deal without agreeing the specifics." Even if she'd not signed many legal documents in her life, she should understand the analogy having spent the last four years in the realm. "I've signed a lot of NDAs for clients in my time, do you want me to talk you through it?" I wasn't an attorney, but the woman who'd helped me set up my business from the legal side of things had taught me the traps to watch for in NDAs early on, once she heard I was going to be a consultant.

"I want to know."

"I'm sure you do. And I'm not saying don't sign, I'm saying understand what you're signing, okay?"

"Okay, explain it to me."

Damon looked amused and maybe a little proud. He passed me the datapad and I scooted my chair round next to Gwen. I took my time talking her through each of the clauses of the Riley Arts agreement. It was basically identical to the one I'd signed when I'd first met Damon. This was, possibly, even broader. After that we worked through the Cestis one, with pauses to ask Cassandra to clarify several points. But in the end, I sat back. "Up to you now."

"It's fine." Gwen grabbed the datapad, scrolled, signed and added her palm scan when asked to. Then repeated the process for the second NDA before handing it back to Damon. "There. So. Tell me about Jack.

Cassandra cleared her throat. "Maggie, can you ask Lianith to leave the room."

Lianith raised her head, eyes narrowed. *"Trust,"* she said.

"She says we can trust her," I said.

Cassandra stared at the nixling. "I'm glad to hear that. But as a show of good faith, I would prefer you to leave. After all you can't sign the kind of…contract…that Gwen just did."

Lianith made a trilling noise, clearly disgruntled. But she jumped down and stalked out of the room.

Cassandra watched her go and then made a little 'go on' jerk of her head in my direction.

Right. Apparently I was going to do the honors. How do you tell your sister your father is a criminal genius? "Jack made his money in tech. He came up with a few early innovations in holographics. Those made him rich. Then he moved into investing and got richer."

Damon nodded at me, not disagreeing with anything.

I explained about meeting Jack at the *Serenity Falls* tournament. Gwen listened in silence. When I got to the part about Jack locking me into a game, she said, "Wait, what? How is that possible?"

"It shouldn't be," Damon said. "And we've already rolled out updates to prevent it happening in any VR environment I control."

"Can you only do it to someone with a chip?" she asked, looking distinctly freaked out.

Damon's brows shot up. "I'm not sure. I don't think we've tested it with just a headset. Jack used a cuff that covers the chip."

"We should test that," I said. "A headset, I mean."

"How do you test it?" Gwen asked, eyes wide.

"We have a VR environment set up with the kill switch programming disabled. Once you're in, someone has to let you out," Damon said

"And people *volunteer*?" Gwen squeaked.

"Well, my team trust each other. And it's only a select few."

She squirmed uneasily. No need to ask what she thought about it.

"Callum can get out of it without any help," I said, trying to be reassuring.

"With magic?"

"Yes, though we're not entirely sure how it works. I've

done it a few times, but I can't do it reliably. Maybe you could, as you're half-Fae."

She shook her head, "I don't think I want to try."

"That's fair. No one will make you. And, like Damon said, there's nothing to worry about in any regular game."

"What did he want?" Gwen asked. "Jack, I mean."

"We're not sure. Me, maybe." I glanced at Cassandra.

Who only flapped her hand at me. "Tell her the rest of it."

So I did. That Jack had hinted at working with darkness, not to mention had summoned imps and burned my house down in his escape.

When I finished, Gwen had lost all the color in her face again. I put a hand on her forearm. "It's okay. It's a lot, I know, but he can't get to us here."

The fact that he hadn't been seen in the US since fleeing was one of the few things helping me sleep at night.

"He's working with a demon? That can't end well," Gwen managed.

"Not for him, no," Cassandra said. "People who make deals with demons usually end up dead. One way or another."

Gwen swallowed hard. "You actually think he wants to summon one? What can that bring except death and destruction?"

So she'd learned something about demons in her time in the realm.

"Demons are masters of persuasion. They convince people it's all going to work out. Well, people they don't outright take over," Cassandra said. "People who try usually want power or money. They all underestimate how powerful demons are. They think they'll summon a demon and control it, rather than the other way around. That they'll be the exception. Which is crazy, but by the time someone starts summoning imps, they're not completely sane by any usual measure. They're not thinking about death and destruction. But we are."

The Cestis didn't let a witch who had been tainted by demons live. I'd been tested for demon taint twice. I was under no illusions what would have happened to me if I'd failed.

"Which is why you need to learn some basic magic," Cassandra said. "Hopefully you'll never come anywhere near Jack, but if you do you need strong shields and some control of your magic. If you don't control it, someone else might be able to control you."

Okay, so she wasn't pulling her punches now.

"Right," Gwen said, chewing her lip. "Maggie, how did your mom meet Jack?"

"I don't know. We only have that one picture of them. But my mom went off the grid well before she had me. Managed to stay under the radar. The Cestis didn't know I existed until she died. Which was not long after I turned thirteen. Once my grandparents found me and registered my birth properly, they knew about me." Or so I assumed. "But I didn't show any power, so they left us alone."

"You didn't show power at thirteen? That's when it happens for witches, right?" Gwen asked.

"My mom bound my power," I said. "There was nothing for me to use."

Gwen was all wide pale blue eyes now. "To a demon. How did you survive?"

"As far as we can tell, it was because Maggie didn't consent herself. The demon used her power, but couldn't take her over. Whatever Sara did, the rite she used protected Maggie," Cassandra said.

"But your magic did come in?" Gwen asked.

"When I met Damon, I got a chip to help him with a job. We think the chip changed my energy signature enough to somehow break the bond. Like Cassandra said, we don't know anything about the binding, or how my mom did it, so we don't know why having a chip broke it."

Cassandra muttered something under her breath. My mother was fortunate the Cestis had never managed to get their hands on her.

Though, either way, I'd still have lost her. It was an old pain, but sometimes it still stabbed me like new. I bit it down and summoned a smile. "And that's enough of a history lesson. Cassandra, is your tea ready?"

Chapter Twenty

THE NEXT FEW days grew slowly less awkward as Gwen and I tried to adjust to our new reality.

True, she spent a fair bit of time gaming or in her room on her datapad, but she also started to talk about her life at boarding school, and I shared some of my time with my grandparents, both of us tentative in our overtures to navigate this new relationship. I could see her start to relax after all the bombshells. She started to talk about UC again, and played with Lianith, smiles replacing the tense expression she'd worn for the first twenty-four hours after we found out about Jack.

Cassandra had started to teach her the basics of energy fields and she'd taken to it quickly, though she found the whole color thing funny. She kept whispering colors to me whenever she met someone new. Though she'd looked pleased when she'd discovered my aura was blue like hers.

On Thursday, I offered to take her on a hike on one of the reestablished trails around the headlands and she accepted. Though she punctuated the walk with commentary about people's colors as we went.

"That guy's kind of khaki," she muttered at me when a tall, wiry, Asian guy jogged past us, his breathing loud and his face contorted in a grimace that suggested he wasn't enjoying the exercise.

"Probably hungover," I muttered back and she laughed, the smile making her eyes flash as bright as the blue of her running shorts. "Come on, let's keep going."

Moving while we talked seemed to make things go a little easier, and Gwen smiled with delight as we reached the highest lookout, with all of San Francisco and the bay spread out at our feet.

"It's a beautiful city," she said, looking down.

"It is. Not like it was, but you can't argue with this." I swept an arm out at the view.

"Earthquakes." She shivered, hugging her arms around herself. "I've never been in one."

"Well, if it makes you feel any better, the seismologists don't think there's likely to be another major earthquake here for quite some time. Probably several hundred years. Which is not to say that we won't get tremblers, but you get used to those." I didn't mention that I wasn't used to tremblers. She hadn't been in the Big One. She shouldn't have the same over-reaction to minor quakes that I did.

"Perhaps. It's not something we have to think about in England." She chewed her lip, staring down at the view as though she expected everything to start rattling any second.

She was right about that. England had to deal with rising seas and the warming of their famously cold climate, but I hadn't heard reports of earthquakes.

"The buildings are all much safer than they used to be," I said. "And the warning systems improve all the time."

"Why did you stay? Even though, you know…."

She meant my grandfather dying. We'd talked a little about that as well.

I gestured at the view again. "This is home. The first real home I ever had. I didn't want to abandon it when it was having a hard time."

Her expression turned sad. "I've never felt like that about a particular place. My aunt and I moved a few times when I was small, and then she dumped me at school. My room in her apartment in Canterbury always felt like something of an afterthought. I had a few things there, but not many. And I only stayed with her a few weeks a year."

I nudged her shoulder. "Well, once you decide what you want to do for school, you can put down some roots for a while. It doesn't have to be forever, but most of those programs are three or four years, at least. That's long enough to decide if you want to stay here." I waved a hand again, this time aiming at the view of the ocean. "There are tech hubs in other parts of the world, you know. This isn't your only option."

"No," she said, "but I want to learn from the best, and the best is here." She grinned at me. "You know that, right?"

"Yes. But I'm kind of biased when it comes to him."

"He's very smart, isn't he?" she said. "And hot, if you like older guys."

Older guys? I tried not to splutter, telling myself she was only twenty-two. To her, Damon was ancient. Like me. "I do," I gurgled eventually.

"I can tell. And he likes you right back, that's obvious," she grinned and held up a hand for a high five. "Go, big sis."

I laughed and slapped her hand. "I'm no slouch in the brain department myself, and I'm guessing neither are you, if you've got the marks to get into one of these programs."

"We'll see," she said. "I've been trying to study up on some things Yoshi told me about. Things move quickly in the tech world. Everything I learned before is out of date."

"You'll catch up soon enough." The sun was starting to lower slightly. It would be less fun navigating our way back down in darkness. Besides, after the exercise, my stomach was growling.

"We should get back," I said and started the descent.

Damon was sitting on the bed when I came out of the bathroom wrapped in a towel, once again blessing the luxury of high-tech showers. The steam and hot water had revived me after such a long hike.

"You're home early," I said, suddenly feeling even better.

"Wanted to see how you were doing." He leaned back on the bed, studying me appreciatively. "How did it go?"

"Yeah, it was good, I think. It's becoming easier for both of us."

"Great." He nodded his head toward the door. "There was some mail for you. A messenger brought it to the gate. I left it on your desk."

"Package?" I asked. I did get the odd delivery. Packages from clients and office supplies and that kind of thing. I'm sure if I asked, Damon would get Amy to magically restock my office as she did his, but this was my business still. I paid the bills.

"No, an envelope. Are you expecting any documents?"

Not many people sent actual mail these days. There were a few who stuck to traditions like cards on birthdays and celebrations. Cassandra sent Christmas cards, but she didn't do it for all the other holidays. It was probably an invite to a charity lunch or something. I got them regularly since Damon and I had gone public. So far, I always declined and Damon made a donation instead. Which is probably what they wanted, more than dealing with little old me who didn't have the kind of wealth they were interested in.

"Thanks, I'm going to go work for a bit before dinner, unless you want me for something."

"Always." His eyes went hot. "But you have to work. And so do I."

Darn. I should have dropped the towel when I first spotted

him. But now I'd have to wait. "Any news?" I asked, wandering into the walk-in closet to grab clean clothes.

"Cassandra rang earlier. They've confirmed the Wheatley on the database isn't a real person."

"So that's another point for Team Jack then," I said, emerging with the clothes. I dropped them onto the bed and sat next to Damon.

He slid an arm around my shoulders. "Seems like it."

I sighed. "Fine, I'll see you for dinner."

I dressed and marched down to my office, trying to recapture the happy buzz of hiking endorphins to chase away the small ribbon of ick the confirmation had given me. It was silly. I knew it was Jack. Had known it since I'd first seen the photo.

The envelope was on my desk, as Damon had said. Nothing special about it. Bigger than the usual invite and the paper was office supply yellow not fancy white or cream. Maybe a formal notification from the DNA database or something? I didn't know if they sent a confirmation by mail. There was no return address. Just a printed address label with my name and the address.

I tore the edge and pulled out the contents without thinking and found myself staring at a photograph of Gwen and me on the hike.

What the fuck?

I nearly dropped the photo. But instead, I made myself turn it over.

You did not tell me you had a guest. U.

This time I did drop the photo. Or flung it away from me. *Usuriel* was sending me photos?

Oh, crap. Usuriel knew about Gwen.

I grabbed the photo and headed for Damon.

He came to his feet when he saw my face. "Something wrong?"

I waved the picture. "Usuriel's still watching me."

"What?" He grabbed the photo. "This is today?"

"Yes. He knows Gwen's here." I'd known he'd find out sooner or later. I just didn't count on it being sooner.

Damon's face darkened. "Well, he can't get to her here."

"I don't know that he wants to."

He held up the photo. "If he doesn't, why does he have people following you?"

I waved a hand in frustration. "How am I supposed to know? I'm not the Lord of the Nichtkin."

"I know." He tossed the photo back onto the desk, but I got the feeling he wanted to tear it to pieces. "I hate this."

"Trust me, you don't hate it more than me." We both stared down at the photo. All my happy endorphins had vanished.

"So, what do you want to do?" Damon asked after a minute, his voice calmer.

"Ignore it. Anything else seems like unhelpful escalation. I'll tell Cassandra."

"Are you going to tell Gwen?" Damon asked, not disagreeing.

"No. She's just starting to settle in. Let's leave it for now. Can you put this somewhere she won't stumble across it? And ask Amy to hold any mail that might come for Gwen? We should make sure Usuriel doesn't send one to her."

"Yes and yes. I'll put this in the safe," he said. Something in his tone suggested he'd like to lock me away in a safe, too. I had half a mind to let him.

Worrying about Usuriel and Jack made it hard to focus on work. On Friday, I found myself checking the security logs and the camera feeds, instead of concentrating on what I was supposed to be doing. Just before twelve, I gave up and went to find Gwen.

She was in the game room lying back in one of the game chairs, headset on, eyes closed, engrossed in whatever she was doing.

I hesitated on the threshold. Opportunity for sisterly bonding, or should I give her space? I didn't know, but blowing up shit in a game might make me feel better.

I crept across the room and slid into the chair next to hers. She didn't react, which told me she was deep in the game.

I put my wrist against the control panel.

:CONTACT:

The foyer formed around me. "Madge, I'm do-not-disturb for an hour. Unless Damon calls."

"Of course, Maggie," came the reply.

Good. I didn't want to be interrupted if I could avoid it. Not when our sister time had been going smoothly. I waved a hand to summon the menu, delving into the admin system to see what game Gwen was playing.

Serenity Falls. Again. It seemed to be turning into her favorite. Fine with me. Better than Archangel. Which I still avoided. Too many memories of my demon.

And we were doing well in *Serenity Falls.* We'd fallen into a rhythm working together without having to try too hard. She was more impulsive than I was, but I chalked that up to her being younger and less experienced. I knew more about the pitfalls in the game. She was still exploring. Which she did in a systematic and thorough way that reminded me of, well, *me.*

Maybe there was something in this genetics business after all.

Though I was less certain of that every time I watched her running on the treadmill before breakfast. I mean, I ran, too, but I did it so I could make it through my lessons with Callum without puking. Gwen enjoyed it. She even sang along to the songs she got Madge to pump through her earphones. And sounded good doing it.

I was happy if I could keep my breathing mostly under control. I'd chase endorphins in other ways. The naked-Damon-involved kind of ways.

I tracked down Gwen's location in the game, but hesitated again. What if she thought I was being too try-hard? We were still strangers, even though we were sisters, and there was still distance between us. Suddenly uncertain, I procrastinated for a moment, and pulled up my messages.

I didn't keep in contact with many of the gamers I'd known through Nat anymore, but I played with Benji and some of the other Righteous developers every so often and hung out with Lizzie watching Zee train.

Damon, Lizzie and Zee wouldn't use game messages to get hold of me, but some of the Righteous crew might. I'd dropped them a note before all the nonsense with Ajax and Jack had come up, telling them I'd be beta testing *Infinite Rise* and there'd been a trail of messages ever since.

I checked the latest chat in those, added my two cents and then ran my eye over the short list of other messages. A couple of administrative things from the system and one message request. From someone I didn't know. Interesting. My profile was private. Though, I wasn't impossible to get to. No one was truly unreachable if you wanted to invest enough time and effort.

The username was Night&Mirrors, I snorted to myself. Gamers had been around for a long time, and yet their ability to pick silly usernames still amused me. Gwen's was BritDont-Quit33. Damon's was simply Righteous when he gamed publicly. At home we used our names. The status bubble next to Night&Mirrors showed they were currently online. I flicked open the message.

I would like to talk to you.

No signature. Just the one line.

I snorted again, preparing to consign it to the depths of the spam filter. Then something pinged in my brain.

Night&Mirrors. Usuriel's territory was sometimes called the Court of Mirrors.

It couldn't be, could it? Surely *Usuriel* wasn't gaming?

I mean, he could, of course. Callum did, and no doubt Usuriel could put his hands on tanai who could explain to him how to game and get him whatever equipment he wanted, barring a chip. But what was he doing in the game and, more to the point, how did he find me?

My first instinct was to disengage and get the hell out of there. But that would leave Gwen logged in while Usuriel was online. It wouldn't take me long to pull her out, but the Fae moved fast and a few seconds might be all the time he needed.

But he hadn't approached Gwen. He'd approached me.

What the hell did he want? Surely his charming photo had been enough to let me know he was still watching. I tried to figure out his angle, dialing down the sensory feedback to my avatar so the instinctive fear died down to unease, letting me focus.

While I was hesitating, another message pinged.

> The system informs me that you are online. I would like to talk.

Well, that was certainly arrogant enough to be Usuriel.

> Who is this?

The response came almost instantly.

> Lord of the Night.

> Lord Usuriel?

> Is there another Lord of the Night?

I rolled my eyes so hard I risked spraining my eyeballs. Arrogance at its finest. Damon might pull his master of the universe attitude at times to get things done, but he didn't tip over into outright arrogant. He didn't think he was better than other people.

Usuriel, on the other hand, did. But if he wanted to talk, in-game might be safer than in person.

Yes, he could probably use magic here, but he could hardly lock me in. He might have a viddeck, but I doubted he'd figured out Jack's nasty little trick. Callum knew how to get out of it, but he didn't know how the system was locked down in the first place.

I thought fast. I didn't want to join Usuriel in a game. Cerridwen had managed to get someone to plant a summoning in a game. I didn't want to end up under another compulsion, forcing me to meet Usuriel wherever he was hiding.

But here, on Damon's home system, I had access to quarantined environments that I controlled completely. I sent Madge a request to try to identify the user of the account and pulled up a new sterile test space. Those weren't connected to anything else, other than a quarantined server, and they had multiple levels of firewalls and security around them.

The test space formed around me, another plain white box, only differentiated from the foyer by the fact I used a different, less-stark shade of white for the walls. I double-checked all the security and sent Usuriel an invite before I lost my nerve.

I'd barely taken a breath when he materialized on the other side of the small room.

His avatar wore a long black velvet coat over tight leather pants and a black T-shirt that had enough sheen that it was probably supposed to be silk. The hair was lighter than it had been at Decker's, but still not as light as in the realm. And the face was handsome, but not alarmingly so. The eyes, while dark, almost startlingly so against the blond, were not fully black. Definitely trying to pass as human.

Had he been interacting with humans in the game?

I tightened my grip on my mental shields. Just because he looked more human, didn't mean it was safe to treat him as though he was.

"Lord Usuriel," I said, politely.

He nodded. "Maggie Lachlan."

Nerves prickled down my spine. This could be anyone. Another Fae. Someone sent by Usuriel. A tanai related to the Nichtkin. "All right," I said, "if it's really you, prove it. Tell me something that only you would know."

"I know what it's like to kiss you," he said.

I glared at him. "You're not the only man who knows that, my lord, and if you are hoping for a civil conversation, I suggest you think of something else."

"You parted my shields in the realm," he said in a low rumble of a voice. It was part annoyed, part…alluring.

Ick. I slammed my shields down harder. If he thought he could sway me with his Fae charm or whatever the hell you called his particular brand of pushing past unearthly toward creepy but still somehow enticing beauty.

But he knew about what I'd done to his shields. The only people who knew the details of what I'd done in the realm were people I'd trust with my life not to share them. And I doubted that Usuriel had shared the story. He wouldn't want any Fae to know that a mere human had beaten his power, however briefly. That would be a blow to his status.

"Okay," I said, "let's assume it's you. What did you want to talk to me about?"

"You did not tell me you had a guest," he said, taking a step closer.

I stiffened and thrust out a hand. "Stay right where you are. Also, you did not ask, my lord."

His eyes narrowed. "The little tanai you stole from me."

"I didn't steal her from anyone. We had a deal and I fulfilled it. Everything fair and in accordance with the contract. Despite you trying your best to wriggle your way out of it." I was two seconds away from booting him out. But I wanted to know how much he knew about Gwen. "So I'm not sure why she's of any interest to you. Or why you are having us followed for that matter."

"I told you I would be watching."

Great, so he was stalking me, not Gwen. If he was telling the truth.

"I am merely curious as to why she is no longer in London. I would have thought your Cestis there would have been taking care of her."

"She's a grown woman. She can go wherever she wants."

"So she came here?"

"She's interested in a career in game design," I said, hoping I wasn't revealing too much. "San Francisco is the best place in the world for that."

"And your Damon Riley is helping her?"

"She's staying with us while she makes some decisions." That was noncommittal.

"Kind of you to open your home to a stranger."

"Is kindness such an odd concept to you, my lord? Humans do not always think of obligations and favors as the Fae do. Sometimes we merely do what is right."

"Foolish," he muttered.

"Perhaps. But Gwen is not your concern. She is none of the Fae's concern. Period."

"She seems to be nobody's concern, other than yours," Usuriel said. "Did her father disown her, too?"

I went still. Was he asking or did he know something about Jack? "That's Gwen's business, not yours," I said firmly. "But now, you know she's here and that should be the end of it. You have no claim on her that I am aware of, my lord. So unless you want me to involve Lady Cerridwen in this matter, I suggest you leave us alone."

"I am entitled to protect my people."

"Neither Gwen nor I are a threat to your people."

"That is for me to decide."

"Within the realm, perhaps. Your authority ends once you step through the door."

"She is tanai."

"But not of your family." I said firmly. "Unless you are making a claim otherwise? Is her mother one of yours?"

His mouth flattened. "No. Whoever her mother is, she has not made herself known."

And looking at Gwen, it was hard to believe she came from one of the Nichtkin. Usuriel's illusions aside, I had no doubt whatsoever I'd never seen his real face. "This conversation is going in circles, my lord. And I have other business."

He scowled. "You are here in one of these game worlds. You cannot be so busy."

"My work involves these game worlds. The same cannot be said for you."

"I grew curious after your adventure in my realm. About what you and your Damon Riley do. It is like a dream of a kind and I rule dreams and nightmares."

Yeah, not creepy at all. "So you got someone to teach you to game?"

"I have not spent all my time locked up in the realm, Maggie. The door here was closed, but others were open and I visit your world often enough. There are tanai who are mine. It was not difficult to find one to show me this thing."

Thankfully, I hadn't been anywhere near a public game system since we'd returned from the UK. And Damon had done only that one exhibition game at Decker's.

A dumb part of my brain suggested I should try locking him in here. Find out if he, too, could leave a game without needing a kill switch. I squished it hard. No sharing secrets with the scary Fae lord with a chip on his shoulder. "Well, it's nice to have a hobby."

My brain caught up with my previous thought. I hadn't been gaming, but Gwen might well have. She could use her datapad to link up to the public game networks. Or had she asked Damon for a link? The account we'd made for her didn't have access to anything sensitive. But if Gwen had been gaming…had Usuriel been watching her? Maybe even before she came to San Francisco?

So many questions. None of them I was willing to ask because he would want something in return.

"You do not spend much time in the game. At least, not where you can be found."

I raised an eyebrow. "As you can imagine, Damon protects what is his as well."

"Your guest on the other hand, is here often."

Fuck. He *had* been spying on Gwen. "How do you know that?"

"There was quite a stir when she returned from the realm. And there are those who remember her from before she came to us. It was not hard to find her."

In other words, someone she'd known at university or one of the tanai she'd met had sold her out to Usuriel.

Charming. I cursed them mentally, wishing I could turn them all into frogs. Or bugs. I was going to have to talk to her about staying off the public links for a while. And about whether her username was from before she went into the realm. And about Usuriel, because she'd need a good reason to not go onto the links when she was probably trying to build some networks and meet people who gamed here.

"She has been talking to someone in game. Quite often. Especially the last few days."

I bristled. He shouldn't know that. Unless whoever had helped him find Gwen was helping him poke around in places he shouldn't necessarily have access to. I was going to do my best to find out which tanai had helped him. And then hand them over to Mitch. "How do you know that?"

He shrugged. "Perhaps she is not as security conscious as you and Damon."

"Well, she's allowed to talk to people." I used my chip to access the menu and start a search for links between Gwen's account and Usuriel's. And to download the activity on hers. If Usuriel was telling me this, he thought he had a reason.

"This person sought her out."

"That happens, too." I didn't point out he was doing a fine line in stalking himself.

"I do not think they are who they are pretending to be. Their account has no history of other activity in other games. It was created recently."

"How recently?" I really needed to find his source.

"On your Monday this week. Late in the day."

The day I'd received my notification from the database. The day Jack would have, too. Telling him Gwen was back in the world—assuming he'd known she'd been out of it. Crap. I tried to keep the reaction off my face, but Usuriel wasn't fooled.

"Not so sanguine, now?" he said. "I know something else happened that day. A few hours before the account was made."

I gave him a flat stare. "If you're waiting for me to ask you what, you'll be waiting a while. I have no desire to be in your debt. So you can tell me or not." I sent a few more inquiries though my chip, trying to see if I could slip into the back of Usuriel's account. Usuriel might be a Fae lord, but I was the freaking queen of tech even before I'd met Damon, and working with Damon had only taught me how to be even better. And sneakier. I doubted Usuriel or whoever was helping him could get around me.

"May I share an image with you?"

Better than sending it through the mail like an old-fashioned stalker. I triple-checked the security on the space, deploying every defense the system had. Bad things could be hidden in image files. "Go ahead," I said, hoping I wasn't taking a gamble I was going to lose.

An image blinked into view a few feet from me, hanging in the air. It was somewhat grainy, but not so much that I couldn't recognize Jack. At a recharge stop. Like the ones that had replaced gas stations up and down the interstates. The background was too fuzzy for me to make out any identifying features. "Where was this taken?"

"New Mexico, I believe."

Fuck. Too close for comfort. And right next to Mexico. Which still had a border less tightly controlled than the one we shared with Canada. Jack was smart enough to know Damon would be watching the airports and ports here. But he couldn't cover every entry point to the country. I grabbed a copy of the image before Usuriel could snatch it away and shoved it into a secure storage file, locking it down. "And it's from Monday?" Mitch's team could verify that later.

"Yes. That is Jack Miller, is it not?" Usuriel asked.

"It is," I admitted.

"And you cannot be foolish enough to claim he does not present a threat."

"No." I gritted it out.

"So it is interesting, is it not, that on the day he is first seen back in this country, the account who sought Gwen out was also created. I don't know how you feel about coincidences, Maggie Lachlan, but I do not trust them."

Me either. Thank God I'd dialed back the feedback from my avatar or my hands would have been shaking. "You think Jack is talking to Gwen?"

"Perhaps." The eyes on his avatar darkened, as though his true nature was breaking through. I let my sight slide into the magic, trying to be subtle about it in case he was about to try something. There was the faintest hint of black smoke around the avatar, but nothing to suggest he was actively using magic. "Which makes me wonder, Maggie. Because we know he has been interested in you in the past. And your Damon. But why is he interested in her?"

Shit. Nope, this conversation was done. I killed the room and booted Usuriel from the system. I'd deal with the consequences of pissing him off later. Pausing only to trigger the admin version of Gwen's kill switch, too, I wrenched myself out of the game and sat up in my chair, breathing hard.

Gwen sat up with a start, confusion clear on her face at the sudden interruption. "Maggie? Do you need me? Damn, I was hoping you'd join me. I worked out how to get out of the game. You know, the way you told me Callum can?"

I blinked at her, my brain not quite catching up. "You did?"

"Yes, want me to show you?"

I did but it would have to wait. "Not now. We need to talk to Damon."

"Isn't he at work?"

Crap. Yes. He was. "I'll call him. Or Cassandra."

She was starting to look worried. "Did something happen?"

"Don't get mad, but I need to ask you a question."

"O-kay."

"Your username. Is it one you used before? Before you went into the realm, I mean?"

"Yes." She looked confused. "I never closed my account and I was still paying for a link. I never intended to stay in the realm so long, so I didn't shut down anything before I went in. I was in Halls, so I didn't have a lease or a car or any other big regular expenses."

I stomped on the big sister urge to lecture her about financial responsibility. It would be the pot calling the kettle black. At her age I'd signed up for a gym at one point in a fit of Nat-urged-on enthusiasm. I'd taken classes about a month, then ignored it for about three years before I cancelled my membership. And presumably her university would have stopped taking money when they decided she wasn't coming back. I wondered how long that had taken? Had anyone raised an alarm? Or had the tanai handled it somehow?

"And have you been talking to anyone from the public links in game?"

"I've played a few sessions with someone. I met them in the game. Is there a problem?"

"Maybe. I'm not sure how to tell you this but Lord Usuriel has been in San Francisco."

The color drained from her face and she shrank back into the chair, her skin looking like chalk against the dark leather. "What does he want?"

I had to avoid telling her Usuriel had asked about her. Sticking to Jack was less likely to completely freak her out. "He got interested in Jack after we left the realm. He found out who we were after, somehow. And I think he sees Jack as a threat because of the demon connection. He's been looking for him, too. But he hadn't found him. But today, he sent me a photo of Jack. He said it was taken in New Mexico. Earlier this week."

"Mexico?"

"New Mexico." I jerked my head roughly in the direction of the state. I couldn't expect Gwen to have a solid understanding of American geography. I didn't know all the counties or whatever they were in England. "It's two states east from here. Along the border."

"So Jack's in the States?"

Apparently it was possible to turn paler than chalk. Or greener, maybe. "Hey, take a breath."

She ignored me. "He's in the US?"

"Seems that way. If the photo's real."

"Is he coming here?" Her voice was high, too breathy.

"I don't know. But breathe. This person you're talking to in the game. When did you meet them?"

"Tuesday. I went to the supply market on that weird desert crossing level and we started chatting."

"So the day after Meredith ran your DNA?"

"Ye-es. What, you think it's Jack?"

"I don't know. Have they told you anything about themselves?" No point asking about what avatar they used. Avatars could resemble anyone or anything.

"Not really. They're into old sci-fi movies, said they liked to cook and hike. They—he—seemed nice."

Male, then. Dammit. Though, again, there were gamers who didn't play their biological sex. "He hasn't asked to meet?"

"He mentioned hanging out at one of the clubs one night, but nothing definite."

"If he tries to firm something up, put him off. No meeting him. Not until we know what's going on." I sent a message to Maia, asking her to pick us up. Jake replied, reminding me it was Maia's day off. "Jake's coming to get us."

"Where are we going?" Gwen asked.

"To see Cassandra. Maybe Cerridwen can work out what Usuriel's up to."

"It sounds like he's being helpful," she said tentatively. As though she couldn't quite believe it.

"Fae don't just help. Or rarely. So let's—" I stopped as both of our datapads chimed near identical alarms. I checked mine. "Crap, I forgot you have your follow-up with Meredith today." I chewed my lip. "Do you want to reschedule?"

"You can talk to Cassandra and Damon while I'm doing whatever needs to be done there, can't you?". She held out her arm. "The surgical shield is starting to lift. And it itches. I'm dying to take it off. Or get a new one."

"How itchy?" I asked. Hopefully it wasn't another allergy. But surely she'd have mentioned it by now.

"Enough to be annoying. But I feel fine otherwise. Still, Jack can't know I'd be going to the hospital. Let alone with you."

I wasn't so sure about that. But if we took Jake, it should be fine. We could head to Cassandra's after, or meet her at the Riley campus, which was even more heavily guarded than the house. And I could understand Gwen wanting to know if her arm was healing okay.

"Okay. Hospital, then Cassandra. Let's go."

Chapter Twenty-One

"Don't worry, everything is going to be fine." I said to Gwen once we were on our way to the hospital. Jake had arrived in one of the security team's Jeeps. Fine by me. They were as well armored as the cars and, because they didn't have the dividers between the front and back seats, felt less formal. Even though Jake still insisted we both sit in the back. I'd retrieved the photo file from the game and forwarded it to Damon, Mitch and Cassandra. So far, no one had called me back.

"Saying something doesn't necessarily mean it's true."

"Jack hasn't managed to get anywhere near Damon or me since his first attempt. He won't get to you. Damon's team will be checking all the security links they can get their hands on. The city feeds, everything. If he shows his face in public, they'll find him."

"What if he's not wearing his face?" Gwen pointed out. "If he's a strong witch, he could alter his appearance, couldn't he?"

Well, crap. Yes. Jack was more than capable of that kind of illusion. One of his minions had imitated Yoshi at the tournament. "We can't rule it out. But you can't change things like retina scans or palm scans." At least I hoped you couldn't. "So he's not going to get very far anywhere with decent security. I know for a fact he's flagged on every Riley system there is. And Cassandra's house is warded against him, too." Lizzie and Zee had enough of a taste of Jack's magic when we'd fought him at my house to be able to add some specific wards against him.

Gwen chewed her thumbnail, staring at the back of Jake's head. She squinted in a way I was coming to recognize, before she muttered. "Orange."

She was right. Jake's aura was a clear sunny orange.

I smiled. As nervous tics went, aura checking was kind of cute. But if she was nervous, it was time to be the calm older sister. "Right, we can both sit here and stew for the next fifteen minutes or you can tell me how you got out of the game."

She stopped chewing. Straightened in her seat a little, looking glad of the distraction. "I kind of just…did?"

I snorted. "That's not that helpful. Explain to me what you were thinking about?"

"Well, you said Callum could do it. So I wondered if it was like moving things in the realm, or moving it around you."

"Like the Ways?"

"No, those are for long distances. Leaving the game isn't going far. And it's all in your head. A switch in your reality. From the game back to the real world."

Clear as mud. "So you moved yourself?"

A shrug. "Not exactly. I tried to see the energy fields in the game but I couldn't really get anything. But I could feel it around me. The way you can feel the magic in the realm—you can do that, can't you?"

"Yeah." It felt like an ocean of power, one waiting to send a tsunami to drown me. But for Gwen, being tanai, it would be different. Friendlier, perhaps. Or, at least, familiar.

"So, I felt it and I could feel where it was connected to me.

So I pushed at the connection and it…broke, I guess? It's hard to describe. But it worked. I was out of the game."

"You're sure you didn't use the kill switch?"

She nodded. "I'm sure. Well, as sure as I can be without a witness. I did it a few times and one time I put my arms inside my T-shirt so I couldn't hit the kill switch and it still worked."

Right. Wearing a headset, she'd have been thinking of hitting the physical switch on the chair. Not giving a mental command like you could with a chip. "Well, that's given me things to think about." My attempts had always focused more on breaking the illusion the game was creating in my brain, rather than my specific connection to the tech. Callum had never said anything about that. But maybe he did it differently.

"Does it help?" she asked, looking hopeful. Kind of like a student waiting to hear she got a good grade from her teacher. "I'm not sure how else to explain it."

I smiled. "It does. I'll have to try it for myself." I hadn't been practicing often since we'd returned from the realm. Callum had been busy, so we'd only managed a few hours of gaming. I should pin him down. Or try Gwen's approach.

Though I also wanted to see her with Callum, so he could test her magic from a Fae perspective. With what she'd managed to do with the game and the ease with which she'd picked up seeing the energy fields, I suspected Cassandra's assessment of Gwen's potential was correct.

I was still thinking about Gwen's approach when we reached the hospital. I accompanied Gwen up to see Meredith, who checked out her arm, pronounced herself satisfied with the progress and replaced the surgical shield with a fresh one. When she was typing up notes, Gwen leaned over and whispered, "Very green."

I laughed. It was true. Meredith's energy field was a soothing verdant green.

She also had good hearing. She stopped typing. "You can see my energy field?" she asked Gwen.

"Yes."

"Well, that's useful. But pay attention to whoever is teaching you. Magic isn't the same out here as in the realm."

"I'm following orders," Gwen said.

Meredith rolled her eyes. "Okay. We're done. You have an appointment in another week. We'll do some final tests and you'll be good to go. You might have a scar, of course."

"Scars are cool," I said. "She can make up stories about how she got it."

Gwen giggled. "Shark attack."

"And on that note, the two of you are free to get on with your day." Meredith politely waved us to her door. We made our way back down to the parking garage where Jake was waiting for us. Gwen kept coming up with new stories for a scar. My favorite was skiing accident while chasing a yeti.

I was still laughing about that when we started across the Bay Bridge. The silliness of it was a relief, but the reality that we were heading to Cassandra's to talk about Usuriel's news about Jack was starting to push aside the momentary reprieve. "Cassandra will probably have cookies," I said. "Or biscuits, you'd call them. What's your favorite flavor?"

Gwen didn't answer. I glanced sideways and realized she'd gone very still, staring at the back of Jake's head. I nudged her arm gently and when she looked round, raised an eyebrow at her.

Her eyes were wide, the color gone from her face. She mouthed something I couldn't quite make out.

"What?" I whispered sharply.

She nodded once in Jake's direction. "Not orange. *Blue*."

Blue? What? It took a few seconds for my brain to catch up. Jake's aura was orange. But auras didn't change color. So this wasn't Jake…it was someone else.

Someone with a blue aura. Like Jack….I reached for my

magic, but before I could think what to do in such close quarters, whoever it was twisted casually in his seat and tossed a handful of…glittering dust in our direction. I heard something I thought might be 'two for the price of one' as my vision dissolved in jagged sparking light before the darkness rose up and sucked me down into its depths.

I woke up to the sensation of someone lifting my arm. I jolted, but didn't move, as though my body didn't quite want to respond. I thrashed—or tried to—but barely managed to twitch. Fear ripped through me, clearing the remains of sleep and bringing the image of Jake and glittering dust back to me.

We'd been taken. And I was still affected by whatever it was that had been thrown at us. My head felt like it was bathed in acid, pain rippling from temple to temple in nasty waves that made my stomach heave. I clamped my jaw shut and forced my eyes open.

Jack Miller stood beside me, his hand clamped around my right wrist, though the sensation was oddly distant. He wore a Riley Security uniform. *Bastard.*

I tried again to move. My arm stayed right where it was. He smiled at me and I dropped my gaze, taking in my surroundings. A room. White walls, beige carpet. A beige door off to my right. A desk I could half see to my left. Light coming from behind me. A bank of windows? So, an office? The surface beneath me felt soft, but not like a bed. A sofa, maybe? I couldn't see more, because I couldn't turn my head.

Where the hell had he taken me? And what had he done with Gwen? And Jake?

"Awake are you?" Jack said, his tone perfectly conversational as though we were discussing the weather. "I imagine you don't feel so good. That particular cocktail is rough, but you should feel better in an hour or so. Not that it matters how you feel. It will decide what it wants to do with you once it's here. Maybe it will send you through to the one who wants you so much."

It? I tried to think through the pain. Nausea rolled over me again as I realized. A demon. He was talking about summoning a demon. Or a lesserkind. Not that a lesserkind was any better.

"Let me go and you might survive this," I snarled. My tongue felt thick in my mouth, so the words came slowly, stripped of the threat I intended.

"That's optimistic of you," he said. "But I think I'll take my chances. Now that I have my daughter, this will all be much easier."

Fuck. He'd just admitted it. I was suddenly grateful for the drug slowing my reactions, keeping them off my face. He was our father. Fury rolled through me, and I closed my eyes, not wanting him to see, wrestling it under control. He'd said daughter, not daughters. He didn't know about me. I had to use that. Keep the secret. Focus on Gwen.

He had Gwen. Bastard. I pushed the anger away and opened my eyes. I managed to move my head, enough to see more of the room. Definitely an office. But no sign of Gwen.

Where was she?

I had to think. An office building. Probably an abandoned one unless he owned it? There were plenty of industrial parks scattered around San Francisco and its surrounding cities that had never gone back into business after the Big One. Too many, in fact. It was one of the rebuilding projects Damon was still working on with the city consortiums.

Too many. Making us hard to find. And plenty of scope to stash Gwen somewhere that might not even be in the same building.

I swallowed. "Some father you are. What makes you think she'll want to have anything to do with you?"

He still looked unruffled, his pale blue eyes all ice, no

emotion. The same color as Gwen's, but hers were warm. Jack was cold to the core.

"It's not ideal, I'll admit. But she's not like you, Maggie. She hasn't got the Cestis at her beck and call, and she has no idea how to use her magic like a witch. I made sure of that from the start. Of course, this would have been easier if she hadn't decided to leave London, but what's done is done. She'll help me in the end, whether she wants to or not."

Help him what? Summon a demon? I stared at him, hoping he could feel the loathing. At least he didn't seem to have realized he was my father, too. Which could be bad for me. He'd have no compunction about killing me if he thought I was just an inconvenient witch.

I had to think. It took a huge amount of power to summon a demon. Could Jack manage it? He'd summoned imps. Was he strong enough to call a lesserkind. Who could then summon a demon. Not to mention take Gwen over. And with Gwen's magic, maybe Jack could manage to bring a demon through.

Fuck. We should have spent more time teaching her how to shield.

"You'll still die." I managed. "No one survives a demon. Not for long."

"Too many idiots try. I'm far from an idiot."

I would have laughed if he wasn't so terrifying. If he believed what he said, then he was insane, not just stupid. No point trying to reason with a crazy man. I had to play along and buy myself time to get us out of here.

I pictured my hand smashing into his nose, the way Callum had taught me, but my wrist barely twitched. What the *fuck* had he drugged me with? I had to move my wrist a certain way to activate the panic button in my chip. I tried again, failed, and bit back a curse.

Jack laughed. "Much as it's charming to see you again,

Maggie, I have places to be. And so do you." He held up a cuff in the hand not holding my arm.

I tried to jerk away, knowing what it was, but his grip and the drug or spell or whatever it had been held me motionless. "This will keep you quiet until I need you. If I do." He slid the cuff into place and snapped it closed.

Pain pulsed through my head, worse than before, and suddenly I was inside an unpleasantly familiar plain white room.

He'd locked me into a VR environment.

Again.

But this time, Jack didn't know I had a potential escape route. And I didn't want to let him suspect I wasn't as freaked out as I'd been the first time. I scrambled to my feet, cursing and demanding to be let out, just like I had then.

"Feel free to waste all that energy, darlin'." His voice boomed out of nowhere. "You'll be easier to handle in the end."

"Fuck off and die." I didn't have to fake that response.

No response. Had he gone? Was he watching? Pinky had freed me the last time I'd been locked in one of these things. He didn't know I didn't need the cuff removed this time. So he probably thought I would be stuck until he came for me.

I had no way of knowing. Unsurprisingly there was no response when I waved my hand to try and bring up a menu and only silence met my attempt to send an inquiry to the system through the chip.

Right. So it was free myself, or nothing.

But I had to be sure Jack was gone. So I would wait. Bide my time. Let the drug clear my system, though the lingering pain of being forced into the VR by the chip was now making it hard to tell if my headache was easing at all. I sank down to the floor, resting my head in my hands, breathing slowly. Let him think I was slumped there, despondent.

Instead I tried to push the pain away, move it outside my

shields. I knew little about healing, and was usually bad at what I'd tried, but it seemed to help a little. The pain felt more distant, leaving me room to think.

Jack said he needed Gwen, so presumably she wasn't in immediate danger. Well, not of him killing her. But when it came to demons, death wasn't the worst thing that could happen. So I had to try to thread the needle. Give Jack long enough to stop paying attention to me and for the drug to wear off more, but not long enough to let him hurt Gwen.

And hope he didn't have too many others helping him.

Demon summoning seemed to be a solitary activity. If you wanted the power a demon offered, you probably didn't want to share. Or were more than willing to stab anyone you convinced to help you to keep the power for yourself at the end.

Jack must have help to stay so well hidden for all this time. Not to mention getting back into the country. But even if he had minions, so to speak, I doubted there'd be many of them with him or he wouldn't have come for us himself.

I didn't have a weapon, but I could fight and I could sneak around like a pro thanks to Callum. So I'd cross the deal-with-minions bridge if I had to.

Besides, Damon would be looking for me. Once Cassandra realized we were late, she'd raise the alarm. Presumably Jack was smart enough to ditch the car, but that wouldn't stop Damon. He'd find me.

I couldn't afford to believe otherwise.

I started counting my breaths, waiting for the pain in my head to ease, soothing the coil of anger and fear in my gut. I'd deal with how I felt about knowing Jack was my father when we were all safely out of here. I could use the emotion for fuel, but it couldn't control me. I'd reached thirty minutes by the time the pain receded, time enough to focus, to dial into my magic and get ready to try to break out.

Hopefully no one was watching me. Jack had no reason

to think I could get free and if he was arrogant enough to think his cuff was enough and no one needed to be guarding me, then I was delighted to use his delusion against him.

I tested the simple way first, sending a disengage command to the system. Nothing. Which didn't surprise me.

Right. So we were going to do this the other way. And while I was sure that if I gave into my panic, I would be able to use the emotion to break myself free as I had in the past, Gwen's way—if I could use it—would be faster. And less draining.

Find the energy. Break the energy.

I closed my eyes again, focusing on the sensations around me. I could feel the hum of the game, the sensation of being in VR, familiar as breathing these days. I tried to feel my magic, to feel the energy I gave off. To see where the two connected.

There.

A thread. The faintest hint of connection hovering at my wrist.

See the energy, break the energy.

Here goes nothing.

I shaped my magic into a spike, much like I would if I was trying to attack the way Callum had been teaching me. And, taking a final breath, hoping I wasn't about to set fire to myself out in the real world, I stabbed the spike at the connection.

Pain. I bit my lip, determined not to scream. If someone was watching, I wasn't going to give myself away before I even got started.

The pain ebbed. I cracked my eyes open just enough to check where I was.

It had worked. I was back in the office.

Yeah, take that you arrogant asshole, I thought viciously. I tore the cuff off, then waited to see if anyone came bursting through the door. When they didn't after a few minutes, I sat up carefully.

My head throbbed like it was on fire. I waited it out, breathing slowly until it felt safe to risk turning my head to see where I was.

Yep, an office. Blandly corporate. The UV screens on the windows seemed to be mostly intact and there was still enough outside light to tell me that either only a few hours had passed, or I'd been out more than a day. Surely I'd be hungrier and thirstier if that was the case? I pushed to my feet, trying to get a better view out of the windows.

I'd been right about the abandoned office park part as well. The building I was in faced a row of what I had to assume were similar office-type buildings. The pavement of the parking lot was cracked in several places, weeds growing through it. The painted lines outlining each parking spot were mere suggestions, worn away by weather and time.

There was nothing beyond the buildings to give me a clue where I was. Just more industrial-looking structures. No lights on in any of them. No cars anywhere. No sign of occupancy.

So, no immediate chance of help. Not that I wanted to drag innocent bystanders into this.

I flexed my wrist, activating the panic button in my chip. But I had no idea where I was or how long it might take Damon's team to find me. So I was rescuing my damn self. And my damned sister. I studied the sun again through the UV shields. Midafternoon. I was going to assume it hadn't been a full day. The room was cold, the air smelled damp and dusty, which suggested a recently revived cooling system. Which didn't help me figure out the time. But I was going with still Friday. After all, Jack hadn't summoned a demon yet. Or I'd be dead. Or enslaved.

He needed time to convince Gwen to help him.

I had to find her first.

So. I'd have a better chance if I had a weapon. Or two. I

turned my head slowly, not wanting to set off the headache again. There were shelves on one wall, but they were empty. There was also a small filing cabinet in a corner, but its drawers were half open and I could see they were empty as well.

Which left the desk. Two closed drawers, one narrow, one deep.

I pushed myself up, wobbled slightly, clenched my jaw and crossed the room. The drawers slid open smoothly. The top one was empty. Not so much as a paperclip.

But the second one…the second one held…my backpack? I stared at it blankly. Was Jack that arrogant? So sure of his cuff holding me that he didn't even bother to ditch my belongings?

Crazy, I reminded myself. Crazy and convinced he was winning. A dangerous combination, but one I could use against him. He thought I wouldn't be able to get out. More fool him.

I eased the backpack out of the drawer and pushed the tiny spot underneath one of the pocket flaps where a panic button was sewn between the layers of fabric. I pressed it, just in case the one in my chip hadn't worked. My datapad was gone, so was the small penknife I kept stashed in one of the inner pockets, suggesting Jack wasn't entirely stupid. As I searched through the backpack, Cerridwen's bracelet rattled against one of the clips.

Oh, good. Jack hadn't taken that either.

I sent a small burst of power into it. The Fae equivalent of a panic button. Might as well summon all the cavalry. Particularly if Jack was planning to bring demonkind to this party. That done, I shoved it into the pocket of my jeans and kept rifling through the pack.

I hadn't been carrying a gun, but as far as I could see, Jack hadn't taken anything besides my datapad and knife. The tiny torch, a bottle of ibuprofen, a few protein bars and the small pouch I used to carry around a lip balm, Band-Aids, gum, and other basic necessities. I dry swallowed two of the ibuprofen, hoping they'd help chase away the last of the headache, forced myself to take a bite of a protein bar, and reached for the hard case I carried my sunglasses around in. The one with the secret section under the lid where I hid my lockpicks.

I slid them into the pocket of my jeans, debated whether I should bring the backpack with me, but slid it back into the drawer. I didn't need extra weight. I crossed to the door, which only had a standard mechanical lock that had been reversed so the nib was on the outside, leaving me with the keyhole.

Perfect. I paused by the door, listening and trying to breathe as quietly as possible. There was no sound at all.

I stretched my senses farther, feeling for magic, reaching for all the skills I'd built in my sessions chasing Cerridwen's illusions around the city. I knew the feel of demon magic now. Could sense it several blocks away. And I doubted Jack had found himself a lair that big.

There. Off to my right. Magic. Bad magic. Greasy, slimy, just-plain-wrongness. I made quick work of the lock with the picks and slipped out through the door. It went against all my instincts, but I headed toward the magic.

The corridor was dimly lit, half the lights dark. Fine by me. I pulled a ward around myself and made my way slowly down the rows of offices until I came to an intersection with another corridor. I glanced down to the left. An exit sign glowed faintly at the end of it.

I took half a step toward it before I stopped. As tempting as it was to get the hell out of there, to see if I could find help, I wasn't going to leave Gwen here.

Help is coming, I told myself firmly and turned back in the other direction.

I made it about twenty feet before someone stepped out of a doorway behind me and clapped a hand over my mouth, dragging me back into the room.

Chapter Twenty-Two

I struggled, kicking and flailing and felt a flash of satisfaction when whoever had me grunted in pain before a loud *"STOP STRUGGLING"* rang in my head.

"Callum?" I went limp with relief.

"Who else?" His hands wrapped around my upper arms, keeping me upright.

"I thought you must be one of Jack's thugs."

"I am not. So stay still and I will let you go. Be quiet though. Can you stand?"

I nodded and after a few seconds he let me go, stepping back. I whirled, not believing it was really him. Callum, dressed in his hunting leathers, looking darkly deadly, was the best thing I'd seen all day. I grinned idiotically, resisting the urge to hug him. Until I saw he wasn't alone. Usuriel stood a few feet behind him, almost blending into the darkness except for the pale gleam of his hair. He, like Callum, was dressed in black leather. His seemed to suck the light out of the air.

My smile died.

"What is he doing here?" I shot Callum a glare.

He scowled back. *"Supposedly helping."*

"Why?"

"I am not entirely sure. Nevertheless, he is here and given what I can sense in this place, that is a good thing."

"It's rude to converse when others can't hear you, wolf," Usuriel drawled.

I ignored him but switched to normal conversation. "How did you find me?"

"Your bracelet. Cerridwen sensed you were in trouble and reached out to Cassandra. Damon had already called her. His team noticed the car you were in taking an unusual route. And then its tracker was cut off."

"Are they here too?"

"Damon and his…forces are securing the perimeter. The Lady Cassandra and her colleagues are elsewhere in the building. Or they should be."

"Gwen's here," I said. "We have to find her."

"We have to stop whatever that magic is," Usuriel said, tipping his head in the direction I'd been headed. "No one is safe if it continues."

"I think Jack is trying to summon something."

"Yes. And his protections are strong. But I do not feel the little tanai with him. She was that way," Usuriel said, jerking his head left.

I stared at him. "You can sense her?"

"I remember what her magic feels like. I know the magic of everyone who has spent time in my realm." He smirked, reminding me *I* had spent time in his realm. "She used it not long ago."

"Jack locked me into a VR again," I said to Callum. "He might have done the same to her. If he has a way to make it work with a headset. She told me she worked out how to get out, but I don't know if she can do it every time. Or if Jack's watching her. He wasn't watching me. But he said he wanted her, not me. Wants to use her in his summoning."

"I would imagine he's quite focused on completing his

working," Usuriel said. "Which does not give us long to stop him. Depending on what ritual he has chosen."

Callum nodded. "I agree. Jack is the target we need to deal with. Damon's men have been tasked with finding whoever Jack brought with him. There do not seem to have been many of them."

"Well, it's hard to find a bunch of nutjobs who all think playing with demons is fun," I said, trying to sound as though a large part of me wasn't screaming inside at the thought of facing another demon. "How do you want to do this?"

"You should make your way outside, find Damon's men," Callum said. "Get to safety."

"That's not what you've been training me for."

"No, but this is more than you are ready for."

I scowled at him. "I fought a demon before."

"You cannot call lightning inside a building. Not without killing everyone else in the room. Usuriel and I have a better chance of stopping Jack. You should leave." Callum folded his arms across his leather-clad chest.

"I'm not leaving Gwen."

Usuriel raised a brow at this.

Callum looked resigned. "You are going to be stubborn about this, aren't you? Like you were in the realm?"

"She still needs help." He could say whatever he wanted, but I wasn't changing my mind. I had to change his, so we wouldn't waste time arguing. "It's her Jack wants, not me. He needs her somehow. We can't let him have her."

"What use does he have for an untrained tanai?" Callum asked.

Right. They didn't know Gwen was Jack's daughter. "Untrained makes her more vulnerable," I said. "Perhaps he thinks he can use her magic somehow to bring the demon through? Bind her, maybe?"

"He would need power over her for that," Usuriel said sharply. "A bond of magic…or blood." He stepped toward me. "What hold does he have over her? Did he do something in the game?"

Callum looked at him sharply. I cut him off before he could ask about the game.

"Not as far as I know. She admitted to talking to him. Or someone. I didn't have time to confirm who it was." God, had that only been this morning? "But they've never met. He couldn't have bound her without meeting her, could he? She didn't act like she was under a compulsion. And besides, he's a witch, not Fae. I don't even know if witches can do that."

"Witches can do many things," Callum muttered. "But we are wasting time." He turned to Usuriel. "Maggie is right. If Jack wants the tanai, freeing her might be the quickest way to thwart his plans."

"If he completes the summoning while we try, we will all pay the price," Usuriel objected.

"You two go after Jack, I'll find Gwen," I said.

"You will get yourself killed," Callum growled.

"Are you saying I'd be safer going with you to face a demon?"

He bared his teeth at me. "You should leave."

I opened my mouth to argue but a wave of slimy magic pulsed across the room, cutting off my words.

Usuriel and Callum both pivoted toward the magic, like hunting hounds sighting prey.

"Go," I said. "I'll find Gwen."

Callum turned back to me, mouth twisting.

"Go. Stop Jack. I'll be fine." That was probably a big fat lie but maybe, being Fae, he wouldn't realize.

"She is right, s'ealg oiche," Usuriel said. "We should hurry."

For once he was on my side. I started to move back to the door, wanting to get out of there before he changed his mind.

Callum caught my wrist. "Wait."

I tugged at his grasp. "I should go."

Magic pulsed over me and I gasped. He stepped back. "Some strength for your ward. Now go."

I ran, every nerve straining as I headed in the direction Usuriel had told me to go, searching for Gwen's magic, hoping like hell he wasn't somehow double-crossing us. Whatever Callum had done had strengthened more than my wards. The lingering effects of Jack's drug and breaking out of the VR had vanished. As I worked my way through a confusing tangle of interconnecting corridors, I caught glimpses of the grounds outside the building, a fleeting impression of a weedy stretch of grass sloping down to a footpath in one spot and more empty parking spots in another. No glimpse of anyone else. If Damon's security guys were out there, they were doing a damned good job staying out of sight.

I pulled my attention back to my surroundings. Good guys out there, but bad guys in here. Concentrate on them. And Gwen.

A noise up ahead brought me skidding to a halt, arms flailing to stop myself from crashing into the wall. It sounded like something thudding against a surface. Like someone trying to force a door open.

I set off again, scanning the door handles and straining to hear more. I knew I'd found the right one when I spotted one with the lock on the outside, like mine had been. But that made life easy. No need to pick a lock. A quick check for wards—clear, thank God—and I yanked the door open. Gwen nearly fell through, tumbling into me.

I caught her and pulled her close for a hug, feeling her trembling against me, breath shaky. I gave her thirty seconds, then pushed her gently back, to look at her. "Are you okay?"

Her face was tear-stained, her eyes bloodshot, the pupils

wide with fear. Her hair looked wild as though she'd been pulling on it.

"Yes. It was Jack. Jack's here. He woke me up, but I couldn't move. He said something about behaving like a good daughter. You were right, he's an asshole." Fury briefly replaced the fear in her eyes. "Then he put a headset on me and he…he locked me into VR. Like you said. But I got out. Thank God. That was awful." She swallowed hard, stopping her stream of words. "But I couldn't open the door. Where are we?"

"I'm not sure. But help is here, we'll be fine." I tried to sound sure about that, but if Callum and Usuriel didn't stop Jack, we were all probably dead.

Don't think about that. We were going to make it out. And I would be making sure Gwen learned how to pick locks, and half a hundred other things to keep her safe, once we did.

"Help? The Cestis?"

"Yes. And Callum. And…Lord Usuriel." I didn't want her to panic and try to run if Usuriel suddenly appeared. "They're here to stop Jack."

"Good." She nearly spat the word. "He's…crazy. He was talking about demons and there was this thing…with him."

I froze. A thing. "An imp?"

She shuddered. "No. Bigger. It was awful. Kind of gray looking. Gray and wrong. It wanted to touch me, but Jack said 'no'. It didn't seem happy."

Fuck, fuck, fuck. A lesserkind. If lesserkind were already involved we were in deep shit. New plan. Get the fuck out of the building.

This corridor ended in a dead end, but I remembered the exit sign I'd seen before Callum had grabbed me. "We'll figure out what it was later," I said. "We're leaving. This way."

I half-dragged Gwen after me as I broke into a run, trying not to sprint flat out in deference to her shorter legs. She kept pace with me easily enough, making me vow to copy her more dedicated approach to time on the treadmill.

I retraced my path as best I could, trying to keep the feel of the demon magic on my left, so we were heading away from it. I'd faced a demon on my own once. I knew damned well I'd only survived through desperation and pure luck. And it had cost me the closest thing I'd had to a sister at the time. Nat's death for my life.

I wasn't going to make the same mistake. This time, I would save my sister and let the experts deal with the demon.

But all my good intentions came to a screeching halt when we turned into what I thought was the final corridor to find a lesserkind blocking our path.

Gwen's cry of shock cut off as I shoved her behind me, raising my hands. I had to fight to keep them steady as the lesserkind's acrid rotting scent, worse than a thousand imps, hit me and it blinked void-black eyes at me. Those eyes were pure evil. Pure malice. They made Usuriel's seem perfectly human.

"Not so fast, witch." The words were rough, the s's hissing faintly over a mouthful of sharp black teeth. Not exactly like the one who'd controlled Ajax. But similar enough. Taller than an imp, built more on human lines, but every angle and curve of its body subtly wrong even without the gray skin and lack of hair.

Bile rose in my throat, sick terror flooding through me.

No. I had to save Gwen. No time to be scared.

Could I kill it? There was a chance. With enough fire, a lesserkind would burn. But I didn't yet know how to call the kind of white-hot fire the Cestis had used to deal with Ajax's. But I reached for my magic anyway. If I didn't try, we would die.

"Foolish witch." It lifted a hand, its claws glistening like an oil slick under the flickering lights. "You cannot kill me."

"I can try," I said.

"Not unless you want the girl to die, too," the lesserkind said. Its mouth turned up in something that couldn't be called a smile, but was viciously triumphant. Was it bluffing? I risked a glance over my shoulder, keeping my hands up.

A second lesserkind, stood behind Gwen, holding a jagged black knife to her throat.

Her eyes were wide and frantic as she gagged against the hand over her mouth.

Cold terror swept through me. I turned back, trying to stay calm. "You can't hurt her. Jack wants her."

"Jack wants a witch. You will do. Your power is known."

"My power is mine," I snarled.

"We shall see. But if you want the small one to live, then you will come with me, witch. No tricks."

Gwen made a muffled noise of protest but I knew I had no choice. I slowly lowered my hands, nodding. "Okay. We'll come."

Presumably it would take us to Jack. And into the path of Usuriel and Callum, I hoped. Maybe even the Cestis.

The lesserkind jerked its head past my shoulder. "We go that way. Start walking." It pulled a knife to match its friend. "My blade is sharp and I am fast, witch. Do not be stupid. My master will reward you if you serve."

Reward me with a quick death, most likely. I wouldn't let it take me. I'd rather die. But Gwen...I couldn't watch her die first. I had to try to keep her safe.

Swallowing down the acid sting of lesserkind stink and bile at the back of my throat, I turned. The second lesserkind—thinner and more mottled gray—began to drag Gwen back-ward, lifting her with ease, so that only the tips of her toes trailed along the carpet, giving her no chance of getting enough purchase to try and fight back. Probably just as well. I was relying on Jack needing her alive, but a lesserkind could kill in a second if it lost its temper. One had killed Ajax with a single blow. Gwen was safer if she didn't struggle.

Her eyes were closed. I didn't blame her. I didn't want to look, either.

But I had no choice. My lesserkind shoved me forward, moving fast until we were in the lead. The thought of the knife at Gwen's throat was enough to stop me trying anything even as my instincts screamed at me to fight or run. Instead, I just walked, the lesserkind's knife pressing into my jacket every time I slowed.

Instead of heading straight toward the demon magic, we went around, leaving through an exit door and going up a flight of cement fire stairs before entering again a floor above.

Did they know the others were here? The Cestis and Riley Arts? Or Callum and Usuriel?

With every step, I hoped someone we knew would appear.

Someone who could help us. Save us.

I would have even welcomed Usuriel with open arms. But there was nothing but more empty corridors and the feel of demon magic growing stronger. Every time I glanced back at Gwen, the sight of tears running down her cheeks felt like a gut punch even though I tried to take it as a good sign. If she was scared enough to cry, I hoped it was a sign she was still the one in charge, that the lesserkind hadn't invaded her mind and seized control.

My shields were slammed shut as tightly as I could slam them. So far I hadn't felt any attempt to breach them from the lesserkind. It knew Gwen was enough to buy my cooperation.

Fear had turned my heart into a jackhammer. The sensation of demon magic was growing, the feel of it feeding my fear as the wrongness of it made every nerve in my body rebel against taking one step closer.

But I did it anyway. Though I moved as slowly as I could, considering there was a lesserkind with a knife at my back and another with a blade at my sister's throat. But any half second I could buy us was a chance for the Fae or the Cestis to reach us.

When we finally stopped at a door with a half-faded sign that read Oakes Conference 1, I nearly laughed. A freaking meeting room. Jack was summoning a demon in a goddamned meeting room? It would have been funny if I wasn't so scared.

I'd spent a lot of hours in anonymous meeting rooms in countless client offices over the years. Now I might die in one. I bit back the choked sound of half-hysterical amusement rising in my throat. The lesserkind carrying Gwen approached the door and it swung inward.

It was a larger room than I'd expected. About forty feet or so long and twenty wide. There was a second door in the far wall, but it was otherwise empty of anything you'd expect to find in a conference room.

Instead there was only Jack, crouched inside a glowing white circle that burned my eyes. He was using chalk to carefully inscribe a second circle with a series of symbols that resembled runes. Only a lot nastier looking than any rune I'd learned. The shape was almost complete.

Fuck. How long did we have until he finished?

The magic, whatever it was, filled the room, battering my senses. It made me want to spit, as though it was physically crawling into my mouth. I stopped in my tracks, then jerked as the tip of the lesserkind's knife pressed into my spine.

The lesserkind prodded me forward and his companion dragged Gwen closer to the circle.

Jack glanced up and his face darkened. "What are they doing here? I don't need her yet."

"Found them," the lesserkind behind me said. It was close enough that its breath blew across the side of my face. "Both free."

"Free? How?" Anger burned in Jack's eyes but he didn't move, holding his chalk in place.

Right. So he couldn't move or he'd ruin his spell.

"Do not know. But we brought them here. No time to waste." The lesserkind sounded annoyed.

The one holding Gwen turned an assessing gaze on the circle. The expression reminded me lesserkind weren't stupid like imps.

"Almost ready," it said to Jack. "Time to bind her or break her and be done."

Jack's face twisted. "Fine. Give me a minute."

He went back to drawing, his hand moving more rapidly. His forehead glistened with the faintest sheen of sweat.

Given the room was even colder than the rest of the building, perhaps Jack wasn't quite so sure of himself after all.

Or else the magic was taking more from him than he might have expected.

So strong. I had no idea how to break it. Gwen's eyes were open, but she was staring at Jack. She didn't know enough magic to help.

Think.

After a minute or so, Jack made a final decisive stroke and lifted the chalk. The glowing ring of light became a column, the magic stretching from floor to ceiling, a ward against whatever he was going to do inside the circle. It was still translucent, so I had a perfect view of the smug smile on Jack's face as he slowly rose to his feet.

My hands flexed with the urge to punch him as he took a deep breath and wiped his forehead, tucking the chalk into a pocket

"All right." He moved to the edge of the circle and pushed a hand through the ward. "Give her here."

"No!" I yelled as the lesserkind with Gwen shoved her toward Jack. He caught her hand and yanked her into the circle. How had he pulled her through the ward? It was strong. Stronger than any ward I'd felt. Was it keyed to her already? What had Usuriel said? Something about blood? Fear fogged the memory, and I couldn't bring it back. Not with Gwen now inside the ward with Jack. Helpless.

She stayed still for a moment, as though dazed, before her attention snapped to Jack.

His smile widened. My hands twitched again. I wanted to rip his heart from his body. Rage burned back the fear a little. But there was still nothing that I could do.

"Now then, daughter. You can do this the easy way or the way that neither you nor I will enjoy so much. The demon won't care. They don't mind pain. But I don't want to hurt you, Gwen. I just need your magic," Jack said.

"No!" She stepped away from him, moving closer to the center of the circle. His hand clamped over her wrist, pulling her back to him.

"Uh-uh," he said, wagging a finger at her. "You don't want to stand there. Especially not once we get started. If you help me, you'll live. You'll benefit, even. You can stand at my side when I have everything. I'll make up for all the years we've lost. But that spot in the center? Nothing will survive there once it opens."

Opens? I stared at the ward, trying to understand the magic. There was a kernel of witch power to it, but the demon magic twisted everything. I had no more chance of pulling it down than I did of flying across the room to save Gwen.

Where the fuck were Callum and Usuriel?

Gwen, to my surprise, hauled back with her free hand and slapped Jack across the face. Hard. Hard enough that his head rocked back and she cried out from the impact. "Why the fuck would I help you?" she snarled.

I grinned viciously, unable to stop myself.

"Little bitch." His own hand swung, but before I could react—try to warn Gwen—Usuriel stepped out of a patch of nothing, a long black sword at the ready. It glowed with something like icy fire and he cut the lesserkind that had held Gwen in half as easily as slicing through butter. Black blood sprayed everywhere as the two halves fell, a streak of it spattering across his face, shockingly dark against his skin.

The lesserkind holding me screeched in outrage. Acting on instinct, I rammed my elbow behind me and then launched myself toward the circle when the lesserkind let me go. Usuriel pivoted, then launched past me, sword swinging. There was another screech, a flare of magic and then another wet thunk, just as someone grabbed me around the waist, stopping me from hitting the ward, swinging me back.

"Stop," Callum growled.

I struggled, arms stretching toward Gwen. "Let me *go*."

"You can't get through it," he snarled. "It will kill you."

I stared up at him and then twisted back to Gwen. My sister was crumpled at Jack's feet, one hand on her cheek. The bastard had knocked her down.

"I'll kill him," I snapped.

"*We* will kill him," Callum corrected. "Now, clear your mind if you want Gwen to survive this."

Usuriel joined us, still holding his sword ready. It was no longer on fire, but black blood was dripping from the blade.

"I didn't know you could kill lesserkind with a sword," I said.

"You could not," he said, his attention fixed on Jack and Gwen. "But I am not you."

Ugh. Even when he was doing the right thing, he was annoying.

But I'd deal with him later. Jack first. He stared down at Gwen, not moving to help her, face impassive. She was crying again. My hand flexed. I wanted to snatch Usuriel's sword and cut Jack down. But it wouldn't work if I couldn't get through the ward. Me dying wouldn't help her.

Feeling as helpless as Gwen looked, I watched her. Then movement on the other side of the circle caught my eye. Lizzie's face appeared. Then Cassandra's. And Ian and Radha.

I stared, thinking for a moment I must be imagining them. But Lizzie gave me a fierce smile and tilted her head to the far door. Where Damon stood, a gun in his hand aimed squarely at Jack. Next to him was Mitch, gun in one hand and the other on Damon's shoulder. I didn't need to be able to hear to know that Mitch was telling his boss not to do anything stupid.

Good. Mitch would keep Damon safe, if at all possible. So I could focus on Gwen.

"The gang's all here", I muttered. Thank fuck for that. "What now?" I asked Callum.

Jack's head snapped toward me. He was smiling again. A shark's smile. And as much emotion as a shark behind his iceberg eyes. He was certainly not bothered by the appearance of the Cestis. Damn. He really trusted his ward. But he'd trusted his tech, too. We'd broken that.

He bent and hauled Gwen to her feet again. "Now, I use this stupid girl for the reason I had her birthed in the first place. None of you can enter the circle. It's locked with my blood. None but mine can enter."

Across from me Cassandra stiffened. She turned her gaze on me, making a tiny nod at the ward.

The ward locked with Jack's blood. And he *didn't* know I was his daughter. I could use that, surely. I just had to wait for the right moment. I braced myself, not taking my eyes off Jack.

He pulled a knife from his belt and pressed it into Gwen's throat. "Now, where were we, daughter? I was explaining to you that it would be foolish to choose the hard way. I'll give you a moment to reconsider. But first, a drop of your blood." He moved the blade, slashing it down toward Gwen's hand. A line of red blood appeared and he caught drips of it on the blade while Gwen stood frozen in shock.

Jack flicked the knife again and three drops spattered in the dead center of the circle, forming a triangle that flared blue-black like the heart of a flame, before sinking into the floor. The floor immediately started to move, swirling like mist. The stink of demon magic grew stronger, fouling the air, making me want to retch or spit.

Jack started talking to Gwen, or chanting, or maybe both, guiding them both closer to the edge of the circle, standing beside her not behind. She watched him like he was a monster from her darkest nightmares, too terrified to look away. The misty patch on the floor expanded, started to turn to black fog and a buzzing like a million enraged wasps filled the air.

If I was going to do something, I didn't have long.

"He said, 'locked with his blood', right?" I said to Callum. Jack's blood. Which ran in my veins. He'd pulled Gwen through. Maybe I could cross it, too.

"Yes. But that does not help us unless you have some on hand. We can break the ward with enough time. Cassandra will begin shortly. Wait."

The center of the circle was almost transparent, a dark void that made every instinct I had scream at me to run. Gwen was crying, shaking her head. Underneath the demon magic I could feel Jack's magic, more human, but corrupt somehow. He was slamming it at Gwen. If she broke—if she gave in and let him take her magic—it would be all over. We'd all die.

"No time." I snatched one of Callum's daggers from the sheath at his hip and sliced my palm open. Blood welled up and it stung like hell but I ignored it. Jack hadn't noticed, too focused on Gwen.

Hoping like hell I was right and not about to die, I let the dagger fall and bolted for the circle, hand outstretched. I registered Damon shouting my name, then there was a snapping hiss as the blood on my hand connected with the magic, then a flare of pain like acid, but the ward parted, letting me in.

Jack spun as I broke through the ward, mouth dropping open. A blast of magic from behind shoved me forward, so I crashed into Gwen and Jack. Desperately, I reached for Gwen, twisted the two of us to try to stay clear of the roiling bubble of darkness in the center of the circle. It was starting to expand. And the column of light looked…fainter. Had I broken the ward? Or at least damaged it so it might break? I could feel the magic the Fae and the Cestis were pouring at it, a pounding sensation that rang through me like a huge bell tolling. Maybe I had done something. Enough to give the others a starting point to break the ward entirely.

Not that I intended to stay inside it while they did. Not with demon magic still pulsing around us, stronger with every breath. I shoved Gwen toward the ward, pushing her out, away from the bubbling fog and demon stink, hoping like hell she'd run. Be safe. Survive. Even if I didn't.

"You! How?" Jack snarled from behind me. I whirled to face him, saw the deadly gleam of knife in his hand.

I barely had time to wish I'd kept Callum's dagger before Jack lunged at me.

I dodged instinctively, all the months of training with Callum paying off. As Jack stepped past me, I pivoted and kicked, connecting solidly with his arm. The knife went flying, landing in the circle of fog and vanishing.

I had no time to celebrate that small victory. Jack lunged again, landing a punch on my left shoulder which made me yelp. But I wasn't left-handed, and I snapped back a punch of my own, catching his stomach. He fell back, off balance, wheezing and staring at me.

Didn't think I could fight, did you?

My focus narrowed to just him, all the tactics Callum had drilled into me running through my head. Before I could make a move, there was a blinding flash of white and the ward vanished. The buzzing stopped for a second, then seemed to redouble, making my spine crawl as the circle of fog crept outward.

"Maggie, get *back*."

Damon's voice. I obeyed it without thinking.

A gunshot cracked, cutting through the buzz, Jack crumpled forward, clutching his side. His knees hit the edge of the fog and his eyes widened in terror. "No!" He tried to jerk back but the black fog flowed over him, around him, and then swallowed him whole.

The sense of demon magic vanished so quickly, it was like I'd gone deaf.

I stood trembling, staring at a charred circle of cement where the fog had been. The symbols Jack had drawn had vanished. So had he.

I lifted my head and my eyes found Cassandra's. "What the hell just happened?"

"A summoning can't work without the summoner," she said, somewhat wide-eyed. "And he's…gone."

"Dead?" I asked. My gaze sought Damon's. His gun was still raised and the harsh satisfaction on his face told me he was the one who'd shot Jack.

"Your guess is as good as mine," Cassandra said. "Though demons don't generally deal kindly with those who disappoint them."

Epilogue

"*Please* change your mind," I said desperately to Gwen five days later.

We were standing in the kitchen of my house in Berkeley. There'd been plenty of fallout from Jack. The rest of the night was still half a blur in my memory.

Damon had swept in and carried me out of the room, and one of his security guys—I had no memory of who—dealt with the gash on my hand.

After that Cassandra had ordered us out of the building and Gwen and I had been bundled into a car and driven back to the city. Meredith had been waiting at Damon's house to finish the job of patching us up. I'd waved her off after she sealed the wound on my hand, but she'd spent a long time talking to Gwen, who was shocky and shaken, withdrawn like she had been in Slovenia. Meredith gave her something to help her sleep.

The next morning Cassandra and Lizzie had turned up, smoke stained and bleary eyed. They'd torched the office complex—owned, as it turned out, by one of the companies in the chain that owned Ajax's apartment—and cleansed the site with Cerridwen's help. Usuriel left before Cerridwen arrived.

Cassandra and Lizzie had also checked Gwen and I over, looking, I assumed for demon taint. But neither of the lesserkind had broken through our shields and—to my astonishment and relief—no one had fucking mentioned demonstone.

Mitch found Jake in the trunk of a car in the lowest level of St. Isidore's parking lot. He was dehydrated and had a nasty concussion, but was going to be okay.

Gwen had stayed pale and quiet. She'd retreated to the game room, playing old tech games involving cute animals and magical farms, Lianith curled in her lap.

I'd joined her once or twice, but she'd made it clear that, while she was happy for the company, she wasn't ready to talk about what had happened.

"Give her time," Damon said. So did Lizzie and Audrey and Cassandra.

The second night, Lianith woke me and I followed her out to the garden. This time it wasn't a nixling waiting for me, but Usuriel.

He inclined his head at me. Not quite a nod of approval but almost.

"What are you doing here?" I asked, still too exhausted to even wonder how he'd breached our wards.

"I came to see if you are well," he said in a tone that was somewhat less scary than his usual Lord of the Nichtkin, Elder power, hear-me-and-tremble voice.

"The Cestis already checked me for demon taint. Perhaps they should examine you, my lord. You're the one who splashed himself in lesserkind blood. Which was well-done, if messy." It was as close as I would come to saying thank you to him. Thanks implied a debt.

"I would speak to your sister," he said, not deigning to dignify my dig with a response.

I opened my mouth to refuse, and realized it was pointless. The secret of my parentage was out. The Fae present understood well enough what me being able to pass through Jack's blood-locked ward meant. Cerridwen had had words with me about not telling her. I assumed she had the same conversation with Cassandra.

The atmosphere had been distinctly awkward. Callum and Gráinne had both been making themselves scarce. But Lianith had stayed put.

Hopefully her staying was a sign that I hadn't completely fallen out of Cerridwen's good graces or set human-Fae relations back a few centuries.

"She's sleeping," I said.

"There is a light on in her window." He tilted his head in the direction of Gwen's room before he returned those dark eyes to me, his expression cool.

I could tell him she'd been sleeping with the light on the last two nights, but it wouldn't help. He knew where her room was. If he could break the wards of the garden, no doubt he could enter the house if he tried.

"I'll go ask her if she wants to talk to you. But I'm not going to force her."

He inclined his head again.

When I'd shaken Gwen awake and explained, I'd expected her to refuse. Instead, she said she'd talk to him. She and Usuriel retreated to the kitchen garden to talk. I'd stayed with Lianith on the stairs to the deck, wishing desperately for Fae hearing.

Nearly thirty minutes passed before Gwen came back. Without Usuriel.

She wouldn't tell me what he wanted. Just said, "You don't need to worry about me. Go back to bed," before proceeding to do that herself.

But now, in the hazy light of a foggy summer morning she had told me Usuriel had offered her a place in his court if she wished to return to the realm. And that she wanted to go.

"Why on earth would you go back there?" I asked blankly.

"No demons," she said simply. "I'm sorry, Maggie, I'm not you. I'm not a hero. Those…things. I never want to see one again."

"Is Usuriel's court any better?"

"He saved us," she pointed out. "And there are no demons in the realm."

Saving us had been something of a group effort. And I'd been the one to free her from Jack's circle. But as much as the need to point that out burned on my tongue, I didn't think it would help.

"He knows you're half-Fae, half-witch. He might want to use that to his advantage."

She pushed her hair back from her face, irritation clouding her eyes. "I know that. I want you and the Cestis to negotiate for me. Make sure he doesn't."

I gaped at her. "You want me to help you run away again?" Help her to leave me behind? Just when we'd found each other?

"Yes. If you care about me. I'm telling you this is what I need."

I'd wanted to scream. But I couldn't refuse.

Which was why, two days later, we stood in my kitchen. Negotiations concluded. Usuriel agreed that I could see Gwen now and then in Cerridwen's territory. If she wanted to see me. I'd tried to claim the right of family but he'd shot me down, saying that only worked for the Fae half of the equation.

But we'd nailed down an agreement permitting Gwen to leave if she chose and avoided her swearing service to Usuriel. And confirming Morgaine would bring no claim against Gwen for leaving as abruptly as she had. Gwen would be an honored guest. Unless she decided otherwise.

We hadn't been able to do much about Gwen's unknown mother but Usuriel had agreed to keep Gwen safe and let us know immediately if her mother revealed herself and tried to make any sort of claim. It was the best we could do. I wanted to lock her in a basement until she came to her senses, of course, but I couldn't do that. She had to make her own choices.

I only hoped she'd keep her head. I didn't trust Usuriel on this. He'd tried so hard to keep me out of the realm. Now, knowing that Gwen was a likely demon target, why did he want her?

But I hadn't been able to change her mind, though it was breaking my heart. I'd only just found her and now she was going to leave.

"Change your mind," I said again, voice catching.

She hugged me gently. "I'm sorry. I can't. Not now. I need to feel safe. He can give me that."

Bitter laughter choked me. She trusted Usuriel to protect her over us. I hoped that choice wasn't going to haunt us all.

But I climbed into the car with her, after Usuriel signed the agreement, and Damon and I rode with her to the Rose Garden and the door.

I even managed to let her go after hugging her one last time. Then leaned into Damon, not sure my legs were going to hold me up.

The door opened and Usuriel walked through first. He turned to watch Gwen follow and his black eyes caught mine. The smile that flickered across his face was entirely too self-satisfied to make me feel any better. I fought my urge to drag Gwen back to the car and safety. I had no right to do it.

She'd made her choice. Safety, not family.

When the door closed, I pressed my face into Damon's chest and sobbed, heartbroken.

"It's okay," he whispered. "I've got you. I'll always be here."

I clung to him harder. Gwen had chosen safety. But Damon was my safe place. And though it felt like a piece of my heart had cracked all over again, it would have to be enough.

For now.

THE END

Join my VIP readers to get an EXCLUSIVE TechWitch short story

PRE-ORDER Maggie and Damon's next adventure
WICKED LIES

A note from M.J.

I hope you loved reading WICKED DEEDS. I always love writing Maggie and Damon's books and the next one will be WICKED LIES.

As an indie author, it really helps me when readers get the word out about my books, so if you enjoyed the book, please consider leaving a review at the store where you purchased it and tell your friends!

If you want to stay up to date with all my news, find out about new releases and sales, then please sign up to my newsletter at www.mjscott.net or using the QR code below.

Acknowledgements

Writing a book takes a lot and authors don't do it alone. Thank you for all the support from my family and friends (non writers for putting up with writer brain, writers for understanding writer brain). Thank you to Deranged Doctor for yet another fabulous cover! And thank you to all the readers who tell me how much they love the books, it makes the hard writing days much better!

Shadow Kin

Blood Kin

Iron Kin

Fire Kin

Romance (writing as Melanie Scott)

The Cloud Bay series

Don't Blame Me

Right Where You Left Me

You Belong With Me

The New York Saints series

The Devil in Denim

Angel in Armani

Lawless in Leather

Playing Hard

Playing Fast

About the Author

M.J. Scott is an unrepentant bookworm who grew up in a family that fed her a properly varied diet of books. This cemented her story addiction and love of fantasy and romance. So it's not surprising she grew up to write books with both. When not wrestling with the magical worlds in her head, she can generally be found reading, doing something crafty, binge watching, and avoiding housework. She lives in Melbourne, Australia in a small house packed with books, cats, and craft supplies. She also writes romance as Melanie Scott. Her website is www.mjscott.net.